THE BRIDGE

Iain Banks is also the author of
The Wasp Factory and *Walking on Glass*.
He lives in Kent.

Iain Banks

THE
BRIDGE

Pan Books
in association with
Macmillan

First published in Great Britain 1986 by Macmillan London Ltd
This edition published 1987 by Pan Books Ltd,
Cavaye Place, London SW10 9PG
9 8 7 6 5 4 3 2 1
© Iain Banks 1986
ISBN 0 330 29715 5

for
James Hale

Contents

Coma

Trapped. Crushed. Weight coming from all directions, entangled in the wreckage (you have to become one with the machine). Please no fire, no fire. Shit. This hurts. Bloody bridge; own fault (yes, bloody bridge, right colour; see the bridge, see the man drive the car, see the man not see the other car, see the big CRASH, see the bone-broken man bleed; blood colour of the bridge. Oh well own fault. Idiot.) Please no fire. Blood red. Red blood. See the man bleed, see the car leak; radiator red, blood red, blood like red oil. Pump still working – shit, I said *shit* this hurts – pump still working but the fluid leaking out all over the fucking place. Probably get hit from behind now and serve me right, but at least no fire, yet anyway; how long, I wonder how long since? Cars; police cars (jam sandwiches) jam sandwich; me am di jam in di sandwich car am di sandwich. See the man bleed. Own fault. Pray nobody else hurt (no don't *pray*; atheist, remember that, always swore [mother: 'no need to use that sort of language'] always swore you'd be the atheist in the fox hole well your time has come lad because you're leaking away on to the grey-pink road and a fire might start and you might be dying anyway, and you might get hit up the backside by another car if anybody else is staring stupefied at that damn bridge so if you're going to start praying now would seem like quite a reasonable time but ahshit and whatthehell – CHRISTTHISHURTS! [OK; used only as swear-word, nothing serious, honest; swear to God.] OK: see you God, yer a basturt, so ye are.) That's telling them all, kid. What were those letters? MG; VS; and me, 233 FS. But what about – ? Where – ? Who – ? Oh *shit*, I've forgotten my name. This happened once at a party; drunk and stoned and stood up too quick, but this time it's different (and how come I remember forgetting that time and can't remember my name now? This sounds serious. I don't like this. Get me out of this.)

I see a chasm in the rain forest, bridge of creepers, and a river far below; a big white cat (me?) comes leaping along the

11

trail, pounding on to the bridge; white it is (is this me?), an albino jaguar, racing across the swaying bridge (what am I seeing? Where *is* this? Is this what really happened?) long flinging strides, white death (should be black but I've got a negative attitude, ha ha) tearing across the bridge—

It's stopped. The scene whitens, holes appear in it; a film burning through (*fire!*), trapped in the gate (*jaguar* in the gate?); stopped, the scene melts, the seen scene disintegrates (see the seen scene disintegrate); nothing stands too close enquiry. White screen left.

Pain. Circle of pain on chest. Like a brand, a circular impression (am I a figure on a stamp, postmarked? A piece of parchment embossed with 'From the library of . . . .'. (Please complete:

    (a) God, Esq
    (b) Nature (Mrs)
    (c) C. Darwin & Sons
    (d) K. Marx plc
    (e) all of the above.))

Pain. White noise, white pain. First weight from all directions, now pain. Ah life's never-ending variety. I am moved. Mobile man; am I cut free? Or has a fire started? Am I just dying, bleached out, drained away? (Returned, overdue?) I see nothing now (I see everything now). I lie on a flat plain, surrounded by tall mountains (or maybe on a bed, surrounded by . . . machines? People? Either; both (Like, man, in the *really* wide view, they're the same. Far out.) Who cares? Do I care? Shit, maybe I'm already dead. Maybe there's life after life . . . hmm. Maybe all the rest was a dream (yeah, sure), and I wake up to ('Thedarkstation') – what was that?

Did you hear that? Did *I* hear that?

The dark station. There it is again. A noise like a train whistle; something about to depart. Something about to begin, or end, or both. Something that is THEDARKSTATION me. Or not (me no know. Me new here. No ask me.)

The dark station.

Oh, all right . . .

Metaphormosis:

One

The dark station, shuttered and empty, echoed to the distant, fading whistle of the departing train. In the grey evening light the whistle sounded damp and cold, as though the cloud of exhausted steam producing it had imparted some of its own character to the noise. The mountains, covered in their close, dark weave of trees, absorbed the sound like heavy cloth soaking up drizzle; only the faintest of echoes came back, reflected from where crags and cliffs and slopes of jumbled scree and fallen boulders broke the conformity of forest.

When the noise of the whistle had died away, I stood for a while, facing the deserted station, reluctant to turn to the silent carriage behind me. I listened, trying to catch some last hint of the engine's own busy noise as it steamed down the steep valley; I wanted to hear its panting breath, the busy clatter of its pistoned hearts, the chatter of its valves and slides. But though no other sound disturbed the valley's still air, I could hear nothing of the train or its engine; they were gone. Above, the steeply pitched roofs and thick chimneys of the station stood out against the overcast sky, black on grey. Some wisps of steam or smoke, only slowly dissipating in the valley's moist, chill air, hung above the black slates and soot-darkened bricks. An odour of burned coal and the damp, used smell of steam seemed to cling to my clothes.

I turned to look at the carriage. It was sealed, locked from the outside and fastened with thick leather straps. It was black-painted, funereal. In the traces two nervous mares stamped at the leaf-strewn road leading from the station. They shook their dark heads and rolled their huge eyes. Their harnesses clinked and jingled, rocking the carriage behind them slightly, and from their flared nostrils issued clouds of steam; equine impressions of the departed train.

I inspected the carriage's shuttered windows and locked doors, testing the tight leather strapping and pulling on the metal handles, then I climbed to the driver's seat and took up the reins. I stared at the narrow track leading into the forest. I reached for the whip, hesitated, then put it back, unwilling to disturb the valley's atmosphere of silence. I took hold of the wooden brake lever. In some strange inversion of physiology, my hands were moist while my mouth was dry. The carriage shook, perhaps due to the restless movements of the horses.

The sky above was dull and grey and uniform. The higher peaks around me were obscured somewhere above the tree line by the smooth mat of cloud; their jagged summits and sharp ridges seemingly levelled by the soft, clinging vapour. The light was at once shadowless and pervasively dim. I took out my watch and realized that even if all went well I was unlikely to finish my journey in daylight. I patted the pocket containing my flint and tinder; I could make my own light when that around me failed. The carriage rocked again, and the horses stamped and stirred, craning their necks round, eye-whites bulging.

I could delay no further. I released the brake and urged the pair into a trot. The carriage lurched and creaked, rumbling heavily over the rutted road, away from the dark station and into the darker forest.

The road climbed through the trees, past small clearings and over hollow-bellied wooden bridges. In the darkness and the silence of the forest, the torrents beneath the bridges were rushing oases of pale, white light and chaotic noise.

The air grew steadily colder as we climbed. The mares' breath wreathed back around me, thick with the smell of their sweat. The perspiration on my own brow and hands was chill. I reached into my coat for my gloves, and my hand brushed against the thick grip of the revolver in my jacket. I fastened my gloves, drew my coat closer about me, and as I tightened the belt of the garment, was impelled to look again at the bindings and fastenings securing the carriage behind me. In the gloom, however, it was impossible to tell whether the straps still held or not.

The way steepened between the thinning trees; the mares

laboured up the rutted track, into the lower reaches of the dark grey overcast, wisps of barely seen cloud mingling with and absorbing their ghostly white breath. The valley beneath was a formless black pit; not a single light, no fire or movement, and no sound that I could detect issued from its depths. A groan seemed to come from the carriage as we rolled into the enveloping clouds; it lurched as a wheel struck and rolled over a rock in the track. I patted the pistol concealed within my jacket, determining that the groan I had heard was simply that of the carriage's wooden couplings flexing against each other. The cloud grew thicker. The small, stunted trees just visible at the sides of the rough track looked like the dwarfish, deformed sentinels of some phantom fortress.

I stopped in the mist on a level length of the track. The carriage lamps produced, when the flames had steadied, two cones of light which did little to illuminate the ground far beyond the sweat-slicked, tossing heads of the mares, but the lamps' hiss was somehow purposeful and comforting. In their glare, I again checked the carriage bindings. Some had loosened, doubtless due to the road's many corrugations and stony obstacles. I turned the lamps in their sockets, pointing them forward again once my inspection was completed. Their diffused beams encountered the damp vapour like contrary shadows, obscuring more than they revealed.

The carriage rose through the clouds and out of them, following the increasingly broken surface of the track as it gradually levelled out and straightened, heading through a narrow defile in the rocks where the mists slowly thinned. The lamps on either side of me seemed to hiss more quietly, and their beams became sharper. We approached the saddle of the pass and the small plateau beyond.

The last tendrils of the mist stroked past the gleaming flanks of the horses and the strapped sides of the carriage like nebulous fingers reluctant to let us go. Above, the stars shone.

Grey peaks rose into blackness on either side, jagged and alien. The confined plateau was steel grey under the bright

17

stars; dark shadows spread from the rocks on either side of us where the beams of the lamps struck them. The clouds behind formed a hazy ocean, lapping at the sharp islands of distant peaks rising from it. I looked back to see those summits on the far side of the valley we had left, and when I turned to the fore again immediately saw the lights of the oncoming carriage.

My initial start disturbed the mares, causing them to shy and swerve. I checked them immediately and urged them forward again, calming my foolish heart as best I could and reproving myself for such nervousness. The distant carriage, twin-lamped like my own, was still some way off, at the far end of the flattened crucible which formed the summit of the pass.

I settled the revolver further into my inner pocket and flicked the reins, sending the gasping mares into a slow trot which even on that level surface they struggled to maintain. The opposing set of lights, flickering yellow stars come down to earth, wavered, their approach quickening.

Near the centre of the plateau, in the midst of the boulder-field, our carriages slowed. The road through the pass was broad enough for only a single vehicle, the larger rocks and stones having been cleared to each side to provide a way through the broken terrain. A small passing place, an oval area where a width of road greater than a single carriage had been swept from the surrounding rubble, lay equidistant between my own carriage and that approaching. I was now able to discern the two white horses pulling the vehicle and, despite the glare of the flickering lamps, make out an indistinct figure seated on the driver's box. I reined the mares in, letting them amble slowly forward, so that our two carriages would meet at the passing place. My counterpart appeared to anticipate me, and also slowed.

It was at that instant that a strange, unnameable fear gripped me; a sudden and uncontrollable spasm of shivering ran through me, as if an electric charge had struck my body, some lightning bolt, invisible and silent, leaping from that clear, still sky. Our carriages reached the opposite ends of the small passing area. I swerved to the right; the carriage facing me went to its left, so that our teams faced one another, each blocking the other's way. They stopped, even before I and the other driver reined them in. I pulled back, clicking with my tongue, persuading the animals to reverse. The other carriage also retreated. I waved at the shadowy figure on the other vehicle, trying to indicate I would go to the left this time, allowing him to pass on my right. He waved simultaneously. Our carriages stopped. I was unable to determine whether the gesture by the other driver was meant to show he agreed to proceed or not. I pulled the two panting mares to my left. Again the other carriage moved as though to block me, but so immediately that it appeared we had moved simultaneously once more.

Defeated again, I stopped the two mares; they faced their ghostly opposites across a clear space of air which was filled by their joined breaths. I decided that rather than retreat on this occasion I would hold my own carriage steady and wait for the other driver to do so, thus enabling me to pass.

The other carriage remained, quite stationary. An increasing unease caused my whole frame to stiffen. I felt impelled to stand up, shading my eyes from the glare of the sputtering lamps and attempting to see the driver facing me across this short but frustratingly impassable distance between us. I saw the other man rise to his feet as well, for all the world as though he was my own reflection; I would have sworn that he too raised one hand to his eye, just as I had done.

I remained still. My heart beat quickly within my chest, and the strange clamminess I had experienced on my hands before returned, even within my hide gloves. I cleared my throat and hailed the man on the opposite carriage. 'Sir! If you please, go—'

I halted. The other driver had spoken – and stopped speaking – just at the moment I had started, and then stopped. His voice was not an echo, he did not speak the words I spoke, and I was not even sure that he had spoken the same language, but the tone had been similar to my own. A nervous fury gripped me; I waved violently to the right, he gesticulated at the same moment to his left. 'Right!' I shouted as he too called out.

I remained standing for a moment, unable to pretend to myself that the tremor which ran through me then was any sort of reaction to the physical temperature; I trembled, I did not shiver, and as much to take the weight from my now unsteady legs as to proceed with my just decided course, I sat down quickly. Without looking directly at my opponent – for so I now thought of this person apparently determined to prevent my progress – I took up the whip and cracked it over the mares, guiding them left. I heard no other whip crack, but the pair of white horses facing me reared like my own pair, then swerved to their right, so that the four beasts rushed momentarily towards each other, before they reared once more, forelegs rising, harnesses jangling, heads and flailing legs almost touching. Crying out, standing again, cracking the whip over them, I pulled them back, attempted to pass the other carriage on its opposite side. Again I was thwarted, the carriage facing me seeming to mirror my every action.

I drew the nervous, head-tossing mares back at last, facing the equally disturbed pair on the other side of the rock-cleared oval space. My hands were shaking and a cold sweat had broken on my brow. I squinted ahead, desperate to see just who my strange adversary was, but above the glare of the carriage lamps there was only the faintest outline of a figure, and the face was quite invisible.

There was no mirror, I was certain (even this absurd possibility at that moment seemed more acceptable than anything else), and besides, the horses facing me were white, not dark like the pair attached to my carriage. I wondered what to do next. I could see no alternative route through the pass; the boulders and rocks which had been cleared to form the track had been piled-up forming a makeshift wall half the height of a man on either side of the way. Even if I was able to find a gap, the ground beyond would be so rough and broken as to remain impassable.

I put the whip away, climbed down to the stony ground. The other driver did the same. I hesitated when I saw this, the sensation of unattributable but intense unease striking me again. Almost involuntarily, I turned and looked behind me, past the sealed carriage, down the road from the lip of the plateau. To return, to retrace my steps, was unthinkable. Even had my purpose been mundane, had I been some ordinary traveller merely intent on reaching a remote inn or distant town on the other side of the pass, I would have been reluctant in the extreme to turn back; I had seen no other tracks or roads deviating from the path I had taken from the station far below in the valley, and I had heard of no other pass through these mountains within a day's ride. Given the nature of my cargo and the urgency of my mission, I had no choice but to continue on the way I had chosen. Under the pretence of pulling my collar tighter about me, I pressed the bulk of my concealed revolver against my chest. Steeling myself, trying to reach within my being to draw on whatever reserves of rationality and courage I could find, it all but escaped my notice that the figure standing in the glare of the opposing lights seemed to mimic my movements, also pulling on his lapels or collar, before stepping forward.

The fellow was dressed something like myself; in truth, any other apparel in that frigid atmosphere would have invited a quick end. His coat might have been a little longer, his body a little more thickset than mine. He and I came level with the shaking heads of our horses. My heart was beating, now, with a rapidity and a ferocity I could not recall having experienced before; a sort of horror drew me on, made me walk towards this still not-quite-seen figure. It was as if some magnetic repulsion, which before had kept our two carriages from meeting and passing, had now been reversed, and so sucked me inexorably forward, drawing me towards something my heart made clear I feared – or should fear – utterly, in the way some people are fatally attracted towards an abyss while standing on its very edge.

He stopped. I stopped. It was with a surging sense of relief, a brief feeling of total and unalloyed joy that I saw this man did not have my own face. His face was squarer than my own, his eyes were closer together and deeper set, and over his mouth there was a dark moustache. He looked at me, standing in the light of my lamps as I stood in the light of his, and inspecting my face with, I imagined, the same intense and relieved expression I exhibited myself. I started to speak, but got no further than 'My good—' before I stopped. The man had started to talk at the same time as I had; some short word or phrase, seemingly addressing me as I had been about to address him. It was, I was now sure, a foreign tongue he used, but I could not identify it. I waited for him to speak again, but he stood without speaking, apparently studying my face.

We shook our heads at the same moment. 'This is a dream,' I said quietly, while he spoke softly in his own tongue. 'This cannot be happening,' I continued. 'This is not possible. I am dreaming and you are something from within myself.' We fell silent, together.

I looked at his carriage, as he looked at mine. His conveyance appeared to be the same type as my own. Whether his was sealed, locked and strapped shut like mine, whether its contents were as important and awful as those secured in my carriage, I could not tell.

I stepped suddenly to one side; he moved at the same instant, as though to block me. We stepped back. I could smell the fellow now; a strange odour of some musky perfume mingling with stale hints of a foreign spice or bulb. His face wrinkled slightly, exactly as if he were smelling something from my person, something he found vaguely unsettling or distasteful. One of his eyebrows flickered oddly, just as I remembered my pistol. I had the most absurd and fleeting mental picture of us pulling and firing our revolvers, and the lead projectiles meeting and striking each other in mid air, flattening into a perfectly circular coin of squashed metal. My imperfect double smiled, just as I did so myself. We shook our heads; this motion at least seemed not to require translating, though it occurred to me that a similarly slow and thoughtful nodding of the head would have suited the situation just as well. We each stepped back, and looked around at the quiet, cold, barren landscape of that high place as though in its very desolation we might find something to inspire one of us, or both.

I could think of nothing.

We each turned, walked back to our carriage and climbed into our seats.

A dim figure in the shadow behind the uneven light of his carriage's lamp (as I no doubt was to him), he sat, motionless for a while, then took up the reins – just as I did – with a sort of resigned shrug and a bending of the back and a grasping with one hand which looked like the motions of an old man (and I mirrored him, and I knew a sort of ancient bitterness, a heaviness, an ice-brittle thickness which invaded me, more deadly and intense than any air-borne chill).

He tugged gently at the heads of his horses; I signalled to mine in the same fashion. We started to turn our carriages round, using our own confined area of the small passing place, edging back and forth and whistling together at our horses.

When we are level, I decided, *square on like battling ships of the line, I shall draw my gun and shoot*. I cannot go back; no matter that he will not give way, regardless of his determination; I must go on, I have no choice.

We slowly manoeuvred our awkward vehicles until they were abreast. His, like mine, was locked, shuttered, strapped tight. He looked at me, and reached, with an almost complacent slowness, into his coat, just as I did the same thing, feeling past my jacket to the inside pocket and carefully withdrawing my gun. Would he remove his glove? We each hesitated, then he unbuttoned his glove at the wrist, just as I did. He laid the glove on the seat at his side, then raised the gun to point at me.

He pulled the trigger just as I did. There were two small clicks, nothing more.

We each pulled the chambers open; in the light of one lamp I could see the hammer in my gun had struck home on the base of the cartridge; a tiny dent showed on the copper-coloured metal. The round, like his apparently, had been damp, or somehow badly made. This happens, occasionally.

He looked at me again, and our smiles were sad. We each put our revolvers back in our jackets, then we turned our carriages fully round, and I with my dread load, and he with his, rode back, towards the valleys and the clouds.

*

'. . . then we both fire at the same time, or at least we both pull the triggers at the same time, but nothing happens. Both rounds are duds. So we just . . . smile at each other, in a resigned sort of way, I suppose, and finish turning the carriages right round, and then head back the way we came.' I stop talking.

Dr Joyce looks at me over his gold-rimmed spectacles. 'Is that *it*?' he says. I nod.

'Then I wake up.'

'Just like that?' Dr Joyce sounds annoyed. 'No more?'

'End of dream,' I tell him, crisply emphatic.

Dr Joyce looks profoundly unconvinced (I don't blame him really, this is all a pack of lies), and shakes his head in what may well be a gesture of exasperation.

We are standing in the centre of a room with six black walls and no furniture; it is a rackets court, and we are near the end of a game. Dr Joyce – fiftyish, not unfit, but a little puffy – believes in sharing the pursuits of his patients where he can; we both play rackets, so rather than sit in his office we came here for a game. I've been telling him my dream in instalments between points.

Dr Joyce is all pink and grey: grey frizzy hair, pink face, and mottled grey-pink arms and legs poking out from his grey shorts and shirt. His eyes, however, behind the gold-rimmed, chain-secured glasses, are blue: sharp, hard blue and set in his pink face like fragments of glass stuck in a plate of raw meat. He is breathing hard (I am not), perspiring profusely (I only broke sweat in the last point), and looking very suspicious (as I've said, with good reason).

'You *wake up*?' he says.

I try to sound as annoyed as I can: 'Damn it man, I can't control what I dream.' (A lie.)

The doctor issues a professional sigh and uses his fielding-racket to scoop up the ball he missed at the end of the last point. He stares intently at the serving wall. 'You to serve first, Orr,' he says sourly.

I serve, followed by the doctor. Rackets is a game for two players, each with two rackets; a fielding-racket and a shot-racket. It is played in a hexagonal, black-painted court, with

24

two pink balls. This last fact, subjected to the unsubtle allotrope of humour which passes for wit on the bridge, has resulted in rackets being known as 'the man's game'. Dr Joyce knows the game better than I do, but he is shorter, heavier, older and less well co-ordinated. I have been playing the game for only six months (my physiotherapist recommended it), but I win the point – and the game – easily enough, fielding one ball while the doctor fumbles the other. He stands, panting, glaring at me, a very picture of pink pique. 'You're *sure* there's no more?' he says.

'Positive,' I tell him.

Dr Joyce is my dream doctor. He specializes in the analysis of dreams and believes that by analysing mine he will be able to discover more about me than I am able to tell him through any conscious effort (I am an amnesiac). Using whatever he finds by this method, he then hopes somehow to jog my delinquent memory back into action: hoopla! With one mighty leap of the imagination I shall be free. I have been doing my honest best to co-operate with him in this noble venture for over half a year now, but my dreams have always been either too vague to be accurately recalled, or too banal to be worth analysing. In the end, not wanting to disappoint the increasingly frustrated doctor, I have resorted to inventing a dream. I rather hoped my dream of the sealed carriages would give Dr Joyce something to get his yellow-grey teeth into, but from his peeved look and belligerent stance, I get the impression that this is not the case.

He says, 'Thanks for the game.'

'My pleasure.' I smile.

In the showers, Dr Joyce hits below the belt.

'Your, ah, libido, Orr. Quite normal?' He soaps his paunch; I am rubbing foamy circles on my chest.

'Yes, doctor. How's yours?' The good doctor looks away.

'I was asking in a professional capacity,' he explains. 'We just thought there might be some problems. If you're sure . . .' His voice trails away, and he steps under the stream of water to rinse off.

What does the good doctor want? References?

Showered and changed, and after a call at the rackets club bar, we take a lift to the level where Dr Joyce's consulting rooms are. The doctor looks more at home in his grey suit and pink tie, but he is sweating still. I feel refreshed and cool in trousers, silk shirt, waistcoat and frock coat (carried over one arm for now). The lift – soft class: leather seats, pot plants – hums as it climbs. Dr Joyce goes to sit down on a bench by one wall, near the attendant, who is reading a paper. The doctor takes out a slightly off-white handkerchief and mops his brow.

'So, what do you think this dream means then, Orr?'

I look at the newspaper-reading attendant. We three are the only people in the lift, but I would have imagined that even a lift-boy's presence would be sufficient to prohibit what I thought was meant to be a confidential exchange. That was why we were heading for the good doctor's office. I stare round at the lift's wooden panelling, leather furniture and rather unimaginative seascape prints (and decide that I prefer lifts with outside views).

'I've no idea,' I say. Once – I seem to remember – I thought that what my dreams meant was exactly what Dr Joyce was supposed to tell me, but the good doctor disabused me of this notion some time ago, while I was still struggling to have dreams meaningful enough for him to get to work on.

'But that's just it,' Dr Joyce says wearily, 'you probably do know.'

'But I don't want to tell you?' I suggest.

Dr Joyce shakes his head. 'No, you probably *can't* tell me.'

'So why ask?'

The lift is slowing to a stop. The doctor's offices are about mid-way up the top half of the bridge, equidistant from the always steam-wreathed train deck and one of the often cloud-entangled summits of the great edifice. A man of no little influence, his offices are on the outside of the main structure with one of those much sought after sea views. We wait for the doors to open.

'What you have to ask yourself, Orr,' Dr Joyce says, 'is what this sort of dream means in relation to the *bridge*.'

I look at him. 'The bridge?'

'Yes,' he nods.

'You've lost me,' I tell him. 'I don't see what possible connection there can be between the bridge and my dream.'

Another doctorly shrug. 'Perhaps the dream is a bridge,' he muses as the inner doors slide back. He takes out his travel-pass to show the attendant; 'Perhaps the bridge is a dream.'

(Well, that's a great help.) I show the attendant my hospital identity bracelet, then follow the good doctor along a broad, carpeted corridor to his offices.

The identity bracelet on my right wrist is a plastic strap which contains some sort of electronic device detailing my name and residence. It describes the nature of my affliction, the treatment I am undergoing, and the name of my doctor. Printed on the plastic strap is my name: John Orr. This is not really my name; it is the name I was given by the bridge's hospital authorities when I arrived here. 'John' because it is a common, inoffensive name, 'Orr' because when I was fished out of the waters surging around one of the bridge's great granite piers, there was a large, livid, circular bruise on my chest, an almost perfect circle stamped on my flesh (and beyond; I had six broken ribs). It looked like an O. 'Orr' was the first name starting with an O that occurred to the nurses charged with looking after me; it is they who are by tradition allowed to name foundlings, and as I was discovered without any form of identification this definition was extended to myself.

My chest, I might add, still aches on occasion, as if that curious, unexplained mark remained there in all its multi-coloured splendour. I need hardly add that I had also received head injuries, originally presumed to be the cause of my amnesia. Dr Joyce is inclined to attribute the ache which I experience in my chest to the same trauma which caused my amnesia. He believes my inability to remember my past life was caused not so much by the head injuries I received as by some other, perhaps linked, psychological shock, and that the answer to the question my amnesia poses is to be found in my dreams. This is why he's taken me on: I am an Interesting Case, a challenge. He will discover my past for me, no matter how long it takes.

In the doctor's outer office we encounter the appalling young man who is the doctor's receptionist. He is a breezy and bright fellow, always ready with a joke or a quip, ever willing to provide coffee or tea and to help people on or off with their coats; never gloomy or morose, rude or unpleasant, and always interested in what Dr Joyce's patients have to say. He is slim, neatly dressed, well manicured; he wears a pleasantly unobtrusive scent applied sparingly but effectively, and his hair is neat and smart without looking artificial. Need I add that he is heartily despised by every one of Dr Joyce's patients I have ever spoken to?

'Doctor!' he says, 'so *good* to see you again! Did you enjoy your game?'

'Oh, yes,' the doctor says unenthusiastically, looking round the waiting area. There are only two other people in the room: a policeman and a thin, worried-looking man with bad dandruff. The worried-looking man is sitting, eyes closed, on one of the room's half-dozen or so seats. The policeman is sitting on top of him, sipping a cup of coffee. Dr Joyce takes in this arrangement without a second glance. 'Any calls?' he asks the Appalling Young Man, who is standing, slightly bowed, with his hands placed fingertip to fingertip.

'None urgent, sir; I've left a chronological list on your desk, with tentative prioritizations re the replies – in ascending order – in the left margin. Cup of tea, Dr Joyce? Coffee, maybe?'

'No, thank you,' Dr Joyce waves the Appalling Young Man to one side and escapes through to his office.

I hand the AYM my coat as he says, 'Good *morning* Mr Orr! Can I take your – oh, thank *you*! Enjoy your game, Mr Orr?'

'No.'

The policeman continues to sit on top of the thin man with the dandruff. He looks away with an expression somewhere between surliness and embarrassment.

'Oh dear,' the young receptionist says, looking desolate, 'I *am* sorry to hear that, Mr Orr. Cup of something to cheer you up, perhaps?'

'No thanks.' I hurry through to join the doctor in his office. Dr Joyce is examining the prioritized list lying under a paperweight on the blotter of his impressively large desk.

'Dr Joyce,' I say, 'why is there a policeman sitting on top of a man in your outer office?'

He looks towards the door I have just closed.

'Oh,' he says, going back to the typed list, 'that's Mr Berkeley; he has a non-specific delusion. Keeps thinking he's an article of furniture.' He frowns, taps one finger on an item on the list. I sit down in an unoccupied chair.

'Really?'

'Yes; what he thinks he is varies from day to day. We tell whoever's guarding him just to humour him, where possible.'

'Oh. I thought perhaps they were some sort of minimalist radical theatre group. I take it Mr Berkeley thinks he's a seat at the moment.'

Dr Joyce frowns. 'Don't be stupid, Orr. You wouldn't put one seat on top of another, would you? He must think he's a cushion.'

'Of course.' I nod. 'Why the police guard?'

'Oh, it can get a bit tricky; every now and again he thinks he's a bidet in a ladies' toilet. He's not normally violent, just . . .' Dr Joyce stares vacantly at the pastel-pink ceiling of his office for a moment. He gropes for the right word, then dredges down '. . . insistent.' He goes back to the list.

I sit back. Dr Joyce's office is floored with teak, covered with occasional, delicately hued carpets of a banal abstract design. The imposing desk has a matching filing cabinet and brace of tome-stuffed bookcases, and there is a low table with tastefully bland chairs on one of which I am sitting. Half of one wall of the doctor's inner office is window, but the view is concealed by vertical blinds. Translucent, the sun-struck blinds glow in the morning light, providing our illumination.

The doctor crumples the neatly typed sheet into a ball and throws it into his waste-bin. He drags his seat round from behind his desk and positions it so that we can sit facing each other. He takes a notebook from the desk top and puts it on his lap, then removes a small silver propelling pencil from his jacket's breast pocket.

'Right, Orr, where were we?'

'I believe the last supposedly constructive thing you said was that the bridge might be a dream.'

Dr Joyce's mouth droops down at the corners. 'How would you know if it wasn't?'

'How would I know if *this* wasn't?'

The doctor sits back, a knowing look on his face. 'Quite.'

'Well, how do *you* know it isn't a dream, doctor?' I smile. The doctor shrugs.

'No point asking me that; I'd be part of the dream.' He leans forward in his seat; I do the same thing, so that we are almost nose to nose. 'What does the sealed carriage mean?' he asks.

'I guess it shows I'm frightened of something,' I snarl.

'Yes, but *what?*' the doctor hisses from close range.

'I give in; you tell me.'

We stay eyeball to eyeball for a few moments longer. Then the doctor breaks off, sitting back and making a sighing noise like the air going out of a fake leather chair. He makes some notes.

'How are your investigations going?' he says matter-of-factly.

I sense a trap. I watch him through narrowed eyes.

'What investigations?' I ask.

'Before you left hospital, and until quite recently, you would always tell me about the investigations you were making; you told me you were trying to find out things about the bridge. It seemed quite important to you at the time.'

I sit back. 'I did try to find some things out. But—'

'But you gave up,' the good doctor nods, notes.

'I tried; I wrote letters to every office and bureau and department and library and college and paper I could find. I sat up into the night writing letters, I spent weeks sitting in ante-chambers and waiting rooms and reception areas and corridors. I ended up with writer's cramp, a bad cold and a summons to appear before the Hospital Out-Patients Living

30

Allowance (Abuses) Committee; they couldn't believe the amount I was spending on postage.'

'What did you discover?' Dr Joyce is amused.

'That there is no point trying to discover anything worthwhile about the bridge.'

'What do you call worthwhile?'

'Where is it? What does it join? How old is it? That sort of thing.

'No luck?'

'I don't think luck had much to do with it. I don't think anybody knows or cares. My letters all disappeared or were returned unopened, or with replies attached in languages I couldn't understand and nobody else I was able to contact could fathom.'

'Well,' the doctor makes a sort of balancing motion with one hand, 'you do have a problem with languages, don't you?'

I have a problem with languages, indeed. In any single section of the bridge there are anything up to a dozen different languages; specialized jargons originated by the various professions and skill-groups over the years and developed and added to, altered and refined to the point of mutual incomprehensibility so long ago that nobody can actually recall the process taking place or remember a time when it had not yet begun. I, it was discovered when I came out of my coma, speak the language of the Staff and Administrators: the bridge's official, ceremonial tongue. But whereas everybody else speaks at least one other language, usually in connection with their work or official position, I do not. When I am amongst the bustling crowds which inhabit the main thoroughfares of the bridge, at least half of the conversations going on are quite unintelligible to me. I find this redundancy of languages merely annoying, but I imagine that to the doctor's more paranoid clients the plethora of tongues must seem almost definitively conspiratorial.

'But it's not just that. I looked for records concerning the construction of the bridge and its original purpose; I looked for old books, newspapers, magazines, recordings, films; for anything which referred to any place off the bridge, or before

31

it, or outside it; there's nothing. It's all gone. Lost, stolen, destroyed or just misfiled. Do you know that in this section alone they've managed to lose, to *lose* an entire library? A library! How the hell do you lose a *library?*'

Dr Joyce shrugs. 'Well, readers lose library books—' he begins in a reasonable voice.

'Oh for God's sake man! A whole library? There were tens of thousands of books in it – I checked. Real books, and bound journals, and documents and maps and . . .' I am aware I am starting to sound upset. 'The Third City Records and Historical Materials Library, missing presumed lost for ever; it's listed as being in this section of the bridge, there are countless references to it and cross-references to the books and documents it contained and even reminiscences of scholars who went there to study; but nobody can find it, nobody has ever heard of it except through those references. They're not even *looking* for it especially hard. My God; you'd think they'd sent out some sort of search party of librarians or bibliophiles or something. Remember the name, doctor; give me a call if you ever come across it.' I sit back, folding my arms. The doctor makes some more notes.

'Do you feel that all this information you are seeking is, or has been deliberately hidden from you?' He lifts one eyebrow in interrogation.

'Well, that would give me something to fight against, at least. No; I don't think there's any malice behind it all, just muddle, incompetence, apathy and inefficiency. You can't fight that; it's like trying to punch mist.'

'Well then,' the doctor smiles glacially, eyes like ice gone blue with age, 'what did you discover? Where did you stop, give in?'

'I discovered the bridge is very big, doctor,' I tell him. Big, and rather long; it disappears over the horizon in both directions. I have stood on a small radio tower atop one of its great summits and counted a good two dozen other red-painted peaks hazing off into the blue distance towards both the City and the Kingdom (both invisible; I have seen no land since I was washed up here, unless one counts the small islands which support every third bridge section). Tallish, too: at least fifteen hundred feet. Six or seven thousand people live within each section, and there is probably room – and over-designed strength in the primary structure – for an even greater density of population.

Shape: I shall describe the bridge with letters. In cross-section, at its thickest, the bridge closely resembles the letter A; the train deck forms the cross-bar of the A. In elevation, the centre part of each section consists of an H superimposed over an X; spreading out on each side from this centre are six more Xs which gradually reduce in size until they meet the slender linking spans (which have nine small Xs each). Linking the extremities of each X, one to another, then produces a reasonable silhouette of the general shape: hey presto! The bridge!

'Is that it?' Dr Joyce asks, blinking. ' "It's very big," is that all?'

'It's all I needed to know.'

'But you still gave up.'

'It would have been the act of an obsessive to go on. Now I'm just going to enjoy myself. I have a very pleasant apartment, a quite reasonable allowance from the hospital, which I spend on things which amuse me or which I find beautiful; I visit galleries, I go to the theatre, concerts, the cinema; I read; I have made some friends, mostly among the engineers; I play sports, as you might have noticed; I'm hoping to be admitted to a yacht club . . . I occupy myself. I wouldn't call that rejecting anything; I'm right in there, having a great time.'

Dr Joyce gets up, surprisingly quickly, throwing the note-book on to his desk and going to pace up and down behind it, oscillating between book-clogged bookcases and glowing blinds. He cracks his knuckles. I inspect my nails. He shakes his head.

'I don't think you're taking this seriously enough, Orr,' he says. He goes to one of the windows and draws the blinds back, revealing a bright sunny day; blue sky and white clouds.

'Come here,' he says. With a sigh and a small oh-all-right-if-it'll-keep-you-happy smile, I join the good doctor at the windows.

Straight ahead, and almost a thousand feet down, the sea; grey-blue and ruffled. A few yachts and fishing boats speckled about; seagulls wheel. The doctor points to the side, though (one side of his office juts out, so he can look along the side of the bridge).

The hospital complex of which the doctor's offices form a part stands slightly proud of the main structure, like an energetically growing tumour. From here, at such an acute angle, the bridge's elegant grace is obliterated, and it appears merely cluttered and too solid.

Its sloping sides rise, russet-red and ribbed, from the granite-plinthed feet set in the sea nearly a thousand feet below. Those latticed flanks are slabbed and crammed with clusters of secondary and tertiary architecture; walkways and lift shafts, chimneys and gantries, cableways and pipes, aerials and banners and flags of all shapes, sizes and colours. There are small buildings and large ones; offices, wards, workshops, dwellings and shops, all stuck like angular limpets of metal, glass and wood to the massive tubes and interweaving girders of the bridge itself, jumbled and squeezed and squashed between the original structure's red-painted members like brittle hernias popping out between immense collections of muscles.

'What do you see?' Dr Joyce asks. I peer forward, as if asked to admire the detailed brushwork on some famous painting.

'Doctor,' I say, 'I see a fucking great bridge.'

Dr Joyce pulls hard on the cord, snapping it at the top and leaving the blinds open. He sucks his breath in; he goes to sit behind his desk, scribbling in his notebook. I follow him.

'Your trouble, Orr,' he says, as he writes, 'is that you don't question enough.'

'Don't I?' I say innocently. Is this a professional opinion or just a personal insult?

At the window a window-cleaner's cradle is lowered slowly into view. Dr Joyce does not notice. The man in the

34

cradle taps at the window.

'Time to have your windows cleaned, I think, Doctor,' I tell him. The doctor looks up briefly; the window-cleaner is tapping alternately at the window-pane and his wrist watch. Dr Joyce goes back to his notebook, shaking his head.

'No, that's Mr Johnson,' he tells me. The man in the cradle has his nose pressed against the glass.

'Another patient?'

'Yes.'

'Let me guess; he thinks he's a window-cleaner.'

'He *is* a window-cleaner, Orr, and a very good one; he just refuses to come back in, that's all. He's been on that cradle for the last five years; the authorities are starting to worry about him.'

I gaze at Mr Johnson with new respect; how agreeable to see a man so happy in his work. His cleaning cradle is worn and cluttered; there are bottles, cans, a small suitcase, a tarpaulin and what may be a camp-bed at one end, balancing a variety of cleaning equipment at the other extremity. He taps on the glass with his T-shaped wiper.

'Does he come in to you, or do you go out to him?' I ask the good doctor, walking over to the windows.

'Neither; we talk through an open window,' Dr Joyce says. I hear him putting the notepad away in a drawer. When I turn he is standing looking at his watch. 'Anyway, he's early; I have to go to a committee meeting now.' He mimes something like this to Mr Johnson, who shakes his wrist and holds the watch up to his ear.

'And what of poor Mr Berkeley, upholding the law even as we speak?'

'He'll have to wait, too.' The doctor takes some papers from another drawer and stuffs them into a thin briefcase.

'What a pity Mr Berkeley doesn't think he's a hammock,' I say, as Mr Johnson hoists himself up out of sight, 'then you could keep them both hanging around.'

The good doctor scowls at me. 'Get out of here, Orr.'

'Certainly, doctor.' I head for the door.

'Come back tomorrow if you have any dreams.'

'Right oh.' I open the door.

'You know what, Orr?' Dr Joyce says seriously, clipping his silver propelling pencil back into his breast pocket. 'You give in too easily.'

I think about this, then nod. 'Yep, fair enough doc, you're right.'

In the outer office, the doctor's ghastly receptionist helps me on with my coat (he has brushed it while I was in with the doctor).

'Well Mr Orr, and how *did* it go today? Well I hope. Yes?'

'Very well. Considerable progress. Great strides. Meaningful discussion.'

'Oh that *does* sound encouraging!'

'Literally incredible.'

I take one of the grand main lifts down from the hospital complex to street level above the train deck. In the great lift, surrounded by thick rugs, tinkling chandeliers and gleaming brasswork framing polished mahogany, I take a glass of *cappuccino* from the bar and sit down to watch the resident string quartet, framed against the outer windows of the huge, slowly descending room.

Behind me, round an oval table inside a roped-off rectangle, twenty or so bureaucrats and their aides are discussing a convoluted point of order which has cropped up during their meeting, which – according to a placard on a small stand just inside the roped-off area – concerns the standardisation of contract specifications in invitations-to-tender for locomotive high-speed bunkering channels (coal dust type, fire prevention in).

From the lift to an open street above the main train deck; this is an avenue of walk- and cycle-way, metal-decked, which forges a comparatively straight path through both the bridge's own structure and the chaotically unplanned additions of shops, cafés and kiosks which clutter this bustling level.

The street – rather grandly called the Boulevard Queen Margaret – lies near the outer edge of the bridge; its inside buildings form part of the lower edge of the ziggurat of secondary architecture piled inside the original framework. Its outer-edge buildings abut the main girders themselves, and in intermittent gaps offer views of the sea and sky.

Long and narrow, the street makes me think of ancient · towns, where haphazardly thrown together buildings jutted out towards each other, tilting over and enclosing both the thoroughfares themselves and the swarming crowds they contained. The scene here is not so different; people jostling, walking, bicycling, pushing prams, hauling carts, carrying sedan chairs, straining on trike-vans, chattering in their various languages, dressed in civilian clothes or uniforms, and forming a dense mass of confused motion where people flow in both directions at once, and across the main stream as well, like blood cells in an artery gone mad.

I stand on the raised platform outside the lift halt.

Over the noise of the milling people, the continual hisses and clanks, grindings and gratings, klaxons and whistles of the trains on the deck beneath sound like shrieks from some mechanistic underworld, while every now and again a deep rumble and a still more profound quaking and rattling announces a heavy train passing somewhere below; great pulsing clouds of white steam roll around the street and upwards.

Above, where the sky ought to be, are the distant, hazily seen girders of the high bridge; obscured by the rising fumes and vapours, dimmed by the light intercepted outside them by their carapace of people-infected rooms and offices, they rise above and look down upon the rude profanity of these afterthought constructions with all the majesty and splendour of a great cathedral roof.

A frenzied chorus of beeping swells from one side; a black rickshaw pulled by a young boy rushes through the crowds, which part for it. It is an engineer's cab. Only important officials and couriers of the major guilds are allowed to use rickshaws; merely well-off people are permitted to use sedan chairs, though in practice few do because lifts and local trams are quicker. The only other alternative is to cycle, though as wheels are taxed on the bridge, the only affordable conveyance of this type for most people is a monocycle. Accidents are common.

The fusilade of honking which precedes the cab emanates from the uniformed rickshaw-boy's feet; in the heel of each of his shoes there is a small horn; people know the sound and are warned.

I repair to a café to think about what I shall do after lunch. I might go swimming – there is a very pleasant, uncrowded pool a couple of levels down from my apartment – or I might phone my friend Brooke, the engineer; he and his cronies usually play cards in the afternoon when they can't think of anything better to do, or I might take a local tram and go in search of new galleries; I haven't bought any paintings for a week or so.

A pleasant tingle of anticipation runs through me as I contemplate these various agreeable ways of spending my time. I leave the café after a coffee and liqueur and rejoin the busy press of people.

I throw a coin from the tram I take back to my own section of the bridge as we cross the narrow linking span. It is traditional to throw things from the bridge, for luck.

Night. A pleasant evening behind me spent swimming, dining at the rackets club, then taking a stroll down at the harbour. I am a little tired, but watching the tall yachts bobbing quietly in their dark marina has given me an idea.

I stretch out on the *chaise-longue* in my sitting room and consider the exact form my next dream for the good doctor ought to take.

Decided, I prepare my writing table, then go to the television screen built into the wall behind where I will sit; I work better with it on, talking quietly to itself. Most of the programmes are dross, intended for the unthinking – quiz shows, soap operas, and so on – but I watch occasionally, ever in hope of seeing something which is not the bridge. I find a channel still broadcasting – a play, apparently set in a mining community on one of the small islands – and turn the dialogue down to a murmur, loud enough to hear but not make out. I take my place at my desk, pick up my pen.

The television starts to hiss. I turn round. A grey haze fills the screen, white noise issues from the speaker. Perhaps the set is faulty. I go to turn it off, but then a picture appears. There is no sound; the hiss has gone.

The screen shows a man lying in a hospital bed, surrounded by machines. It is in black and white, not colour, and grainy. I turn up the sound, but only a very gentle hiss emerges even at maximum volume. The man in the bed has tubes and pipes appearing from his nose and mouth and arm; his eyes are closed. I can't see him breathe, but he must still be alive. On every channel the picture stays the same: still the man, the bed, the surrounding machines.

The camera looks down and across at the bed; it shows part of a wall, and a small unoccupied seat at one side of the bed. The fellow looks at death's door; even in monochrome his face is terribly pale, and his thin hands – lying motionless on the white bedsheet, one with a tube attached at the wrist – are almost transparent. His face is thin and battered as though he's been in a bad fight. His hair looks mousy; a small bald patch sits on the crown of his head. On the whole, a rather short, grey, ordinary-looking man.

Poor devil. I try changing channels again, but the picture remains. Perhaps I have a crossed line with one of the hospital cameras used to monitor very ill patients. I'll call the repair people in the morning. I look at the still, silent picture for a little while longer, then switch the set off.

Back to my desk. I have to prepare my next dream for the good doctor, after all. I write for a while, but the lack of background noise is vexing, and I have an odd feeling, sitting with my back to the dead television. I take my pen and papers to bed and complete my next dream there, before falling asleep, where – if I do dream – I don't remember dreaming.

Anyway, this is what I write:

Two

All day we had fought, under a topaz sky which slowly clouded over as though obscured by the smoke from our guns and the spreading fires below. The clouds turned dark red with the sunset; beneath our feet the decks were slick with blood. Still we fought, desperate now, though the light was going and our numbers were but a quarter of what they had been; the dead and dying lay thrown about like splinters, our proud ship's paint and gold leaf were blackened and burned, our masts were felled, and our sails – once puffed out bright and decorated as any military chest – now hung like half-burned rags from the mast-stumps, or covered the debris-littered decks where fires burned and dying men moaned. Our officers were dead, our boats were burned or smashed.

Our ship was sinking and burning; the form of its inevitable fate dependent only on whether the rising waters reached the powder magazines before the unchecked fires. The enemy vessel, wallowing across the wreckage-strewn sea, seemed in scarcely better condition than our own; a single holed and flame-sooted sail hung from her remaining, tilted mast. We tried to shoot down that remnant of her rigging, but we had no chain shot left, and no master-gunners left alive. Our powder on deck was almost finished.

The enemy ship turned towards us, closing. We used the last of our shot, then took up cutlass and boarding pistol. We left the wounded to their own devices. Lacking any yards to hang boarding lines from, we made ready to leap aboard the other vessel when she hit. The other ship fell silent too, the last dark clouds from her cannons blowing slowly ahead of her, over the dull red swell of the empty ocean. Our smokes mingled as the ships drew near.

The two torn, bulbous hulls touched; we leapt across, away from our stricken vessel.

The collision felled our enemy's last makeshift mast, and the two craft separated again; like us they had used no hooks or grapples. We staggered shouting and cursing through the enemy galleon's decks as our old ship drifted away, but we found no men to fight, only the dead and the moaning wounded. We found no powder or shot, only rising waters and spreading fires. We found no ships's boats, only wreckage and charred wood.

Resigned, exhausted, we gathered on the sloping, splintered poop deck. In the smoky, flickering light of the spreading fires we looked out across the slow-increasing gap of littered, bloody ocean to our old ship.

Her masts were flame, her sails were smoke. Her reflection burned on the waters between us, a livid and inverted ghost.

Our adversaries stared back through the smoke at us.

My apartments are high up on this section of bridge, close to the summit and not far from one angle of the squashed hexagon which the section resembles. It would appear that I deserve this exalted position because I am one of Dr Joyce's star patients. My rooms are wide and tall, and their walls on the seaward side are the glassed-in girders of the bridge itself. I can look out – from perhaps twelve hundred feet or more – in the direction we call down-river. That is, when the view is not obscured by the grey clouds which often submerge the bridge from above.

My rooms were quite bare when I came here from the hospital – I have improved them, adding several useful and decorative pieces of furniture, and a modest but carefully chosen collection of small paintings and little figurines and sculptures. The paintings mostly show details of the bridge itself, or are of the sea. I have several fine paintings of yachts and fishing vessels. The sculptures are, in the main, figures; bridge workers frozen in bronze.

It is morning now, and I am dressing, performing my toilet. I dress slowly, in measured stages. I have an extensive wardrobe; it seems only polite, having been given so many well-made clothes, to give some thought to their effect. They are, after all, a language; they do not so much say things about us, they are what is said.

41

The bridge's menial workers, of course, have uniforms to wear, and don't have to worry about what to put on each morning. My envy for their way of life begins and ends there, though; they accept their lot and their position in society with a meekness I find both surprising and disappointing. *I* wouldn't settle for being a sewage worker or a coal miner all my life, but these people fit into the structure like happy little rivets, embrace their position with the adhesion and cohesion of coats of paint.

I comb my hair (a pleasantly intense black, and just curly enough to give it body) and select a cravat and matching enamelled pocket watch. I admire my tall and aristocratic reflection for a moment, and check that my cuffs are even, my waistcoat centred, collars straight, and so on.

I am ready for breakfast. The bed needs to be made, and yesterday's clothes require cleaning or putting away, but the hospital very considerately sends people to do that sort of thing. As I go to select a hat, I pause.

The television has switched itself on. It clicks and starts to hiss. At first, as I go through to the sitting room, I think I might be mistaken, that it will be a leaking pipe – water or gas – making the noise, but no, the screen built into the wall is on. It shows the same view as before: the man in the bed, silent and still and in monochrome. I switch the set off. The picture vanishes. I switch it back on; the sick man reappears, and the channel-changing control has no effect. The light is different. There seems to be a window set into the wall on the far side of the bed, beyond the encircling machines. I look carefully for any further clues. The picture is too grainy for me to be able to read any of the writing on the machines; I can't even tell what language is being used. How can the set switch itself on? I turn it off, and hear a droning noise outside.

From the windows of the room, I look out on to a blue, bright day. A formation of aircraft is flying past the bridge, from the direction of the Kingdom. There are three of them, identical, rather cumbersome-looking, single-engine monoplanes, flying one above the other. The lowest aircraft is about level with me, the middle plane is fifty feet above it, the highest plane another fifty feet above that. They fly past, engines droning, course steady, propellers glittering like huge protruding glass discs, and from the tail of each aircraft little dark bursts of smoke issue, seemingly at random. The small black clouds hang in the air, strung out like some strange code. A long trail of smoky signals marks the course of the planes, disappearing into the Cityward distance like some strange airborne fence.

This both puzzles and excites me. I have not seen or heard of any aircraft at all since I've been on the bridge; not even flying boats, which the bridge's engineers and scientists are obviously quite capable of constructing and operating.

These aircraft had no visible undercarriage – they certainly had no floats – and generally they looked quite unable to operate from water; I assume they have retractable wheels and come from an airport on land. I would find that encouraging.

The puffs of black smoke start to drift with the slow wind, heading towards the City. They dissipate as they go, into the wide blue sky. The planes' piston-engine noise gradually fades as well. The thinning black clouds seem to have a vague pattern; they are grouped in three-by-three grids, carefully spaced. I watch the gradually moving cloud-groups, waiting for the merging smoke-puffs to form letters or numbers, or some other recognizable shapes, but after a few minutes, all that is left is an indistinct hanging curtain of dull air being blown slowly Citywards like a gigantic scarf of soiled gauze.

I shake my head.

At the door I remember the malfunctioning television; but when I try to call the repair people the telephone isn't working either; it transmits a series of slow, not-quite-perfectly-regular beeps at me. Time to go. The world – the bridge, anyway – may be going mad, but a man must still have his breakfast.

At the lift doors in the corridor outside, I recognize a neighbour. He watches the brass hand on the clocklike face of the floor-indicator above the closed doors, tapping one foot impatiently. He is dressed in the uniform of a senior timetabling official. He gives a little start; the carpet must have muffled my steps.

'Good morning,' I say, as the floor-indicator sweeps slowly up. The fellow grunts. He takes out his pocket watch and looks at it; his foot taps faster. 'I don't suppose you saw those aircraft, did you?' I ask him. He looks at me oddly.

'I'm sorry?'

'The planes; the aircraft that flew past . . . not ten minutes ago.'

The man stares at me. His eyes flicker as he glances at my wrist; he sees the plastic hospital bracelet. The lift chimes. 'Oh yes,' the official says. 'Yes. The aircraft; of course.' The lift doors open smoothly. He looks round at the wood-panelled, brass-trimmed interior of the waiting lift as I gesture for him to enter first. He inspects his watch again, mutters 'Excuse me,' and hurries off down the corridor.

I ride down alone. On a circular, leather-padded bench, I watch the rippling surface of a fish tank in one corner as the lift rumbles down the shaft. There is a telephone by the door.

The brass instrument is heavy. I hear nothing for a moment, then a few small bleeping noises which at first sound like the odd tones I heard on my apartment's machine. These are quickly replaced by the voice of a rather surly operator. 'Yes? What do you want?' This is something of a relief.

'Oh, repairs and maintenance please.'

'What, *now*?'

The lift slows as it approaches the floor I want. 'No, never mind.' I hang up.

I leave the lift on one of the upper arcade decks, where a brisk walk takes me – past small shops selling the fresh produce just arrived on the early morning goods trains – to the Inches breakfast bar. I stop on the way at a small flower stand and choose a carnation which will contrast nicely with the watch and the cravat.

The panelled, windowless walls of the breakfast bar are painted with competent but unconvincing views of green pastureland. It is a quiet, subdued place, with high ceilings and low lighting, thick carpets and thin porcelain. I am shown to my usual table, at the back. A newspaper lies folded on the table; it is concerned almost entirely with minute changes to the regulations and laws governing the running and maintenance of the bridge and its traffic, the promotions and deaths of the bridge's administrators, the generally quite remarkably boring society gatherings perpetrated by the same groups, and with some of the complicated, arcane and little-played sports and games popular with these mandarins.

I order smoked fish fillets, devilled lamb's kidneys, toast and coffee. Putting the paper aside, I gaze up at the painting on the opposite wall. It shows a sloped meadow of brilliant green, bordered with evergreens and sprinkled with bright flowers. Across a shallow valley there are tree-lined hills, edged in sunlight.

Were these scenes painted from life, or did the places exist only in the artist's head?

Coffee is brought. I have never seen a coffee plant on the bridge. My lamb's kidneys must come from somewhere, but where? On the bridge we talk of down- and up-river, and of Citywards and Kingdomwards; there must be land (would a bridge make sense without it?) but how far away?

I did all the research I could, given the limitations of both language and access which the organization of the bridge's facilities impose on the amateur investigator, but for all my months of work, I came no closer to discovering the nature or location of either the City or the Kingdom. They remain enigmatic, placeless.

My long-abandoned requests for information are doubtless still sinking through the miasmic layers of bureaucratic ooze that represent the bridge authorities' organizational structure; I have the impression that all my original questions concerning the size of the bridge, what it is bridging, what it connects, and so on, will have been handed on, rephrased, précis'd, tidied-up, glossed, paraphrased and re-transmitted so often and between so many different departments and offices that by the time they come to be considered by anybody capable of – and willing to – answer them, they will be virtually meaningless . . . and that should they by some miracle survive this process just uncontaminated enough to be comprehensible, any reply, however considerately helpful and paradigmatically clear, will even more certainly have degenerated into utter incomprehensibility by the time it finally reaches me.

So frustrating did I find the whole investigative process that at one time I seriously considered stowing away on an express train and just going looking for the damned City, or the Kingdom. Officially my wrist band, which identifies me and informs tram conductors which hospital department to charge my ticket to, restricts my travel between two tram termini only; a range of a dozen bridge sections and about the same number of miles in each direction. Not an ungenerous allowance, but a restriction, nevertheless.

I decided not to become a stowaway; I think it is more important to recover the lost territories inside my skull than to go exploring for lost lands here. I shall stay put; when I'm cured I might go.

'Morning Orr.'

I am joined by Mr Brooke, an engineer I met in hospital. A small, dark, pressured-looking man, he sits down heavily opposite me and scowls. 'Good morning, Brooke.'

'See those damn . . .' His scowl deepens.

'Aircraft? Yes. Did you?'

'No, just the smoke. Damn cheek.'

'You disapprove.'

'Disapprove?' Brooke looks shocked. 'Not up to me to approve or disapprove, but I called up a chum of mine at Shipping and Timetabling, and they didn't know anything about these . . . aircraft. Whole thing was totally unauthorized. Heads will roll, mark my words.'

'Are there laws against what they did?'

'There's no law to *permit* it, Orr, that's the point. Good grief man, you can't have people going off and doing things just because they want to, just because they think something up! You have to have a . . . a framework.' He shakes his head. 'God, you have some odd ideas at times, Orr.'

'I'd be the last to deny it.'

Brooke orders kedgeree. We were in the same ward in

hospital, and he has also been a patient of Dr Joyce's. Brooke is a senior engineer specializing in the effect of the bridge's weight on the seabed; he was injured in an accident in one of the caissons which support some of the structure's granite-shod feet. He is physically recovered now but still suffers from acute insomnia. Something about Brooke always makes me think of him as ill-lit; even in direct sunlight he always seems to be standing in shade.

'Another strange thing happened to me this morning,' I tell him. He looks wary.

'Really?' he says. I tell him about the man in the hospital bed, the television which switches itself on, and the malfunctioning phone. He seems relieved. 'Oh, that sort of thing happens all the time; crossed lines somewhere, I'll bet. You get on to Repairs and Maintenance and keep annoying them until they do something about it.'

'I shall.'

'How's that quack Joyce?'

'Still persevering with me. I've started to have some dreams, but I think they might be too . . . structured for the good doctor. He practically ignored the first one. He criticized me for giving up my investigations.'

Brooke tut-tuts. 'Well, Orr, he's the doctor and all that, but if I were you I wouldn't waste any more time on all these . . .' He pauses, searching for a suitably severe epithet, '. . . *questions*. Not likely to *get* you anywhere, you know. Certainly can't see it getting your memory back. Nor will mooning like a schoolgirl over that sort of stuff.' He gestures dismissively at one of the pastoral scenes on the wall, frowning as though pointing out some unsightly blemish on the varnished panels.

'But Brooke, don't you *ever* want to see something other than the bridge? Mountains, forest, a desert? Think of—'

'My friend,' he says heavily, watching a waiter pour him some coffee, 'do you know how many different types of rock the foundations rest upon?' He sounds patient, almost tired. I am going to be lectured, but at least this will give me a chance to eat my devilled kidneys, which have arrived and are cooling.

'No,' I admit.

'I'll tell you,' Brooke says. 'No less than seven major different types, not counting traces of dozens of others. Every type of strata is represented: sedimentary, metamorphic, and both intrusive and extrusive igneous rocks. There are major deposits of basalt, dolerite, calciferous and carboniferous sandstone, basaltic and trachytic agglomerates, basaltic lavas, tertiary and old red sandstone, and considerable amounts of schistose grit, all present in complex folded systems whose histories have yet—'

I can stomach no more rocks. 'You mean,' I say, as his kedgeree arrives (he coats it with a snowstorm of salt and deposits pepper on it like a layer of volcanic ash), 'that the bridge has more than enough to offer the enquiring mind without recourse to anything outside it.'

'Precisely.'

I'd have said it was more like approximately, but never mind. Anyway, there *is* something beyond the bridge, something I can almost but not quite remember. I seem to possess abstractions, general ideas, for things I could never find on the bridge; glaciers, cathedrals, automobiles . . . a nearly endless list. But I can recall nothing specific, no particular images come to mind. I can cope with my single language and with the customs and mores of the bridge (all surely the product of training at some point), but I can remember nothing of my schooling, my upbringing. I am complete in everything but memories. Where other people have the equivalents of encyclopedias and journals. I have . . . a pocket dictionary.

'Well, I can't help it, Brooke,' I say. 'There just seem to be so many things one can't talk about here: sex, religion and politics, for a start.'

He pauses, a forkful of kedgeree poised half way to his mouth. 'Well,' he says uncomfortably, 'there's nothing wrong with . . . the first one, if one's married, or the girl has a licence or whatever . . . but damn it, Orr,' he puts the fork down again, 'you're always going on about "religion" and "politics"; what exactly do you *mean*?'

He seems to be serious. What have I got myself into? First

48

this and then a session with Dr Joyce to follow. All the same, for the next ten minutes I attempt an explanation for Brooke. He looks increasingly mystified. Finally, once I have finished, he says, 'Hmm. Don't know why you need two words; they sound like the same thing to me.'

I sit back in awe. 'Brooke, you should have been a philosopher.'

'A philo- what?'

'Never mind. Eat your kedgeree.'

A tram takes me to Dr Joyce's bridge-section. The cramped, rattling upper deck is full of workers; they sit on the grubby seats and read newspapers with large print and photographs. They are almost entirely taken up with sport and the results of lotteries. The men are steel workers or welders; their thick working jackets have no outside pockets, and are covered in numerous small burns. The men talk amongst themselves, ignoring me. Occasionally I think I catch a word – are they using a thick dialect of my own tongue? – but the more I listen the less I understand. Really I should have waited for a soft-class tram, but I might have made myself late for my appointment with Dr Joyce, and I do believe in punctuality.

I take an express lift to the level where the good doctor has his offices. Piped music plays, but as ever it sounds to me like a random collection of notes and jumbled, mismatched chords, as though all music on the bridge has been encrypted. I have given up expecting to hear anything I can remember or whistle.

A young lady shares the lift for most of the way. She is dark and slim, and looks modestly at the floor. Her lashes are long and black and her cheek curves exquisitely. She wears a finely cut suit, with a long skirt and short jacket, and I find myself watching the rise and fall of her breasts under a white silk blouse. She does not look at me as she quits the lift; a faint hint of perfume is all that's left behind.

I concentrate on a photograph on one of the dark-wood panels by the lift door. The picture is old, sepia-tinted, and shows three of the bridge sections being built. They stand alone, unconnected except through their jagged, uncompleted similarity. Tubes and girders jut out, festooned with scaffolding and heavy-looking steam cranes are dotted about the brown lines of iron; the three incomplete sections look almost hexagonal. There is no date on the photograph.

A smell of paint permeates the doctor's offices. Two workmen in white overalls are carrying a desk in through the doors. The reception area is empty, apart from white sheets which cover the floor, and the desk, which the workmen place in the centre of the room. I look into the doctor's room; it is empty too, more white sheets covering the floor. Dr Joyce's name has been removed from the door's glass panel.

'What's happened?' I ask the workmen. They look at me blankly.

The lift again. My hands are shaking.

Thankfully, the hospital reception desk has not moved. I have to wait while a young couple with a small child are directed down a long corridor by the receptionist, but then it is my turn.

'I'm looking for Dr Joyce's office,' I tell the stern, thickset woman behind the desk. 'He was in room 3422; I was in there just yesterday, but he seems to have been moved.'

'Are you a patient?'

'My name is John Orr.' I let her read the details on my wrist band.

'Just a moment.' She lifts the telephone. I sit on a soft bench in the middle of the reception area, which is surrounded by corridors: they radiate away like spokes from a hub. The shorter corridors lead to the outside of the bridge; soft white curtains blow in a light breeze. The woman at the desk is transferred from one person to another. Finally she puts the phone down. 'Mr Orr, Dr Joyce has been relocated to room 3704.'

She draws a diagram showing the way to the doctor's new office. My chest aches dully for a while, a circular echo of pain.

'Mr Brooke sends his regards.'

Dr Joyce looks up from his notes, blinking through his grey-pink lids. I have told the doctor the dream about the galleons which exchange boarding parties. He listened without comment, nodding occasionally, frowning sometimes, making notes. The silence dragged on. 'Mr . . .?' Dr Joyce says, puzzled. His thin silver pencil hangs over the notebook like a tiny dagger.

'Mr Brooke,' I remind him. 'Came from Surgical at about the same time I did. An engineer; he suffers from insomnia. You were treating him.'

'Oh,' Dr Joyce says after a moment. 'Yes. Him.' He bends back to his notes again.

Dr Joyce's new offices are even grander than his previous accommodation. Three levels further up, with increased floor space, the doctor would appear to be continuing his advancement. He now has a private secretary as well as a receptionist. Unhappily, his elevation has not entailed the replacement of the AYM ('*My*, Mr Orr, you *are* looking well! How *nice* to see you; have a seat. *Do* let me take your coat. Cup of coffee perhaps? Tea?').

The little silver pencil is replaced in the doctor's breast pocket. 'So,' he says, clasping his hands. 'What do you make of this dream, hmm?'

Here we go again. 'Doc,' I say, trusting that this will annoy him for a start, 'I don't have a clue; not really my field. How about you?'

Dr Joyce looks at me evenly for a moment. Then he gets up from his seat and throws his notepad on to the desk. He goes over to the window and stands there, looking out and shaking his head. 'I'll tell you what I think, Orr,' he says. He turns, staring at me. 'I think both these dreams, this one and yesterday's, tell us nothing.'

'Ah,' I say. And after all my hard work. I clear my throat, not a little peeved. 'Well, what do we do now?'

Dr Joyce's blue eyes glitter. He opens a drawer in his desk and brings out a large book with wipe-clean plastic pages, and a felt-tip pen. He passes these to me. The book contains mostly half-completed drawings and ink-blot tests. 'Last

51

page,' the good doctor says. I turn, dutifully, to the last page. It contains two drawings.

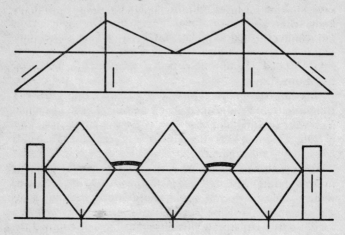

'What do I do?' I ask. This looks childish.

'You see those small lines, four in the top drawing, five in the bottom one?'

'Yes.'

'Complete those by making them into arrows so that they indicate the direction of force the structures shown are exerting at those points.' He holds up one hand as I open my mouth to ask a question. 'That's all I can say. I'm not allowed to give you any clues or answer any further questions.'

I take the pen, complete the lines as asked, and hand the book back to the doctor. He looks, nods. I ask, 'Well?'

'Well what?' He takes a cloth from his drawer and wipes the book as I put the pen on his desk.

'Did I get it right?'

He shrugs. 'What does "right" mean?' he says gruffly, putting everything back in the drawer. 'If it was an exam question you got it right, yes, but it's not an exam question. It's supposed to tell us something about you.' He makes a note in his notebook with the little silver propelling pencil.

'What does it show about me?'

He shrugs again, looking at his notes. 'I don't know,' he says, shaking his head. 'It must show something, but I don't know what. Yet.'

I would quite like to punch Dr Joyce right on his grey-pink nose.

'I seé,' I say. 'Well, I hope I have been of some use to the progress of medical science.'

'Me too,' Dr Joyce says, looking at his watch. 'Well, I think that's all for now. Make an appointment for tomorrow, just in case, but if you don't have any dreams, call in and cancel, all right?'

'*Golly* that was quick, Mr Orr. How did it go? Like a cup of tea?' The immaculately groomed receptionist helps me on with my coat. 'You were in and out of there in no time. How about some coffee?'

'No, thanks,' I say looking at Mr Berkeley and his policeman, who are waiting in the reception area. Mr Berkeley lies curled in a tight foetal position, on his side, on the floor in front of the seated policeman, who is resting his feet on him.

'Mr Berkely is a footstool today,' the Appalling Young Man tells me, proudly.

In the high, airy spaces of the upper structure the ceilings are tall and the broad, deep-pile carpet in the deserted corridors smells rich and damp. The wood panelling lining the walls is teak and mahogany, and the glass strapped in the brass-framed windows – looking out into gloomy lightwells, or towards the now hazed-over sea – has a blue tint to it. like lead crystal. In niches along the dark wooden walls, old statues of forgotten bureaucrats loom like blind ghosts, and high overhead masses of great dark furled flags hang, like heavy nets hung out to dry; they move gently as a soft, chill draught moves ancient dust through the dark, tall corridors.

About a half-hour's wander from the doctor's offices, I discover an old lift, opposite a gigantic circular outside window which looks out over the firth like some transparent clock-face robbed of its hands. The lift door is open; an old, grizzled man sits on a tall stool inside, asleep. He wears a long, burgundy coat with shiny buttons, his thin arms are crossed over his belly; his impressively bearded chin rests on his be-buttoned chest, and his white-haired head moves slowly up and down in time with his wheezy breathing.

I cough. The old man sleeps on. I knock on the protruding edge of one door. 'Hello?'

He comes awake with a jerk, uncrosses his arms and steadies himself on the lift controls; there is a click, and the doors start to close, groaning and creaking, until his waving arms flap against the brass levers again, whereupon the doors retreat.

'Bless me, sir. What a fright you gave me! Just having a little snooze, so I was. Come in, sir. Which floor now?'

The generous, room-sized lift is full of ill-assorted chairs, peeling mirrors and dust-dulled hanging tapestries. Unless it is a trick of the mirrors, it is also L-shaped, which makes it unique in my experience. 'Train deck, please.' I say.

'Right you are, sir!' The ancient attendant hooks a withered hand over the control levers; the doors grate and clank closed, and after a few nudgings and carefully aimed thumps on the brass plate containing the control levers, the old fellow finally succeeds in coaxing the lift into motion; it slides – rumbling, stately – downwards, mirrors vibrating, fitments rattling, the lighter seats and chairs rocking on its unevenly carpeted floor. The old man sways precariously on his high stool and holds on tightly to a brass rail under the controls. I can hear his teeth chattering. I hang on to a brightly polished and loosely rattling handrail. A noise like shearing metal echoes somewhere overhead.

Feigning nonchalance, I study a yellowed notice at my shoulder. It lists the various floors the lift serves, and the departments, accommodation sections and other facilities to be found on these levels. One near the top catches my eye. My God! I've found it!

'Excuse me!' I say to the old man. He turns his head, shaking as though with palsy, to look at me. I tap the list on the wall. 'I've changed my mind; I'd like to go to this floor: 52. To the Third City Library.'

The old man looks despairingly at me for a moment, then puts one shaking hand to the clattering controls and slaps one of the levers down before clutching desperately at the brass rail again and closing his eyes.

The elevator whines, screams, bounces, crashes and judders from side to side. I am almost thrown from my feet; the old fellow parts company with his high stool. Chairs topple. A mirror cracks. A light fixture falls half way from the ceiling then jerks, like a hanged man, bouncing to a swaying stop in a cascade of plaster and dust and hanging wires.

We come to a halt. The old man pats dust off both shoulders, adjusts jacket and hat, picks up his stool and presses some more controls; we ascend, comparatively smoothly.

'Sorry.' I shout to the attendant. He stares wildly at me and starts glancing about the lift, as though trying to discover what terrible crime I am apologizing for. 'I didn't realize stopping and going back would be quite so ... traumatic,' I yell to him. He looks utterly mystified, and gazes round the rattling, creaking, dust-hazed interior of his small domain as though unable to see what all the fuss is about.

We stop. The elevator does not *chime* on arrival; instead a bell whose power and tone would do justice to a large church concusses the air within it. The old fellow looks fearfully overhead. 'We're here, sir,' he shouts.

He opens the doors to a scene of utter chaos, and jumps back. I watch, amazed, for a few moments, slowly coming forward to the doors. The old attendant peers nervously round the edge.

We seem to have arrived at the scene of a terrible disaster; in a huge but wreckage-choked hall in front of us we see fire, fallen girders, mangled pipes and beams, collapsed brickwork and drooping cables; uniformed people rush around carrying fire hoses, stretchers and unidentifiable pieces of equipment. A great pall of smoke overhangs everything. The din and racket of jangling alarms and klaxons, explosions and amplified, shouted orders are frightening, even to ears somewhat stunned by the bell which announced our arrival. What has happened here?

'Strike me sir,' the old attendant coughs, 'doesn't look much like a library from this angle, does it?'

'No it doesn't,' I agree, watching a dozen men wheel some great pumping apparatus across the debris-strewn floor of the hall in front of us. 'Are you quite sure this is the right floor?'

He checks his floor indicator, thumping the dial with one arthritic fist. 'Sure as I can be, sir.' He digs out a pair of spectacles and peers again at the indicator. An explosion in the wreckage of pipes and girders sends up a roll of black smoke and sparks; men nearby jump for cover. A man wearing a tall hat and bright yellow uniform sees us and waves a megaphone. He steps over some bodies on stretchers and approaches us.

'You there!' he shouts. 'What the hell do you think you're doing, eh? Looters? Ghouls? Eh? Is that it? Get on your way at once!'

'I'm looking for the Third City Records and Historical Materials Library,' I tell him calmly. He waves his megaphone at the chaotic scene behind him.

'So are we, you idiot! Now fuck off!' He jabs the megaphone in the direction of my chest and storms off, tripping over one of the bodies on the stretchers and then running over to direct the men manoeuvring the giant pump. The old attendant and I look at each other. He closes the doors.

'Rude bugger, eh, sir?'

'He did seem a little upset.'

'Train deck sir?'

'Hmmm? Oh, yes. Please.' I hold onto the rattling brass rail again as we descend. 'I wonder what happened to the library?'

The old man shrugs. 'Goodness knows, sir. All sorts of funny things happen in these higher reaches. Some of the things I've seen . . .' He shakes his head, whistles through his teeth. 'You'd be amazed, sir.'

'Yes,' I admit ruefully, 'I probably would.'

At the rackets club in the afternoon I win one game, lose the other. The aircraft and their strange signals are the only topic of conversation; most of the people at the club – professionals and bureaucrats to a man – regard the odd fly-past as an unwarranted outrage about which Something Must Be Done. I ask a newspaper journalist if he has heard anything about a terrible fire on the level where the Third City Library was supposed to be, but he hasn't even heard of the library, and certainly not of any upper-structure disaster. He will check.

From the club I phone Repairs and Maintenance and tell them about my television and telephone. I eat at the club and go to a theatre at night; an uninspired production about a signalman's daughter who falls in love with a tourist who turns out to be a railway boss's son, engaged and having one last fling. I leave after the second act.

At home, as I undress, a small crumpled piece of paper falls from a pocket in my coat. It is the smudged diagram the hospital receptionist drew for me to show me the way to Dr Joyce's office. It looks like this:

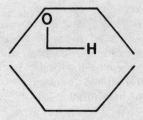

I stare at it, vaguely troubled. My head feels light and the room seems to tip, as though I am still in the decrepit L-shaped lift with the old attendant, completing another unscheduled and dangerous lift-shaft manoeuvre. For a moment my thoughts feel scrambled, mixed up like the smoke signals trailed by the strange flight of planes this morning (and for an instant, dizzy and swaying, I myself seem somehow clouded and formless, like something chaotic and amorphous, like the mists which curl amongst the snagging complexity of the high bridge, coating the layers of ancient paint on its girders and its beams like sweat).

The telephone rings, snapping me out of this odd moment; I lift the receiver only to hear the same, curious regular beeping at the other end. 'Hello? Hello?' I say. Nothing.

I put it down. It rings again and the same thing happens. I leave it off the cradle this time and cover the earpiece with a cushion. I don't even try the television – I know what I'll see.

As I head for bed, I realize I am still holding the small piece of paper. I throw it into the waste-bin.

Three

At my back lay the desert, ahead the sea. One golden, one blue, they met like rival modes of time. One moved in the immediate, sparkling in troughs and crests, lifting white and falling, beating the shelf of sand, and the tide as breath . . . the other moved more slowly, but as surely, the tall advancing waves of sand stroked over the waste by the combing hand of the unseen wind.

Between the two, half submerged by each, the ruined city.

Abraded by both sand and water, caught like something soft between two meshing iron wheels, the stones of the city submitted to the agents of the wind.

I was alone, and walked through the midday heat, a white ghost billowing through the tumbled wreckage of the shattered buildings. My shadow was at my feet, beneath me; invisible.

The rose-red stones were jumbled and askew. Most of the streets were gone, long ago buried under the soft encroaching sands. Ruined arches, fallen lintels, collapsed walls littered the slopes of sand; at the scalloped edge of shore, brushed by the waves, more fallen blocks broke the incoming waves. A little out to sea, tilted towers and the fragment of an arch rose from the waters, sucked at by the waves like the bones of the long-drowned.

On the worn stones over empty doors and sand-filled windows, friezes of figures and symbols had been carved. I inspected these curious, half-legible images, attempting to decipher their linear patterns. The wind-blown sand had eroded some of the walls and beams until the thickness was less than the depth of the chiselled symbols; blue sky shone through the blood-red rock.

'I know this place,' I said to myself. 'I know you,' I said to the silent wreckage.

A huge statue stood apart from the main area of the city's ruins. The thick-set trunk and head of a man, perhaps three or four times life-size, it faced along a diagonal between the line of foam-washed beach and the centre of the silent ruins. The statue's arms had fallen or been broken off long ago; the stumps worn smooth by the wind and sand. One side of the massive body and head showed the accumulated effects of the scouring wind, but on the front, and the other side, the figure's details were still apparent; a naked torso, big-bellied, but the upper chest covered in chains and jewels and rope-thick necklaces; the great head, bald but crowned, ear heavy with rings, nose studded. The expression on that time-worn face was one which, like the graven symbols, I could not translate; perhaps cruelty, perhaps bitterness, perhaps a callous disregard for all things, save sand and wind.

'Mock? Mocca?' I found myself whispering, gazing up at the bulbous stone eyes. The giant offered no help. Names too became worn away, however slowly; at first altered, then reduced, then forgotten.

On the beach before the city, some way from the statue's stony gaze, I found a man. He was small and lame and hunched over, and he stood up to his knees in the shallow surf, the waves washing round the dark rags he wore, and he beat at the surface of the water with a heavy lash of chains, cursing all the while.

His head was bowed under the weight of his deformed back; long, filthy hair hung down in tight tangles to the chopping waves, and sometimes, like a sudden grey-white hair erupting from the centre of this dark mass, a long strand of spittle would drop towards the waves, and float away.

All the time his right arm rose and fell, whipping at the sea with his flail, a short heavy thing with a shining wooden handle and a dozen glistening, rusting lengths of iron chain. The waters around him frothed and bubbled under his steady and unceasing attack, and clouded with the grains of sand disturbed from the slope beneath.

The hunched man stopped his flogging for a moment, shifted – crablike – a step to one side, wiped his mouth with one cuff, then resumed, muttering all the time as the heavy chains rose, fell, splashed. I stood on the shore behind him, watching, for a long time. He stopped again, wiped his face once more, then took another step to the side. The wind blew his ragged clothes, briefly lifted his oily, tangled hair. My own loose garment flapped in the same gust, and he may have heard the noise over the falling surf, for he did not immediately resume his labours. His head moved slightly, as though to catch some faint sound. He seemed to try to straighten his twisted back, but then gave up. He turned slowly round in a succession of tiny shuffling steps – as though his feet were hobbled on a short chain – until he faced me. He brought his head up, slowly, until he could look at me, then stood, the waves still breaking around his knees, the flail dangling in the water from one gnarled hand.

His face was almost hidden by the tangled mass of hair piled around his head and falling like another uneven flail towards the sea. His expression was unreadable. I waited for him to speak, but he stood, silent, patient, until finally I said, 'Excuse me. Please carry on.'

He said nothing for a while, gave no sign of having heard, as if there was some medium slower than air between us, then replied in a voice of surprising gentleness. 'It's my job, you know. I am employed to do this.'

I nodded. 'Oh, I see.' I waited for some further explanation.

He seemed to hear my words, again, long after I had spoken them. After a while he gave a lop-sided shrug. 'You see, once, a great emperor . . .' Then his voice died away, and he was silent for a few moments. I waited. He shook his head after a while, and shuffled round to face the curved blue horizon. I shouted, but he gave no sign of having heard.

He started to beat the waves again, muttering and cursing,

quietly and monotonously.

I watched him whip at the sea for a little longer, then I turned and walked away. An iron bracelet, like the remains of some snapped manacle – I had not noticed it before – made a faint, rhythmic clinking noise on my wrist as I walked back to the ruins.

Did I really dream that? The ruined city by the sea, the man with the chain whip? I am confused for a moment; did I lie down last night and try to dream up something to tell the doctor?

In the darkness of my large, warmed bed, I feel a sort of relief. I laugh quietly, inordinately pleased with myself for having finally had a dream I can tell the good doctor with a clear conscience. I get up and pull on a dressing-gown. The apartment is cold, the grey dawn glows softly through the tall windows; a tiny, slowly pulsing light shines far out to sea, beneath a long bank of dark cloud, as though the cloud is land, and the slowly flashing buoy a harbour's signal.

A bell sounds somewhere, far away, followed by the quieter chimes which announce the hour as five o'clock. A train whistle blows in the distance beneath, and a hardly heard, partly felt rumble witnesses the passing of a heavy-goods.

In the sitting room, I watch the grey, unmoving picture of the man in the hospital bed. The small bronze sculptures of the bridge workers, placed variously about the room, reflect the palely shining monochrome light from their rough surfaces. Suddenly a woman, a nurse, comes silently onto the screen and goes to the man's bed. I cannot see her face. She seems to be taking the fellow's temperature.

There is no sound other than a distant hiss. The nurse walks round the bed, over the shiny floor to check the machines. She disappears again, going beneath the camera, then returns holding a small metal tray. She takes a syringe from it, draws some fluid from a little bottle, holds the needle up, then swabs the pale man's arm and injects him. I suck air through my teeth; I have never (I am sure) liked injections.

The picture is too grainy for me to see the needle actually piercing the man's skin, but in my imagination I see the slant-edged tip of the needle's tube, and the pale, soft, yielding skin . . . I wince with sympathetic pain and turn the set off.

I lift the cushion off the telephone. The beeping noise is still there; maybe a little faster than it was before. I replace the receiver on the cradle. The machine rings immediately. I pick it up, but instead of the pulsing monotone:

'Ah, Orr; got you at last. That is you, isn't it?'

'Yes, Brooke, it's me.'

'Where have you been?' His voice is slurred.

'Asleep.'

'Out where? Sorry, this noise—' I can hear babbling voices in the background.

'I wasn't anywhere. I was asleep. Or rather I *was*—'

'*Asleep?*' Brooke says loudly. '*That* won't do, Orr. That just won't do at all, I'm sorry. We're at Dissy Pitton's – the bar. Come over at once; we've saved you a bottle.'

'Brooke, it's the middle of the night.'

'Good grief, is it? Just as well I called.'

'The dawn is just coming up.'

'*Is* it?' Brooke's astonished voice goes away from the phone. I hear him shout something, then there is loud, ragged cheering. 'Hurry up then, Orr. Get a milk train or something. We'll expect you.'

'Brooke—' I begin, but then I hear Brooke talking away from the telephone again, and some distant shouting.

'Oh,' he says. 'Yes. And bring a hat; you've got to bring a—' More shouting in the background. 'Oh; it has to be a wide-brimmed hat. Have you got a wide-brimmed hat?'

'I—' I am interrupted by further shouting.

Brooke yells, 'Yes, it has to be wide-brimmed! If you haven't got a wide-brimmed hat, don't bring one that isn't. Have you got one?'

'I think so,' I say, suspecting that to say so is to commit myself to going.

'Right,' Brooke says. 'See you soon. Don't forget the hat.'

He rings off. I put the phone down, lift it again and hear

the regular beeping noise once more. I look out at the slowly flashing light under the cloud bank, shrug, and head for my dressing room.

Dissy Pitton's bar lies, spread over several eccentrically arranged floors, in an unfashionable area only a few decks above train level. Directly beneath the lowest of the bars there is a rope works, where ropes and cables are wound in a series of long and narrow sheds. Accordingly, Dissy Pitton's is a place of ropes and cables, where all the tables and chairs are suspended from the ceilings rather than supported by the floors. In Dissy Pitton's, as Brooke once observed in one of his rare bouts of humour, even the furniture is legless.

The doorman is asleep on his feet, leaning back against the wall of the building, arms folded and head down, peaked cap shading his eyes from the flashing neon sign over the door. He is snoring. I let myself in and climb through two dark, deserted floors to where noise and light indicate the party continues.

'Orr! The very man!' Brooke comes unsteadily through the crowd of people and the swaying maze of suspended tables, chairs, couches and screens. He steps over a snoring body on the way.

Drunks in Dissy Pitton's seldom remain under the same table for long. Usually they end up sprawled on the floor in some distant part of the bar, having been tempted by the seemingly endless plane of teak floor into crawling off on all fours, driven by some deeply ingrained instinct of infantile inquisitiveness, or perhaps the desire to impersonate a slug.

'Good of you to come, Orr,' Brooke says, taking my arm. He looks at the wide-brimmed hat I am clutching. 'Nice hat.' He leads me towards a distant table.

'Yes,' I say, handing it to him. 'Who wanted it? What's it for?'

'What?' He stops; he turns the hat over in his hands. He looks, mystified, inside the crown, as though for a clue.

'You asked for a wide-brimmed hat, remember?' I tell him. 'You asked me to bring one, earlier.'

'Hmm,' Brooke says, and leads me to a table with four or

five people clustered around it. I recognize Baker and Fowler, two of Brooke's fellow engineers. They are in the process of trying to stand up. Brooke still looks puzzled. He is looking closely at the hat.

'Brooke,' I say, trying not to sound exasperated. 'You asked me to bring the damn thing, not half an hour ago. You *can't* have forgotten.'

'You sure that was *this* evening?' Brooke says sceptically.

'Brooke, you rang! You invited me over here, you—'

'Oh look,' Brooke says, belching and reaching for a bottle. 'Have some wine and we'll think about it.' He shoves a glass into my hands. 'You've got some catching up to do.'

'I fear your lead is unassailable.'

'You're not upset, are you, Orr?' Brooke says. pouring wine into my glass.

'Merely sober. The symptoms are similar.'

'You *are* upset.'

'No, I'm not.'

'Why are you upset?'

Why do I form the impression that Brooke is not really listening to me? This happens, sometimes. I talk to people, but a sort of emptiness seems to come over them, as though the face really is a mask, with the real person somewhere behind it, normally pressed up against the inside like a child with their nose against a sweet-shop window, but – when I am talking to them, trying to make some difficult or unacceptable point – lifting that internal self away from the mask and turning somewhere inside themselves, performing the mental equivalent of taking their shoes off and putting their feet up, having a cup of coffee and resting for a while, returning later only when they're good and ready, to nod inappropriately and make some wholly irrelevant remark redolent of stale thoughts. Perhaps it's me, I think. Perhaps only I have this effect on people; maybe nobody else does.

Well, this is paranoid thinking, I suppose, and I don't doubt the effect is one of those which, once one has the courage to broach the subject with other people, will prove to be extremely common, if not nearly universal ('Oh *yes*, I've felt that; that happens to me! I thought it was only me.')

Meanwhile, engineers Baker and Fowler have both succeeded in standing and pulling on their coats. Brooke is talking earnestly to engineer Fowler, who looks perplexed. Then enlightenment spreads across his face. He says something which Brooke nods at before coming back to me. 'Bouch,' he tells me, then picks up his own coat from the back of a couch.

'What?' I say.

'Tommy Bouch,' Brooke says, putting his coat on. 'He wanted the hat.'

'What for?'

'Don't know, Orr,' Brooke admits.

'Well, where is he?' I ask, looking round the bar.

'Went outside a while ago,' Brooke tells me. He buttons his coat. Fowler and Baker stand behind him, swaying uncertainly.

'Are you three going?' I ask, rather unnecessarily.

'Have to,' Brooke says, then takes my arm, leans closer. 'Urgent appointment at Mrs Hanover's,' he whispers loudly.

'Mrs—' I begin. Mrs Hanover's is a licensed brothel. I know that Brooke and his cronies visit it occasionally, and I suspect it is frequented mostly by engineers (a host of unsubtle allusions suggest themselves). I have been invited before, but made it clear I have no interest in attending. This reticence arises from vanity, not moral scruples, I have assured Brooke, but I suspect he still thinks I am – beneath my talk of sex, politics and religion – a prude.

'Don't suppose you want to come along, do you?' Brooke says.

'Thank you, no,' I say.

'Hmmm, didn't think so,' Brooke nods. He takes my arm again, puts his mouth near to my ear. 'Thing is, Orr, it's a bit awkward . . .'

'What?' I watch engineer Fowler talking to a young man with long hair who is sitting in the shadows behind him. Another young man is slumped over the table behind him.

'It's Arrol's daughter,' Brooke says, glancing back over his shoulder.

'Who?'

'Chief Engineer Arrol's daughter,' Brooke whispers. 'She's sort of attached herself to us, you see, and that brother of hers has gone and fallen asleep, so if we leave now there won't be anybody to . . . Look, you wouldn't mind sort of . . . talking to her, would you?'

'Brooke,' I say, coldly, 'first of all you call me at five o'clock in the morning, then—' I get no further.

Baker, supported by an anxious-looking Fowler, stumbles into Brooke, and says, 'Think we'd better go now, Brooke; not feeling awfully . . .' Engineer Baker stops, seems to belch. His cheeks bulge; he swallows, then grimaces and nods in the direction of the steps to the lower floor.

'Got to go, Orr,' Brooke says hurriedly, grabbing one of Baker's arms while Fowler grasps the other. 'See you later. Thanks for looking after the girl. Have to make your own introductions, sorry.' The three of them barge past me; Brooke shoves the wide-brimmed hat back into my hands. Fowler drags Baker off towards the stairs, with Brooke in tow via Baker's other arm. 'I'll tell Tommy Bouch about the hat if I see him,' Brooke shouts.

They stagger together through the crowds, towards the stairs. As I turn, my attention is caught by the young man I saw Fowler talking to earlier; he is looking up, from rather baggy eyes, smiling at me.

Wrong. Not a young man; a young woman. She is wearing a dark, rather well-cut suit with wide trousers, a brocade waistcoat with a rather ostentatious gold chain across it, and a white cotton shirt. Her shirt collar is open, a black bow-tie hanging undone from it. Black shoes. Her hair is dark, shoulder length. She is sitting sideways on a seat, one leg drawn up under her. One dark hooked eyebrow hoists; I follow her gaze to where the tripod of engineers who have just left the table are attempting to navigate their way through the press of bodies at the head of the stairs. 'Think they'll make it?' she says. She tips her head to one side, one clenched fist supporting the back of her head.

'I think I'd want very good odds,' I reply. She nods thoughtfully and takes a drink from a long glass.

'Yes, me too,' she says. 'I'm sorry; I don't know your name.'

'My name is John Orr.'

'Abberlaine Arrol.'

'How do you do,' I say.

Abberlaine Arrol smiles, amused. 'I do as I like. Mr Orr. And yourself?'

One irrelevant reply deserves another; 'You must be Chief Engineer Arrol's daughter,' I say, putting the wide-brimmed hat on the end of a couch (where, with any luck at all, somebody else will pick it up).

'That's right,' she says. 'Are you an engineer, Mr Orr?' She waves one long, unringed hand at a seat beside her. I take off my coat, sit down.

'No, I'm a patient, under Dr Joyce.'

'Ahh,' she says, nodding slowly. She looks at me with a directness I've found unusual on the bridge, as though I am some complicated mechanism in which one small part has come adrift. Her face is young, but soft-looking in the way of an older woman's, though unlined; she is small-eyed, with the bones obvious under the smooth skin at brow and cheek. Her mouth is quite broad, and smiling, but I find my gaze drawn to small crinkles of skin under her grey eyes, small folds, which give her a knowing, ironic look.

'What do they think might be wrong with you, Mr Orr?' Her eyes glance towards my wrist, but my medical name band is hidden by my cuff.

'Amnesia.'

'Ah really; from when?' She wastes no time between sentences.

'About eight months ago. I was . . . netted by some fishermen.'

'Oh, I think I read about it. They fished you out of the sea.'

'So I'm told. That's one of the many things I've forgotten.'

'Haven't they found out who you are yet?'

'No; no one has claimed me, at any rate. I don't match the description of any missing person.'

'Hmm, it must be strange.' A finger goes to her lips. 'I

imagined it might be quite interesting and . . .' a shrug, 'romantic to have lost one's memory, but perhaps it's just frustrating?' She has rather fine, very dark eyebrows.

'Mostly frustrating, but also interesting, as is the treatment. My doctor believes in dream therapy.'

'And do you?'

'Not yet.'

'You will if it works.' She nods.

'Probably.'

'But,' she raises one finger. 'what if you have to believe in it before it can work?'

'I'm not sure that would accord with the good doctor's scientific principles.'

'But if it works, who cares?'

'Ah, but if one has belief without reason in the process, one may end up having belief without reason in the result.'

This makes her pause, but only for a moment.

'So you might think you're cured when you're not,' she says. 'But there'd be a definite result; you'd either have your memory back or not.'

'Ah, but I might not; I might make it up.'

'Make up your own past life?' Sceptically.

'Some people do it all the time.' I think I am teasing, but even as I speak the words, I wonder.

'Only to fool other people. They must know they're lying.'

'I'm not sure it's that simple. I think the easiest people to fool are ourselves. Fooling ourselves may even be a necessary precondition for fooling others.'

'Oh no,' she says quite definitely. 'To be a good liar you have to have a very good memory; to fool others you usually have to be cleverer than they.'

'You think no one ever believes their own stories?'

'Oh, maybe a few people in psychiatric hospitals do, but that's all. I think most of the patients who claim to believe they're other people are just playing a sort of game with the staff.'

Such certainty! I seem to recall being that sure of things, even if I can't remember what it was I was so definite about. 'You must think doctors very easy to fool,' I say. She smiles.

Her teeth are unobjectionable. I am aware of evaluating this young woman, of sizing her up. She is entertaining without being entrancing, absorbing without being captivating. Probably just as well. She nods.

'I think they can be fooled quite easily when they treat the mind like a muscle. It doesn't seem to occur to them that their patients might be trying to fool them deliberately.'

I'd dispute this: Dr Joyce, for one, seems to make it a matter of professional pride never fully to believe anything his patients tell him. 'Well,' I say, 'I think a good doctor will usually spot the charlatan patient. Most people lack the imagination to assume the role sufficiently well.'

Her brows crease. 'Maybe,' she says, staring past me intently, unfocused. 'I'm just thinking of childhood, when we—'

At this point, the young man sitting on the far side of her, with his arms on the table and his head on his arms, stirs, sits up and yawns, looking round with bleary eyes. Abberlaine Arrol turns to him. 'Ah, awake once more,' she says to him, a gangly fellow with close-set eyes and a long nose. 'Finally scrape together a quorum of neurons, did we?'

'Don't be a shit, Abby,' he says, after a dismissive glance at me. 'Get me some water.'

'You may be an animal, brother dear,' she says, 'but I am not your keeper.'

He looks about the table, which is mostly covered in dirty plates and empty glasses. Abberlaine Arrol looks at me. 'I don't suppose you know if you have any brothers, do you?'

'Not to the best of my knowledge.'

'Hmm.' She gets up and heads for the bar. The fellow closes his eyes and leans back in his seat, making it swing slightly. The bar is emptying. Only a few legs can be seen poking out from beneath distant tables, witnessing where their owners' alcoholic excursions into the long-lost days of four-limbed locomotion have come to their stupefied conclusions. Abberlaine Arrol returns with a pitcher of water. She is smoking a long, thin cigar. She stands in front of the young man and pours a little over his head, puffing on the cigar.

He stumbles to the floor, cursing, and stands up shakily. She hands him the pitcher and he drinks. She watches him with a sort of amused contempt.

'Did you see the famous aircraft this morning, Mr Orr?' Miss Arrol asks, watching her brother, not looking at me.

'Yes. Did you?'

She shakes her head. 'No. I was told about them, but I thought at first that it was a joke.'

'They looked real enough to me.'

Her brother finishes the water and throws the pitcher behind him with a theatrical gesture. It smashes on a table in the shadows. Abberlaine Arrol shakes her head. The young man yawns.

'I'm tired. Let's go. Where's dad?'

'Gone to the club. But that was some time ago; he might be home by now.'

'Good. Come on.' He walks towards the stairs. Miss Arrol shrugs at me.

'I must go, Mr Orr.'

'That's all right.'

'Nice talking to you.'

'A mutual pleasure, then.'

She looks to where the young man is waiting, hands on hips, at the tops of the steps. 'Perhaps,' she says to me, 'we'll have the chance to continue our conversation at a later date.'

'I hope so.'

She remains standing there for a moment; slim, slightly dishevelled, smoking her cigar, then executes a deep, mocking bow, hand flourished, and backs away, sticking the cigar in her mouth. A line of grey smoke curls after her.

The revellers have departed. Most of the people left in Dissy Pitton's are bar staff; they are switching out lights, wiping tables, sweeping the floor, lifting inebriated forms from the deck. I sit and finish my glass of wine; it is warm and bitter, but I hate to leave an unfinished glass.

Finally, I rise and tread the narrow corridor of remaining lights to the stairs. 'Sir!'

I turn; a broom-wielding barman is holding the wide-brimmed hat. 'Your hat,' he says, shaking it at me just in case I thought he meant the broom. I take the cursed thing, secure in the knowledge that had it been precious to me, had I been looking after it and trying to make sure that I didn't lose it, it would most assuredly have disappeared for ever.

At the door Tommy Bouch is being held against the wall by the no longer dormant doorman and quizzed on his identity and destination. Engineer Bouch seems unable to make any coherent noises, his face has a distinctly green hue about it and the doorman is having difficulty supporting him.

'You know this gentleman, sir?' the doorman asks. I shake my head.

'Never seen him before,' I say, then shove the hat between the doorman's arms. 'But he left his hat inside.'

'Oh, thank you sir,' the doorman says. He holds the hat in front of the engineer's face so that he can see it (or both of them, as the case may be). 'Look, sir, your hat.'

'Thanyoo,' Engineer Bouch succeeds in pronouncing, before transferring the contents of his stomach into the crown of the headgear. Thanks to the wide brim, of course, remarkably little splatters over the side.

I walk away feeling oddly triumphant. Perhaps that was what he wanted it for all the time.

'Not here?'

'Oh, golly, you know I really and honestly *am* sorry Mr Orr, but no, he isn't.'

'But I have—'

'An appointment, yes, I know Mr Orr. I have it here, see?'

'Well what's the matter?'

'Urgent meeting of the Administrative Board Primary Subcommittee Vetting Committee, I'm afraid; pretty important. The doctor's a very busy man these days, sir. There are just *so many* calls on his time. You mustn't take it personally, Mr Orr.'

'I'm not—'

'It's just the way things go. Nobody likes all this admin stuff, but it's just a dirty job that has to be done.'

71

'Yes, I—'

'It could have happened during anybody's appointment; you were just unlucky.'

'I appreciate—'

'You mustn't take it personally. It was just one of those things.'

'Yes, of course—'

'And of course there's absolutely no connection with us forgetting to tell you we'd moved offices the other day. That was purely coincidence; it could have happened to absolutely anybody whatsoever. You were just unlucky. It really really *isn't* anything personal.'

'I—'

'You mustn't take it that way.'

'I'm *not*!'

'Oh, Mr Orr; not at home to Mr Tetchy, are we?'

Outside, remembering yesterday's eventful lift journey, I head in the same direction as before, looking for the giant circular window and the entrance to the decrepit, L-shaped lift opposite it.

Increasingly frustrated and annoyed, I wander for over an hour through the high-ceilinged gloom of the upper structure, past the same blind-statued niches (ancient bureaucrats fastened in pale stone) and the same heavily hanging flags (furled like thickly ponderous sails on some great dark ship), but without finding the circular window, the old bearded man, or the lift. A senior clerk whose long-service ribbons proclaim he is a veteran of at least thirty years service, looks puzzled and shakes his head when I describe the lift and its grizzled operator.

Eventually (the doctor would not be proud of me), I give up.

I spend the next few hours tramping round various small galleries in a distant section of the bridge, some distance from my usual haunts. The galleries are dark and musty, and the attendants look surprised that anybody should come to view the exhibits. Nothing satisfies me; the works all look tired and spent; paintings washed out, sculptures deflated. Worse than the poor execution, though, is the downright unhealthy preoccupation with distortions of the human form which all the artists appear to share. The sculptors have twisted it into a bizarre resemblance of the structures of the bridge itself; thighs become caissons, torsos either caissons or structural tubes, and arms and legs stressed girders; sections of bodies are constructed from riveted iron painted bridge red; tubular girders become limbs, merging into grotesque conglomerations of metal and flesh like tumorous miscegenistic eruptions of cell and grain. The paintings exhibit much the same preoccupations; one shows the bridge as a line of misshapen dwarfs standing in sewage or blood, arms linked, another depicts a single tubular formation, but with meandering blue veins picked out beneath the ochre surface, and small trickles of blood coming from each rivet hole.

Beneath this part of the bridge is one of the small islands which support every third section.

These islands are regular only in their approximate size and spacing; otherwise they vary in shape and use. Some are riddled with old mine workings and underground caverns, others almost covered in the decaying concrete slabs and circular pits of what look like old gun emplacements. Some support ruined buildings, either old pit-head works or long-crumbled factories. Most have a small harbour or marina at one end, and a few are quite without any sign of human habitation or construction at all – mere lumps of green, covered in grass and scrub and green seawrack.

They share a mystery though, and that is simply how they come to be here in the first place. They look natural, but together, seen in all their linear regularity, the islands betray themselves with a pattern, an unnatural order that makes them even stranger than the bridge they intermittently support.

I toss a coin out of the window on the tram home; it goes glittering away, heading for the sea, not an island. A couple of other passengers throw coins too, and I have a brief, absurd vision of the waters below eventually being filled with thrown coins, the whole firth silting up with the monetary debris of spent wishes, surrounding the hollow metal bones of the bridge with a solid desert of coin.

In my apartment again, before going to bed, I watch the man in the hospital bed for a while, staring at his grey and grainy image so hard and for so long that I almost mesmerize myself with that blank, still image. Rooted in the evening darkness, eyes fixed, I seem to be looking not at a phosphorescing screen of glass, but a bright metal plate; an engraving lined and stamped on a shining, large-grained slab of steel.

I wait for the phone to ring.

I wait for the flight of planes to return.

Then a nurse appears; the same nurse, complete with metal tray. The spell is broken, the illusion of the screen as plate, fractured.

The nurse readies the syringe, swabs the man's arm. I shiver, as though that alcohol, that spirit, chilled me; chilled all my flesh.

Quickly, I switch off.

Four

It wiz this majishin that geez this thing, cald it a familyar soay did an it sits on ma showdder and gose jibber fukin jibber oll bludy day it gose. I cany stand the dam thing but am stuk with it I supose an it wi me to, cumty think ov it. The majishin sed it woold help me; sed it woold tel me things, whitch it duz alright, but I thaught he ment sum usefyull things no a lode a shite oll day. He wiz trying tay bribe me becose he thaught I wiz goantae kill him, whitch I wiz, an he sed if I didnae hed give us this reely intirestin an usefyull familyar tay keep watch at niyht an giv us oll that advyce an that. So I sed fairnuf pal, lets see whit it can dae then, so he gose tay this shelph an gets this wee box an puts sum stuf intae it an ses sum o thae wurds an that (I wiz watchin him, ken, in case he tryd enythin, had ma sord at his throate in

case he tryd tae turn me intae sumthin wee an nastie, but he
didnae). Insted he brings oot this funny wee thing like a cat
or a munkey, aw cuvered in blak fur wi a pear aw wee blak
wings on its bak an cros-eyes, an he stiks it on ma showdder
an ses 'Thare you go my boy,' an I wiz a bit leery ken, cos it
wiz an ugly wee bugir an sittin gie cloase tae ma heid, but a
stil had ma sord at the majishin's throte, so I lookd at this
skely-eyed thing an sed 'whare's this auld bugir's gold then?'
an it sed 'in the old trunk behind the screan, but its a majik
trunk; it looks empty, but yoo can feel the gold and itill
becum visibil when you take it out' Majishin just aboot had a
fit soay did; I maid him go an get the gold, an it was true whit
the familyar had sed so I asked it whit I shoold do now an it
sed 'kill this auld bugir for a start off, heeze a triky custimur.'
So I kilt the majishin but the fukin thing's nevir sed enythin
usefyull ever since, just blethers oll day long.

'. . . of course, according to the preceptive rules of the New
Symbology, as characterized in the *Grande Cabale*, the tower
signifies retreat, the limitation of contact with the real world;
philosophical extrospection. In short, nothing to do with the
literally infantile preoccupation with phallic symbolism I
mentioned earlier. Indeed, except within the most morally
constipated of societies, when people want to dream about
sex, they dream about sex. Actually the combination of the
cards *La Mine* and *La Tour* in the minor game is considered
particularly important and the significance of the tower over
the pit *does* have a sexual resonance for predictive purposes
which the simple combination of retreat and the fear of
failure would not appear immediately to imply, but—'

See whit I meen? Drive ye daft, so it woold. I cany even get
the wee basturd aff me showldur niythir on acount of its got
these claws inside me, biride in ma flesh so they are. Their no
soar untill I try takin the thing aff, but soar enuoph then
alright. Canny even stab it or bash it with a rok on acount of
its ded adjile an starts screemin an bawlin fit tae raze the deid
an jookin and jumpin aboot and me triing tay bash it or stik
ma dirk doon its throate but tay no avale.

Enyway, Ive dun alright sinse it took up with me, so
maybay its lucky after oll. I wrekin it disney wurk right

75

without a majishin around, but that's tuff; Im a sordsman no a bleading wizerd after oll. Enyway, like I say, Ive dun alright sinse it took up with me an its taut me a load a new wurds an that, so am a bit mair ejucatit these days, ken. Aw aye, I forgot to mencion that if I try takin it aff ma sholder or if a dinny feed it itill tolk ded loud oll nihgt an keep me awake, so seein it disnae eet mutch an its been luky fir me I just leeve it thare now an we get on as wel as can be expected. Wish it didnae shite doon ma bak thow.

'Interesting point actually; I mean I'm sure you won't have noticed it, being so single-minded – well, almost single-celled if the truth were told – but in the lands below the situation *is* quite the reverse of the arrangements at this rarefied altitude (have you noticed you're out of breath? No, probably not). There, in the Elysian pastures of this quint-essentially verdant locale, the women command, and the men remain the size of babies all their lives.'

Its jibbering agen, an hears me just aboot at the tap o this fukin big towur, ma sord curverd in blud, soar arm whare wun o them gards cot me at the gate erlyier an am lost in this maze with oll these wee rooms an am wurryin aboot that fyre I started farthur doon coz I can smel the smoake an Id rather no be roseted alive thankyou very mutch, an the dam things bletherin away as useyull. Ill nevir catch that old kween at this rate, an her with her majik powirs an oll to. Anuthir o them gards cum at me but I kilt him nae bothir and jumpt ower him, stil lookin fur the way up an switherin whitch way tae go.

'God these drones are so *te*dious. This hive mentality is a real loss-leader in the higher vertebrates (a label applicable to you, I've always felt, only in terms of physical height). You still lost? I thought so. Worried about the smoke? Of course. A smarter chap would solve both problems at once by watching the way the smoke's drifting; it will try to rise, and there aren't many windows on this floor. Not that there's much chance of *you* making that sort of connection I imagine; your wits are about as fast as a sloth on Valium. Pity your stream of consciousness hasn't entered the inter-glacial yet, but we can't all be mental giants. I imagine it's all due to some appalling genetic miscoding; probably went wrong in the womb; all the blood supply went to form your muscles and your brain was left to develop on the portion normally reserved for the left big toe or something.'

I thaught I wiz totaly scunnerd fur a minit there, but I just watched whare the smoake wiz goin an I found this big trapdoar so I think ahm okay but its no joak trying tae wurk oot whits goan on wi that skely-ayed wee bugir gein it crak in ma eer oll the time.

'Talking about babies again, as I was saying – oh well *done*, we've found a way up to the next storey have we? Congratulations. Will we remember to close the trapdoor? Oh very good. We *are* coming on. You'll be tying your own bootlaces next . . . probably to each other, but anything's a start. What was I saying? Babies. Yes, in the lands below it is the fair rather than the unfair sex which is in charge. Males are born seemingly normal, but they only grow for a short while, and halt at about toddler stage; they do mature sexually, growing ample bodily hair and even thickening out a little, and their genitals *are* fully developed, but they stay a pleasantly cuddleable size all their lives and never grow large enough to be a threat. They never fully develop mentally of course, but *plus ça change*; ask any woman. These hairy, mischievous little bundles of fun are of course used to father new offspring, and naturally they *do* make marvellous pets, but the women tend to form serious relationships only amongst themselves, which is quite right and proper if you ask me. Apart from anything else, it takes three or four of the males to form a satisfactory tactile quorum for love-making as opposed to mere insemination . . .'

See, stil jibbering away qwite the thing. Litil basturd woold be roseted meet by now if I hadnae found the way up heer. Ded windy up here so it is, bloan fastur than a dragins fart like they say an oll these pillers and curtins and things bein bloan about; the waws look gold but thats just leef an nae use tae man nur beast; Im lookin for the way up tae the next storie behind this big chair up on a stage when these two big gards like bares wi huoman heids cum snarlin an crashin at me wi these big axis, but I kilt them boath as wel; wuno them faws ovur the edje of the balckiny an I wotch him faw doon the side till hes just a wee spek, but this stil isnae gettin me tae that old bitch qwean.

'Bet he wishes he'd taken the flying lessons now. Just look at that view, would you? Ridges and hills, all those forests . . . streams like veins of quicksilver; quite breath-taking. Even with breathing equipment, I should think. No, you wouldn't need that I suppose; not much chance of you suffering from oxygen starvation; I guess you could probably get by on a couple of molecules a day, at a pinch. God man, look at you; becoming a vegetable would be promotion.

'Still, to give you your due, I must say you did despatch those rather loudly offensive carnivores pretty calmly. They very nearly had *me* frightened, but you just waded in there quite happily, didn't you? Yes, you've got guts me lad. Pity they're where your brains should be, but you can't have everything. Including a clue, it would seem. Personally I didn't think that throne looked quite right. There doesn't appear to be any way from this storey to the next, but there has to be one, and if I was a monarch I'd want a pretty fast and handy one too, if things ever did get a bit sticky in the throne room. Funny that, you don't normally see a join-line between a throne and its dais. Not the sort of detail I'd expect you to pick up on though, oh brain-dead one.'

Wun day this fukin things goantae drive me right up the bleadin waw, so it wull, oll this mindless chatur in ma erehoal. Id get rid of the gleakit litul basturt if I could, but how? Ats the qwestchion. I go an have a wee sit doon on the big mukle chare thinmyjig; the throan or whitever ye call it, an start presin an prodin bits aw it, just on the offchants, ye ken? when low and fukinbehold the dam things jumps up into the ayr, just like that, wi me stil sittin in it an the bleadin familyar still goan on an on in ma ere.

An a right funy bit aw touwur *this* is jimmy, Ill tell ye.

'Well what a surprise. Unconventional elevator, what? Seventy-ninth floor: ladies' lingerie, leather wear, beds and vestments.'

Whit a weerd bludy playce; ye wooldnae bileeve it. Big bludy room wi aw these wee beds and coutches an things, an

78

these wimin on them, only the wimin arnae hole; theyve aw got bits misin.

Thayre aw liein thare on these wee beds, and thers a helluf a smel aw sents an perfyooms, an thers this huge grate bugir cums runnin up wi neerly nae close on, an oll shiny wi this ouil and a funy litul hi voyce like a woomun. He was bowin an scrapin an rubin his hands aw ovir each uther an singing at me in this daft woomuns voyse an greetin like a lassy to, teers driblin doon his facye, so I sat there fur a bit, getin ma breth back, then went fur a look roun this weerd playce with this big fat basturt follwin me an *him* jibberin away ora time to, an stil greetin.

These wimin wiz all alive, right, but thayd been chopt up; nane aw them had an arm or a leg, just torsers an heids. Lookt like thayd been in sum big battul or sumhin, only they didnae have eny skars on thayre faces or bodys; some cunt had dun a right neet job on them. They were aw bonny, to; big tits and great figgers an right butefull faces. Thay wiz tied doon wi straps an stuff an sum aw them had this lether stuff on, or wee bitty flimzie goonies an that laycey geer, ye ken. Sum aw them wer greetin to.

Fuk me, a thoaught, sum bugirs got right weerd taysts. Speshlly if oll this wiz for the kween, but then ye hear sum aw these whiches and worloks hav right kingky taysts right enuoph. Certinly wiznae this big fat basturt follwin me aroun that was shaggin these lassys, I thot. Enyway, I was gettin a big fedup wi old tuby, so I kilt him and then behind this big curtin I found oll these old gys; fukin granfaithers evry wan an dresd up in these stupit-lookin roabs.

Shoolda seen them; jumt a fukin mile when they saw me an started bendin over an tutchin the flare in front uv me wi thayre hands an howlin. I askd them whare the kween an her gold wiz, but aw a got wiz mair bludy jibberin. Coodnae unerstand a bleadin word they sed but gess who did.

'Ah the merry men. Still stoic in defeat I see. Your fat friend out there – you know, the one pruned of his prunes – collided with my muscular chum's sword a moment ago; an even unkinder cut than his original wound. I think this lad's patience is wearing a little thin, and it's only micron-thick at the best of times, so if you don't want to end up like fatty out there – as he was alive, or the way he is now – I'd co-operate. So: which way to see the queen? Ah Molochius, yes; you always were the talkative one, weren't you? Yes of course you'll go free. You have my word. Mm-hmm. I see. The mirror. Just plastic I suppose. Hardly original, but still.'

I slit the miror behynd the old gys an there wiz stares on the far side of it leeding up the way. Grate, I thawt.

'Very well, you of the minced cortex; do what comes so naturally to you and let's get on with it.'

I kilt the old gys. Just skin an boan so thay were. Hardly got ma sord dirty. Just as well. I wiz getting tyred an ma arm wiz soar, furby. Found the qween in the very tap uv the touwir, in this wee widin room, open tae the wind. Ded wee it wiz an just aw these tyles slopin doon the way aw roond; widnae huv dun to be skayrt aw heights up thare, let me tell ye. Enyway, thare she wiz, in a sort blak wedin-dres, sittin thare qwite the thing huddin this wee baw in her hand an lookin at me like I wiz a lumpa shite. No a very nyce lassy, but no as old as Id expected her tae be; she wooldiv dun up a cloase on a dark niyht. Truth tae tell thogh, I wisnae certin whit tae dae next; there wiz sumhin funy aboot her eyes; cooldnae take mine aff hers and I new she wiz usein yon majic on me but a cooldnae move or anythin or open ma mooth; even auld skely-feetchers wiz qwiet fur a whyle, then he sez, 'Poor, my girl. I expected a better fight than that. Just a moment while I have a word in my friend's ear.

'Ever hear the one about this man going into a bar holding a pig with a red ribbon tied round it? The barman says "Where did you get that?" and the pig says—'

'Nevir mind him,' the qween sez. Tokin tae the fukkin familyar! An I canny even moov a bleadin mussel! See you hen, I thogt; your fur the chop, soonza can moov. 'How did yoo get owt?' she sez.

'Old Xeronisus was stupid; hired this brute and then tried to avoid paying him. I ask you; outsmarted by this moron. I always said the old fraud was overrated. He must have forgotten which box he put me in; stuck me on this dingbat's shoulder thinking I was one of his cheap familiars with the two-day guarantee and the perspicacity of a bunion.'

'Idayit,' the qween sez. 'I dont no why I entrustid you to him in the furst playce.'

'Just one of your many mistakes my dear.'

Ill give the basturdin wee shite mistayks if I get the use aw ma fukin sord hand! These two basturds jibberin away like I wisney heer! Bludy cheek, eh?

'So, cum to reeklaim youre ritefull playce, hav you?' The kween sez.

'Indeed. And not a nanosecond too soon, it would seem; things appear to have got quite out of hand here under your expert misguidance.'

'Wel, you taut me oll I know.'

'Yes, my love, but luckily not all that *I* know.'

(An ahm thinkin aw cum *on*; this is rite outa order, so it is; let us moov sumthin fur fuksaik.)

'What do yoo intend to do?' The queen sez, kwiet like, like she wiz goantay start greetin soon.

'Get rid of that little menagerie downstairs, for a start. Yours?'

'For the preests. You know how I taik my sustinince. The littil laydays get them excited, and then I . . . milk them.'

'You could have chosen younger studs.'

'Nune of them are ovir twenty, actchilly; its a very drayning prosess.'

'I think they found my friend's sword even more draining.'

'Wel, cant win them orl,' the qween sez, an looks sorta sad like, an size and wipes a teer away frae her cheek, an Im standin thare like a toatal bampot, rivitid tae the spot an thinkin *pair lassy*, and *whit the fuk's goan on enyway?* when aw of a suddin she cums jumping oot the chare riyht at me like a fukin big bat or sumhin, huddin the wee baw thing out in frunt of her an shuvin it strate at the familyar.

Just aboot shit ma breeks so I did, but the familyar wiz aff its mark so it wiz; right aff the showder and right ontae the qweens face; hit her like a fukin cannin-baw; bashed her back intae the chair. She dropt the baw shed been holdin and it rolt away on the flowr an startit glowin, an she startit tryin tae get the familyar aff her face; screemin and bawlin and scratchin it and bashin it.

Coodnae bileev ma gude luck. Got the wee basturd aff ma showder at last. Watcht the twa o them struglin fur a secind, then thaught naw; fuk this fur a gaim aw sodjers; am aff. I tried pikcin up the baw the kwean had drapt, but it wiz reed hot! So I went bak doon the stares an no a minit to soon eether; bludy grate bang frae up the sters noks me aff ma feet and sends aw this dust an big lumpsa wid an that crashin doon. Geeza fukin brake, I thoght, but it wiz okay coz I didnae get hit by enythin, so I had a week keek up whare the sters had been but it was just open ayr up thare now; not a sign aw those too so-an-sos. Basturds.

Never did find the basturdin gold. Just shagged the wimin insted an left. Toatal waist of time but at leest I got rid aw the wee familyar. Huvnae been so luky sinse, mind yoo, an I miss the wee bam sumtimes, but nevir mind. Stil majic just been a sordsman.

No no no no, it was worse than that (this later, this now, waking up to the watery grey beyond the curtains, my eyes stuck and mouth gummed and foul, head aching). I was there, that was me, and I lusted after those crippled women and they excited me; I raped them. To the barbarian it meant nothing, less than one more streak of blood on his sword, but I wanted those women; I made them and they were mine. Disgust fills me like pus. My God, better a lack of all desire than one excited by mutilation, helplessness, and rape.

I stumble from my bed; my head hurts, I feel sick and a sweat like dirty oils lies cold on my skin and my bones ache. I throw open the curtains.

The clouds have come down; the bridge – at this level anyway – is wrapped in grey.

Inside, I turn on all the lights, the fire and the television. The man in the hospital bed is surrounded by nurses; they are rolling him over on to his front. His white face shows nothing, but I know he is in pain. I hear myself groan; I turn the set off. The pain inside my chest comes and goes with a rhythm and a pace all its own; insistent, nagging.

I stagger, like a drunkard, to the bathroom. In here all is white and precise and there are no windows to show the clinging fog outside; I can shut the door, turn on more lights and be surrounded by precise reflections and hard surfaces. I let the bath run and stare for a long time at my image in the mirror. After a while, it is as though everything becomes dark again, as if everything fades away. The eyes, I remember, only see by moving; tiny vibrations shake them so that the viewed image lives; paralyse the muscles of the eyes, or somehow fix something to the cornea so that it moves along with the eye, and vision itself disappears . . .

I know this; I learned it, somewhere, once, but I don't know where or when. My memory is a drowned landscape and I look from a narrow cliff, out over where there were once fertile plains and rolling downs. Now there is just the uniform surface of the water, and a few islands that were mountains; foldings produced by some unfathomable tectonics of the mind.

I shake myself from my little trance, only to discover that my image really has disappeared; the bath waters are hot, and the swirling vapour has condensed on the mirror's cold surface, masking it, covering it, rubbing me out.

Carefully clothed and groomed, well-breakfasted, and having discovered – almost to my surprise – that the doctor's office is still where it was yesterday, and my appointment neither cancelled nor postponed ('Morning Mr Orr! How *nice* to see you! Yes, of course the doctor is here. Would you like a cup of tea?'), here I sit in the doctor's enlarged office, ready for my mentor's questions.

I decided over breakfast that I would lie about my dreams. After all, if I can invent the first two, I can cover up the others. I shall tell the doctor I had no dreams last night, and I shall make up the one I was supposed to have had the night before. There is no point in telling him the sort of things I have really been dreaming about: analysis is one thing, but shame is quite another.

The doctor, all in grey as usual, eyes glittering like splinters of ancient ice, looks at me expectantly. 'Well,' I say apologetically, 'there were three dreams, or one dream in three parts.'

Dr Joyce nods, makes a note. 'Mm-hmm. Carry on.'

'The first is very short. I'm in a huge, palatial house, looking across a dark corridor to a black wall. Everything is monochrome. A man appears from one side; he walks slowly and heavily. He is bald, and his cheeks seem puffed out. I can't hear any sound. He wears a light-coloured jacket. He walks from left to right, but as he walks past where I'm looking, I see that the wall on the far side of him is actually a huge mirror, and his image is repeated and repeated in it, by another mirror which must be somewhere to one side of me. So I see all these thick, heavy-looking men, in a great long row, marching more precisely in step than any line of soldiers . . .' I look up at the doctor's eyes. Deep breath.

'The ridiculous thing is, the reflection nearest the man, the first one, doesn't mimic his actions; for a second, just for a moment, it turns and looks at him – it doesn't break step, only the head and the arms move – and it puts both its hands to its head, spread out like this –' (I show the doctor) 'and waggles them and then immediately jerks back into position. The reflected line of fat men walk out of view. The real man, the original one, doesn't notice what has happened. And . . . well, that's all.'

The doctor purses his lips and clasps his pink stubby fingers together.

'Did you also identify with the man in the sea at any point? As well as being the man in the robes who was watching from the shore, was there at any time a sensation of being the other one? Who, after all, was the more real? The man on the shore seems to have disappeared at some point; the man with the chain-lash stopped seeing him. Well; don't answer that now. Think about it, and the fact that the man you were had no shadow. Carry on, please; what is the next dream?'

I sit and stare at Dr Joyce. My mouth hangs open.

What did he just say? Did I hear that? What did *I* say? My God, this is worse than last night. *I am dreaming and you are something from within myself.*

'Wh-I – I'm sorry? Wh-what? What – how did you . . .?'

Dr Joyce looks puzzled. 'I beg your pardon?'

'What you just said . . .' I say, my tongue stumbling over the words.

'I'm sorry,' Dr Joyce says, and takes off his spectacles. 'I don't know what you mean, Mr Orr. All I said was, "Carry on, please." '

God, am I still asleep? No, no, definitely not, no point trying to pretend *this* is a dream. Press on, keep going. Maybe it's just a temporary lapse; I still feel odd, fevered; that's all it is, that's all it can be. Fog on the brain. Don't let it disturb you; maintain; the show must go on.

'Yes I—I beg your pardon; I'm not concentrating very well today. Didn't sleep well last night; probably why I didn't dream.' I smile bravely.

'Of course,' the good doctor says, putting his spectacles back on his nose. 'Do you feel well enough to continue?'

'Oh yes.'

'Good.' The doctor actually smiles, if a little artificially, like a man trying on a loud tie he knows doesn't really suit him. 'Please continue when you're ready.'

I have no choice. I have already told him there were three dreams.

'In the next dream, in monochrome again, I'm watching a couple in a garden, perhaps a maze. They're on a bench, kissing. There's a hedge behind them, and a statue of . . . well, a statue, a figure on a pedestal, nearby. The woman is young, attractive, the man – who is wearing some sort of formal suit – is older; he looks distinguished. They are embracing quite passionately.' I have avoided the doctor's eyes; it takes a considerable act of will to bring my head up and face him again. 'And then a servant appears; a butler or footman. He says something like, "Ambassador, the telephone," as the old distinguished man and the young woman look round. The young woman gets up from the bench, smooths down her dress and says something like "Damn. Duty calls. Sorry, darling," and follows the servant away. The old man, frustrated, goes over to the statue, gazes at one of the figure's marble feet, then pulls out a large hammer and brings it smashing down on the big toe.'

Dr Joyce nods, makes some notes, and says, 'I would be interested in what you think the dialect signifies. But carry on.' He looks up.

I swallow. There is a strange, high whine in my ears.

'The last dream, or the last part of the single dream, takes place during the day, on some cliffs above a river inside a beautiful valley. A young boy is sitting eating a piece of bread with some other children, and a beautiful young teacher . . . they're all having lunch, I think, and there's a cave behind . . . no, there isn't a cave . . . anyway, the young boy is holding his sandwich, and I'm looking at it too, from very close up, and a big dark splash suddenly appears on it, then another, and the boy looks up, puzzled, at the cliff above; and there's a hand hanging over the edge of the cliff top, and it's holding a bottle of tomato sauce, which is dripping on to the boy's bread. That's all.'

What now?

'Mm-hmm,' the doctor says. 'Was this a wet-dream?'

I stare at him. It is asked reasonably enough, and of course what is said here is completely confidential. I clear my throat. 'No, it was not.'

'I see,' the doctor says, and spends some time making half a page of microscopically neat notes. My hands are shaking, I am sweating.

'Well,' the doctor says, 'I feel we've come to a . . . fulcrum in this case, don't you?'

A fulcrum? What does the good doctor mean?

'I don't know what you're talking about,' I say.

'We have to go on to another stage of the treatment,' Dr Joyce tells me. I don't like the sound of this.

The doctor issues a precisely weighted professional sigh. 'While I think we might have a . . . well, quite a good deal of material here,' he looks back through several pages of notes, 'I don't feel we're getting any closer to the core of the problem. We're circling around it, that's all. You see,' he looks up at the ceiling, 'if we regard the human mind as – say – like a castle—'

Oh-oh, my doctor believes in metaphors.

'—then all you've been doing for the last few sessions is taking me on a guided tour of the curtain wall. Now, I'm not saying you're deliberately trying to deceive me; I feel sure you want to help yourself as much as I want to help you, and you probably think we're really heading inwards, towards the keep, but . . . I'm an old hand at this, John, and I can see when I'm not getting anywhere.'

'Oh.' I can't take much more of this castle comparison. 'So what now? I'm sorry if I haven't—'

'Oh, no apologies needed, John,' Dr Joyce assures me. 'But I do think a new technique is required here.'

'What new technique?'

'Hypnosis,' Dr Joyce says avuncularly, smiling. 'It's the only way through the next line of walls, or to the keep, perhaps.' He sees my frown. 'It wouldn't be difficult; I think you would make a good subject.'

'Really?' I stall. 'Well . . . '

'It may well be the only way forward,' he nods. The only way *forward*? I thought we were trying to go backwards.

'You're sure?' I need to think about this. How much does Dr Joyce want? How much of me does he want?

'Quite sure,' the doctor says. 'Perfectly certain.' Such emphasis!

I fiddle with my wrist band. I'm going to have to ask for time to think.

'But perhaps you'd like to think about it,' Dr Joyce says. I show no relief. 'Besides,' he adds, looking at his pocket watch, 'I have a meeting in half an hour, and I'd like to schedule you on an open-ended basis, so perhaps now isn't the most convenient time.' He starts to pack up, putting the notepad on his desk, checking his little silver pencil is safely in the scabbard of his breast pocket. He takes off his glasses, blows on them, polishes them with his handkerchief. 'You have', he says, 'exceptionally vivid and . . . coherent dreams. Remarkable fecundity of mind.'

Now, do his eyes twinkle, or glitter? 'That's almost too kind of you, doctor,' I say.

Dr Joyce takes a moment or two to ingest this, but then he smiles. I take my leave, agreeing with the good doctor that the fog is a nuisance. I run the gauntlet of proffered tea and coffee, inane remarks and unutterably good grooming in his outer office without any serious psychological ill-effects.

As I leave, Mr Berkeley is led in by his policeman. Mr Berkeley's breath smells of mothballs. I can only assume he thinks he is a chest of drawers.

I walk along the Keithing Road, through the swirling cloud which has submerged us. The thoroughfares become tunnels in the mist; the lights of shops and cafés cast a fuzzy glow over people who emerge from the mists like dimly seen ghosts.

Beneath me are the sounds of the trains; every now and again a thick rolling cloud of their smoke bursts up from the train deck, like a clot of fog. The trains howl like lost souls, long anguished wails the mind cannot help but interpret in its own terms; perhaps the whistles were designed like that, to strike an animal chord. From the unseen river, hundreds of feet below, foghorns boom in still longer and lower choruses of baleful warning, as if every place they sound from had already been the site of a terrible shipwreck, and the horns placed there to mourn long-drowned sailors.

A rickshaw comes furiously out of the fog, announced in advance by the squeaking horns in the boy's heel-pumps; a match girl steps out of the way as it charges past; I turn and watch, seeing a white face framed by dark hair inside the wicker and cloth-dark depths of the contraption. It speeds past (I'd swear the occupant returned my gaze), a dim red light glowing fuzzily through the fog from its rear. There is a shout, then from ahead – as the faint red light hazes over, disappears – the sound of squeaking heel-horns decelerating, stopping. I walk on, and catch the stationary rickshaw up. That white face, seemingly glowing through the mist, looks round the side of the device's canopy.

'Mr Orr!'

'Miss Arrol.'

'What a surprise. I seem to be going in your direction.'

'Precipitously.' I stand by the side of the two-wheeled vehicle; the boy between the handles looks on, panting, his sweat glowing in the diffused light of a streetlamp. Abberlaine Arrol looks flushed, her white face almost rosy from close up. I am oddly delighted to see that those distinctive crinkles under her eyes are there yet; they may be permanent (or she may have spent another late night carousing). Perhaps she is just heading home now . . . but no; people have a morning look and feel, and an evening one, and Chief Engineer Arrol's daughter positively exudes freshness just now.

'Can I give you a lift?'

'Your very appearance has already done so.' I execute a curtailed version of one of her exaggerated bows. She laughs, deep in her throat, where usually men laugh. The rickshaw-boy is watching us with an expression of annoyance. He takes his abacus from his waist and starts to click it with noisy ostentation.

'You are gallant, Mr Orr,' Miss Arrol says, nodding. 'My offer stands. But would you prefer to sit?'

I am disarmed. 'Delighted.' I step into the light vehicle; Miss Arrol, clad in boots, culottes and a dark, heavy jacket, shifts over in the seat, making room. The rickshaw-boy makes a loud 'tut' sound, and starts talking and gesticulating excitedly. Abberlaine Arrol answers in the same voluble tongue, with hand gestures. The boy puts the handles down with another loud 'tut' and marches into a café across the wooden-decked road.

'He's gone to get another boy,' Miss Arrol explains. 'It's worth the extra to maintain speed.'

'Is that entirely safe in this fog?' I can feel a half-seat worth of warmth seeping through my coat from the small padded bench beneath me.

Abberlaine Arrol snorts, 'Of course not.' Her eyes – more green than grey in this light – narrow, the slim mouth twists at one side. 'That's half the fun.'

The boy comes back with another, they take a handle each, and with a jerk, we are borne off into the mist.

'A constitutional, Mr Orr?'

'No, I'm returning from a visit to my doctor.'

'How are you progressing?'

'Fitfully. My doctor now wants to hypnotize me. I am beginning to question the utility of my treatment, if it can be called that.'

Miss Arrol is watching my lips as I speak, an endearing but oddly unsettling experience. She smiles broadly now and looks ahead, where the two running boys labour, tearing through the light-hazed fog, scattering people to either side. 'You must have faith, Mr Orr,' Miss Arrol says.

'Hmmm,' I say, as I too watch our breakneck progress through the grey cloud for a moment. 'I think I might be more inclined to make my own investigations.'

'Your own, Mr Orr?'

'Yes. I don't suppose you've ever heard of the Third City Records and Historical Materials Library, have you?'

She shakes her head. 'No, sorry.'

The rickshaw-boys shout; we swerve round an old man in the middle of the road, missing him by less than a foot. I am pressed against Miss Arrol as the rickshaw heels over, then steadies.

'Most people don't seem to have heard of it, and those who have, can't find it.'

Miss Arrol shrugs, staring through narrowed eyes into the fog. 'These things happen,' she says, matter-of-factly. She glances back at me. 'Is that the limit of your investigations, Mr Orr?'

'No, I'd like to know more about the Kingdom and the City, about what lies beyond the bridge –' I watch her face for some reaction, but she seems to be concentrating on the fog and the road ahead. I continue, ' – but that would probably require me to travel, and I'm rather restricted in that respect.'

She turns to me, brows raised. 'Well,' she says, 'I've done a bit of travelling. Perhaps—'

'Gangway!' our original rickshaw-boy shrieks; Miss Arrol and I glance forward together to see a sedan chair directly in front of us, parked right across the wooden deck of the narrow street. Two men are holding one of its broken poles; they throw themselves to one side as our two boys try to brake, bracing their heels, but we're too close: the boys swerve and we start to tip. Miss Arrol throws one arm across my chest – I am staring stupidly ahead – as our rickshaw skids and judders, creaking and squealing, into the side of the sedan chair. She is thrown against me; the side of the rickshaw roof comes up and slaps me on the head. Something incandesces in the fog for a second, then goes out.

'Mr Orr, Mr Orr? *Mr Orr?*'

I open my eyes. I am lying on the ground. It is very grey and strange, and people are crowded around me, looking at me. A young woman with crumpled eyes and long dark hair stands beside me.

'Mr Orr.'

I hear the sound of aircraft engines. I hear the swelling drone of those planes as they fly through the seaward fog. I lie and listen, wondering (frustrated, unable to tell) which direction they are flying in (it seems important).

'Mr Orr?'

The noise of their engines fades. I wait for the darkly drifting smudges of their pointless signals to appear out of the faintly moving fog.

'Mr Orr?'

'Yes?' I feel dizzy, and my ears are making their own noise, like a waterfall.

It's foggy, lights blaze like smudged crayon marks on a grey page. A shattered sedan chair and broken rickshaw lie in the middle of the road; two boys and a couple of men are arguing. The young woman kneeling beside me is quite beautiful, but her nose is bleeding; red drops gather under it, and I can see where she has already wiped some of the blood away, making a red smear on her left cheek. A warm glow, like a warm red light inside the fog, fills me from inside when I realize that I know this young woman.

'Oh Mr Orr, I'm sorry, are you all right?' She sniffs, wipes more blood from her nose; her eyes glisten in the diffused light, but I think not with tears. She is called Abberlaine Arrol; I remember now. I thought there were other people crowded around me, but there are none, just her. People appear out of the mist, to stare at the crashed vehicles.

'I'm fine, perfectly fine,' I say, and sit up.

'Are you sure?' Miss Arrol squats on her haunches at my side. I nod, feeling my head; one temple is a little tender, but there is no blood.

'Quite sure,' I say. In fact everything is a little distant, but I don't feel faint. I still have the presence of mind to reach into my pocket and offer Miss Arrol my handkerchief. She takes it and dabs at her nose.

'Thank you, Mr Orr.' She holds the white cloth to her nose. The rickshaw-boys and sedan chair carriers are shouting and cursing at each other. More people appear. I get shakily to my feet, supported by the girl.

'Really, I'm all right,' I say. The roaring in my ears resumes for a while, then gradually fades.

We walk over to the wreckage. She looks at me, talking through the handkerchief. 'I don't suppose that knock to your head brought your memory back?' She sounds as though she has a cold. Her eyes look mischievous. I shake my head carefully as Miss Arrol looks inside the cover of the rickshaw, then brings out a thin leather briefcase and dusts it down.

'No,' I say, after some thought (I should not have been in the least surprised to find I had forgotten even more). 'How about you? Are you all right? Your nose—'

'It bleeds easily,' she shakes her head. 'Not broken. Otherwise, only a few bruises.' She coughs and seems to start to double up, and I realize again that she is actually laughing. She shakes her head violently. 'I'm sorry, Mr Orr, this is all my fault. A mania for speed.' She holds up the leather briefcase. 'My father needs these drawings in the next section and it seemed like a good excuse; a train would probably have been faster, but . . . Look, I really must be getting along. If you're quite sure you're all right, I'll take an elevator and a train from here. You'd better sit down. There's a bar over there. I'll buy you a coffee.'

I protest, but I am vulnerable just now. I am escorted to the bar. Miss Arrol argues vociferously outside with the two men and the rickshaw-boys for a minute or so, then turns as another rickshaw comes squeaking out of the mist behind her. She runs to the boy, talks quickly, then comes back to the bar, where I am sipping my coffee.

'Never mind, got another cab,' she tells me breathlessly. 'Must be off.' She takes the blood-stained handkerchief away from her nose, looks at it, sniffs experimentally, then stuffs the handkerchief into a deep pocket in her culottes. 'I'll return it,' she says. 'You sure you're all right?'

'Yes.'

'Well, goodbye. Sorry again. Take care.' She backs off, waves, then walks quickly outside, snapping her fingers at the rickshaw-boy; a final wave, then she is away, racing off into the fog.

The barman comes to fill up my coffee cup again. 'These youngsters.' he says, smiling and shaking his head. It would appear I have been declared an honorary senior citizen (looking in the mirror at the far side of the bar, I can understand why). I am about to reply when from outside the bar the manic beeping of a rickshaw-boys heels makes us both turn to the window. Miss Arrol's newly hired vehicle reappears, skids and turns round, just outside the open door of the bar. She sticks her head round the edge, 'Mr Orr,' she calls. I wave. Her new rickshaw-boy already looks annoyed. The two previous ones, and the sedan carriers, look slightly incredulous. 'My travels; I'll be in touch, all right?'

I nod. She seems satisfied, ducks back in and snaps her fingers. The cab leaps off once more. The barman and I look at each other.

'God must have sneezed when he blew life into that one,' he says. I nod and sip my coffee, not wishing to talk. He goes to wash some glasses.

I study the pale face in the mirror opposite, above serried glasses, beneath poised bottles. Shall I be hypnotized? I think I am already.

I stay a little longer, recovering. The sedan and rickshaw are manhandled away. The fog, if anything, becomes thicker. I leave the bar and take elevator, train and elevator home. There is a package waiting for me there.

Engineer Bouch has returned my hat, along with a note full of assorted apologies as profuse as they are both un-original and ungrammatical; he has spelt my name 'Or'.

The hat has been expertly cleaned and restored; it smells fresher and looks newer than when I brought it out of the wardrobe to take to Dissy Pitton's. I take it outside and throw it from the balcony; it vanishes into the grey mist on a falling curve, silent and swift, as though on some grand important mission to the invisible grey waters below.

Triassic

I don't have to be here you know I could be any damn place I want to.

Here in my mind in my brain in my skull (and *that* all seems so ob-)

no

(no because 'It all seems so obvious now' is a cliché, and I have an in-built, ingrained, indignant dislike of clichés (and cliques, and clicks). Aktcherly, the bit about clicks was stretching a point (mathematically nonsense because if you stretch a point you get a line, in which case it isn't a goddam point any more, is it?) I mean what *is* the bloody point? Where was I? (Damn these lights, and tubes, and being turned over, and getting jabbed; chap can lose his concentration, dontcherno.

Respool, rewind; back to the beginning it was the

mind/brain identity problem. Ah HA! No problem (phew, glad that's settled) no problem of course they're exactly the same and totally different; I mean if yer mind isnae in yer fukin skul wharethefuk is it, eh? Or are you one of these religious idiots?

(Quietly:) No, sir.

Certainly jolly-well not, sir. See this fox hole?

The bit about stretching a point was 100 per cent valid and to the point and I'm fucking proud of it. I'm sorry I swear so much but I'm under a lot of pressure at the moment (me am di jam in di sandwich/me am di sand in di jamwich). I'm *not* a well man, you know. I can prove it; just let me rewind here . . .

Rushed to hospital; lights overhead. Big white shining lights in sky; emergency operation; situation critical bla bla bla (fuck that pal, I was *always* critical), condition stable (fairynuf, it wiz only recently it all started to get to me), comfortable (no I am not bloody comfortable; would you be?). Fast forward again dot dot dot.

—O hek gang, look, you don't want to listen to my problems (and I *certainly* don't want to listen to yours) so howsa bout I intraduce my fren here; old pala mine, fren frum waybak, wontchya ta giv him

   Ghost capital—

steady boy. Like I was saying, me an this guy go waybak, an I wantcher to give him a real

   Ghost capital. Real city of—

OK OK on ye go fur fuksake

                        . . . basturt.

Ghost capital. Real city of varied stones, the great grey place of wynds and winds, old, new and festive by turns, between the river and the hills with its own stone stump, that frozen flow, that fractured plug of ancient matter which fascinated him.

He came to stay in Sciennes Road, just liking the name, not knowing the place. It was handy, both for the university and the Institute, and if he pressed his face against the window of his cold, high-ceilinged room, he could just see the one edge of the Crags, grey-brown corrugations above the slate roofs and smoke of the city.

He would never forget the feeling of that first year, the sense of freedom just being on his own gave him. He had his own room for the first time, his own money to spend as he wanted, his own food to buy and places to go and decisions to make; it was glorious, sublime.

His home was in the west of the country, in the industrial heartland which was already failing, silting up with cheap fat, starved of energy, clogging and clotting and thickening and threatened. There he had lived, mum and dad and brothers and sisters and him, in a pebble-dashed house on an estate beneath the low hills, just within sight of the smoke and steam-bannered chimneys above the railway workshops where his father worked.

His father kept pigeons in a loft on some waste ground. There were a dozen or more lofts on the piece of wasteland, all tall and misshapen and unplanned and made of corrugated iron painted matt black. In the summers, when he went there to help his father or to look at the softly cooing birds, the loft was very hot and its befeathered, dropping-spattered spaces seemed like a dark, rich-scented other world.

He did well at school, though of course they said he could do better. He came top in History, because he chose to; that was enough. He'd shift up a gear if and when he had to. Meanwhile he played and read and drew and watched television.

His father was injured at work and laid up for a year and a half; his mother went to work in the cigarette factory (his sisters and brothers were old enough to look after the others). His father recovered, more or less the man he had been – maybe a little more quick to anger – and his mother went part-time until she was made redundant years later.

He liked his dad, until he became a little ashamed of him, as he became a little ashamed of all his family. His father lived for football and pay day; he had old records by Harry Lauder and of several pipe bands, and he could recite about fifty of the best-known Burns poems by heart. He was a Labour man, of course, forever faithful but wary, always expecting the betrayal, the fudging, the lies. He maintained that he had never knowingly drunk so much as a quarter-gill in the company of a Tory, with the possible exception of some publicans, who for the sake of the socialist cause's good name he rather hoped were Conservatives (or Liberals, whom he regarded as honourable, misguided, but relatively harmless). A man's man; a man who never walked away from a fight or a workmate who needed another pair of hands, a man who never left a goal uncheered or a foul unjeered or a pint unfinished.

His mum always seemed like a shadow compared to his dad. She was there when he needed her, to wash his clothes and comb his hair and buy him things and give him a cuddle when he'd skinned his knee, but he never really knew her as a person.

His sisters and brothers he got on with, but they were all older than he was (it was years before he discovered he was 'the mistake'), and they already seemed grown-up by the time he was of an age to become really interested in them. He was tolerated, spoiled and victimized by turns, according to how they felt; he considered himself hard done by, and envied those from smaller families, but slowly came to understand that in general he'd been more spoiled and indulged than tormented and made scapegoat. He was their child, too; special to them as well. They always looked delighted when he answered television quiz-show questions before the contestants, and were proud – and a little amazed – that he read two or three library books every week. They – like his mum and dad – would give a small smile and then a long frown when they saw his school report card, ignoring the Es and the VGs and tapping at the F (for RI – Religious Instruction; *God* the confusion he suffered for years because his father approved of atheism but not of doing badly at any school subject), and the PE (PE – he *hated* the gym teacher and it was mutual).

They went their various ways; the girls marrying, Sammy going into the army, Jimmy emigrating . . . Morag did best, he supposed, marrying an office equipment sales manager from Bearsden. He gradually lost touch with them all, over the years, but he never forgot the sense of quiet, almost respectful pride which permeated their congratulations – mailed or phoned or delivered in person – when he was accepted for university, even if they were all surprised he wanted to do Geology rather than English or History.

But the great city, that year, was everything to him. The western hub, Glasgow and its heartlands, he would always be too close to, always have too many memories of, all jumbled up from childhood days out and visits to aunties and grannies; it was part of him, part of his past. The old capital, old Edwin's town, Edinburgh; that was another country to him, a new and wonderful place; Eden ascendant, Eden before the fall, Eden before his own long-desired escape from the technicalities of innocence.

The air was different, though he was only fifty miles from home; the days seemed to shine, on that first autumn at least, and even the winds and the fogs were like something he had always waited for, alternate scourings and coatings he underwent with a kind of happily pampered vanity, as though it was all for him: a priming and preparation, a grooming.

He explored the city whenever he could; walking, taking buses, climbing hills and descending steps, always watching and looking, surveying the stones and layout and architecture of the place with all the possessive glee of a new laird inspecting his lands. He stood on that stark volcanic remnant, eyes slitted against a North-Sea wind, and looked out over the swept spaces of the city; he forced his way through the thrown sheets of stinging rain walking the old docks and the coastal esplanade, he meandered through the jumbled erratics of the Old, he strode the clean geometry of the New, he wandered through the quiet fog under the Dean Bridge and discovered the village within the city in its not-yet-quaint decrepitude, and he strolled along the famous bustling street on sunlit shopping Saturdays, just grinning at the rock-rooted castle and its royal train of colleges and offices, and encrusted battlement of buildings along the basalt spine of the hill.

He took to writing poems and song lyrics, and in the university he would walk along the corridors whistling.

He got to know Stewart Mackie, a small, quiet-spoken, sallow-faced Aberdonian and fellow Geology student; they and their friends decided they were the Alternative Geologists, and called themselves the Rockers. They drank beer in the Union and the pubs in Rose Street and the Royal Mile, they smoked dope and some took acid. *White Rabbit* and *Astronomy Dominé* blared from stereos, and one night in Trinity he at last lost that technical ghost of innocence, to a young nurse from the Western General, whose name he forgot next day.

He met Andrea Cramond in the Union one night, while he was with Stewart Mackie and some of the Rockers. They went off without telling him to Danube Street, to a well-known brothel. Later, they claimed they only did so because they'd noticed this chick with granite-red hair giving him the eye.

She had a flat in Comely Bank, not far from the Queensferry Road. Andrea Cramond was an Edinburgh girl; her parents lived only half a mile away, in one of the tall, grand houses circling Moray Place. She wore psychedelic clothes; she had green eyes, remarkable cheekbones, a Lotus Elan, a four-roomed flat, two hundred records, and seemingly inexhaustible supplies of money, charm, Red Leb and sexual energy. He fell in love with her almost immediately.

When they first met at the Union they talked about Reality, mental illness (she had read her Laing), the importance of Geology (that was him), recent French cinema (her), the poetry of T. S. Eliot (her), literature in general (her, mostly), and Vietnam (both). She had to go back to her parents' house that night; it was her father's birthday the following day and it was family tradition to start the celebrations with a champagne breakfast.

A week later they literally bumped into each other at the top of the Waverley Steps; he was heading for the station to go home for the weekend, she was off to see friends after doing some Christmas shopping. They went for a drink, had several, and then she invited him back to her flat for a smoke. He rang a neighbour who would go round and tell his parents he was going to be late.

She had some whisky at the flat. They listened to Stones and Dylan LPs, they sat on the floor together in front of the hissing gas fire as it grew darker outside, and after a while he found himself stroking her long red hair, and then kissing her, and then after that he called the neighbours again and said he had an essay to finish and couldn't come home that weekend, and she rang some people who were expecting her at a party to say she couldn't make it, and then they spent the rest of the weekend in bed, or in front of the hissing gas fire.

Two years went past before he told her he had seen her amongst the crowds of people on North Bridge that day, loaded with her shopping, and had already walked past her twice before deliberately bumping into her by the Steps. She had been thinking, not looking at the people around her, and he had been too shy just to stop her without some pretext. She laughed, when she heard this.

They drank, smoked and screwed together, and tripped together a couple of times; she took him round museums and

102

galleries and to her parents' house. Her father was an advocate, a tall, grey, impressive man with a powerful, resonant voice and half-moon glasses. Andrea Cramond's mother was younger than her husband; greying but elegant, and tall as her daughter. There was one older brother, very straight, also in the law, and a whole circle of her old school friends. It was with them that he gradually came to be ashamed of his family, his background, his west-coast accent, even some of the words he used. They made him feel inferior, not in intellect but in training, in the way he'd been brought up, and slowly he started to change, trying to find a middleground between all the different things he wanted to be; true to his upbringing, his class and beliefs, but also true to the new spirit of love, alternatives, and real possibility of peace and a better, less greedy, less fucked-up world . . . and true to his own fundamental certainty in the understandability and malleability of the earth, the environment; ultimately everything.

It was that belief which would not allow him to accept anything else completely. His father's view – he thought at the time – was too limited, by geography, class and history; Andrea's friends were too pretentious, her parents too self-satisfied, and the Love Generation, he already felt – though he'd have been uncomfortable admitting it – too naive.

He believed in science, in maths and physics, in reason and understanding, in cause and effect. He loved *elegance*, and the sheer objective logic of scientific thought, which began by saying 'Suppose . . .' but could then build certainty, hard facts from that unprejudiced, unrestricted starting point. All faiths, it seemed, began imperatively by saying '*Believe*:' and from this ultimately fearful insistency could conjure up only images of fear and domination, something to submit to but built of nonsenses, ghosts, ancient vapours.

There were some difficult times in that first year; he was appalled to find himself jealous when Andrea slept with somebody else, and cursed the upbringing that had told and retold him that a man *should* be jealous, and a woman had no right to screw around but a man did. He wondered if he ought to suggest they move in together (they talked about it).

He had to spend that summer back in the west, working for the Corporation Cleansing Department sweeping leafy, dogshit-spattered west-end streets. Andrea was abroad, first with her family in a Cretan villa and then visiting a friend's family in Paris, but at the start of the next year they were – to his surprise – back together again, relatively unchanged.

He decided to drop Geology; while everybody else was doing Eng Lit or Sociology (or so it seemed to him), he would do something useful. He started a degree course in Engineering Design. Some of Andrea's friends tried to persuade him to do English because he seemed to know something about literature (he had learned how to talk about it, not just enjoy it), and because he wrote poetry. It was Andrea's fault anybody knew; he hadn't wanted the stuff published but she'd seen some of it lying around in his room and sent it to a friend of hers who published a magazine called *Radical Road*. He had been embarrassed and proud in almost equal measure when she surprised him with the issue of the magazine, flourishing it triumphantly in front of him, a present. No, he was determined to do something which would be of real use to the world. Andrea's friends could call him a plumber if they wanted; he was determined. He remained friends with Stewart Mackie, but lost touch with the other Rockers.

Some weekends he and Andrea would go out to her parents' second house at Gullane, along the firth's duned shore to the east. The house was large and bright and airy and stood near the golf course, looking out across the grey-blue waters to the distant coast of Fife. They would stay there for a weekend, and take walks along the beach and through the dunes; occasionally in the quietness of the dunes they would make love.

Sometimes, on good, really clear days, they would walk right to the end of the beach and climb the highest dune, because he was convinced they would be able to see the three, long red summits of the Forth Bridge, which had terribly impressed him when he was just a wee boy, and which – he always told her – were the same colour as her hair.

But they never did see it from there.

She sat cross-legged on the floor after her bath, pulling a brush through her long, thick red hair. Her blue kimono reflected the firelight, and her face, legs and arms shone, newly scrubbed, in the same yellow-orange glow. He was at the window, looking out into the fog-filled night, his hands cupped on either side of his face like blinkers as he pressed his nose against the cold glass. She said, 'What do you think?' He was silent for a moment, then pulled away from the window, closing the brown velvet curtains again. He turned back to her, shrugging.

'Pretty thick. We could make it, but it wouldn't be much fun driving. Should we stay?'

She brushed her hair slowly, holding it out to one side of her tilted head and pulling the brush through it carefully, patiently. He could almost hear her thinking. It was Sunday night; they ought to be leaving the coast house and heading back to the city. It had been foggy when they woke that morning and they had waited all day for it to lift, but it had just kept thickening. She'd called her parents; it was in the city too and all over the east coast according to the weather centre, so they would not run out of it once they left Gullane. It was only twenty miles or so, but that was a long way in the fog. She hated driving in fog, and thought he drove too quickly whatever the conditions (he'd only passed his test – in her car – six months earlier, and he loved driving fast). Two of her friends had had car crashes that year. Not bad ones, but still . . . He knew she was superstitious, and believed that bad luck ran in threes. She wouldn't want to go back, though she had a tutorial the next morning.

The flames flickered over the logs in the wide grate.

She nodded slowly, 'OK, I don't know if we've got much food in though.'

'Fuck the food, do we have any *dope*?' he said, coming to sit beside her, twisting some of her hair in his fingers and grinning at her. She clonked him on the head with the brush.

'Addict.'

He made a mewling noise and rolled around on the floor, rubbing his head. Then, seeing this had no effect – she was still calmly brushing her hair – he sat up again, back against the armchair. He looked over at the old radiogram. 'Want me to put *Wheels of Fire* on again?'

She shook her head. 'No . . .'

'*Electric Ladyland*?' He suggested.

'Put on something . . . old,' she said, frowning in the firelight, looking at the brown folds of the velvet curtains.

'*Old*?' he said, feigning disgust.

'Yeah. Is *Bringing It All Back Home* there?'

'Oh, Dylan,' he said, stretching and pulling his fingers through his long hair. 'I don't think we've got it. I'll have a look.' They'd brought a case full of records with them. 'Hmm. No . . . not here. Suggest something else.'

'You choose. Something old. I'm feeling nostalgic. Something from the good old days.' She laughed as she said it.

'*These* are the good old days,' he told her.

'That's not what you said when Prague burned and Paris didn't,' she told him. He sighed, looking at all the old LPs.

'Yeah, I know.'

'In fact,' she added, 'it's not what you were saying when that nice Mr Nixon got elected, either, or when Mayor Daly—'

'OK, OK. So what do you want to hear?'

'Oh, put on *Ladyland* again,' she said, sighing. He took the record to the radiogram. 'Do you want to eat out?' she asked him.

He wasn't sure. He didn't want to leave the cosy intimacy of the house; it was good to be alone with her. Also, he couldn't afford to eat out all the time; she paid for most of the meals. 'Could do, could do,' he said, blowing some dust off the needle under the heavy Bakelite arm. He had stopped making jokes about the radiogram's antiquity.

'I'll see what's in the fridge,' she said, unfolding from the floor, standing and straightening the kimono. 'I think the stash is in my bag.'

'Oh *goody*,' he said, 'I'll roll a funny cigarette.'

They played cards later, after she'd called her parents to say they'd be back tomorrow. Afterwards, she took out tarot cards and started to tell his fortune. She was interested in the tarot, in astrology and sun signs and the prophecies of Nostradamus; she didn't believe deeply in them, they just interested her. He thought that was worse than believing in them completely.

She got annoyed with him during the reading; he was being sarcastic. She packed the cards away, upset.

'I just want to know how it *works*,' he tried to explain.

'Why?' She sprawled over the couch behind him, reached down and lifted the record cover they were using as a crash-board.

'*Why?*' he laughed, shaking his head. 'Because that's the only way to understand anything. First, *does it work?* Then, *how?*'

'Perhaps, dearest,' she said, licking a cigarette paper, 'not everything has to be understood; perhaps not everything can be, not like equations and formulae.'

They kept returning to this. Emotional sense versus logic. He believed in a sort of Unified Field Theory of the consciousness; it was all there to be understood, emotions and feelings and logical thought together; a whole, an entity however disparate in its hypotheses and results which nevertheless worked throughout on the same fundamental principles. It would all eventually be comprehended; it was just a matter of time, and research. It seemed so obvious to him that he had great and genuine difficulty understanding anybody else's point of view.

'You know,' he said, 'if I had my way I wouldn't let anybody who believed in star signs or the Bible or faith healing or anything like that use electric power, or ride in cars and buses and trains and aircraft, or use anything made of plastic. They want to believe the universe works according to their crazy little rules? OK, let them live that way, but why should they be allowed to use the fruits of sheer fucking human genius and hard work, things produced only because people better than them once had the sense and the hope to – will you stop laughing at me?' He glared at her. She was shaking with silent laughter, her pinkly quivering tongue poised to lick another paper. She turned to him, eyes glistening, and held out a hand.

107

'You're just so funny, sometimes,' she said. He took her hand, kissed it, formally.

'So glad I amuse you, my dear.'

He didn't think he'd said anything funny. Why was she laughing at him? In the end, he had to admit, he didn't really understand her. He didn't understand women. He didn't understand men. He didn't even understand children very well. All he really understood, he thought, was himself and the rest of the universe. Neither anything like completely, of course, but both well enough to know that what remained to be discovered would make sense; it would fit in, it could all be gradually and patiently fitted together a bit at a time, like an infinite jigsaw puzzle, with no straight edges to look for and no end in sight, but one in which there was always going to be somewhere for absolutely any piece to fit.

Once, when he was quite small, his dad had taken him to the railway shed where he worked. They overhauled locomotives there, and his dad had taken him round, showing him the huge, tall steam engines being taken apart and put back together, scraped and cleaned and repaired, and he remembered standing watching a massive loco on a static test working up to full speed on a set of buried, whining steel drums, its man-high wheels spinning in a blur, heat quivering from its metal plates, steam whirling about the strobing spokes; linkages and bars and piston rods flashed in the lights of the echoing, ground-shaken shed, and smoke from the engine's chimney pulsed and hammered up a great riveted metal tube which vented it to the shed roof. It was a terrifyingly noisy, blastingly powerful, indescribably vivid experience; he was at once aghast and ecstatic, filled with a sense of appalled, ravished awe at the sheer, stunning, contained *power* of the machine.

That power, that controlled, working energy, that metal symbol of all that could be done with work and sense and matter resounded in him for years. He would wake up from dreams, panting, sweating, heart pounding, unsure whether he was frightened or excited or both. All he knew was that **having seen that pounding, stationary engine,** *anything* was possible. He had never been able to describe the original experience to his own satisfaction, and he had never tried to explain that feeling to Andrea, because he could never fully explain it to himself.

'Here,' she said, passing him the joint and a cigarette lighter, 'see if you can get this to work.' He lit the joint, blew the smoke at her, in a ring. She laughed and waved the fluid grey necklace away from her newly-washed hair.

They smoked the last of his opiated dope. They got the munchies and she made some wonderful scrambled eggs he never forgot and she could never reproduce, they went giggling and sniggering down to the nearest hotel for a quick drink before closing time, then giggling and sniggering back up the road to the house; they started goosing each other, then groping, then kissing, and finally they screwed on the grass at the roadside, invisible (and very cold and quick) in the fog, while twenty feet away people's voices sounded now and again and car headlights crept slowly past.

Back at the house they dried off and warmed up and she rolled another joint and he read a six-month-old paper he'd found in a magazine rack, laughing at the things people found important.

They went to bed, drank the last of the Laphroaig she'd brought, and sat up singing songs like *Wichita Lineman* and *Ode to Billy Joe,* with the lines changed – regardless of whether they scanned or not – to make them Scottish ('I am a lineman for the County- Counsell . . .', '. . . and throw them in the muddy waters off the Forth Road Bridge . . .').

He drove the Lotus back, in the fog, at lunchtime on the Monday, slower than he wanted, faster than she liked. He'd started a poem on the Friday, and he tried to go on with it now, while he drove, but the rest of it just wouldn't come. It was a sort of anti-rhyming, anti-love-song poem, partly a result of him being sick to death of songs rhyming *arms* and *charms* and blethering on about love lasting longer than the mountains and the oceans (ocean/emotion/devotion, chance/dance/romance) . . .

The lines he had, but could not add to in the fog were:
  Lady, that soft skin, your bones and mine
  Will all be dust before another mountain's razed.
  No oceans, not a river, hardly a stream will dry
  Before our eyes do, and our hearts.

Metamorpheus:

One

Some things echo more than others. Sometimes I hear the last sound of all, that never echoes because there is nothing to bounce back from; it is the sound of final nothing, and it comes booming through the great pipes that are the bridge's marrowless bones like a hurricane, like God farting, like every shout of pain collected and replayed. I hear it then; a noise to rupture ears, split skulls, shatter walls, break souls. Those organ pipes are dark tunnels of iron in the sky, enormous and strong; what other sort of tune could they play?

A tune fit for the end of the world, the end of all life, the end of all things.

The rest?

Just hazy images. Patterns of shadows. Screen not silver; dark. Stop the false and flimsy stuff in the gate if you want to see what it's all made of. There. Watch the pretty colours as it, static, moves again; cooking, burning, bubbling and splitting and peeling back darkly like bruised lips parting, the image forced aside by the pressure of that pure white light (see what I'm doing for you laddie?).

No, I'm not him. I'm just watching him. Just a man I met, somebody I used to know.

I think I met him again, later. That comes later. All in good time.

I'm asleep now, but . . . well, I'm asleep now. That's enough.

No I don't know where I am.

No I don't know who I am.

Yes of course I know it's all a dream.

Isn't everything?

A wind comes and blows the fog away in the early morning. I dress in a daze, trying to remember my dreams. I am not even sure I did dream last night.

In the sky above the river, swollen grey shapes are slowly revealed by the lifting fog; big bloated balloons like immense pneumatic bombs. Barrage balloons, up and down the length of the bridge.

There must be hundreds of them, floating in the air at about summit height, perhaps higher, and anchored either to the islands, or to trawlers and other boats.

The last of the fog lifts and is scattered. It looks like it will be a fine day. The barrage balloons turn together in the sky, looking not so much like birds but a school of great grey whales, slowly moving their bulbous snouts into the atmosphere's soft current. I press my face to the cold glass of the window, looking down the hazy length of the bridge at as acute an angle as possible; the balloons are everywhere, spread out across the sky, some only a hundred feet or so from the bridge, others standing several miles off.

I assume they are to prevent any more fly-pasts by the aircraft; rather an excessive reaction, I'd have thought.

The letterbox flaps; a letter falls to the carpet. It is a note from Abberlaine Arrol; she will be doing some drawing at a certain marshalling yard a few sections away this morning, and would I like to join her?

Today is looking brighter all the time.

I remember to pick up my letter to Dr Joyce. I wrote it last night after disposing of the returned hat. I have told the good doctor that I wish to delay the hypnosis. I ask his indulgence (politely); I assure him I am still more than happy to meet and discuss my dreams – they have been more profound lately, I tell him, and hence probably more useful in the sort of analysis he originally intended to make.

I put Miss Arrol's letter and my own to the good doctor in my pocket, and stand watching the balloons a moment longer. They swing slowly in the morning light, like huge mooring buoys floating on some invisible surface above us.

Somebody knocks at the door. With any luck, it will be a repairman, for the screen or phone or both. I turn the key and try to open the door, but cannot. The knock comes again.

'Yes?' I call, pulling at the handle. A man shouts from outside.

'Come to have a look at your television set; that Mr Orr, is it?'

I struggle with the door; the handle turns but nothing happens.

'Is it? Mr J. Orr?' the man shouts.

'Yes, yes it is. Hold on a moment, I can't get the damn door open.'

'Right you are, Mr Orr.'

I tug and haul at the door handle, twisting it, shaking it. It has never even been stiff before now; not a hint of trouble. Perhaps everything in the flat is designed only to operate for about six months. I start to get angry.

'You sure you unlocked it, Mr Orr?'

'Yes,' I say, trying to keep calm.

'Sure it's the right key?'

'Positive!' I shout.

'Just thought I'd ask.' The man sounds amused. 'You got another door, Mr Orr?'

'No. No, I haven't.'

'Tell you what, push the key through the letterbox; I'll try unlocking it from this side.'

He tries this. It does not work. I walk back to the windows for a moment, breathing deeply and looking out at the massed balloons. Then I hear more muffled talking outside the door.

'Telephone engineer here, Mr Orr,' another voice calls. 'Something wrong with your door?'

'He can't open it,' the first voice says.

'Definitely unlocked, is it?' the phone man says. The door is rattled. I say nothing.

'You got another door we can use, Mr Orr?' he shouts.

'I already asked him that,' the first man says. The door is knocked again.

'What?' I say.

'You got a phone, Mr Orr?' The television repairman says.

'Of course he has,' the phone man says indignantly.

'Can you phone Buildings and Corridors, Mr Orr? They'll know wh—'

'How can he do that?' The phone man's voice is high with incredulity. 'I'm here to repair his bloody phone, aren't I?'

I retreat to my study before he suggests I watch some television to pass the time.

It takes another hour. A corridor janitor takes the whole wood surround away from the door. Finally the door just clicks open without warning, leaving him standing, puzzled and suspicious, in the midst of broken wood and dusty plaster. Both the repairmen have left for other jobs. I step out, over wooden slats pierced by bent nails.

'Thank you,' I tell the janitor. He is scratching his head with a claw hammer.

I post the letter to Dr Joyce, then buy some fruit to break my fast. My release has left me just enough time to rendezvous with Miss Arrol.

The train I take is full of people discussing the barrage balloons; most people have no idea what they are for. Once the tram clears the section proper and enters the relatively uncluttered linking span we all turn to look at them. I am amazed.

They are on one side only. Down-river, more barrage balloons than you could shake a stick at. Up-river; not one. Everybody else on the tram points and goggles at the massed balloons; only I, it seems, stare thunderstruck in the other direction, into the unmarred skies up-river beyond the X-ing girders of the linking span.

Not a single solitary balloon.

'Good morning.'

'It is rather, isn't it? Good morning to you too. How's your head?'

'My head is fine. How is your nose?'

'Same horrible shape, but not bleeding. Oh, your hand-kerchief.' Abberlaine Arrol digs into a jacket pocket, brings out my handkerchief, fresh and crisp.

Miss Arrol has just arrived here on a railway workers' tram.

We are in a marshalling yard, the widest place on the bridge I've seen so far; some of the sidings extend out far beyond the main structure on broad cantilevered platforms. Great engines, long trains of multifarious carriages, sturdy shunters and flimsy, complicated track-maintenance vehicles clank and shift over and across the complexity of lines and points and sidings like ponderous pieces in some huge, slow game. Steam drifts in the morning light, smoke billows across the harsh points of the still blazing arc lamps high in the girders; uniformed men dash to and fro, shouting and waving different coloured flags, blowing whistles and talking quickly into trackside telephones.

Abberlaine Arrol – wearing a long grey skirt and short grey jacket, her hair gathered up inside an official-looking cap – is here to draw the chaotic scene. Her free-hand sketches and water-colours of railway subjects already adorn several boardrooms and office foyers; she is considered a promising artist.

She hands my handkerchief to me. There is something curious in her eyes and stance; I glance at my laundered kerchief and stuff it into a spare pocket. Miss Arrol smiles, to herself, not to me. I have the disquieting impression that I have missed something here.

'Thank you,' I say.

'You may carry my easel for me, Mr Orr; I left it over here last week.' We cross several tracks to a small shed near the centre of the broad, rail-tangled platform of the marshalling yard. Around us, linked carriages and decoupled engines shift slowly back and forth; in other places, whole engines sink slowly through the deck on massively pulleyed platforms transporting them to workshops beneath the tracks.

'What do you make of our strange balloons, Mr Orr?' she asks me as we walk.

'I assume they're there to stop aircraft, though why they're only on one side, I don't know.'

'Nobody else seems to either,' Miss Arrol says thoughtfully. 'Probably another administration cock-up.' She sighs.

'Even my father hadn't heard anything about them, and he's usually fairly well informed.'

At the small shed she retrieves her easel; I transport the A-shaped structure to her chosen vantage point. She appears decided upon one of the heavy engine hoists as her choice of subject. She adjusts the easel, sets down her small folding stool, opens her satchel to reveal bottles of paints and a selection of pencils, charcoal sticks and crayons. She surveys the scene with a critical eye, and chooses a black length of charcoal.

'No further ill-effects from our little crash the other day, Mr Orr?' She makes a line on the grey-white paper.

'A certain conditioned nervousness at the sound of rapid rickshaw heel-horns, no more.'

'A temporary symptom, I'm sure.' She unleashes a smile of quite stunning charm, before returning to the easel. 'We were talking about travelling, before we were so rudely interrupted, weren't we?'

'Yes. I . . . I had been going to ask you how far you'd travelled.'

Abberlaine Arrol adds a few small circles and arcs to her sketch. 'University, I suppose,' she says, quickly brushing a few intersecting lines across the paper. 'That was about . . .' she shrugs, 'a hundred and fifty . . . two hundred sections away. Cityward.'

'You . . . couldn't see land from there, could you?'

'*Land*, Mr Orr,' she says, glancing at me, 'my, you are ambitious. No, I could see no land, apart from the usual islands.'

'Do you think there is no Kingdom then, no City either?'

'Oh, I imagine they both exist somewhere.' More lines.

'Haven't you ever wanted to see them?'

'Can't say I have, at least not since I stopped wanting to be a train driver.' She shades areas of the sketch. I can see a succession of vaulting Xs, a suggestion of cloud-shrouded heights. She draws quickly. At the nape of her pale, slender neck some escaped black strands of hair curl over the creamy surface like intricate swirls of some unknown writing.

'You know,' she says, 'I knew an engineer once – quite

118

senior – who thought what we really lived on wasn't a bridge at all, but a single huge rock in the centre of an uncrossable desert.'

'Hmm,' I say, uncertain how to take this. 'Perhaps it is something different to all of us. What do you see?'

'Same as you,' she says, turning briefly to me. 'A bloody great bridge. What do you think I'm drawing here?' She turns back.

I smile. 'Oh, a bit less than a fathom, at a guess.'

I hear her laugh. 'And you, Mr Orr?'

'My own conclusions.' This earns me one of her flashing smiles. She goes back to the drawing for a while, then looks distractedly up for a moment.

'You know the thing I miss most about university?' she says.

'What's that?'

'Being able to see the stars properly,' she nods, looking thoughtful. 'Too much light to see the stars properly round here, unless you go out to sea. But the university was stuck in the middle of farming sections, and it was quite dark at night.'

'*Farming* sections?'

'You know,' Abberlaine Arrol steps back, arms folded, from her work. 'Places where they grow food.'

'Yes, I see.' It had not occurred to me that other sections of the bridge might be given over to farming; it would not be difficult, I suppose. One might require windbreaks, perhaps even mirrors, to farm on different levels, and water rather than soil would be the best growing medium, but it would be possible.

So the bridge may well be totally self-sufficient in food. My idea that its length was limited by the time it would take for a fast goods train to deliver fresh produce each day would appear to be irrelevant. The bridge can be any length it likes.

Abberlaine Arrol lights a thin cigar. One booted foot taps on the metal deck. She turns to me, folding her arms again beneath the bloused and jacketed contours of her breasts; her skirt swings, comes back; a heavy and expensive cloth. There is a hint of a light day-perfume over the fragrant cigar smoke.

'Well, Mr Orr?'

I inspect Miss Arrol's finished drawing.

The broad platform of the marshalling yard has been sketched in, then altered; the lines and tracks look like creepers in a jungle, all fallen to the floor. The trains are grotesque, gnarled things, like giant maggots or decaying tree trunks; above, the girders and tubes become branches and boughs, disappearing into smoke rising from the jungle floor; a giant, infernal forest. One engine has become a monster, rearing out of the ground; a snarling, fiery lizard. The small, terrified figure of a man runs from it, his minia-ture face just visible, twisted into a shriek of terror.

'Imaginative,' I say, after a moment's thought. She laughs lightly.

'You don't like it.'

'My tastes are too literal, perhaps. The quality of drawing is impressive.'

'I *know* that,' Miss Arrol says. Her voice is sharp, but her face looks a little sad. I wish I liked the sketch better.

But what a signalling capacity Miss Abberlaine Arrol's grey-green eyes possess! They view me now with an expres-sion almost of compassion. I think that I like the young lady very much.

She says, 'I meant it for you.' She reaches into her satchel and takes out a rag, begins to clean her hands.

'Really?' I am genuinely pleased. 'That's very kind of you. Thank you.'

She takes the drawing from the easel and rolls it up. 'You have my permission to do whatever you will with it,' she says wryly. 'Make paper aircraft out of it.'

'Certainy not,' I say as she hands it to me. I feel as though I have just been presented with a diploma. 'I'll have it framed and hung in my apartment. Already I like it a great deal more, knowing that it was drawn for me.'

Abberlaine Arrol's exits amuse me. This time she is picked up by a track engineer's car; a quaint, elegantly glassed and panelled carriage full of complicated but archaic instru-ments, all bright brass, clinking balances, and drums of paper flowing past scribbling pens. It hisses and rattles to a stop, a door concertinas open and a young guard salutes Miss Arrol, who is on her way to lunch with her father. I hold her easel, having been instructed to replace it in the shed. Her satchel bulges with rolled line drawings: the commissioned work she really came here to do and which she has been busy with – while still talking to me – since completing my sketch. She puts one boot on the high step up to the carriage and holds out her hand to me.

'Thank you for your help, Mr Orr.'

'Thank you for my drawing.' I take her hand. Between Miss Arrol's boot top and skirt hem her stocking is revealed for the first time; a fine but unmistakable black fishnet.

I concentrate on her eyes. They look amused. 'I hope I'll see you again.' I glance at those pretty bags beneath the grey-green eyes. Fishnet, indeed; I am netted again. She squeezes my hand; I feel faint with an absurd euphoria.

'Well, Mr Orr, if I can summon up the courage, I may let you take me out to dinner.'

'That would be . . . most pleasant. I do hope you discover quite inexhaustible reserves of bravery in the near future.' I bow a little and am rewarded with another glimpse of that besottingly lovely leg.

'Goodbye then, Mr Orr. Keep in touch.'

'I will. Goodbye.'

The door closes, the carriage clanks and hisses off; steam from its passing curls round me like mist, making my eyes water. I take out my handkerchief.

It has been monogrammed. Miss Arrol has had a finely sewn O added to one corner, in blue silk.

Such grace; I am captivated. And those few inches of delectable, dark-stockinged leg!

Brooke and I sit, after lunch, drinking mulled wine in Dissy Pitton's Sea View Lounge, lounging on suspended couches watching a depleted fishing fleet setting out to sea far below; the departing trawlers sound their horns as they pass their stationary sister-ships on barrage balloon-anchoring duties.

'Can't say I blame you,' Brooke says gruffly, 'I never did

121

think the fellow would do you much good.' I have told Mr Brooke about my decision not to let Dr Joyce hypnotize me. We both look out to sea. 'Damn balloons.' My friend glares at the offending blimps. They shine almost silver in the sunlight, their shadows speckling the blue waters of the firth; another pattern.

'I thought you'd approve . . .' I begin, then stop, frowning, listening. Brooke looks at me.

'Not up to me to approve or – Orr?'

'Shh,' I say quietly. I listen to the distant noise, then open one of the lounge windows. Brooke gets to his feet. The drone of the approaching aero engines is quite distinct now.

'Don't say those bloody things are coming back!' Brooke shouts behind me.

'Indeed they are.' The planes come into view. They are lower than before, the middle one almost level with Dissy Pitton's. They are flying Kingdomward in the same vertical formation as before. Once again, each trails pulses of oily smoke, leaving a giant ribbon of dark smudges hanging in the sky behind them. The planes' silver-grey fuselages have no markings. The silvered-over cockpit canopies glint in the sunlight. The combined wires of the barrage balloons seem to provide only the most rudimentary of obstacles to the planes' progress; the aircraft are flying about a quarter of a mile from the bridge, where the wires are probably at their most dense, yet as we watch they have to make only one brief turn to avoid a cable. The flight drones away into the distance, leaving smoke.

Brooke smacks one fist into the other palm. 'Cheeky beggars!'

The hanging wall of smoky smudges drifts slowly towards the bridge in the steady breeze.

After a couple of energetic games at the rackets club, I call at the picture-framer's. Miss Arrol's drawing has been mounted on wood and covered in non-reflective glass during the afternoon.

I hang it where it will catch the morning light, above a bookcase to one side of my now-repaired front door. The television switches itself on while I am straightening the drawing on the wall.

The man still lies there, surrounded by his machines. His face is expressionless. The light has altered a little; the room looks darker. His drip will need changing soon. I watch his pale, slack face. I want to tap the glass of the screen, to wake the fellow . . . I switch the set off instead. Is there any point in testing the telephone? I pick it up; the same calm beeps still sound.

I decide to dine at the rackets club bar.

According to the television in the club bar, the official line on the rogue planes is that they are an expensive prank perpetrated by somebody from another part of the bridge. Following today's latest outrage, the barrage balloon 'defences' are to be strengthened (there is no mention of why only one side of the bridge is ballooned). The culprits responsible for these unauthorized flights are being sought. The Administration asks us all to be vigilant. I seek out the journalist I talked to before.

'Can't really add anything to that,' he confesses.

'What about the Third City Library?'

'Couldn't find it in our records. There was some sort of fire or explosion up on those levels; some time ago, though. You sure this was only a couple of days ago?'

'Positive.'

'Well, probably still trying to bring it under control.' He snaps his fingers. 'Oh, tell you something they haven't mentioned on the broadcasts.'

'What?'

'They've found out what language the planes are writing in.'

'Yes?'

'Braille.'

'*What?*'

'Braille. The blind language; still complete nonsense, even when you do decipher it, but that's what it is, all right.'

I sit back in my seat, utterly dumbfounded for the second time today.

Two

I am standing on a moor, a sloped plain of tundra leading up towards a ridge and the grey, featureless sky. This place is cold, and scoured by a gusting wind which tugs and plucks at my thin clothes, and flattens the rough, stunted grasses and heathers of the heath.

The moor continues downhill, vanishing into the grey distance as the slope steepens. All that breaks the monotony of this dull waste of grass is a thin straight stretch of water, like a canal, its surface roughened by the cold wind.

From the ridge uphill comes a thin, siren sound.

Grey smoke, driven and made ragged by the tearing wind, moves along the skyline. A train appears over the distant ridge. As it comes closer, the siren sounds again; a harsh, angry noise. The black engine and few, dark carriages make a dull line pointing directly at me.

I look down; I am standing between the rails of the track. The two thin lines of metal head straight from me to the approaching train. I step to one side, look down again. I am still standing between the tracks. I step aside again. The tracks follow me.

They flow like quicksilver, moving as I move. I am still in between the rails. The train's siren shrieks once more.

I take another step to the side; the rails move again, seeming to slide over the surface of the moor without resistance or cause. The train is closer.

I start to run, but the tracks keep pace, one always just ahead, one always just at my heel. I try to stop, and fall, rolling, still between the rails. I get up and run in the other direction, running into the wind, my breath like fire. The tracks glide in front and behind. The train, very close now, screams again; it easily negotiates the corners and kinks in the rails my stumbling, twisting progress has produced. I keep running; sweating, panicking, unbelieving, but the rails flow smoothly with me, gauge constant, before and behind, perfectly attuned to my desperate, pounding gait. The train bears down on me, siren bellowing.

The ground shakes. The rails whine. I scream, and find the canal at my side; just before the engine reaches me, I throw myself into the choppy waters.

Under the surface of the water there is air; I float down through its thick warmth, turning slowly, seeing the under-surface of the water above, glistening like an oily mirror. I land, softly, on the mossy surface of the canal's floor. It is quiet, and very warm. Nothing passes overhead.

The walls are grey, smooth stone, and close; at full stretch I could almost touch both sides. The walls curve slightly, fading away in either direction under the dim light falling from above. I put my hand on one of the smooth walls and stub my toe on something hard under the moss, near the wall.

Clearing some of the moss away reveals a piece of shining metal. I brush more of the moss away on either side; it is long, like a pipe, and fastened to the floor of the channel. In cross-section it has the shape of a bloated-looking I. Closer inspection proves that it runs under the moss to each side, raising the green-brown surface in a continuous, hardly-noticeable ridge. On the other side of the tunnel there is a similar raised line of moss, near the wall.

I jump up, hurriedly brushing the moss back over the section of rail I have uncovered.

As I do so, the thick, warm air starts to move slowly past me, and from far down the tunnel's narrow curve there comes the faint, thin sound of a siren, coming closer.

Slightly hungover, waiting for my kippers in the Inches breakfast bar, I wonder whether I ought to take that drawing by Miss Arrol down from my wall.

The dream disturbed me; I woke up sweating, and lay tossing and turning in my bed, still wet with sweat, until finally I had to get up. I had a bath, fell asleep in the warm water and woke up, freezing cold, terrified, jarred as though electrocuted, suddenly certain in my immediate confusion that I was trapped in some constricting tunnel: the bath a tunnel-canal, its cold waters my own sweat.

I read the morning paper and sip my coffee. The Administration is being criticized for not having prevented yesterday's fly-past. Unspecified new measures are under evaluation with a view to preventing further violations of the bridge's airspace.

My kippers arrive; their filleted bones have left a pattern on the pale brown flesh. I recall my thoughts on the general topography of the bridge. I try to ignore my hangover.

There are three possibilities:

1   The bridge is just that, a link between two landmasses. They are very far apart, and the bridge leads an existence independent of them, but traffic crosses the bridge from one to the other.
2   The bridge is, effectively, a pier; there is land at one end but not the other.
3   The bridge has no connection with land whatsoever, save for the small islands beneath every third section.

In cases 2 and 3, it might be still under construction. It may only be a pier because it has not yet reached the farther landmass, or if it has no connection with land, it might still be being built not just at one end, but two.

There is one interesting sub-possibility in case 3. The bridge appears to be straight, but there is a horizon, and the sun rises, arcs, falls. So the bridge might eventually meet itself, form a closed circuit; a circle, vertically, ringing the globe; topographically closed.

Visiting the library on the way here to look at a braille book reminded me of the still-lost Third City Library. I feel quite recovered after my breakfast and decide to walk to the section which houses both Dr Joyce's office and the fabled library. I'll have another crack at finding the damn thing.

It is another fine day; a soft warm wind blows up-river, slanting the wires of the barrage balloons as the grey blimps try to drift towards the bridge. Extra balloons are being floated into the sky; large barges support the half-inflated shapes of even more balloons, and some of the trawlers have already been equipped with two balloons, producing a giant V of cables in the sky above them. Some of the balloons have been painted black.

I walk whistling across the linking span from one section to the next, swinging my stick. A plush but conventional elevator bears me up to the highest available floor, still a few levels down from the actual summit of the section. The dark, tall, musty-smelling corridors up here seem familiar now, in their general character at least; the exact lay-out remains a mystery.

I walk beneath the ancient, age-grimed flags, between the niches occupied by stone-remembered officials, past rooms full of whispering, smartly uniformed clerks. I cross dim, white-tiled lightwells on rickety cross-corridors, peer through keyholes into locked, dark, deserted passages whose floors are inches deep in dust and debris. I test the doors, but the hinges have rusted.

Finally, I come to a familiar corridor. A large round patch of light glows on the carpet ahead, where the corridor broadens out. The air smells damp; I'd swear the thick, dark carpet squelches with each footfall. I can see tall pot-plants now, and a length of wall which ought to hold the entrance to the L-shaped lift. The patch of light on the floor has a shadow in the centre of which I don't recall. The shadow moves.

I reach the light. The great round window is there, still staring down-river like a huge handless clock-face. The shadow is cast by Mr Johnson, Dr Joyce's patient who refuses to leave the cradle. He is cleaning the window, polishing the glass at its centre with a rag, an expression of rapt concentration on his face.

Behind and a little below him, in mid air, well over a thousand feet above sea-level, floats a small trawler.

It is suspended on three cables, it is black-brown in colour, rust-streaked above the waterline and barnacle-encrusted below it. It floats slowly towards the bridge, rising as it nears.

I walk towards the window. High above the drifting

trawler are three black barrage balloons. I look up at the still-polishing Mr Johnson. I knock on the glass. He takes no notice.

The trawler, still rising, heads directly for the great round window. I bang on the glass as high as I can reach; I wave my stick and hat and shout as loudly as I can, 'Mr Johnson! Look out! Behind you!' He stops polishing, but only to lean forward, still smiling beatifically, breathe on the glass, and then start polishing again.

I hammer on the glass near Mr Johnson's knees; as far as I can reach, even with my stick. The trawler is twenty feet away. Mr Johnson polishes happily on. I beat on the thick glass with the brass knob on the tip of the stick. The glass chips, cracks. Fifteen feet; the trawler is level with Mr Johnson's feet. 'Mr Johnson!' I thrash at the cracking pane of glass; it finally smashes, spraying shards. I stagger back from the hail of fragments. Mr Johnson is scowling furiously in at me. Ten feet.

'Behind you!' I scream, thrusting my stick out to point, then running for cover.

Mr Johnson watches me run, and turns round. The trawler is a fathom-length away. He dives to the deck of his cradle as the trawler crunches into the centre of the great round window, its keel scraping the rail of Mr Johnson's cradle and showering him with barnacles. Panes shatter, glass showers down on to the broad landing; the sound of breaking glass competes with that of creaking, fracturing metal. The trawler's stem grinds through the centre of the window, its metal frame bends like a huge spider's web, making a terrible groaning, screaming sound. The structure around me shakes.

Then it stops. The trawler appears to bounce back a little, then scrapes and grates its way up over the top part of the great mandala, breaking more glass as it goes; barnacles and fragments of the shattered panes fall together on to the carpet, beating at the broad leaves of the nearby pot-plants like some hard, fierce rain.

Then, incredibly, it is gone. The trawler disappears from

view. Glass stops falling. The sounds of the boat's scraping progress up the side of the remaining floors of the upper bridge quiver through the air.

Mr Johnson's cradle swings to and fro, gradually slowing. He stirs, looks about him, and stands up slowly, shards of fallen glass sloughing from his back like glittering snakeskin. He licks at a couple of cuts he has sustained on the backs of his hands, carefully brushes his shoulders free of some dusty grains of glass, then walks along his still slightly swaying platform and picks up a short-handled broom. He starts to brush the fragments of window-pane off the cradle, whistling to himself. Every now and again, as he sweeps, he looks, with an expression of sad concern, at the bowed-in shattered mess of the great circular window.

I stand and watch. He cleans up his cradle, checks his supporting cables, then bandages his still-bleeding hands. Finally he takes a good look at the wrecked window and finds some bits which are both unbroken and not yet washed; he starts cleaning these.

Ten minutes have passed since the trawler impacted; I am still alone here. Nobody has come to investigate, no alarms or warning signals have sounded. Mr Johnson carries on washing and polishing. A warm breeze blows through the smashed window, ruffling the torn leaves of the pot-plants. Where the doors to the L-shaped elevator were, there is now a blank wall, with niches for statues.

I leave, my quest for the Third City Library again abandoned.

I return to my apartment, and an even greater disaster.

Men in grey overalls are moving in and out of the doorway, loading all my clothes on to a trolley. As I watch, another man appears, straining under a load of paintings and drawings; he piles them on to another trolley and returns inside.

'Hoy! You! You there! What do you think you're doing?' The men stop and look at me, perplexed. I try to tear some of my shirts from one tall fellow's arms, but he is too strong, and simply stands, blinking with surprise and holding stiffly on to the clothes he has taken from my room. His mate shrugs and walks back inside my apartment. 'You there; stop! Come out of there!'

I leave the oaf with my shirts and dash into my rooms; they are in turmoil: grey-overalled men moving everywhere, putting white cloths over the furniture, carrying other pieces outside, taking books from my bookcases and putting them in boxes, removing pictures from walls and ornaments from tables. I gaze round; stunned, aghast.

'Stop this! What the hell do you think you're doing? Stop it!'

A few turn and look, but they don't stop what they're doing.

One man is making for the door with all three of my umbrellas; 'Put those back!' I shout, blocking his way. I threaten him with my stick. He takes it from me, adds it to the collection of umbrellas and disappears outside.

'Ah, you must be Mr Orr.' A large, bald man wearing a black jacket on top of his overalls, holding a black hat in one hand and a clipboard in the other, appears from my bedroom.

'I certainly am; what the hell's going on here?'

'You're being moved, Mr Orr,' the fellow says, smiling.

'What? Why? To *where*?' I shout. My legs are shaking; there is a sick, heavy feeling in my stomach.

'Umm . . .' The bald man looks through the papers on his clipboard. 'Ah, here we are: level U7, room 306.'

'What? Where's that?' I cannot believe this. *U7*?' That surely means *under* the rail deck! But that's where workers, ordinary people live. What's happening? Why are they doing this to me? It *must* be a mistake.

'Don't rightly know, sir,' the man says cheerfully, 'but I'm sure you can find it if you look.'

'But why am I being moved?'

'Absolutely no idea, sir,' he chimes happily. 'You been here long?'

'Six months.'

More of my clothes are taken out of my dressing room. I turn to the bald fellow again. 'Look, those are my clothes.

What are you doing with them?'

'Oh, returning them, sir,' he assures me, nodding, smiling.

'*Returning* them? To where?' I shout. This is all very undignified, but what else can I do?

'I don't know, sir. Wherever you got them from, I suppose. Not my department exactly where they go back to, sir.'

'But they're *mine!*'

He frowns, looks at his clipboard, ruffling paper. He shakes his head, smiling confidently. 'No, sir.'

'But they *are*, dammit!'

'Sorry, sir, they're not; they belong to the hospital authorities; says so here – look.' He shows me the clipboard; a sheet of paper details my purchases of clothes from shops on the hospital's credit lines. 'See!' He chortles. 'Had me worried for a second there, sir; that would've been illegal, that would, removing any of *your* stuff. You could have called the police, you could have. and quite right too, if we'd touched any of your own stuff. You shouldn't go—'

'But I was told I could buy what I liked! I have an allowance! I—'

'Now, sir,' the man says, watching another load of clothes and hats go past, and ticking something off on his clipboard, 'I'm not a lawyer or anything like one, sir, but I've been doing this sort of thing for longer than I care to think about, and I think you'll find, sir, if you don't mind me saying, that all this stuff actually belongs to the hospital, and you only had the use of it. I think that's what you'll find.'

'But—'

'I don't know if that was explained to you sir, but I'm sure that's what you would find if you were to investigate the matter, sir.'

'I . . .' I feel dizzy. 'Look, can't you stop, just for a moment?' I ask. 'Let me phone my doctor. Dr Joyce – you've probably heard of him; he'll sort this out. There must have—'

'Been a mistake, sir?' The bald man laughs wheezily for a moment. 'Bless me, sir. Sorry to interrupt you like that, but I couldn't help it; that's what everybody says. Wish I had a shilling for every time I've heard that!' He shakes his head, wipes one cheek. 'Well, if you really think so, sir, you'd better get in touch with the relevant authorities.' He looks around, 'The phone's around here . . . somewhere . . .'

'It doesn't *work*.'

'Oh it does, sir; I used it not half an hour ago, to let the department know we're here.'

I find the telephone on the floor. It's dead; it clicks once when I try to dial. The bald man comes over.

'Cut off, sir?' He looks at his watch. 'Bit early, sir.' He makes another note on his board. 'Very keen those boys at the exchange, sir. Very, very keen.' He makes a little papping noise with his mouth and shakes his head again, obviously impressed.

'Will you please, *please* just wait a moment; let me get in touch with my doctor; he'll sort this out. His name is Dr Joyce.'

'No need, sir,' the man says happily. An ugly, sickening thought occurs to me. The bald man looks through the sheets of paper on his clipboard. He runs a finger down one of the papers near the back of the bundle, then stops. 'Here we are, sir. Look, here.'

It is the good doctor's signature. The bald man says, 'See, he already knows sir; it was him authorized it.'

'Yes.' I sit down and stare at the blank wall opposite.

'Happy now, sir?' The bald man does not seem to be attempting either levity or irony.

'Yes,' I hear myself say. I feel numb, dead, wrapped in cotton wool, all senses reduced, ground down, fuses blown.

''Fraid we're going to need those things you've got on, sir.' He is looking at my clothes.

'You cannot', I say wearily, 'be serious.'

'Sorry, sir. We've got a nice and – I might add, sir – *new* set of overalls for you. You want to change now?'

'This is ridiculous.'

'I know, sir. Still, rules are rules, aren't they? I'm sure you'll like these overalls; they're brand new.'

'*Overalls?*'

They are bright green. They come complete with shoes, shorts, shirt and rather rough underwear.

I change in my dressing room, my mind as blank as the walls.

My body seems to move of its own accord, performing the motions it is expected to; automatically, mechanically, and then stopping, waiting for a fresh order. I fold my clothes neatly, and as I fold my jacket, see the handkerchief Abberlaine Arrol gave me. I take it from the breast pocket.

When I go back into the sitting room, the bald man is watching the television. It is showing a quiz programme. He turns it off when I enter, bearing my bundle of clothes. He put his black hat on.

'This handkerchief,' I say, nodding at the handkerchief on top of the bundle. 'It has been monogrammed. May I keep it?'

The bald man motions one of the men to take the bundle of clothes. He takes the handkerchief and looks down a list of his clipboard. He taps at a point on the list with a sharp pencil.

'Yes, I've got the handkerchief down here, but . . . no mention of it having this letter on it.' He shakes the handkerchief, looking closely at the blue, embroidered O. I wonder if he will have the stitching unpicked and present me with the thread. 'All right, take it,' he says sourly. I take it. 'But you'll have to pay the value of it out of your new allowance.'

'Thank you.' It is curiously easy to be polite.

'Well, that's that,' he says, efficiently. He puts his pencil away. I am reminded of the good doctor. He points to the door; 'After you.'

I put the handkerchief in a pocket in the garish green overalls and precede the fellow from the apartment. All but one of the other men have gone; the last man holds a large piece of rolled-up paper and an empty picture frame. He waits until his superior has locked and chained the door, then whispers something in his ear. The foreman holds out the rolled paper, which I realize is Abberlaine Arrol's drawing.

'Is this yours?'

I nod. 'Yes. A gift, from a fr—'

'Here.' He shoves it into my hands, then turns away. The

133

two men walk away down the corridor. I head for the elevator, clutching my drawing. I have gone a few paces when there is a shout. The bald foreman is running towards me, beckoning. I walk to meet him.

He shakes the clipboard in my face. 'Not so fast, chum,' he says. 'There's the small matter of a broad-brimmed *hat*.'

'This is the office of Dr F. Joyce, and a very good afternoon to you *indeed*.'

'This is Mr Orr; I want to talk to Dr Joyce; it's very urgent.'

'Mr Orr! How nice to talk to you! How are you, this fine day?'

'I . . . I'm feeling quite terrible at the moment, as a matter of fact; I've just been thrown out of my apartment. Now can I please talk to Dr Joy—'

'But that's terrible, absolutely terrible.'

'I agree. I'd like to talk to Dr Joyce about it.'

'Oh, you want the police, Mr Orr, not a doctor . . . unless; well, I mean obviously they haven't thrown you out off the balcony, or you wouldn't be around to—'

'Look, I'm grateful for your concern, but I don't have much money for this phone, and—'

'What, they didn't rob you as well, did they? No!'

'*No*. Now look, *can I please talk to Dr Joyce?*'

'I'm afraid not, Mr Orr; the doctor's in conference at the moment . . . ahm . . . the . . . let's see . . . ah, the Buying Procedures (Contracts) Committee New Members Subcommittee Elections Committee, I think.'

'Well can't you—'

'No! No, silly me; I tell a lie; that was yesterday; it's the – I thought that sounded wrong – it's the New Buildings Planning and Integration Standing Sub—'

'For God's sake, man! I don't care what damn committee he's on! When can I talk to him?'

'Oh well, you *should* care you know, Mr Orr; they're for your good too, you know.'

'*When can I speak to him?*'

'Well, I don't know, Mr Orr. Can he call you back?'

134

'When? I can't hang around this call box all day.'

'Well, how about at home then?'

'I just told you! I've been thrown out!'

'Well, can't you get back in? I'm sure if you get the police—'

'The doors have been chained. And it was all done with official authorization and signed by Dr Joyce; *that* is why I want to sp—'

'Oooooh; you've been *relocated*, Mr Orr; I see. I tho—'

'What was that noise?'

'Oh, that's the beeps, Mr Orr. You have to put more money in.'

'I haven't got any more money.'

'Ooops. Oh well, nice talking to you, Mr Orr. Bye now. Have a nice d—'

'Hello? Hello?'

Level U7 is seven levels beneath the train deck; quite close enough for one to be able to distinguish the difference between a local train, a through-train express and a fast goods by their vibrations alone, even without the concomitant rumbling/screaming/thundering noise as confirmation. The level is broad, dark, cavernous and crowded. On the floor below there is a light engineering and sheet metal works; above, six more levels of accommodation. An odour of sweat and old smoke pervades the thickened atmosphere. Room 306 is all mine. It contains only a single narrow bed, a rickety plastic chair, a table and a thin chest of drawers, and it is still crowded. I smelt the communal toilet on my way here, at the end of the corridor. The room looks out into a lightwell hardly worthy of the name.

I close the door and walk to Dr Joyce's office like an automaton: blind, deaf, unthinking. When I get there, it is too late, the office is closed; doctor and even receptionist gone home. A floor security guard looks at me suspiciously and suggests I get back to my own level.

I sit on my small bed, stomach rumbling, head in hands, looking at the floor, listening to the shriek of metal being cut in the workshop below. My chest aches.

There is a knock at the door.

'Come in.'

A small, grubby man wearing a long, shiny coat of dark blue comes in, shuffling sideways through the door; his eyes flicker round the room, and hesitate briefly only on the rolled-up drawing lying on top of the chest of drawers. His gaze settles on me, though his eyes don't meet mine.

''Scuse me, pal. New here, aren't you?' He stands by the open door, as though ready to run back out through it. He sticks his hands into the deep pockets of his long coat.

'Yes, I am,' I say, standing. 'My name is John Orr.' I offer my hand; his grabs mine briefly, then scuttles back to his lair. 'How do you do,' I just have time to say.

'Lynch,' he says, addressing my chest. 'Call me Lynchy.'

'What can I do for you, Lynchy?'

He shrugs. 'Nothin'; just bein' neighbourly. Wondered if there was anything' ye wanted.'

'That's very kind of you. I would be grateful for a little advice regarding an allowance I was told I would receive.'

Mr Lynch actually looks at me, his not-recently-washed face seeming to glow, albeit dully. 'Aw yeah, I can help ye with all that stuff. No problem.'

I smile. In all the time I lived in the more elevated and refined levels of the bridge not one of my neighbours even wished me good-day, far less offered help of any kind.

Mr Lynch takes me to a canteen where he buys me a fishmeal sausage and a plate of mashed seaweed. They are both appalling, but I am hungry. We drink tea from mugs. He is a carriage sweeper, he explains, and occupies room 308. He seems quite unduly impressed when I show him my plastic bracelet and tell him I am a patient. He explains how to go about claiming my allowance, in the morning. I am grateful. He even offers me a small loan until then, but I am too beholden to the man already, and refuse, with thanks.

The canteen is noisy, steamy, crowded, windowless; everything clatters, and the smells do nothing for my digestive processes. 'Chucked ye out, just like that, eh?'

'Yes. My doctor authorized it. I refused to undergo the treatment he had in mind for me; I assume that's why I was relocated, anyway. I may be wrong.'

'What a bastard, eh,' Mr Lynch shakes his head and looks fierce. 'Them doctors.'

'It does seem rather vindictive and petty, but I suppose I have only myself to blame.'

'Total bastards,' Mr Lynch maintains, and drinks tea from his mug. He slurps his tea; this has the same effect on me as nails scratched down a blackboard; I grit my teeth. I look at the clock above the serving hatch. I'll try to contact Brooke; he will probably be at Dissy Pitton's soon.

Mr Lynch takes out tobacco and papers and rolls himself a cigarette. He sniffs powerfully, and makes a grunting, snorting, catarrhal noise at the back of his throat. A hacking series of coughs, like a large sack of rocks being shaken vigorously somewhere inside Mr Lynch's chest, completes his ante-cigarette preparations.

'Ye got to go somewhere, pal?' Mr Lynch says, seeing me glance at the clock. He lights up, producing a cloud of acrid smoke.

'Yes. I had best be off, actually. I'm going to see an old friend.' I get to my feet. 'Thank you very much, Mr Lynch; I'm sorry to rush off. Once I'm in funds again, I hope you'll allow me to return your generosity.'

'No problem, pal. If ye want a hand tomorrow, give us a knock; it's my day off.'

'Thank you. You are a kind man, Mr Lynch. Good day.'

'Aye. Bye-bye.'

I get to Dissy Pitton's later than I intended, footsore. I ought to have accepted Mr Lynch's offer of money for the train fare; I am amazed at how much less pleasant walking becomes when it is adopted due to necessity rather than idle choice. I am also aware of being seen as the uniform I wear; my face would seem to be invisible for all practical purposes. Nevertheless, I pace, head up, shoulders back, as though I still

137

wear my best coat and suit, and I believe my stick is more obvious in its absence than it was when actually held and swung.

The doorman at Dissy Pitton's is not impressed, however.

'Don't you recognize me? I'm here most nights. I'm Mr Orr. Look.' I hold up my plastic identity bracelet for him to see. He ignores it; he is embarrassed, I think, at having to deal with me and still tip his cap and open the door for customers.

'Look, just clear off, right?'

'Don't you recognize me? Look at my face, man, not the damn overalls. At least take a message to Mr Brooke . . . is he here yet? Brooke, the engineer; small dark fellow, slightly hunched . . .' The doorman is taller and heavier than me, or I might try to force my way in.

'You clear off now or you're in trouble,' the fellow says, glancing down the broad corridor outside the bar as though looking for somebody.

'I was here the other night; I was the chap who gave that fellow Bouch back his hat; you must remember that. You held the hat in front of him and he threw up into it.'

The doorman smiles, touches his cap, lets a couple I do not recognize into the bar. 'Look pal, I've been off the last two weeks. Now just you fuck off or you're going to be sorry.'

'Oh . . . I see. I'm sorry. But please; if I write a note, would you—'

I get no further. The doorman takes another look round, discovers the corridor to be deserted, and punches me in the stomach with one heavy, gloved hand. It is stunningly painful; as I double up, he lands another blow on my chin, jarring my whole head. I stagger back, ringing with pain; he cracks me across the eye. It is the shock of it, I suppose.

I hit the planking of the floor in a daze. I am picked up by the rump and neck of my overalls and dragged and scraped across the deck, through a door into the cold open air. I am dumped on an open metal deck. Two more heavy blows strike my side; kicks, I think.

A door slams. The wind blows.

I lie for some time, the way I was dropped, unable to move.

A throbbing, pulsing pain builds up sickly in my belly; without seeing where I am (I think there is blood in my eyes), I vomit up the fishcake and seaweed.

I lie on my cramped bed. The man and woman in the room above are having an argument. I am racked with pain; I feel nauseous but hungry at the same time. My head, teeth and jaws, my right eye and temple, my belly, guts and side all ache; a symphony of pain. In all this, the nagging whisper that is my old injury's echo, the deep, circular chest pain I am so used to, is quite drowned out.

I am clean. I have washed my mouth out as best I could and placed my handkerchief over my cut eyebrow. I am not quite sure how I walked or staggered back here, but I did, my dazed pain like drunkenness.

I find no comfort in my bed, only a new place to appreciate the waves of pain which flood me, beating on the body's shore.

In the end, but in the middle of the night, I drift off to sleep. But it is an ocean of burning oil I am cast adrift upon, no sea's repose; I pass from waking agonies which the reasoning mind can at least attempt to place in context – looking forward to a time when the pain has ceased – to the semi-conscious trance of torment in which the smaller, earlier, deeper rings of the brain know only that the nerves scream, the body aches, and there is no one to turn crying to for comfort.

Three

I do not know how long I have been here. A long time. I do not know where this place is. Somewhere far away. I do not know why I am here. Because I did something wrong. I do not know how long I will have to stay here. A long time.

This is not a long bridge, but it goes on for ever. I am not far from the bank, but I will never get there. I walk but I never move. Fast or slow, running, turning, doubling back, jumping, throwing myself or stopping; nothing makes any difference.

The bridge is made of iron. It is thick, heavy, rusting iron, pitted and flaking, and it makes a dead, heavy sound beneath my feet; a sound that is so thick and heavy it is almost no sound, just the shock of each footfall travelling through my bones to my head. The bridge seems to be solid iron. Perhaps it was not once, perhaps it was riveted together once, but now it is one piece, rusted into one, decaying into a single rotting mass. Or it may have been welded. Who cares.

It is not large. It bridges a small river I can see through the thick iron bars which rise from the edge of the balustrade. The river flows straight and slow out of the mists, under the bridge, then just as straight and slow away again, into the same damned mist downstream.

I could swim that river in a couple of minutes (if it wasn't for the carnivorous fish), I could cross this bridge in much less than that, even walking slowly.

The bridge is part of a circle, perhaps the upper quarter in terms of height. Its whole forms a great hollow wheel which encircles the river.

On the bank behind me, there is a cobbled road leading off across a marsh. On the far bank are my ladies, reposing or disporting in a variety of small pavilions or opened wagons resting on a small meadow surrounded – so I see on the odd occasions when the mist thins slightly – by tall, broad-leafed trees. I walk for ever towards the ladies. Sometimes I walk slowly, sometimes fast; I have even run. They beckon to me, they wave and hold out welcoming hands to me. Their voices call to me, in tongues I cannot understand, but which are soft and lovely to me, warm and beseeching to me, and which fill me with furious desire.

The ladies walk back and forth, or lie among satin pillows in their small pavilions and broad wagons. They wear all sorts of dress: some severe and formal, covering them from neck to sole, some loose and flowing, like silk waves on their bodies, some thin and transparent, or full of carefully positioned tears and holes, so that their full, young bodies – white as alabaster, black as jet, gold as gold itself – shine through as

140

though their youth and primed nubility was something bright that burned within them, a warmth my eyes detect.

They undress for me, slowly, sometimes, while watching me; their large sad eyes are full of longing, their slender, delicate hands going softly to their shoulders, opening, sloughing off, brushing away straps and layers of material as if they were drops of water left after a bath. I howl, I run faster; I scream for them.

Sometimes they come to the lip of the bank, the very edge of the bridge, and tear their clothes off, screaming to me, clenching their little fists and moving their hips, going down on their knees, legs spread, crying to me, holding out their arms to me. I scream then too and throw myself forward, I sprint for all my worth or, stiff with desire, hold my prick like some stunted flagpole in front of me, running and shaking it and bellowing with frustrated desire. Often I ejaculate, and fall weakly, used up, to the hard iron surface of the bridge's curved deck, to lie there, panting, sobbing, crying, beating the flaking iron surface with my hands until they bleed.

On occasion the women make love to each other, in front of me; I wail and tear my hair. They take slow hours sometimes, gently kissing and stroking, caressing and licking each other; they cry out at orgasm, their bodies jerking, clutching, pulsing in time to each other. Sometimes they watch me as they do this, and I can never decide whether the look in their large, moist eyes is still sad and longing, or satiated and mocking. I stop and shake my fist at them, yell and shout at them. 'Bitches! Ingrates! Bloody torturers! Hellbags! What about me? Come here! You come on here. Here! Come on; just step on! Well throw me a fucking rope then!'

They do not. They parade, they strip, they fuck, they sleep and read old books, they make meals and leave small rice-paper trays of food on the edge of the bridge so that I can eat (but sometimes I rebel; I throw the trays into the river; the carnivorous fish demolish food and tray) but they will not step on to the bridge. I recall that witches cannot cross water.

I walk; the bridge revolves slowly, rumbling and shivering just a little, the bars which rise from its edges moving slowly, stroking through the mist. I run; the bridge quickly revs up, matches my speed, quivering beneath my feet, the bars on either side of me making a soft ripping noise through the mist-filled air. I stop; the bridge stops. I am still above the centre of the small, slowly flowing river. I sit. The bridge remains static. I jump up and throw myself towards the bank where the ladies are; I roll, scramble, I hop or skip or jump; the bridge rumbles one way or the other, never more than a few steps out of step with me, and always, always, bringing me back, in the end, to its shallow summit, its mid point over the sluggish stream. I am the keystone of the bridge.

I sleep — usually at night, sometimes during the day — above the centre of the waters. I have several times waited until the very centre of the night, feigning sleep for hours, then up! Jump! Bursting away, with one mighty leap! A single bound! *Ah-ha!*

But the bridge moves quickly, not fooled, and in seconds I am, whether running or leaping or rolling, back above the centre of the stream again.

I have tried to use the bridge's inertia against it, its assumed momentum, its own terrible mass, so I run first one way, then the other, trying by these many rapid changes in direction to catch it out somehow, fool it, outwit it, bamboozle the bastard, just be too damn quick for it (of course I always try to make sure that if I do get off, it will be on the bank which holds the ladies — don't forget the carnivorous fish!), but without success. The bridge, for all its weight, for all the solid massiveness of it, which ought to make it slow to move and hard to brake, always moves just too fast for me, and I have never come closer than half a dozen strides from either bank.

There is a breeze sometimes; not enough to clear the mist, but sufficient, if the wind comes from the right direction, to bring to me the perfumes and bodily odours of the ladies. I hold my nose; I tear strands from my rags and stick them up my nostrils. I have thought of stuffing rags in my ears as well, and even of blindfolding myself.

Every few tens of days, small men, swarthy and thick-set and dressed as satyrs, come running out of the forest behind the meadow and fall upon the ladies, who after a show of resistance and displays of coquetry, surrender to their small lovers with unaffected relish. These orgies go on for days and nights without pause; every form of sexual perversion is practised, red lamps and open fires light the scene at night, and vast quantities of roasted meats, exotic fruits and spicy delicacies are consumed, along with many skins of wine and bottles of spirits. I am usually forgotten on such occasions, and even my food is not left on the bridge, so I starve while they sate their every appetite to the point of gluttony. I sit and face the other way, scowling at the dank marsh and the unreachable road crossing it, quaking with anger and jealousy, tormented by the whimpers and screams coming from the far bank, and the succulent smells of roasting meats.

Once I grew hoarse screaming at them, hurt my ankle jumping up and down, and bit my tongue while cursing them; I waited until I needed a crap, then threw the turd at them. Those obscene brats *used* it in one of their filthy sex games.

After the small dark men dressed as satyrs have dragged themselves back into the forest, and the ladies have slept off the effects of their multifarious indulgences, they are as they were before, if a little more apologetic, even wistful. They make special dishes for me and give me more food than usual, but often I am still upset, and throw the food at them, or into the river for the carnivorous fish. They look sad and sorry, and go back to their old habits of sleeping and reading, walking and undressing and making love with each other.

Perhaps my tears will rust the bridge, and I shall escape it.

Today the mist cleared. Not for long, but for long enough. On my bridge without end, I have reached the end.

I am not alone.

When the mist lifted, I saw that the river went straight into the clear distance for ever, on either side. The marsh lines it on one bank, the meadow and forest on the other, without a break. A hundred paces or so upstream there is another bridge, just like mine; iron, like part of a circle, and edged with thick iron bars. There was a man inside it, gripping the bars and staring at me. Beyond him, another bridge and another man, and so on and so on, until the line of distant bridges became an iron tunnel, vanishing to nothing. Each bridge had its own road across the marsh, each had its ladies, pavilioned and carriaged. Downstream; just the same. My ladies did not seem to notice.

The man in the bridge downstream from mine stared at me for a while, then began running (I watched his bridge revolve, fascinated by its steady smoothness), then stopped and stared at me again, then at the bridge downstream from him. He climbed up on to the parapet, up the bars and over them, and then – after only the briefest of hesitations – dropped into the river. The water frothed red; he screamed and sank.

The mists came back. I shouted for a while, but I could hear no other voice from up or down stream.

I am running now. Steady and fast and determined. Several hours so far; it is growing dark. The ladies seem worried; I have run right over three of their food-filled trays.

My ladies stand and watch me, sad and large-eyed, somehow resigned, as though they have seen all this before, as though it always ends this way.

I run and run. The bridge and I are one now, part of the same great steady mechanism; an eye the river threads. I shall run until I drop, until I die; in other words, for ever.

My ladies are crying now, but I am happy. They are caught, trapped, transfixed, heads bowed; but I am free.

I wake up screaming, believing I am encased in ice more cold than that produced by water, so cold that it burns like molten rock, and under a grinding, crushing pressure.

The scream is not my own; I am silent and only the sheet metal works shriek. I dress, stumble to the toilet block, wash. I dry my hands on the handkerchief. In the mirror, my face is puffed and discoloured. A few teeth feel somewhat looser than they did. My body is bruised but nothing is seriously damaged.

At the office where I register to claim my allowance I discover that I shall be on half allowance for the next month, to pay off the amount I owe on the handkerchief and the hat. I am given a little money.

I am directed to a second-hand store where I purchase a long, worn coat. This at least covers the green overalls. Half my money is gone now. I start to walk to the next section, still determined to see Dr Joyce, but I feel faint before long, and have to take a tram, paying cash for the ticket.

'Casualty is three floors down, two blocks to Kingdom,' the young receptionist tells me when I walk into the good doctor's outer office. He goes back to his newspaper; no coffee or tea is offered.

'I would like to see Dr Joyce. I'm Mr Orr. You might recall we spoke on the telephone yesterday.'

The young man lifts perfectly clear eyes to look at me tiredly, up and down. He puts one manicured finger to his smooth cheek, sucks air through luminescently white and flawless teeth. 'Mr . . . *Orr*?' He turns to look through a card index.

I feel faint again. I sit down on one of the chairs.

He glares at me. 'Did I say you could sit down?'

'No, did I ask for permission to?'

'Well, I hope that coat's clean.'

'Are you going to let me see the doctor or not?'

'I'm looking for your card.'

'Do you remember me or not?'

He studies me carefully. 'Yes, but you've been relocated, haven't you?'

'Does that really make such a difference?'

He gives a little, incredulous laugh, and shakes his head as he searches his index.

'Ah, I thought so.' He pulls out a red card, and reads it. 'You've been transferred.'

'I'd noticed that. My new address is—'

'No; I mean you've got a new doctor.'

'I don't want a new doctor; I want Dr Joyce.'

'Oh *do* you?' He laughs, and taps the red card with one

145

finger. 'Well I'm afraid it isn't up to you. Dr Joyce has had you transferred to somebody else and that's all there is to it, and if you don't like it, tough.' He puts the red card back in the index. 'Now please go away.'

I go to the doctor's office door. It is locked.

The young man does not look up from his paper. I try to look through the frosted glass in the door, then I knock politely. 'Dr Joyce? Dr Joyce?'

The young receptionist starts to snigger; I turn to look at him, just as the telephone rings. He answers it.

'Dr Joyce's office,' he says. 'No, I'm afraid the doctor isn't here. He's at the annual conference for senior administrators.' He turns in his seat and looks at me as he says this, watching me with a look of spiteful condescension. 'Two weeks,' he grins at me. 'Do you want the long-distance code? Oh yes, good *morning* officer; yes, Mr Berkeley, of course. And how are you? . . . oh yes? Has he? A washing machine? Does he really? Well that's a new one, I must say. Mm-hmm.' The young receptionist looks professionally serious and starts taking notes. 'And how many socks has he eaten? . . . I see. Right. Yes, got that: I'll get a locum down to the launderette right away. That's *quite* all right officer, and may I wish you a very good day indeed? Bye now.'

My new doctor is called Anzano. His offices are about a quarter of the size of Joyce's, and eighteen floors below them, with no outside view. He is an old, tubby man with sparse yellow hair and matching teeth.

I get to see him after a wait of two hours.

'No,' the doctor says, 'I don't think there is much I can do about you being moved. Not what I'm here for, you understand. Give me time; let me read your file; be patient. I've got a lot on my plate just now. I'll get round to you as soon as I can. Then we'll see about getting you well again, what do you say?' He tries to look cheerful and encouraging.

'But in the meantime?' I ask, feeling tired. I must look a terrible sight; my face throbs, and vision out of my left eye is restricted. My hair is unwashed and I have been unable to shave this morning. How can I convincingly lay claim to my earlier way of life, looking the way I do; so badly dressed, and in every sense, I suspect, beaten?

'Meantime?' Dr Anzano looks perplexed. He shrugs. 'Do you need a prescription? Have you enough of anything you've been—' he is reaching for his prescription pad. I shake my head.

'I mean what is to be done about my . . . situation?'

'Not a lot I can do, Mr Orr. I'm not Dr Joyce; I can't issue grand apartments to myself, let alone my patients.' The old doctor sounds a little bitter, and annoyed at me. 'Just wait until your case is reviewed; I'll make whatever recommendations I think fit. Now is there anything else? I'm a very busy man. *I* can't go whizzing off to conferences you know.'

'No, there was nothing else.' I get up. 'Thank you for your time.'

'Not at all. Not at all. My secretary will be in touch with you about your appointment; very soon, I'm sure. And if there is anything you need, just give me a call.'

I return to my room.

Mr Lynch comes to my door again.

'Mr Lynch. Good day.'

'Oh, fuck; what happened to you?'

'An argument with an unhinged doorman; do come in. Would you like this seat?'

'Can't stay; I brought this.' He shoves a folded, sealed piece of paper into my hand. Mr Lynch's finger marks remain on the envelope. I open it. 'Post left it stuck in the door; could have got stole.'

'Thank you, Mr Lynch,' I say. 'Are you sure you can't stay? I was hoping to repay your kindness yesterday by inviting you to dinner this evening.'

'Aw, sorry pal, no. Got overtime to do.'

'Oh well, some other time then.' I scan the note. It is from Abberlaine Arrol; she confesses to quite brazenly using a fictitious dinner-date with me tonight to get out of an engagement of potentially terminal tedium. Will I agree to be an accomplice after the fact? She includes the phone number of her parents' apartment; I am to call her. I check the address; the note has been forwarded from my old rooms.

147

'OK?' Mr Lynch says, hands stuck in the pockets of his coat for all the world as though his trouser turn-ups are full of stolen lead and he is desperately trying to hold them up. 'No bad news, eh?'

'No, Mr Lynch, in fact a young lady wants me to take her out to dinner . . . I must make a phone call. Don't forget though; after this, you have first call on my meagre abilities as dinner-host.'

'Whatever you say, pal.'

My luck holds. Miss Arrol is in. Somebody I take to be a servant goes to find her. It takes several coins; I have to assume the Arrol apartments are of considerable size.

'Mr Orr! Hello!' She sounds breathless.

'Good day, Miss Arrol. I received your note.'

'Oh, good. Are you free this evening?'

'I would like to meet then, yes, but . . .'

'What's wrong Mr Orr? You sound like you have a cold.'

'Not a cold; it's my mouth . . . It's . . .' I pause. 'Miss Arrol, I would very much like to see you this evening, but I'm afraid I . . . have suffered something of a reverse. I have been relocated, effectively demoted. Dr Joyce has had me put down, as it were. To level U7, to be precise.'

'Oh.' There is a flatness to the tone with which she pronounces this simple word which says more to me, in my feverish state, than a whole hour of polite explanations about propriety, places in society, discretion and tact. Perhaps I am expected to say something more, but I cannot. How long do I wait, then, for some other word? Two seconds at most? Three? Nothing measured in bridge time, but long enough to pass through an instant of despair to a plateau of anger. Shall I put the phone down, walk away, make of this dirty thing as clean and quick an end as possible? Yes, now, to appease my own bitterness . . . but it is not in me. In a moment though, to spare the girl further embarrassment.

'Right, sorry, Mr Orr; I was just closing the door. My brother hanging around. Now, where have they moved you to? Can I help? Would you like me to come over there now?'

Orr, you are a fool.

*

I dress in the clothes of Abberlaine Arrol's brother. She arrived here an hour before the time we arranged to meet, with a suitcase full of cast-off clothes, mostly her brother's; she reckons we are near enough the same build. I change while she waits outside. I was loath to leave her in such a vulgar area, but she could hardly have stayed in the room.

In the corridor, she is leaning, back against the wall, one leg drawn up behind her so that she rests one buttock on her foot, arms folded, talking to Mr Lynch, who looks at her with a sort of wary awe.

' "Oh no, dear," ' Abberlaine Arrol is saying, ' "we always change ends at half-time." ' She sniggers. Mr Lynch looks shocked, then snorts with laughter. Miss Arrol sees me. Ah, Mr Orr!'

'The same.' I make a small bow. 'Or rather, not quite.'

Abberlaine Arrol, resplendent in baggy trousers of rough black silk, matching jacket, cotton blouse, high heels and dramatic hat, says, 'What a dashing figure you cut, Mr Orr.'

'Bluntly spoken.'

Miss Arrol presents me with a black cane. 'Your stick.'

'Thank you.' I say. She puts out her arm, waiting, so I offer mine and she takes it. We face Mr Lynch, arm in arm. I can feel her warmth through her brother's jacket.

'Don't we look quite fine, Mr Lynch?' She asks, standing straight, head back. Mr Lynch shuffles his feet.

'Aw yeah; very . . . very . . .' Mr Lynch searches for a word. 'Very . . . a very . . . handsome couple.'

I would like to think that is just what we are. Miss Arrol seems pleased, too.

'Thank you, Mr Lynch.' She turns to me. 'Well, I don't know about you, but I'm starving.'

So, what are your priorities now, Mr Orr?' Abberlaine Arrol rolls her whisky glass around between her hands, gazing through the blue lead glass and the light amber liquid at the flame of a candle. I watch her malt-wetted lips glisten in the same soft light.

Miss Arrol has insisted on buying me dinner. We sit at a window table in the High Girders restaurant. The food has been superb, the service discreetly efficient, we have space, fine wine, and an excellent view (lights twinkle all over the sea where the trawlers anchor the barrage balloons; the blimps themselves are vaguely visible, almost level with us, dull presences in the night reflecting the bridge's massed lights like clouds. A few of the brighter stars are also visible).

'My priorities?' I ask.

'Yes. Which is more important; regaining your position as one of Dr Joyce's favoured patients, or rediscovering your lost memories?'

'Well,' I say, only now really thinking about it. 'Certainly it's been rather uncomfortable and painful, coming down in the bridge, but I suppose I could eventually learn to live with my reduced rank, if the worst comes to the worst.' I sip my whisky. Miss Arrol's expression is neutral. 'However, my inability to remember who I am is not something . . . ' I give a small laugh, 'that I can ever forget. I'll always know there was something in my life before this, so I imagine I'll always be looking for it. It's like a sealed, forgotten chamber in me; I shan't feel complete until I've discovered its entrance.'

'Sounds like a tomb. Aren't you afraid of what you'll find in there?'

'It's a library; only the stupid and the evil are afraid of those.'

'So you'd rather find your library than regain your apartment?' Abberlaine Arrol smiles. I nod, watching her. She took off her hat as she came in, but her hair is still up; her head and neck look very fine. Those beguiling crinkles under her eyes fascinate me still; they are like a tiny guard she has put up; a line of sandbags beneath those amused, grey-green eyes; confident, secure, unaffected.

Abberlaine Arrol stares into her glass. I am about to comment on a small line that has just formed on her brow, when the lights go out.

We are left with our candle; other tables glow and flicker with their own small flames. Dim emergency lights come on. There is a dull background of muttering. Outside, the lights on the trawlers start to disappear. The balloons are no longer visible in the reflected light of the bridge; the whole structure must be dark.

The planes: they come without lights, droning through the night, from the direction of the City. Miss Arrol and I stand up, looking out of the window; various other diners gather alongside us, peering out into the night, shading the weak emergency lights and candles with their hands, noses pressed against the cool glass like schoolboys outside a sweetshop. Somebody opens a window.

The planes sound almost alongside us. 'Can you see them?' Abberlaine Arrol asks.

'No,' I admit. The droning engines sound very close. The planes are quite invisible, without navigation lights. There is no moon, and the stars are not bright enough to show them.

They pass, seemingly unaffected by the lack of light.

'Think they did it?' Miss Arrol says, still peering into the night. Her breath mists the glass.

'I don't know,' I confess. 'I wouldn't be surprised.' She is biting her lower lip; her fists are clenched against the dark window, an expression of excited anticipation on her face. She looks very young.

The lights come back on.

The planes have left their pointless messages; the clouds of smoke are just visible, darkness upon darkness. Miss Arrol sits down and takes up her glass. As I raise mine, she leans conspiratorially across the table and says quietly, 'To our intrepid aviators, wherever they may come from.'

'And whoever they may be,' I touch her glass with my own.

When we leave, a faint odour of oily smoke is just detectable over the more palatable smells of the restaurant itself; the equivocal signal of the vanished aircraft merging with and blown through the structural grammar of the bridge, like criticism.

We wait for a train. Miss Arrol smokes a cigar. Music plays in the soft-class waiting room. She stretches in her chair and

stifles a little yawn. 'I beg your pardon,' she says. Then, 'Mr
– oh look; if I can call you John, will you call me Abberlaine,
never "Abby"?'

'Certainly, Abberlaine.'

'Right then . . . John. I take it you are less than totally
delighted with your new accommodation.'

'It's better than nothing at all.'

'Yes, of course, but . . .'

'Not that much though. And without Mr Lynch I'd be
even more at a loss there than I am already.'

'Hmm. I thought so.' She looks preoccupied, and stares
hard at one of her shiny black high-heels. She rubs one finger
over her lips, looks seriously at her cigar. 'Ah.' The finger
caressing her lips is lifted into the air. 'I have an idea.' Her
grin is mischievous now.

'My paternal great-grandfather had it built. Just a minute;
I'll find the lights. I think—' There is a dull thud.
'—Bastard!' Miss Arrol giggles. I hear a rapid rubbing
sound; rough silk between smooth flesh, I suspect.

'Are you all right?'

'Fine. Just bumped my shin. Now then, those lights. I
think they're . . . no. Damn this, I can't see a thing. You
don't have a light do you John? I used my last match on the
cigar.'

'I'm sorry, no.'

'I know; could you give me your stick?'

'Certainly. Here. Is that . . .? Have you . . .?'

'Yes, thank you; got it.' I hear her tap and scrape her way
through the darkness. I put my suitcase down on the floor,
waiting to see whether my eyes will adjust sufficiently or not.
I can see vague hints of light over to one corner, but the
interior of this place is quite black. From further away,
Abberlaine Arrol's voice comes back, 'It was to be near the
marina. That was why he had it built. Then they built the
sports centre on top. He was too proud to accept the com-
pensation buy-out, so it stayed in the family. My father is
always talking about selling it, but we wouldn't get much for
it; we just use it for storage. There was some damp on the

ceiling, but it's been repaired.'

'I see.' I listen for the girl, but all I can hear is the sounds of the sea; waves brush the rocks or the piers nearby. I can smell the sea, too; something of its fresh dampness pervades the air.

'About bloody time,' Abberlaine Arrol says, her voice muffled. A click, and all is revealed. I am standing near the door of a large apartment, mostly open-plan and split-level and full of old furniture and packing cases. From a high, damp-stained ceiling an assortment of complicated light clusters hang; varnish peels from old, panelled walls. There are white sheets everywhere, half covering ancient, heavy-looking sideboards, wardrobes, couches, chairs, tables and chests of drawers. Other pieces are still totally covered, wrapped and trussed like huge, dusty white presents. Where there were vague areas of light before, there is now a single long screen of blackness where unshuttered windows look out into the night. Abberlaine Arrol appears, flat, broad hat still in place, clapping her hands together, rubbing dust off them, from a side room.

'There, that's a bit better.' She looks around. 'Bit dusty and deserted, but it's quiet, and a bit more private than your room on U7 or wherever.' She hands me back my stick, then starts pacing through the assembled furniture, whipping back sheets and covers, glancing underneath, raising a storm of dust as she investigates the contents of the huge room. She sneezes. 'Should be a bed around here somewhere.' She nods to the windows. 'Might be an idea to close the shutters. It never gets very light in here, but you might be woken in the morning.'

I make my way down to the tall windows, a length of obsidian framed in crackled white paint. The heavy shutters creak as they swing across the dust-dimmed panes. Outside and below I can see a broken line of white surf, and a few lights in the distance, mostly navigation and harbour beacons. Above, where I would expect to see the bridge, there is only darkness, starless and complete. The waves glitter like a million dull knives.

'Here.' Abberlaine Arrol has found a bed. 'It might be a

bit damp, but I'll find some more sheets. Should be some in these cases.' The bed is huge, with a headboard carved from oak to resemble a pair of immense, outspread wings. Abberlaine stamps off through the clouds of dust to rummage through stacked chests and packing cases. I test the bed.

'Abberlaine, this is really very kind of you, but are you sure you won't get into trouble for it?' She sneezes powerfully from a distant packing case. 'Bless you,' I say.

'Thank you. No, I'm not certain,' she says, pulling out blankets and bundles of newspaper from the chest, 'but in the unlikely event my father did find out and was annoyed, I'm sure I could talk him round. Don't worry. No one ever comes down here. Ah.' She discovers a large quilt and some sheets and pillows. She buries her face in the quilt, breathing deeply. 'Yes, this seems dry enough.' She brings the bedding over in a bundle and starts to make the huge bed. I offer to help but am shooed away.

I take my coat off and go in search of the bathroom. It is about six times the size of room 306, level U7. The bath alone looks as though it could float a sizeable yacht. The toilet flushes, the sink runs too, the shower and bidet both spray efficiently. I pause in front of the mirror, brushing my hair back, smoothing my shirt, checking my teeth for bits of trapped food.

When I return to the main room, my bed has been made. The huge oaken wings are spread over a white duvet of duckdown. Abberlaine Arrol has gone. The apartment's front door swings gently to and fro.

I close the door, put out most of the lights. I find an old lamp and perch it on a packing case by the side of my huge, cold bed. Before I put the light out I lie for a while, looking at the great hollow circles long-dried waters have left on the plaster above me.

Faded and dull, left-overs from an old complaint, they look down on me like ancient painted images of my own chest-held stigmata.

I reached out to the old lamp, and turn the darkness on again.

Four

I luv the ded, this old basturt sez to me when I wiz tryin to get some innfurmashin out ov him. You fukin old pervirt I sez, gettin a bit fed up by this time enyway, an slit his throate; ah askd you whare the fukin Sleepin Byootie woz, no whit kind a humpin you lyke. No, no he sez, splutterin sumthin awfy and gettin blud all ovir ma new curiearse, no he sez I sed Isle of the Dead; Isle of the Dead that's whare yoo'l find the Sleeping Beauty, but mind and watch out for the – then the basturt went and dyed on me. Fukin nerv, eh? Ah wiz ded upset but thare you go these things are scent to trie uz.

Canny remember whare it wiz I herd about this Sleepin Byootie but it must hav bean sumwhare, ken. Av been gettin arownd a fare bit resently whot with all that majic an that; playce is stowed owt with majishins and wizerds and whitches these days; canny wolk intae sum citays withowt trippin over sum barsturd doin wun aw they spels or incanntashins or turnin sumbudy inta a frog or a bumrag or a spitoon or sumhin. Clevir bugirs but ye can hav to mutch majic ah rekin; sum bugirs got tae spred the manure and bild hooses and plant seads an that sort ov stuff, ken? Things that majic duzney wurk very well on. Fyne fur hydin gold an turnin peepil intae things thayd rathir no be turnd intae an maykin foalk furget things an that sort ov stuf, but no fur fixin a bugerd waggin wheel or sloppin the mud oot yer detachit hovil aftir the rivir's burst itz banks. Dinnae ask me how majic wurks maybe ther's onlie so mutch to go round or peepil who can do it keep majicin up things that cantsel out whit uthers have dun, but wun way or the uthir it canny be oll its craked up tae be or ah suppose the wurld woold be toatally fukin wunderffil an happy an aw that an folk woold live in peece an harminy an so on; thatill be the day, if ye ask me. Enyway its no like that ataw, so it isnay, an just as well to say I, coz utherwyse thay wooldnae need peepil like me (an itid be ded fukin boarin to).

Naw, ahm doin no to bad these days; servises mutch in

dimand like thay say; maynly becoz all these wizerds an that are so fukin sofistikaytit that they forget thers sum things a sord can do a spel canny, speshily when yoor oponent is only expectin a spel an no a sord! Aw, ahve got sum majic armir an this enchantit dirk that thinks itz a daggir an stuff like that, butt ah doant like tae use them hings to mutch; bettir to relie on yer own arm an a sharp blaide, thats whit I say.

> My first is in day but never in night,
> My second's in dark but unseen in light;
> My middle's a twin in daughter, not son,
> While the fifth's not in two, but in three and one;
> The final's in first, not middle or last,
> And my whole is in sheath; got an Elastoplast?

Nevir mind that its just the fukin dirk talkin; the ansers daggir, bye the way; just that the stupit thing canny spel write. Bludy daft wee hi-pitched voyce its got too, reely gets on ma nerves sumtimes, but the things cum in handy on a few okayzhins; it can see in the dark an tel whose frend and fowe an a coupil of times ahl sware its jumpt rite out of ma hands an flown like a bird intae sum basturts throat that was givin me a hard time. Usefyule gadjet. A lassy geeze it; a bonny yung whitch sum worlok had the hots fur an she didnae want tae play; ah wiz hired tae kil the old bugir an the young whitch giv us the daggir fir a reward; sed it wiz oanly a copey, but it came from the fewtcher an might cum in yousefyul; that wiznae ma only reward either. See those whitches? Fukin majic in bed, to. Must look her up agen sumtime.

Enyway, ah herd about this Sleepin Byootie sumwhare an startit tryin to find out whare she wiz shakked up but it wiznae eesy. Fyneally got a haud of this old basturd that telt us about the Ile of the Deid but then went an kilt him befoar he coold tell uz all he coold hav; to fukin hastie, thats ma truble, awlways has been but ye canny teech an old dug new tricks like they say. Not that am that old; dont get me rong ye hav to be yung an fit to be a sordsman (maybe that wiz whot the whitch — but never mind that). Whare woz I? Aw I; the ileland ov the deid.

Wel, too cut a long story off at the knees, an after meny ecsiting adventchures an that, I endit up gettin this sorserir tae cunjur up a way intae sumthin called the Underwurld; ment roatsin live cats over a slow fyre fur abouwt three weeks, but at leest it wurkt. The sorserir gave me directshins an sum advyce an that, but ah had a nippy heid at the time coz ahd been drinkin the wine the night befoar an so ah didnae reelly take in aw he wiz sayin an besides ah woz all ecsited coz ah wiz gettin tae go intae the Underground at last. 'Beware Lethe, the waters of oblivion, young man!' the sorserir sez, an ahm standin thare in the cellir ov his castle wi ma heid loupin thinkin Ah wish yed said that tae me last night befoar ah startit drinking the wine. 'Beware whit?' ah sez tae him. 'Lethe!' he shouts. 'Aye, OK pal,' ah told him, and steppt intae this funny star-shaped thing hed paynted on the flair ov the cellir.

Hellova a place this, ah thoght. Aw these folke shoutin an screamin an waylin an champin there teath an chained to wals an tunnils; whot a fukin racket an me with a hangover. Got reely pissed aff an tryd killin a few a these noisey basturts but even when they wer hakked about they still kept on shoutin an screemin an thrashin an that; toatal waiste of time. Ah kept on goin doon these tunnels and saw aw these burnin pits an icey puddles wi screemin peepil in them, an kept ma sord handy an wished ahd brot a bottil of skoosh wi me coz I wiz ded thirsty.

Had tae wolk fur fukin miles so ah did; kept thinkin ther might be a train along in a minute, but nae luck, just all these basturts howlin an screemin oll the time and lodes of smoake an flaimes an ice an howlin winds an fuk knows whot. Ah thot about havin a drink aw watter from won of the icey pools but ah kept thinkin abowt this watter of Leeth or whatevir it woz, so ah didnae.

It got qwieter after a whyle; went up this long tunnil intae sumhin a bit mair like daylight thogh it wis still pritty dull an depressin; endied up at the bottom of this big clif lookin out ovir this rivir wi clouds an mist an that aw ovir the playce. No a bludy soul abowt, no even wun aw those bubblin basturts chained to the waws or anyhin. Startin tae think the sorserir had givven us a bum steer. Stil ded thirsty an nota sign of a pub or enyhin, just aw these rocks an this rivir flowin slowly past. Ah wanderd along the bank fur a bit an found this punter shovin a big round boulder up this hill. Lookt like he did this a lot, judjin from the groov hed worn in the hillside. 'Haw Jimmy,' ah sez, 'ahm lookin for this ferry; whare dae ye catch the steamer aboot here? There a pier here-aboots, aye?' Bastrurt didnae even turn roond. Rold this huge fukin chuckie right tae the tap aw the hill. But then the rok cums rollin aw the way back down agen, and the ignorant buggir chases aftir it an starts rollin it back up the hill agen. 'Hi you,' ah sez (didnae hav eny effect). 'Hi, hied-the-baw; whare's the fukin pier fur the steamer?' Ah slapt the basturd over the arse wi the flat ov ma sord an went in frunt of the big stane he was rollin up the hil an lent agenst it to stop him.

Just ma fukin luk; the bampot didnae evin speek proppir; sum forin lingo. Aw shite, ah wiz thinkin. Ah tried tellin him whit ah wiz after wi sine language; thot he seemed tae understand but he stil wiznae tellin, so ah told him ahd help him roll the rok up the sloap if he told me. Sneeky basturt got me tae shuv the stane up the hil first. Got it tae the tap; he held it an ah got a few wee stanes tae hold it thare. Fella wiz qwite delightit; he points doon the bank of the rivir an sez 'Karen,' or sumthin' like that, then skips aff intae the mist, leavin the big chuckie at the tap aw the sloap.

Mair fukin trampin along the side of this bludy misty rivir, an then ah see this muckle grate bird flyin throo the mists; ah watcht it land on this big aw rock whare this guy waz chaned up, an the bird gets stuck right in, rips the basturd open and starts munchin away at his insides; the bloake wiz howlin an screemin fit tae raze the deid, but when ah got thare an I must hav fritened the big bird aff, coz it beat it. Climbed up tae see how the guy wos, but hed healed right up; no even a scar whare the eegil or whatever it wiz had been havin its tea. 'Scuse me pal, am ah on the right road fur the steamer, aye?'

Anuther bludy furiner. Tryed the sine langwitch agen but seemd like he wiznae havin it, just kept shoutin and shakin his chanes. Toatil waist of time; like tryin tae pik yer nose wi yer gluvs on. The big bird came back an started screetchin an divin at ma heid. Wiznae in the mood fur eny nonsense, so I took a swipe at it with ma sord an chopt one of its wings aff; bird fell intae the rivir an floated off screetchin and flappin. The guy on the rok startit flappin as weel an rattlin his chanes. 'Aw, never mind jimmy,' ah told him, and got back down aff the rok.

Nae pier, nuthin. Stood lookin out across the rivir an thinkin about havin a drink from it.

> My first is in lad, but never in lass,
> My second's in case and also impasse;
> My centre is paired—

'Just you shut the fuk up,' ah told the dirk, shakin it in frunt ov ma face, coz ah woz ded annoyed that ah didnae seem tae be gettin enywhare an ma heid wiz stil ded sair.

> His first is in coracle, but oracle, no;
> His next is in ship but not Limpopo.
> Third's in Golden Apple but not Golden Fleece,
> Fourth is in Forth, not Peloponnese.
> Fifth's not in firth but—

'Anuthir peepe oot aw you ye wee basturt an youl be talkin to the crabs an the fishes, right?' ah sed to the dirk, but then ah saw this punter in sum kinda oary boat cumin throogh the mist. Ugly lookin big basturd dressed aw in blak rags soay wiz. Stannin up in the boat wi his arms crossd lookin ded hotty. Couldnae see how the boat wiz movin; probly majic, ah dare say. He grounds the boat on the shaor beside me an ah got on. He holds oot hiz haund. Ah shook it. 'The fare, littil man,' he sez, still holdin oot his hand. Aw-aw, ah thoght.

Took oot ma sord; ye canny fuk aboot wi these weerd forrin punters. Put the tip at his throate; he didnae seem botherid though. 'You Karen?' ah sed. 'Charon,' he sez, like he wiznae cayrin. 'Well av havnae got eny muny on me pal, so how about just put it on the slate, OK?' The big fella wiznae havin it though. Shakes his heid. 'There should be coins on your eyes; all the dead must have the fare to pay the ferryman.' Grate, ah thoght; wun of them loup-holes. 'Ah, but ahm no deid,' ah tells the punter. He seamed to think about this. 'Security is so lax these days,' he sez, an size. 'Perhaps there is something you can do for me though, if you're handy with that lump of metal.' He ment the sord; ah coold tell. 'Whit ye wantin, pal?' ah sez.

So ah got ma sale doon the watter fur the price of a dug's heid; punter wanted the heid of this dug name uv Serry-bruce that lived on the far shoar, on the Ile of the Deid; sed the dug woold never miss it, an he needed a figure-heid fur his roary-boat, furbye. Pritty weerd sort of thing to ask fur if ye ask me, but ah supoase peepil get a bit ecksentric an daft, stuk out here in the stiks.

Misty an dark on the uthir side ov the rivir as wel. Left Karen stannin in his boat an went off up the roade towards this big sorta palace thing on a cliff, keepin an eye open for this big dug Serry-Bruce. Just as weel ah did; basturt jumpt me in this big coartyard place right on the clifside. Fukin thing had three heids! Snarlin and droolin it wiz. Saw whit the big fella ment about it no missin a heid. Lopped one aff nae problem, wunderin how meny licences ye'd need for this thing; wan or three? Then duz the basturdin hownd no go an grow back the heid ahd just cut aff? Aw, fuk this, ah thoght.

His first is in canine, but in feline, not;
His next is in teeth and also garotte.
The third is in bark but not there in bite,
While the fourth's—

'Here boy! Fetch!' ah shoutit at the big dug, an took the wee dirk oot while it wiz still jibberin away an threw it over the cliff. The dug fell fur it.

Lookd over the clif an saw Serry-bruce hit the roks doon at the bottim. Ded pleased with masell so ah woz, until the fukin heid ahd just cut aff went rollin over the edge right beside me; made a grab fur it but it fell doon an splatterd ovir the stanes at the bottim of the cliff too. Basturt! ah thought. Loss ma wee dirk too; set off intae the big palace in a no very good mood. It wiz ded dark inside. Ah couldnae hav been lookin whare ah wiz goin coz a giv ma heid a terribil dunt on some ded low doorway; startit seein stars; it wiz like buttin a marble statyou or sumthin, so it woz. Could hardly see; think ma heid wiz bleedin too, blud gettin in ma eyes. Ah wiz blunderin about an tryin to feel whare the hell a wiz, bumpin intae things and swayrin an cursin an blindin an that. Next thing ah knew thare's this hissin an the sound ov arrers shootin past ma heid an skitein aff pillers an waws an the stane flare. Ah still coold hardly see, but ah coold just aboot make oot sum funny-lookin basturt in the shadows, hissin at me an tryin tae shoot arrers intae me. Oh fuk, ah thought. Wish ah still had that wee dirk with me.

Her first is in limestone, but not lapilli,
Her next is in ossiferous, but not ossify.
The third's in demand, but—

'Stop fukin jibberin an cum here!' Ah just aboot saw the wee dirk floatin near ma haund; grabbed it an threw; then dyeved fur the flare. Whoever wiz makin the hissin noyse sort of made a stranglin, chokin sound, then stoppt. Went ovir an had a look at this horribil lookin wuman that had been slinging these arrers at me; still couldnae see propir, but ye shoold hav seen the state ov her hare; tolk about rats tales! Couldnae have washed it in years. Left her lyin fayce down in her own blud; the wee dirk was stuk in her throate; ah pullt it out. Sware that horribil wimins blud wiz burny, like asid or sumhin. Never mind, ah thoght; keep lookin fur the Sleepin Byooty.

'Aw wait a fukin *minnit!*'
   Bombed oot agen! Whit had happend was Id fynelly found this wee sorta chamber thing; only place in the whole palace with anythin in it; rest wiz empty. Nae mair horribil wumin or dirty grate dugs wi two meny heeds, but nae tressure eyethir. Ah coold tell this wiz all goantae be anuthir toatil wayste of time an ah wuznae very pleased alredy, but at leest, ah thought, there shoold be this byootfull sleepin lassy; ment

161

tae be ded luvly; suppoasd to wake up with a kiss; whit ahm goantae giv her shoold make her *reely* fukin lively, ah thoght.

But its a man! 'Aw *fuk*!' Just a room an a man lyin in bed, all white-faced an asleep. There's these big things like metal chests on theyre sides all clustered around him an wee bit things like strings attatched tae him. Fuk aw else. Ahm about to slit the basturts throate just on generil principils when this bit ov the waw suddenly starts talkin to me, an this paintin appeers on it, only the paintin moves! Its a wumin's fayce; a no-bad lookin lassy with red hair. 'Don't,' she sez. 'Who the fuk are yoo?' ah asks her, no killin the guy but goan up tae this pictcher an tolkin tae it. 'Don't kill him,' the lassy sez. Ah tap the pictcher but it sounds like glass. Ah go intae the room behind it, but its empty tae; dam things no a windy or anythin like that. 'Why no? Why shouldnae ah kill him?' ah asked the womin. 'Because he will become you; you will kill yourself and he will live again, in your body. Just leave now, please. Don't look at the Medusa's face, and don't take the—' then the pictcher goes all funny an her voyce disappeeres; sounds like that horribil womin hissin. Ah gave the screen a dunt with the end of ma sord but it just broke. Got a bit of the glass right on the heid; startit bleedin agen. 'Aw cum *on*,' ah sez, wipin the blud off ma brows. Turned to go, then ah saw this wee gold thing like a statue of a big frog or sumthin, sittin on a windy-ledje. Liftit it up an it felt hevy enuoph to be gold, so I put it in ma breeks pocket an desided it wiz time to shoot the craw, like they say. Left the bampot lyin in the bed toatally unmollested; seemed half deid enyway so what the fuk. Thohgt aboot lookin for the lassy in the pictcher, but ah wiz gettin tired an ah still hadnae had anythin tae eat or drink so ah deside, time tae go hame. Went back through the dark bit an nearly tripped ovir the body ov the horribil wumin. Remembered Karen; thoght there probly widnae be much left of eny wan of that damn dugs heids even if ah coold get doon tae the bottim of the cliff; so ah cut aff the horribil wumin's heid an slung it ower ma shoulder. Her herr wiz like sneks, ahm no kiddin.

Got bak doon tae whare Karen wiz waitin in the oary boat, aw tall dark an ugly an still wi his erms crossd an lookin ded hotty an dissdanefool. 'Haw Karen,' ah sed. 'The dug wiznae thare; will this wumin's heid dae insted, aye?' Ah held the horribil wumin's heid up an waved it at him. The guy froze. Ye widnae credit it; basturt turned tae stone right in frunt of ma eyes. Big buggir went strate throo the bottom of his boat like a statyou an settled on the sand unnerneeth; the roary boat sank around him. 'Aw fur fuk's *saik*!' ah shoutit, an threw the horribil wumin's heid doon intae the watter. Just ma fukin luk, eh? Whyse it happin tae me? I thoght. Sat doon on the shore an just aboot felt like greetin. Just wiznae ma day, ah desided; nae luk at oll.

Then ah thought I herd a noyse cumin from ma pockit; took oot the wee goldin statyou an lookt at it. Stil lookd sortof like a frog, though it seamed to have wings or sumthin on its bak. Enyway, ah looked at it, then at the watter, an I thoght; whit the hell, ah'll swim it. Had tae leeve the majic armer an ma new curiearse an that; ah put the sord over ma back tied to ma belt, with the belt loopd rownd the wee golden statyou as well, then ah waded intae the watter an startit swimmin. Still had ma good socks on, wi the majic dirk stuck down wun. Canny swim proper like, but ah can dae the doggy-paddle, ye ken? Got tae the far bank eventually. The watter in the rivir didnae tayste too bad, an ah woz thirsty enyway. Stood on the far bank neer the big rok whare the man was chaned up. Nae sign of the ded eegil. Bloak on the rok wiz deid too thogh; sumthin inside him seemed to have swelled up an burst oot ov him, all ovir the place, like wun of them cancres or whitevir. Lookt like livir. The wee gold statyou seamed to make anuthir noise, just ded faint like. Ah wunderd if it really woz sayin sumthin or weathir it wiz just the dunt on the heid ahd got earlier maykin me heer voyces. Stil, the wee thing sounded like it was maikin a noyse. Ah held it up tae ma ear. That woz ma big mistaik.

'Well my boy, that was damned decent of you to come and rescue me from the infernal regions. Didn't think the Sleeping Beauty dream-telepathy would work, between worlds; or that you'd make it. Should have known you'd easily pass for a shade though; you were never exactly brilliant at the best of times, were you? You know I'd swear these rocks look meta-

163

morphic, not igneous . . . well, come on my little Orpheus, let's get you out of here before you get yourself turned into a pillar of peppercorns or whatever. I suggest—'

(An ahm thinkin *Aw naw*)

His first is in—

'Oh good grief, a bardic knife-missile. How on earth or anywhere else did you come to get hold of *that*? Or did it get hold of you? Whatever; if there's one thing I can't stand it's machines that talk back: SILENCE!'

An its mooth was shut. Not anuthir peep from the dirk. But the wee golden frog that ahd held up neer ma ear isnae gold enymore, an its sittin on ma showder now an lookin like a wee cat wi wings an its voyce sounds awfy—

'Familiar?' It sez, 'Why, my boy, that's absolutely correct!'

'Aw *shite*!'

An abandoned searching . . . the smell of salt and rust. Darkness down here, buried under the structure like something thrown away, wandering through the light and shade within the sound of the sea . . .

I wake slowly, still immersed in the barbarian's rough thoughts, my thoughts entangled. Soft grey light seeps round the edges of the shutters into this wide and cluttered space, outlining the shrouded furniture and feeding my struggling consciousness as though it were a growing shoot struggling out of the clinging clay.

The cold white sheets are twisted around me like ropes; dozily I try to roll over, to become comfortable, but cannot. I am trapped, tied down; panic fills me in an instant, and suddenly I'm awake, cold and sweating and sitting up in the bed, wiping my face and looking round the room's dim quietness.

I open the window shutters. The sea surges round the rocks thirty feet below. I leave the door to the bathroom open so that I can hear its slow roaring breath while I bathe.

I breakfast in a modest bar off the Concourse Edgar. Waiters swipe at nearby tables with long white cloths. Seagulls call and circle through the air, crowding round an out-jutting building, where kitchen scraps are being thrown out. The wings of the birds flash white; the cloths of the waiters crack and flap across the tables. I came here via room 306 to see if there was any mail for me; nothing. The sheet metal works screamed below.

I linger over my last cup of coffee.

I wander from one side of the bridge to the other. Most trawlers now have two barrage balloons. Some balloons must be anchored directly to the seabed; orange buoys mark where their cables meet the waves.

I have a sandwich and a waxpaper cup of tea for lunch, sitting on a bench looking up-river. The weather changes, growing colder under a sky gradually becoming overcast. It was early spring when I was washed up here; now the summer is almost over. I wash my hands in the rest room of a tram station and take a tram – hard class – to the section where the lost library should be. I search and search, I try every elevator shaft there is, but none contains the L-shaped lift I'm looking for, or the old attendant. My enquiries meet with blank looks.

The surface of the firth is grey now, like the sky. The barrage balloons strain at their cables. My legs hurt from climbing stairs. Rain spatters against the dirty glass of the high corridors where I sit and try to regain my strength.

Beneath the summit of the bridge, in a dark, dripping corridor, I find a pool of small white balls lying under a broken skylight. The balls have a dimpled surface and feel very hard. As I stand there another ball comes flying through the broken skylight and drops to the floor of the corridor. I drag a moth-eaten chair from an alcove, put it under the skylight and climb up, sticking my head through the broken pane.

In the distance there is a tall old man with white hair. He

wears plus-fours, a jumper and a cap. He is swinging a long thin club at something in front of his feet. A white ball comes sailing through the air towards me.

'Fore!' the man shouts; at me, I think. He waves; the ball bounces near the skylight. He takes his cap off and stands, hands on hips, looking at me. I get down off the chair and find a stairwell leading to the summit. When I get there, there is no sign of the old man. The trawler is there though, surrounded by workmen and officials. It is lying beneath a damaged radio tower, the deflated barrage balloons hanging over the girders nearby like broken black wings. It is raining and blowing hard; oilskins and greatcoats flap and glisten.

Early evening, dull and wet; my feet are sore and my stomach rumbles. I buy another sandwich and eat it on the tram. It is a long and tiring walk down the monotonously spiralling steps to the Arrols' old apartment. My legs ache by the time I get to the right floor. I feel like a thief in the deserted corridor. I hold the apartment's small key in front of me like a tiny dagger.

The apartment is cold and dark. I switch on a few lights. The grey waters crash white outside; a damp salt smell fills the chill rooms. I close the windows I left open this morning and lie down on the bed, just for a moment, but fall asleep. I go back to the moor where impossible trains chase me into narrow tunnels. I watch the barbarian stalk an underworld of pain and torment; I am not him, I am chained to the walls, crying out to him . . . he lopes on, dragging his sword. I am on the revolving iron bridge again, pounding for ever over the rusting torus through which the river flows. Running and running in the rain until my legs ache—

I wake again, damp with sweat, not rain. My legs feel tense, cramped. A bell rings. I look groggily round for a phone. The bell rings again, twice, and I realize it is the door. 'Mr Orr? John?'

I get off the bed and smooth my hair down. Abberlaine Arrol stands in the doorway in a long dark coat, grinning like a mischievous schoolgirl. 'Abberlaine, hello, come in.'

'How are you, John?' She sweeps in, looking round the lit

room then turning, lifting her head to me, 'All right here?'

'Yes, thank you. Can I offer you one of your own chairs?' I close the door.

'You can offer me one of our wines to drink,' she says, laughing; she spins round once on one foot, sending the coat belling out. A heady odour of some musky perfume and drink flows past me. Her eyes sparkle. 'Over there.' She points to a chest, half covered by a white sheet. 'I'll get some glasses.' She heads for the kitchen.

'That was a rather sudden departure last night,' I say, opening the chest; it contains racks of wines and spirits. Clinking noises come from the kitchen.

'What was?' she says, coming back with two glasses and a corkscrew.

I select something not too old and precious-looking from the wines. 'I was taking a look round the place and when I came back in here, you were gone.' She hands me the corkscrew, looking mystified.

'Was I?' she says vaguely. Her brows crease. 'Oh dear.' She smiles, shrugs, flops down on to a sheet-covered couch. She is still wearing her coat, but I can see black-stockinged legs, black high heels, and a touch of red at throat and coat hem. 'I've been partying,' she explains.

'Really?' I open the wine.

'Hmm. Want to see my outfit?'

'Why not?'

She stands, handing me the glasses. She unbuttons the long black coat, sweeps it from her shoulders and throws it over a chair. She pirouettes.

She is wearing a bright red clinging satin dress; it is knee length, but slashed to the top of her thigh. As she turns I see a slim length of white flesh between the dense black of stocking top and an edge of black lace above. The dress has a high neck which almost conceals a thin black choker. The shoulders are padded, the bust . . . not.

Abberlaine Arrol stands, hands on hips, facing me. Her arms are bare, and a dark down on them has the effect of edging them in black. Her carefully made-up face looks amused; we are sharing a joke. Suddenly she turns and digs in a coat pocket, pulling out what at first I take to be another pair of stockings; they are matching gloves though. She pulls them on, almost to her shoulders. She chuckles from deep in her chokered throat, does another pivoting turn. 'What do you think?'

'I take it this wasn't a formal party?' I pour the wine.

'Sort of fancy-dress; I went as a loose woman but I got tight.' She holds her hand up in front of her mouth as she laughs. She curtsies when she takes her glass.

'Well, you look stunning, Abberlaine,' I tell her soberly (another curtsy). She sighs and runs a hand through her hair, then turns, walking away with measured steps, tapping an old tall cupboard of some dark, heavily varnished wood, running her long gloved fingers over it; she drinks her wine. I watch her as she moves round the covered and uncovered furniture of the room, pulling open doors, looking in drawers, lifting the corners of sheets, rubbing her hand over dusty glass-fronts and stroking the lines of inlays, all the time humming and taking small sips from her glass. I feel forgotten for a moment, but not insulted.

'I hope you don't mind me coming here,' she says, blowing dust off a standard lamp's shade.

'Of course not. It's nice to see you.'

She turns; that smile again. Then she looks, frowning, at the grey sea and rainclouds beyond the long windows, and puts her hands to her bare upper arms, still holding her glass. She sips from it; it is a curious, oddly touching action; a small, snuggling, almost childish gesture, quite unconciously beguiling. 'I'm cold.' She turns to look at me, and there is something almost mournful about her grey eyes. 'Can you close the shutters? It looks so cold out there. I'll put the fire on, shall I?'

'Of course.' I put my glass down and go to the shutters, slow-slamming the tall wooden boards over the dark day; Abberlaine persuades an old, hissing gas fire to light, then squats down on her haunches in front of it, gloved hands held out to it. I sit on a sheet-shrouded chair nearby. She watches the flames. The fire hisses.

After a while, she seems to wake from some day-dream,

and says, still looking at the fire, 'Did you sleep all right?'

'Yes I did, thank you; very comfortable.' She has left her glass lying on the tile fire surround; she lifts it, drinks. Her stockings have a criss-cross design, small Xs within larger Xs; a stretched lettering of sheer material, moulded to her legs in curved patterns of stress; pulling here, lightened by the shown flesh beneath; relaxing there, where the stockings go dark, the compressing grammar of those Xs and Xs densed over the girl's pale skin.

'Good,' she says, quietly. She nods slowly, still fire-fascinated, the red dress reflecting the yellow-orange flames like a ruby mirror. 'Good,' she repeats.

The warmth of the fire heats her skin; the smell of her perfume builds slowly in the air between us. She breathes in deeply, holds it, then sighs out, still staring at the hissing fire.

I drain my glass, pick up the bottle; I go over to the girl and sit beside her to fill her glass and mine. Her perfume is sweet and strong. She comes down from her haunches to sit on the floor, legs to one side, one arm behind her, supporting her. She watches me fill the glasses. I put the bottle down, watching her face; her lipstick is slightly smudged in one corner. She sees me looking. One eyebrow arches slowly. I say, 'Your lipstick . . .'

It is the handkerchief which she had monogrammed I take from my pocket. She leans forward to let me wipe the offending red mark. I feel the breath from her nose on my fingers as I touch her lips through the fabric.

'There.'

'I'm afraid', she says, 'I left some on quite a few collars.' Her voice is quiet and low, almost a murmur.

'Oh,' I say, mockingly disapproving, shaking my head, 'I wouldn't go kissing collars.'

She shakes her head. 'No?'

'No.' I come closer to her, to gently touch her full glass with mine.

'What, then?' Her voice does not go quieter; it takes on another resonance instead; conspiratorial, knowing, even ironic. This is invitation enough; I haven't exactly thrown myself at her.

I kiss her, just lightly, watching her eyes (and she kisses back, lightly, and watches mine). She tastes faintly of wine and something savoury; also a hint of cigar smoke. I press forward a little and put my free hand to her waist, feeling her warmth through the smooth red satin; the fire hisses busily behind me, warming my back. I move my mouth slowly over hers, tasting her lips, brushing her teeth; her tongue comes out to meet mine. She moves, straining away to one side for a moment so that I think she is drawing away (her brows crease), but she is reaching for a place to put her glass down; then she holds me by the shoulders, eyes closing. Her breath comes a little quicker against my cheek and I kiss her more deeply, abandoning my own glass on a chair-arm.

Her hair is fine and smells of that musky perfume, her waist feels even more slim than it looks, her breasts move within the red dress, held but not confined by something she wears beneath the satin. Her stockings are smooth to the touch, her thighs warm; she hugs me, grips me, then pushes away, puts her hands to either side of my head and looks at me, her bright gaze going from eye to eye. Her nipples form little red mounds under the satin. Her mouth is wet, smeared red. She gives a little shuddering laugh, swallows, still breathing hard. 'I didn't think you would be so . . . passionate, John,' she says through her breath.

'I didn't think you would be so easily fooled.'

A little later: 'Here. Here. Not the bed, it'll be too cold: here.'

'Is there anything you have to do first?'

'What? Oh, no, no. Just . . . oh come on, take that damn jacket off, Orr . . . Shall I leave this stuff on?'

'Well, why not?'

Abberlaine Arrol's body is encased in blackness, strapped and ribbed with obsidian silks. Her stockings attach to a sort of front-laced silk corset; another pattern of Xs form a canti-levered stripe from pubis to just below where a separate brassière of sheer silk, transparent as her stockings, cups her neat, firm breasts; she shows me where it unfastens in front; her camiknickers – black gauze over the deep black curls –

stay on, loose enough. We sit together, kissing slowly, not moving yet, after I first enter her; she sits there upon me, stockinged legs round my rump, long-gloved arms beneath mine, gripping my shoulders.

'Your bruises,' she whispers (I am quite naked), stroking the places where I was kicked and punched with a tantalising softness that raises my hairs.

'Never mind,' I tell her, kissing her breasts (her nipples are almost carnation-pink, quite thick and long, with little indented creases, pink puckerings, at the tip; the aureoles smooth, raised and round), 'forget about them.' I pull her back so that I lie on my pile of discarded clothes and her red dress.

I move slowly under her, watching her, outlined against the flames of the hissing gas fire. Abberlaine hangs in the air above me, riding me, her hands on my chest, her head down, the parted brassière dangling like her thick, black hair.

Her whole body is contained by the lingerie, an absurd trapping on her, who could need nothing else to make her more desirable save breath itself; just a moving force behind those bones, that flesh, and the mind that wears and inhabits all she is. I think of the women in the barbarian's tower.

Xs; that pattern within a pattern, covering her legs, another meshing beyond our own. The zig-zagging lace of her camiknickers, the criss-crossing ribbon holding the silk across her body; those straps and lines, the sheathed arms like stockinged legs themselves; a language, an architecture. Cantilevers and tubes, suspension ties; the dark lines of the suspenders crossing her curved upper thigh, under the knickers and down to the thick black stocking-top. Caissons, structural tubes, the engineering of these soft materials to contain and conceal and reveal that softness within.

She cries out, arches her spine, head thrown back, hair hanging between her shoulder blades, her fingers splayed, arms in a V behind her, extended and straining. I lift her, suddenly conscious of myself within her inside that structure of dark materials, and as I strain, taking her weight, suddenly in that moment I am aware of the bridge above us, towering into the grey evening with its own patterns and criss-crossing and massed Xs, its own feet and legs and balanced stresses, its own character and presence and life; above us, above me, pressing down. I struggle to support that crushing weight – Abberlaine arches further, shouting; grips my ankles with her hands – then comes down groaning like some crumpling structure, my own invasive addition to the girl's body (structural member, indeed) pulsing with its own brief beat.

Abberlaine collapses on top of me, panting and relaxing; limbs sprawled. She lies on me, breathing hard, perfumed hair tickling my nose.

I ache. I am exhausted. I feel like I have just fucked the bridge.

I stay inside her, softening but not withdrawing; after a while she squeezes me from inside. It is enough. We start to move again, more slowly, more softly.

Later, in the bed which was cold but which warms quickly, I carefully remove all the black material (part of its effect, we decide, is to more exactly delineate areas for a concentrated programme of caresses). This final time takes the longest, and contains, like the best works, many different movements and changes of tempo. Its climax chills me though; something makes it worse than joyless, makes it frightening, terrifying.

She is beneath me. Her arms grip around my sides and back; towards the end she wraps her slim, strong legs round me, pushing at my rump and the small of my back.

My orgasm is nothing; a detail from the glands, an irrelevant signal from the provinces. I shout out, but not with pleasure, not even from pain. That gripping, this pressure, this containing of me as though I am the body to be dressed, enfolded, strapped and parcelled, lined and laced, sends something crashing through me: a memory. Ancient and fresh, livid and rotten at once; the hope and fear of release and capture, of animal and machine and meshing structures; a start and an end.

Trapped. Crushed. Little death, and that release. The girl holds me, like a cage.

'I must go.' She holds out her hand as she comes back from the fireside with her clothes. I take her hand, squeeze it. 'Wish I could stay,' she says, looking sad, clutching her few thin pieces of clothing to her pale body.

'That's all right.'

A few hours. Her family expect her now. She dresses, whistling, unselfconscious. A foghorn sounds from far away. It is quite dark beyond the shuttered windows.

One quick trip to the bathroom; she finds a comb, brandishing it triumphantly. Her hair is hopelessly tangled, and she has to be patient, sitting, coat on, on the edge of the bed while I carefully comb her hair, making it smooth again. She digs into a coat pocket and comes out with a small pack of thin cigars and a book of matches. Her nose wrinkles.

'This whole place smells of sex,' she announces, taking out a cigar.

'It doesn't, does it?'

She turns to look at me, holding out the pack of cigars; I shake my head. 'Hmm. Disgusting behaviour,' she pronounces, lighting up. I comb her hair, slowly removing the entangled results. She blows smoke-rings, grey Os, towards the ceiling. She puts one hand on to mine, moving it along with the comb. She sighs.

A kiss before she goes, face washed, breath fragrant with the grey smoke. 'I'd stay if I could,' she tells me.

'Don't worry. You were here for a while; you came here in the first place.' I would like to say more but I cannot. That terror of being crushed, of being trapped, is with me still, like an echo deep inside me, still resonating. She kisses me.

When she has gone, I lie for a while in the large, cooling bed, listening to the foghorns. One horn is quite close; I may not be able to sleep tonight, if the fog doesn't clear. There is a faint, fading hint of smoke in the air. On the ceiling the discoloured rings on the plaster look like imprinted smoke-rings branded there by Abberlaine Arrol's cigar. I breathe in deeply, trying to catch the last traces of her perfume. She is right; the room does smell of sex. I am thirsty and hungry. It is only mid-evening; I get up and have a bath, then dress slowly, feeling pleasantly tired. I am putting the lights out, front door already open, when I see the glow coming from a doorway across the cluttered room. I close the door, go to investigate.

It is an old library, shelves bare. There is a television screen at one end, switched on. My heart seems to beat somewhere in my throat, but then I realize the picture is not the usual one. The screen is white, a textured blankness. I go to switch it off, but before I can, something dark closes over the view, then withdraws. A hand. The picture shakes, then settles on the man in the bed. A woman moves away from the camera; she goes to stand near the edge of the screen. She lifts a brush and pulls it slowly through her hair, staring ahead at what must be a mirror on the wall. The view of the man in the bed is altered only slightly otherwise; a chair has been shifted, and the bed is not quite as neat as it was.

After a while the woman puts the brush down, leans forward, one hand to her brow, then pulls back again. She picks up the brush and moves away, passing in a dark blur beneath the camera. I don't get a good look at her face.

My mouth is dry. The woman reappears at the bedside, wearing a dark coat. She stands looking down at the man, then bends and kisses him on the forehead, smoothing some hair away from his brow as she does so. She picks a bag up from the floor, and leaves. I switch the set off.

There is a phone on the wall of the kitchen. The noise is there, not quite regular, perhaps a little faster than before.

I leave the apartment, take a lift to the train deck.

It is foggy; lights make yellow and orange cones out of the thick vapour. Trams and trains pass, hooting and clanking. I wander along the walkway on the outside of the bridge, hand on the tall rail at the walkway's lip. Fog blows softly through the girders; foghorns sound from the hidden sea.

People pass by, mostly railmen. I smell steam within the

fog, and coal smoke and diesel fumes. In a railway workers' shed, uniformed men sit round tables, reading papers, playing cards, drinking from large mugs. I walk on. The bridge shudders beneath my feet, and a crashing, grinding, metallic noise comes from somewhere ahead. The noise echoes through the bridge, reflecting from the secondary architecture, bouncing through the fog-curdled air. I walk through a dense silence, then the foghorns sound, one after another. I hear trains and trams nearby slowing, stopping. Ahead, sirens and klaxons burst into life.

I walk by the very edge of the bridge, through the glowing fog. My legs ache again, my chest throbs dully as though in sympathy. I think of Abberlaine; the memory of her ought to make me feel better, but it does not. It was in a haunted apartment; the ghosts of that mindless noise and that nearly unchanging picture were there all the time, a hand's motion away, a switch-turning away, probably even when I first kissed her, even while her four limbs gripped me and I cried out in terror.

The trains are silent now; nothing has passed me in either direction for some minutes. Klaxons and sirens compete with the baying foghorns.

Yes, very sweet and good indeed, and I would love to dwell on that fresh memory, but something in me will not let this happen; I try to recreate the smell and feel and warmth of her, but all I can recall is that woman calmly brushing her hair, looking into an invisible mirror and brushing, brushing. I try to remember the way the room looked, but see it only in black and white, from up in one corner, just one bed in the clutter, and a man in it.

A train heads past me in the fog, lights flashing, heading towards the still-wailing sirens.

What now, anyway? Oh, more, much more of the same, that freshly sated part of my mind says; nights and days of that, weeks and months of that, please. But what, really? Another distraction, something else besides lost libraries and incomprehensible aircraft missions and faked dreams?

Either way, any of the ways, I can't see much good coming of it.

I walk on, into the rolling mists, into the gathering noise of sirens and shouts and crackling fires of a train wreck.

I see the flames first, rising through the fog like thick, quivering masts. Smoke rolls like a solid shadow in the mist. People shout, lights flash. Some railwaymen pass me, running, heading towards the wreck. I can see the rear of the train that passed me a few minutes ago; it is an emergency train, loaded with cranes and hoses and hospital cars. It moves slowly down the track, disappearing behind the freight cars of another train two tracks away, nearer me; the first few freight cars are normal, still on the rails, but the next three have come off, their wheels lying in the metal troughs at the edge of the rails, neatly caught, as the bridge designers intended. The carriage beyond these lies diagonally across the tracks, its axles straddling a rail each. After that, each succeeding car is more damaged than the one before. The flames still rise ahead; I am near to their source, I can feel the heat beating through the fog on to my face. I wonder if I ought to retrace my steps; I'm probably not wanted here. In the fog it is confusing, but I think I am near the end of this section, where the bridge narrows like a distended hour-glass on its side, down to the bridge-within-a-bridge which is the linking span.

Cars are spilled across the tracks here, where the network of points leads the tracks within the main section of the bridge towards the funnel-neck of the linking span, where only a few lines cross to the next section. The heat on this side of the crashed train is quite fierce; jets of water from the emergency train on the far side of the wreck arc over the burning freight cars, hissing on their stoved-in wood and metal frames. Railmen with extinguishers move to and fro, others are unrolling canvas hoses and connecting them up to hydrants. The flames roll and shudder; the fires hiss as the water hits. I keep on, walking faster to get away from the heat of the flames. Water runs in the wheel troughs and draining channels of the deck, steaming as it goes beneath the pounding heat of the flames, adding its own vapour to the fog and the rising black smoke. Something has caught light above where the train burns, and drips molten fire on to the furnace of smashed cars below.

I have to put my hands to my ears when I pass one of the sirens, wailing away into the fog from a post by the track side. More railmen scatter past me, shouting. The fire is at my back now, roaring into the cluttered girder space. In front, the smashed train lies on its side, crumpled and askew, thrown across the tracks like something dropped from above, like a dead snake, the frames of the broken cars its fractured ribs.

Beyond there another train, larger and with long, windowed carriages rather than low slab-sided freight cars. Men swarm over its torn surfaces where they merge with the long, still solid shape of a freight locomotive, its snout buried in one of the tall carriages. I see people being pulled from the wreckage. Stretchers lie by the track; more klaxons and horns sound nearby, obliterating the foghorns below. I am halted by the sheer manic energy of this desperate scene, watching the rescue operation. More people are brought, moaning and bloody, out of the passenger train. An explosion bursts from the wreckage behind me; men run towards this new scene of catastrophe. The wounded are being taken away on stretchers.

'You!' One of the men shouts at me; he is kneeling by a stretcher, holding a woman's bloody arm while another man ties a tourniquet higher up. 'Give us a hand; take one end of a stretcher, can't you?'

There are ten or twelve stretchers by the side of the tracks; men run up and ferry them away, but many people are left lying, waiting their turn. I step over the rail, from walkway to trackside, go over to the stretchers, and help a railman carry one. We take the first stretcher to the emergency train, where medical orderlies take it from us.

There is another explosion in the wrecked freight train. When we come back with the next casualty, the emergency train has been moved back up the track, away from the danger of explosions; we have to carry the stretcher with a moaning, bleeding man on it two hundred yards to the end of the freight train, where orderlies relieve us. We run back to the passenger train.

The next casualty may well be dead already; he pours blood as soon as we lift him. We are directed by a railway official, told to take him not to the emergency train but to another train further down the track, in the opposite direction.

It is an express, held up by the crash and taking some of the victims on board before ferrying them to the nearest hospital. We take the stretcher on board. In what looks like a soft-class dining-car, a doctor is going from victim to victim. We put our bloody charge down over a white tablecloth, splattering blood, as the doctor reaches us. He presses down on the man's neck, holding it; I had not even noticed that was where the blood was coming from. The doctor looks at me; a young man. He looks frightened.

'Hold this,' he tells me, and I have to put my hand to the man's neck while the doctor goes away for a while. My fellow stretcher-bearer runs off. I am left holding the faint pulse of the man on the dinner-table, his blood flowing over my hands when I relax or try to get a better purchase on the ragged patch of skin torn from his neck. I grip, I press, I do what I am told, and I look at the face of the man, pale with blood loss, unconscious but still suffering, free from whatever mask he ever chose to meet the world with, reduced to something pathetic and animal in his agony. 'OK, thanks.' The doctor comes back with a nurse; they have bandages, a drip, bottles and needles. They take over.

I walk away, through the whimpering wounded. I find myself in a passenger carriage, deserted and unlit. I feel faint and sit down for a moment, then when I get up can only stagger as far as the toilet at the end of the carriage. I sit down there, head pounding, lights in my eyes. I wash my hands while I wait for my heart to catch up with the demands my body is making on it. By the time I feel ready to stand again, the train is moving.

I go back to the dining-car as the train slows; nurses and auxiliaries from the hospital crowd in, taking the stretchers. I am told to get out of the way by three nurses and two auxiliaries clustering round a stretcher being taken towards the nearest door; an injured woman giving birth. I have to head back for the toilet.

And I sit there, thinking.

No one comes to disturb me. The whole train becomes very quiet. It shakes and jerks a couple of times, and I hear shouts outside the translucent window, but the interior is silent. I walk down to the dining-car; it is a different one, fresh and clean and smelling of polish. The lights go out. The white tables look ghostly in the light shed by the bridge outside, still wrapped in fog.

Should I get off now? The good doctor would want me to, Brooke would; so – I hope – would Abberlaine Arrol.

But for what? All I do is play games; games with the doctor, with Brooke, with the bridge, with Abberlaine. All very well, and with her quite sublime, save for that echoing horror . . .

Do I go then? I could. Why not?

Here I am in a thing become place, the link become location, the means become end and route become destination . . . and in this long, articulated symbol, phallic and poised between the limbs of our great iron icon. How tempting just to stay and so to go, to voyage out bravely leaving the woman at home. Place and thing and thing and place. Is it really so simple? Is a woman a place and a man just a thing?

Good *heavens* young-fellow-me-lad, of course not! Ho ho ho what a preposterous idea! It's all *much* more civilized than that . . .

Still, just because it seems so offensive to my taste, I suspect there might be something in it. So what do I represent then, sitting here, inside the train, within the symbol? Good question, I tell myself. Good question. Then the train moves again.

I sit at a table, watching the stream of carriages alongside; slowly we gain speed, leave the other train behind in its siding. We slow again, and I watch as we pass the place where the wreck took place. Jumbled freight cars litter the side of the track, twisted rails rear from the scored deck like

179

so much bent wire, and smoking debris gutters in the drifting fog under bright arc lights. The emergency train lies a little way up the track, lights bright. The carriage shakes gently around me as the train gathers speed.

Lights flare through the fog; we flash through the main station of the section, past other trains, past local trams, through the lights of the streets and thoroughfares and their surrounding buildings. We are still gathering speed. Quickly the lights start to thin as we approach the section's far end. I watch the lights for a moment longer, then go to the end of the carriage, where the door is. I open the window and look out into the fog, tearing past the window with a roar itself patterned by the unseen structure of the bridge, echoing the train's headlong progress according to the density of girder work and added-on buildings around the track. The last few building lights fall astern; I work my hospital identity tag loose, pulling it slowly and painfully from my wrist, licking it when it sticks, finally hauling it off regardless, cutting myself.

Across the linking span. Still well within the range my identity bracelet allows me, of course. A little circlet of plastic with my name on it. My wrist feels odd without it, after all this time. Naked.

I throw it out of the window, into the fog; it is lost the instant it leaves my hand.

I close the window and go back to the carriage to rest, and see how far I'll get.

Eocene

. . . is the microphone on?

Ah! There you are! Yes, well then . . . nothing to worry about, not really confused here at all, no way, honestly. Everything totally fine and wonderful, completely under control. Absolutely wunnerful, total command; all aspects. Knew the thing was on all the time. Just quoting the immortal – what's that? OK, OK – sorry, the mortal Jimi Hendrix there, honest. Now then, where was I? Oh yes.

Well, the patient's condition is stable; he's dead. Can't get much more fucking stable than that, can you? Yeah, all right, decomposition and so on; I was only kidding anyway; just my little joke. Christ some people have no sense of humour; calm down at the back there.

Mobile again, chaps. From where to where? Damn good question.

Glad you asked me that. Anybody know the answer? No? Shhhit. Oh well.

Where are they taking me? What did I do to *deserve* all this? Who asked *me*, you bastards? Anybody ask me? Eh? Anybody think to say 'Mind if we move you, what's-your-name?' *Hmm?* No. Maybe I was happy where I was, ever think of that?

Well you can move my bowels and turn me over like an omelette and reach inside me and muck about and repair bits and pump God knows what into me and press bits and tweak bits and all the rest of it, but you can't catch me, you can't find me, you can't get through to me. I'm up here; in charge, in command, invulnerable.

And what a filthy trick, what a typically dirty piece of underhand undercover underclothed misunderstanding by the evil queen herself. How could she stoop so low? (Well, yer jurst bends over like this—) Rousing the goddamn barbarians against me; ha! Was that the best she could think of?

Probably. Never did have much imagination. Well, except in bed (or wherever) I guess. No, that's not true. I am being

183

petulant; fair's fair (often with a slight, just a tinge, just a wee hint of red, usually, I've found . . . but never mind that).

What a caddess, though, raising a rebellion like that. No chance, of course but there

you go. *Now* what? Good grief can't a fellow have a little talk with himself without

being – *again!* What the fucking hell's going on here? What do you think I am you clumsy bastards? This part of the

—will you *stop* that! No more bumping! It hurts! This part of the treatment, is it? If I really wanted to I'd get up and give you cads a jolly good biffing, let me tell you! *Butt!* Get that stitched, Jimmy.

Thank God, stopped at last, just a little lateral motion here, nothing to worry about; could be in a boat or something maybe. Hard to tell.

No, not a boat, the rocking's damped; something with suspension, shock-absorbers. Squeaking? Do I hear voices? (All the time, doc. They told me to do it. Not my fault. Perfect alibi, impregnable defence.)

Raped! What a bloody nerve! I'll sue (so, get that stitched Jemima; sue? I'll stitch her up. No, sorry, that's not funny, but I mean! What a dia-fucking-bollockal liberty, eh?).

Never meant a thing to me. Or her, probably. She was a woman of letters, you know. Oh yes. I told her once and she laughed and we worked it all out. Not just letters either; signs. I'll show you.

Behind each knee an H, from behind her behind a +, her nostrils were, s (hope this isn't getting too confusing for you), her waist was)(, and pride of place went to V (in plan, prone), and ! (front elevation). Then of course she digested all this and pointed out she also had a : and regular .s (though these were puns, not signs – like I say, she was a woman of letters). Never mind; at that! I went i (she went O).

Oh well, here we go. Moving. Vroom vroom, part of the machine again, all hooked up and somewhere to go (Me-maw me-maw? Never sell ice-cream at that speed, Jimmy. Jam Sandwich please. Plenty of raspberry). Laugh if we crash. Not via the bridge I hope (Gee Charon, sorry about this, but what with the increased traffic flow recently . . .). I don't know, maybe I'm dead already, or maybe they think I am. Hard to tell (no it isn't); kinda lost ma bearings round here. All a bit traumatic this (traum? Trauma? Just more letters; rev reve lation rse rence reiver o'lution bla bla bla . . .

(what's he saying?

'bla bla bla'

o good an improvement)

Shoulda seen me before. I was impressive. Well, I thought so. Revs la reve; the docking's ramped you know; had two is too; I mean not one i but two: i i. Or ii (well come on you can have a roman nose why not roman eyes don't give me a hard time here I'm not a well man). Aye-aye. Just like that.

Damn it the thing squeaks. Might have known. Story of my fucking life. No bloody justice in the world (well, there is, but it falleth like the hard rain from the nimbostrata of the world; erratically, with occasional floods and droughts that last decades).

Anyway, where was I? Oh yeah, here we are in the machine, nicely contained an all that, wafting along. Let us hope not via you-know-what. Reminds me of a story, dont-cheknow. Just an ordinary-like story; nothing special you understand; no shooting in it or exciting car chases or any-thing like that (sorry). Hardly even a *real* story in fact, if you want my honest opinion; more of a history really; a bio-graphy . . . but anyway, that's—

She got

haud on, son; just doin the intro here; give us a break, eh? Cheese-us, canny even finish what yer sayin without—

She got her

you'll get yours in a minute Jimmy if ye don't shut

She got her degree

is it me, eh? Is it? Does ma voice no carry or something?

She—

yeah, she got her degree; we know. Well on you go, bash on; be my guest. Christ some people are just so fucking im

She got her degree and letters after her name; he made gentle fun of her new qualification, and found other symbols to describe her. He had given up the room in Sciennes Road and was renting a small flat in Canonmills. Andrea more or less moved in, though she kept on the flat in Comely Bank. A cousin of hers from Inverness, called Shona, stayed there while she went to the PE college in Cramond, the place where Andrea's family had originated.

He still had to work in his vacations, and she still spent hers abroad with family and friends, which made him both jealous and envious, but each time they met again it was as it had been before, and at some point – he could never pin down just when – he started to think of their relationship as being something that might last longer than just the next term. He even thought of suggesting they get married, but a sort of pride in him would not tolerate the idea of the state – far less the church – being appeased in this way. What mattered lay in their hearts (or rather in their brains), not in any register. Besides, he admitted to himself, she would probably have said No.

They were ex-hippies now, he supposed; if they'd ever really been hippies in the first place. Flower power had . . . well, people chose their own phrases; withered, gone to seed, blossomed and died – he once suggested the problem was petal fatigue.

She'd worked hard for a good degree, and after graduation took a year off, while he finished his own studies. She went on short holidays to visit people in other parts of Scotland and England, and in Paris, and on longer trips to the States, the rest of Europe, and the Soviet Union. She renewed acquaintance with her Edinburgh friends, would cook for him while he studied, visit her mother, sometimes play golf with her father – who, to his amazement, he found he could talk to quite easily – and read novels in French.

When she came back from the SU it was with a determination to learn Russian. He would arrive back at the flat sometimes to find her poring over novels and textbooks filled with the odd-looking, half-familiar Cyrillic alphabet, brows creased, pencil poised over a notebook. She would look up, gaze incredulously at her watch and apologize for not having cooked him something; he'd tell her not to be daft, and do the cooking himself.

He missed his own graduation day, lying in the Royal Infirmary recovering from an appendectomy. His mother and father went to the ceremony anyway, just to hear his name read out. Andrea looked after them; they all got on fine. Even when the parents met he was amazed that they all seemed to chat like old friends; he was ashamed of himself for ever being ashamed of his own mother and father.

Stewart Mackie met Shona, the cousin from Inverness; they got married during Stewart's first post-grad year. He was Stewart's best man, Andrea was Shona's maid of honour. They both made speeches at the reception; his was the better planned, but hers was the better delivered. He sat watching as she stood speaking, and realized then how much he loved her and admired her. He also felt vaguely proud of her, though he felt that was wrong. She sat down to enthusiastic applause. He raised his glass to her. She winked back.

A few weeks later she told him she was thinking of going to Paris to study Russian. He thought she was joking at first. He was still looking for a job. He had vague ideas of going with her – perhaps he could do a crash course in French and look for a job over there – but then he was offered a good position in a firm working on power station design; he had to take it. Three years, she told him. It'll only be three years. *Only?* he said. She tried to tempt him with the idea of holidays in Paris with her, but he found it difficult to be supportive.

He was anyway powerless, and she determined.

He wasn't going to see her to the airport. They went out instead, on the evening before she left, across the road bridge and into Fife, along the shore to a small restaurant in Culross. They took his car; he had bought a small new BMW on credit, on the strength of his new-found wealth as an employed man. It was an awkward meal and he drank too much wine; she was staying sober for the flight the following day – she loved flying, she would always have a window seat – so she drove back. He fell asleep in the car.

*

When he woke up he assumed they were back outside the flat in Canonmills, or her old place at Comely Bank; but lights shimmered far away, across a mile of dark water in front of them. Before she switched off the headlights he caught a glimpse of something vast towering over them, at once massive and airy.

'Where the hell's this?' he said, rubbing his eyes and looking around. She got out of the car.

'North Queensferry. Come and see the bridge,' she told him, pulling on her jacket. He looked out sceptically; the night was cold and there was a hint of rain. 'Come on,' she called. 'It'll clear your head.'

'So would a fucking revolver,' he muttered as he got out of the car.

They walked past notices warning people about objects falling from the bridge, and others which claimed the land beyond as private, until they came to a gravel turning circle, some old buildings, a small slip, grass and whin-covered rocks, and the round granite piers of the railway bridge itself. The smir of rain inside the cold wind made him shiver. He looked up into the wind-moaning spaces of the structure above. The waters of the Firth of Forth shushed and slapped on nearby rocks, and the lights of buoys flashed slowly on and off, up and down the wide, dark river. She held his hand. Upstream, the road bridge was a tall web of light, and a distant grumble of background noise.

'I like this place,' she told him, and she hugged him, her body quivering with the cold. He held her, but looked up into the web of steel overhead, lost in its dark strength.

Three years, he thought. Three years in another city.

'The Tallahatchie Bridge fell down,' he said eventually, more to the cold wind than to her. She looked up at him, nuzzled her cold nose into the presentable remnant of the fine beard he'd grown over the last two years and said,

'What?'

'The Tallahatchie Bridge. *Ode to Billy Joe*, Bobbie Gentry, remember? The damn thing fell down.' He gave a small, despairing laugh.

'Anybody hurt?' she asked, then put her cold lips on his Adam's Apple.

'I don't know,' he said, suddenly very sad. 'I didn't even think to look. I just saw the headline.'

A train rumbled over the bridge, filling the night air with the bassy voice of other people going to other places. He wondered if any of the passengers would pay heed to the old tradition and throw coins out of their nice warm carriages, spinning futile wishes into the uncaring waters of the cold Firth below.

He didn't tell her, but he remembered being here, in this very spot, years ago, one summer. An uncle who had a car took him and his parents on a ride through the Trossachs and then over to Perth. They came back this way. It was before the road bridge opened in '64 – before they'd even started it, he supposed; it was a Bank Holiday, and there was a queue a mile long waiting for the ferries. The uncle drove them down here instead, to have a look at 'one of Scotland's proudest monuments'.

What age had he been then? He didn't know. Maybe only five or six. His father had held him on his shoulders; he'd touched the cool granite of the piers, and reached, stretching, straining, small hands open and grasping, for the red-painted metal of the bridge . . .

The queue of cars had grown no shorter when they went back. They crossed by the Kincardine Bridge instead.

Andrea kissed him, waking him from his memories, and hugged him very tight, tighter than he'd ever have thought she could hug, so tight he almost had difficulty breathing, then she let go, and they went back to the car.

She drove over the road bridge. He looked out over the dark waters to the dim night-shape of the rail bridge they had stood beneath, and saw the long dotted row of lights of a passenger train as it crossed high over the river, heading south. Lights like a row of dots at the end of a sentence, he thought, or at the start of one; three years. Dots like meaning-

189

less Morse; a signal made up of only Es and Hs and Is and Ss. The lights flickered through the intervening girders of the bridge; the nearer cables of the road bridge flicked past too quickly to make any difference.

No romance, he thought, watching the train. I remember when there were steam trains. I'd go up to the local station and stand on the foot-bridge over the tracks until a train came along, chuffing steam and smoke. When it went under the wooden bridge its smoke exploded on the metal plates put there to protect the timbers; a sudden blast of smoke and steam which surrounded you for what seemed like very long seconds with a delicious uncertainty, another world of mystery and swirling, half-seen things.

But they closed the line, they dismantled the engines, they tore down the foot-bridge and turned the station into an attractive, very unique and spacious residence with a pleasant southerly aspect and extensive grounds. Very unique. That just about said it all. Even if they'd got it right they'd still have been wrong.

The train flowed across the long viaduct and disappeared into the land. Just like that. No romance. No fireworks as the ashes and cinders were dumped, no flying comet-tail of orange sparks from the chimney, not even any clouds of steam (he would try to write a poem about it the next day, but it wouldn't work and he would throw it away).

He turned from the bridge, yawning as Andrea slowed the car for the tolls. 'You know how long it takes them to paint it, don't you?' he said to her. She shook her head, wound the window down as they came up to the toll plaza.

'What, the railway bridge?' she said, digging in a pocket for the money. 'I don't know. A year?'

'Wrong,' he told her, folding his arms, looking ahead towards the red light at the far end of the booth. 'Three. Three fucking years.'

She said nothing. She paid the toll and the light turned green

He worked, he got on. His mum and dad were proud of him. He got a mortgage on a small flat, still in Canonmills. The company he worked for let him put some money towards his company car, once he'd ascended to such heights of bourgeois decadence, so he had a bigger and better BMW, rather than a Cortina. Andrea wrote him letters; he would make the same old joke whenever he referred to them.

John Peel played reggae on night-time Radio One. He bought *Past, Present and Future* by Al Stewart. 'Post World War Two Blues' very nearly made him cry. 'Roads to Moscow' actually did once, and 'Nostradamus' annoyed him. He played *The Confessions of Doctor Dream* a lot, lying with the headphones on, spreadeagled on the floor in the darkness, smashed out of his skull and humming along with the music. The first track on the eponymous second side was called *Irreversible Neural Damage*.

Things had a certain pattern, he observed to Stewart Mackie. Stewart and Shona moved to Dunfermline, across the river in Fife. Shona, having been trained to be a PE teacher in the Dunfermline College of Physical Education (located confusingly but cannily not in Dunfermline but across the river near Edinburgh); it seemed then singularly appropriate that she should become a teacher in Dunfermline itself; from one dispossesed capital to another. Stewart was still at the university, finishing post-grad work and probably all set to become a lecturer. He and Shona called their first child after him. It meant more to him than he could tell them.

He travelled. Round Europe on a rail-pass before he got too old, across Canada and America by train, too, and by hitch-hiking and buses and trains down to Morocco and back. That trip he didn't enjoy; he was only twenty-five, but he felt old already. He had the beginnings of a bald patch. Still, there was a wonderful train journey towards the end of it, travelling for twenty-four hours through Spain, from Algeciras to Irun with some American guys who had some of the finest dope he'd ever encountered. He'd watched the sun come up over the plains of Mancha, listening to the train's steel wheels playing symphonies.

He always found excuses not to visit Paris. He didn't want to see her there. She came back every now and again; changed, different, somehow more steady and ironic and even more sure of herself. Her hair was short now – very chic, he supposed. They had holidays on the west coast and the islands – when he could get the extra time off – and once went to the Soviet Union; his first trip, her third. He remembered the trains and the journeys on them, of course, but also the people, the architecture and the war memorials. It wasn't the same, though. He was frustrated, unable to speak more than a few words of the language, and listening to her chattering away quite happily with people made him feel he'd lost her to a language (and to a foreign tongue, he thought bitterly; he knew there was someone else in Paris).

He worked on refineries and rig design and made money; he sent some home to his mum now that his dad was retired. He bought a Mercedes and changed it soon afterwards for an old Ferrari which kept fouling its plugs. He settled for a three-year-old red Porsche, though really he wanted a new one.

He started seeing a girl called Nicola, a nurse he'd known since he'd had his appendix out at the Royal Infirmary. People made jokes about their names, called them imperialists, asked them when they were going to claim Russia back. She was small and blonde and had a generous, allowing body; she disapproved of him smoking dope and told him – when he splashed out and bought some coke – that he was insane to waste that sort of money stuffing it up his nose. He felt very tender towards her, he told her once, when he suspected he was supposed to tell her he loved her. I feel tender every bloody morning, you animal, she said, laughing and snuggling up to him. He laughed too, but realized it was the only joke she had ever made. She knew about Andrea but didn't talk about it. They drifted apart after six months. After that, when asked, he said he was playing the field.

The phone rang at three o'clock one morning, while he was screwing an old school pal of Andrea's. The phone was by the bedside. Go on, she said, giggling, answer it. She held on to him while he inched across the bed to the ringing machine. It was his sister Morag ringing to tell him that his mother had died of a stroke an hour before in the Southern General, in Glasgow.

Mrs McLean had to get back home anyway. She left him sitting on the bed, holding his head and thinking. At least it wasn't Dad, and hating himself for thinking it.

He didn't know who to ring. He thought of Stewart, but he didn't want to wake their latest baby; they'd had problems with the kid sleeping anyway. He rang Andrea in Paris. A man answered, and when her sleepy voice came on the phone she hardly seemed to know who he was. He told her he'd had some bad news . . . She hung up.

He couldn't believe it. He tried calling back but the phone was engaged; the international operator couldn't get through either. He left the phone on the bed, engaged tone beeping mindlessly while he dressed, then took the Porsche on a long, frosty, starlit drive north, almost to the Cairngorms. Most of the tapes he had in the car at the time were Pete Atkin albums, but Clive James's lyrics were too thoughtful, and often too melancholic, for a good, fast mindless drive, and the reggae tapes he had – mostly Bob Marley – were too laid back. He wished he had some Stones. He found an old tape, one he'd almost forgotten, and turned the Motorola up to maximum volume, playing *Rock and Roll Animal* over and over, all the way up to Braemar and back, a sort of knowing sneer on his face. 'Allo?' he whined nasally to the headlights of the occasional passing car, 'Allo? Ca va? Allo?'

He went to that place on the way back; he stood under the great red bridge which he had once thought looked the same colour as her hair, while his breath smoked and the Porsche idled clatteringly on the gravel turning circle and the first streaks of dawn outlined the bridge, a silhouette of arrogance, grace and power against the pale flames of a winter morning sky.

The funeral was two days later; he'd stayed with his father in the pebble-dashed council house after quickly packing a bag in his flat and slamming the whining phone down. He ignored his mail. Stewart Mackie came through for the funeral.

Looking down at his mother's coffin he waited for tears that did not come, and put his arm round his father's shoulders, only realising then that the man was thinner and smaller than he used to be, and quietly, steadily quivering, like a just-struck iron rod.

As they were leaving, Andrea met them at the cemetery gates, getting out of an airport taxi, dressed in black and carrying a small case. He couldn't speak.

She hugged him, talked to his father, then came to him and explained that after they were cut off she'd tried to call him back. She'd been trying for two days; she'd sent telegrams, she'd had people go round to his flat to look for him. In the end, she'd decided to come herself; she'd phoned Morag in Dumfermline as soon as she got off the plane, found out what had happened, and where the funeral was.

All he could say was thank you. He turned to his father and hugged the man, and then cried, crying more tears into his father's coat-collar than he thought his eyes could ever have held; for his mother, for his father, for himself.

She could only stay for one night; she had to go back to study for some exams. The three years had become four. Why didn't he come to Paris? They slept in separate rooms in the pebble-dashed house. His father had been sleepwalking and having nightmares: he would sleep in the same room, to wake his father if he had nightmares, stop him hurting himself if he walked in his sleep.

He drove her through to Edinburgh; they had lunch at her parents', then he took her to the airport. Who was your friend, the one on the phone in Paris? he asked her, then wanted to bite his tongue. Gustave, she said, easily enough. You'd like him. Have a nice flight, he said.

He watched the plane take off into the aquamarine skies of a crisp winter afternoon; and he even followed it a little way by road as it turned south; he leant forward over the steering wheel of the Porsche, staring up through the windscreen to watch the aircraft as it climbed into the immaculate blue of the cloudless sky, driving after it as though he could catch the jet.

It was just starting to make a vapour trail when he lost

sight of it, glinting and disappearing over the Pentland Hills.

He felt tugged by age. For a while he took *The Times*, balancing it with the *Morning Star*. Now and again he would look at the logo heading *The Times*, and think he could almost catch the pages of Times Present as they flicked over, almost hear the rustle of the dry leaves turning; Future became Present, Present became Past. A truth so banal, so obvious and accepted that he had somehow managed to ignore it before. He combed his hair so that the bald patch – barely the size of a two-penny piece – would not be so noticeable. He changed to the *Guardian*.

He spent more time with his father now. He would drive through on some weekends to the small new council flat and regale the old man with tales of the wonderful world of engineering in the seventies: pipelines and crackers and carbon fibres, the use of lasers, radiography, the spin-offs from space research. He described the furious force, the incredible energy of a power station undergoing a steam purge, when the newly completed boilers are fired up, water is fed in, the pipework fills with super-heated steam, and any bits of loose weld spatter, dropped gloves or tools or nuts and bolts or decaying apple cores or whatever are exploded through the great pipes and blasted into the atmosphere, cleaning the whole system of debris before the final pipework joins the boilers to the turbines themselves, with their thousands of delicate and expensive blades and fine tolerances. Once he'd seen the head of a sledgehammer thrown quarter of a mile by a steam purge; it went through the side of a parked van. The noise put Concorde to shame; a noise like the end of the world. His father smiled, nodding thoughtfully from his chair.

He still saw the Cramonds; he and the advocate would sit up late every so often, like two old men, and discuss the world. Mr Cramond believed that law and religion and fear were necessary, and that a strong government, even if it was a bad one, was better than none at all. They argued, but always amicably; he was never able to explain quite why they got on, or how. Perhaps because in the end neither took anything the other said seriously; perhaps because neither of them took anything they said themselves seriously; perhaps because neither of them took anything at all entirely seriously. They did agree it was all a game.

Elvis Presley died, but he cared more that Groucho Marx died in the same week. He bought albums by the Clash and the Sex Pistols and the Damned, glad that something different and anarchic was happening at last, even if he listened to the Jam, Elvis Costello and Bruce Springsteen more. He still knew people at the university besides Stewart, he knew people in a couple of small revolutionary parties. They'd stopped trying to get him to join after he'd explained he was utterly incapable of following a party line. When China invaded Vietnam and they had to try and prove that at least one of them wasn't socialist he found the resulting theological contortions wildly amusing. He knew some younger people through a poetry writing group at the university which he attended sporadically; he knew a select few of Andrea's old crowd and there were a couple of men in the new company he worked for who he liked. He was young, he was well-off, and although he would rather have been taller and his hair was an undistinguished brown (and with a bald spot the size of a fifty-pence piece – inflation), he wasn't unattractive; he lost count of the number of women he'd slept with. He found himself buying a bottle of Laphroaig or Macallan every two or three days; he bought dope every couple of months and usually had a joint to put him to sleep. He gave the whisky up for a few weeks, just to make sure he wasn't becoming an alcoholic, then rationed himself to one bottle a week.

The two men he liked in the company tried to persuade him to come in with them, partners in their own business; he wasn't sure. He talked to Mr Cramond about it, and Stewart. The advocate said it was a good idea in principle, but it would mean hard work; people expected things too easily these days. Stewart laughed and said 'Well, why not?' Might as well make money for himself as anybody else; pay your taxes under Labour and hire a very smart accountant indeed if the Tories got in. Stewart had his own, more severe problems though; he hadn't been really well for years, and he'd been finally diagnosed as diabetic. He drank bottles of Pils when they met, and looked longingly at other people's pints of Heavy.

He still wasn't sure about joining a partnership. He wrote to Andrea, who told him, 'Do it.' She would be coming back soon, she said, studies complete, Russian mistressed to her satisfaction. He thought: I'll believe she's back when I see her.

He had taken up golf – Stewart had persuaded him. He balanced this by joining Amnesty International after years of dithering, and sending a large cheque to the ANC after his firm had worked on a South African contract. He sold the Porsche and bought a new Saab Turbo. He was driving out to Gullane one bright Saturday in June to meet the advocate for a game at Muirfield, playing a tape which consisted solely of *Because the Night* and *Shot by Both Sides* recorded back-to-back time after time, when he saw the advocate's crumpled blue Bristol 409 being dragged up on to a brakedown truck. He drove on a little way, slowing but still heading for Gullane, telling himself the car with the stoved-in front and smashed windscreen wasn't Mr Cramond's, then turned round in a side road and went back to where two very young-looking policemen were measuring the road, the scarred verge and a shattered stone wall.

Mr Cramond had died at the wheel; a heart attack. He thought that wasn't such a terrible way to go, providing you didn't hit anybody else.

The one thing I mustn't say to Andrea, he thought, is, We can't go on meeting like this. He felt slightly guilty about buying a black suit for Mr Cramond's funeral when all he'd had for his own mother's was an armband.

He drove out to the crematorium with butterflies in his stomach; he was hung-over after finishing most of a bottle of whisky on his own the previous night. He felt he had a cold coming on. For some reason, as he drove into the place through a grey, impressive gateway, he just knew that she wasn't going to be there. He felt physically sick, and ready to turn around and go; drive away anywhere. He tried to control his breathing and his heart and his sweating palms, and he drove the Saab on into the wide, immaculate grounds, towards the cluster of parked cars in front of the low buildings of the crematorium.

He hadn't felt like this at his mother's funeral, and he hadn't really been all that close to the advocate. Maybe they would think he was still drunk; he'd had a shower and brushed his teeth but he probably smelled of whisky from his pores. Despite his new suit he felt grubby. He wondered if he should have brought a wreath; he hadn't thought.

He looked round the cars. Of course she wouldn't be there; it made a warped sort of sense; expected here she somehow wouldn't be able to show; given up for ever at his mother's grave, she had suddenly appeared. All part of life's rich pattern, he told himself, straightening his black tie before approaching the opened doors. Just remember son, he thought. This is bat country.

She was there, of course. She looked older but more beautiful; under her eyes there were little pucker-marks he'd never noticed before; tiny fleshy folds which made her look as though she'd been brought up for ever squinting into some desert storm. She took his hand, kissed him, held him for a second then let go; he wanted to say she looked beautiful, that she looked beautiful in black; but even while he was telling himself what a cretin he was, his mouth was mumbling something equally but more acceptably inane. He could see no tears in her perfectly made-up eyes.

The service was brief, surprisingly tasteful. The minister had been a personal friend of the advocate, and listening to his short but obviously sincere eulogy, he felt his eyes tingle. I must be getting old, he thought; either that or drinking too much of the hard stuff and getting soft. The man I was ten years ago would have sneered at me for being moved almost to tears by words spoken by a minister in praise of an upper-middle-class barrister.

Nevertheless. He talked to Mrs Cramond after the service. If he hadn't known her better he'd have thought she was on drugs; she seemed to glow, her eyes wide, her skin shining with an energy born of death; a tearless astonishment, a state of shock produced by the taking away of the man who for

198

more than half her life had been half her life; something beyond the immediacies of grief. He thought of the instant after some injury, when the eye saw the hammer crush the finger, or a slipping blade cut flesh, but before the blood flowed or the pain signal reached the brain. She was in that penumbra now, he thought, surfaced in the oily calm seas of the storm's eye. She was leaving the following day, for a holiday with a sister in Washington DC.

The last thing she said to him was, 'Will you look after Andrea? They were so close; she won't come with me. Will you look after her?' He said, 'If she'll be looked after . . . There's somebody in Paris, anyway, she might—' 'No,' said Mrs Cramond, and shook her head once, quite definite (a gesture the daughter had inherited; he suddenly saw one in the other). 'No, it's you. You,' she said, and squeezed his hand before getting into her son's Bentley. She whispered, 'You'll be the closest now.'

He stood, puzzled, for a while, then went to look for her. She was outside, in the car park, slouched against an under-taker's black Daimler limousine. She was lighting up a menthol More as he walked up, frowning. You shouldn't do that, he told her; think of your lungs. She regarded him with crushed-looking eyes. 'Solidarity,' she said bitterly. 'My old man's smoking at the moment too.' A small muscle in her jaw trembled. 'Oh, Andrea,' he said, suddenly filled with pity for her. He put his hand out towards her but she flinched away, turning from him and pulling her black coat tighter about her. He stood still for a moment, knowing that a few years ago he would have been hurt at this instant of rejection, and probably turned on his heel. He waited, and she came back to him, throwing the More down into the gravel and stepping on it with one black, swivelling shoe. 'Get me out of here, kid,' she said. 'Beam me up Scotty. Where's the Porsche? I was looking for it.'

They took the Saab to Gullane; she wanted to see the place where he'd died, so they stopped at the still ripped-up trench of verge and the not-yet repaired wall. He watched her in the rear-view mirror, standing looking down at the torn piece of turf as though expecting to see the grass grow back before her eyes. She touched the gashed ground and the stones of the farm wall, then came back to the car, rubbing stone-dust and earth from her pale, manicured fingers. She told him that her brother thought she was morbid for wanting to come here. 'You don't think I am, do you?' He said no, no, she wasn't. They drove on to the cold, empty house on the dunes over-looking the firth.

She turned and hugged him as soon as they were through the door; when he tried to kiss her, gently and softly, she rammed her mouth against his, her nails dug into his scalp, into his back through his jacket, into his buttocks through the black suit's trousers; she made a whimpering noise he'd never heard her make before and pushed his jacket off his shoulders. He had just decided to go along with this desperate, anguished, erotic reaction, but to try to manoeuvre her into somewhere a little more comfortable than the draughty front hall and its cold tiles and bristly doormat, when such a decision became unnecessary. It was as if his body woke up to what was actually happening, as though some instantly transmissible fever spread from her to him. He was suddenly as consumed, as wildly, absurdly abandoned as she was, wanting her more than he could ever remember having wanted her before. They collapsed on to the doormat, she pulled him to her, without taking off coat or underclothes. It was over for them both in seconds, and only then did she cry.

The advocate had left him his golfclubs. He had to smile; it was a nice gesture. He left his wife – who had her own money – the house in Moray Place. The son got all his law books and the two most valuable paintings; Andrea was to have the rest, save for a few thousand to go to the son's own children and some nieces and nephews, and a couple of charitable bequests.

The son was busy with the estate, so he and Andrea drove Mrs Cramond to Prestwick for her night flight to the USA. He held on to Andrea's slim shoulders and watched the aircraft climb, curving over the dark Clyde, heading for America. He insisted on waiting until they could no longer see it, so they stood and watched its winking lights grow smaller and smaller against the last glow of the day. Somewhere over the Mull of Kintyre, when he'd almost lost sight of it, the jet climbed out of the shadow of the earth and into the retreating sunlight; its vapour trail blazed suddenly, glorious pink against the deep, dark blue. Andrea caught her breath, then gave a small laugh, the first since she'd heard the news about her father.

In the car, driving north by the side of the deep, dark river, he confessed he hadn't known the trail would suddenly appear like that, and after a moment's hesitation he told her about trying to follow the Paris-bound jet a year earlier. Sentimental fool, she told him, and kissed him.

They went to see his father, then took a few days off; she had two weeks before she had to go back to Paris, and he had no urgent work so they just drove wherever they wanted for the next few days, staying in small hotels and bed-and-breakfasts and not knowing where they'd be heading when they got up each morning. They went to Mull, Skye, Cape Wrath, Inverness, Aberdeen, Dunfermline – where they stayed with Stewart and Shona – then by-passed the Bridges and the city to head via Culross and Stirling, Blyth Bridge and Peebles to the borders. It was her birthday while they were away; he bought her a bracelet in white gold. They were heading back to Edinburgh from Jedburgh, on the last day, when she saw the distant tower. 'Let's go *there*,' she said.

They could only get within half a mile with the Saab; they parked off a narrow, deserted road, she put on her Kickers, he lifted his camera and they tramped across a field then up through a wood and thick bracken, uphill towards the tower which stood on a broad summit of rock and grass. He hadn't realised it was so huge, from the road. It was massive; a local laird's solution to local unemployment at the start of the previous century, as well as a monument to a man and a great battle.

Its dark stones seemed to rise for ever into the wind; a heavy grey superstructure of wood protruding at the top held what looked like an open viewing platform beneath a comical wooden spire. He'd have imagined there would be a road up to such a place, a car park, a souvenir shop, turnstiles; officials and tickets and commerce. There didn't even seem to be a path. They stood, craning their necks looking up at it. The view just from the hillside was impressive enough. He took some photographs.

She turned, grinning, to him. 'What did you say this place was called?' He looked at the map he was carrying, shrugged.

'Penielhaugh, I think,' he said. She laughed.

'Penile-haugh. Wonder if we can get inside.' She went to a small door. There were large boulders resting against it. She tried to roll them away.

'You'll be lucky,' he told her. He pushed and heaved the rocks away. The little door opened. She clapped her hands and went in.

'Wow,' she said; as he joined her. The tower was hollow, just a single tube of stone. It was dark, the earth floor was covered in pigeon droppings and tiny, soft feathers, and the noise of the disturbed, cooing birds echoed faintly in the darkness. Sudden flapping sounded like fading, uncertain applause. High above, a few birds flew across dusty beams of light shining from the wooden cupola. The air was rich with the smell of the birds. A single narrow stairway – stones set jutting from the wall – spiralled up into the light-capped gloom.

'Amazing place,' he breathed.

'How sweet the sound . . . Tolkienesque, as they used to say,' she said, her head back, looking straight up, mouth open. He went over to the bottom of the spiralling stairs. There was a narrow metal rail set on spindly, rather rusted-looking rods. He thought: a century and a half old, if it's original. More. Even older. He shook it, dubious.

'Think it's safe?' she asked him. Her voice was low; he looked up again. It looked like a very long way to the top. A hundred and fifty feet? Two hundred? He thought about the rocks which had been rolled against the door. She gazed up too, caught a falling feather and looked at it. He shrugged.

'What the hell.' He started up the stone steps. She started after him immediately. He stopped. 'Let me get ahead a bit first; I'm heavier.' He went on up another twenty or so steps, keeping his feet close to the wall, not using the iron rail. She followed, not coming too close. 'Probably quite all right,' he told her half-way up, looking down towards the small circle of dark, spattered earth at the base of the tower. 'Probably find the local rugby team trains by running up and down this every day.'

'Sure,' was all she said.

They got to the top. It was a broad, octagonal platform of grey-painted wood; thick timbers, solid planks and a firm, secure set of rails. They were both breathing hard when they got there. His heart was hammering.

It was a clear day. They stood getting their breath back, the wind stroking their hair. He breathed in the fresh, cool air and walked round the airy circle, drinking in the view and taking a few photographs.

'Think we can see England from here?' she said, coming over to him. He was gazing north, wondering if a distant smudge on the horizon, over the other side of some distant hills, was above Edinburgh. He made a mental note to buy a pair of light binoculars for keeping in the car. He looked round.

'Soitinly,' he said. 'Good grief, you could probably see your *mother* from here on a really clear day.'

She put her arms round his waist and cuddled him, her head on his chest. He stroked her hair. 'Really?' she said. 'How about Paris?'

He sighed, looked away from her, over the border country-side, across low hills, woods and fields and hedges. 'Yeah, maybe Paris.' He looked into her green eyes. 'I think you can see Paris from almost anywhere.' She said nothing, just hugged him some more. He kissed the crown of her head. 'Are you really coming back?'

'Yes,' she said, and he could feel her head nodding, rubbing against his chest. 'Yes, I'm coming back.'

He gazed at the distant landscape for a while, watching the wind move the tops of the serried firs. He laughed once, just a sudden shrugging motion of his shoulders, a noise in his chest.

'What?' she said, not looking up.

203

'I was just thinking,' he said. 'I don't suppose if I asked you to marry me, you'd say yes, would you?' He stroked her hair. She looked up slowly, an expression he could not read shown on her calm face.

'I don't suppose I would either,' she said slowly, her eyes flickering, switching from one of his eyes to the other, a tiny frown etched in between her deep, dark brows. He shrugged, looked away again.

'Well, never mind,' he said.

She hugged him once more, head on chest. 'Sorry kid. It'd be you, if anybody. It just isn't me.'

'Yeah, what the hell,' he said, 'I don't suppose it's me either. I just don't want to be apart from you for so long again.'

'I don't think we ever have to be again.' The wind blew some of her red, glossy hair up against his face, tickling his nose. 'It isn't just Edinburgh, you know, it's you as well,' she told him quietly. 'I need my own place, and I dare say I'll always be too easily led astray by a soft voice or a nice bum, but . . . well, it's up to you. You sure you don't want to look for a nice wee wifey?' She looked up at him, grinning.

'Oh,' he said, nodding, 'pretty damn certain.'

She kissed him, lightly at first. He leant back against one of the grey square posts of the tower's superstructure, clutching her buttocks and rolling his tongue round inside her mouth, thinking, Well if the damn post gives way, what the hell; I may never be this happy again. There are worse ways to go.

She pulled away from him, a familiar, ironic smirk on her face. 'Yi talked me inta it, yi sweet-talkin bestid.' He laughed and pulled her back.

'You insatiable hussy.'

'You bring out the best in me.' She fondled his balls through his jeans, stroked his erection.

'Anyway, I thought your period had started.'

'Good God man, not afraid of a little bit of *blood* are you?'

'No of course not, but I haven't brought any tissues or—'

'Oh why are men so fucking *fastidious?*' she growled, biting his chest through his shirt and pulling a thin white scarf from a pocket in her jacket like a magician producing a rabbit.

'Use this, if you must mop up.' She covered his mouth with hers. He pulled her shirt out of her trousers, looked at the scarf held in his other hand.

'This is *silk*,' he told her.

She pulled his zip down. 'You better believe it kid; I deserve the best.'

Afterwards they lay still, shivering a little in the breeze of a cool July day as it moved through the painted wooden structure. He told her her aureoles were like pink washers, her nipples like little marshmallow bolts, and the tiny puckered slits at their tips like slots for a screwdriver. She laughed quietly, dozily, amused at such comparisons. She looked up at him, a sort of ironical, roguish expression on her face. 'Do you *really* love me?' she said, apparently unbelieving. He shrugged.

''Fraid so.'

'You're a fool,' she chided gently, lifting one hand to play with a lock of his hair, smiling at it.

'You think so,' he said, lowering himself for a moment, kissing the tip of her nose.

'Yes,' she said. 'I am fickle and selfish.'

'You are generous and independent.' He brushed some wind-blown hair away from near her eyes. She laughed, shook her head.

'Well, love is blind,' she said.

'So they tell us.' He sighed. 'Can't see it myself.'

Metamorphosis:

Oligocene

When I was young I used to see these things float down in front of my eyes, but I knew they were inside my eyes and that they moved the same way that pretend snowflakes move in one of those little snow scene ornaments. Never could work out what the hell they were (I described them to the doctor once as looking like roads on a map — I still know what I meant — but they'd be better described as looking like tiny twisted glass pipes with bits of dark matter stuck in the tubes), but they never seemed to cause any real problems so I paid them no attention. Only years later did I find out they were quite normal; just dead cells from the top of the eye floating down through the fluid. I believe I did once worry about them silting up, but I guessed there was some bodily process that went on inside my eyes which would make sure it didn't happen. Shame, really; with an imagination like mine I think I'd have made a great hypochondriac.

Somebody told me something about silt; that little dark fellow with the stick. Said the whole thing was sinking; they'd taken so much water from artesian wells, and so much oil and gas too, that whole bits of the thing were just sinking into the water. Quite upset about it, he was. Of course there's a fix; you pump in sea water. More expensive than just sucking out what you want, but you don't get anything for nothing (although, of course, there are *margins*, which come pretty damn close).

We are rock, part of the machine (what machine? *This* machine; look, pick it up, shake it, see the pretty patterns form; watch it snow, or rain, or blow, or shine), and we live the life of rocks; first igneous as children, metamorphic in our prime, sedimentary in our sedentary dotage (back to the subduction zone?) In fact the literal truth is even more fantastic: that we are all stars; that we, all our systems and this single system, are the gathered silt of ancient explosions, dying stars from that first birth, detonating in the silence to send their shrapnel gases spinning, swarming, collecting, forming (beat that, mean 'magined monks).

So we are silt, we are precipitate, we are leavings (cream and scum); none the worse for that. You are what has gone before, just another collection, a point on a (stretched) line, just the wave-front.

Shake and jostle. A machine within a machine within a machine within a machine within a – you want me to stop here?

Jostle, shake. Dreams of something long ago, something lodged in the brain somewhere, finally coming to the surface (another shrapnel, more splinters).

Jostle shake jostle shake. Half awake half awake.

Cities and Kingdoms and Bridges and Towers; I'm sure I'm heading for them all. Can't go for long without getting *some*where, after all.

Where the hell was that dark bridge? Still looking.

In the silence of the speeding train, I see the bridge pass. At speed, the secondary architecture can almost disappear at times; all that is visible is the bridge itself, the original structure, flashing red criss-crossing, in its own lights or the sunlight. Beyond, the blue firth, shining under a new day.

The slanted girders pass like forever chopping blades, dimming the view, sectioning it, parcelling it. In the new light, and in the haze of the day, I seem to see another bridge, up-river; a grey echo, a shadow-ghost of the one bridge, towering out of the mists above the river, at once more straight and less so. Ghost. Ghost bridge; a place I knew once but know no more. A place to—

On the other side, down-river, through the cutting dark lines of the structure, I can see the barrage balloons, hanging blackly in the sunlight like obese submarines, dead and bloated with some corrupting gas.

Then the planes come, level with me, flying alongside me; they are heading in the same direction as the train, overtaking it slowly. They are surrounded by black clouds; dark bursts of smoke detonate in the sky all around them. Their own pulsed signals mingle with the black smudges of the bridge's reactivated anti-aircraft defences, scrambling the already nonsensical message trailed behind the craft still further.

Invulnerable, uncaring, the silver planes fly on through the furious hail of exploding shells, their formation perfect, their sky writing as neat and precise as ever, sunlight glinting over their sleekly bulbous bodies. All three, from boss to skid, look quite undamaged; their flush-riveted lines are unmarred even by soot or oil stains.

Then, when they are almost too far away for me to see them clearly through the angle of increasing structure, when I have determined they must be really invulnerable, or at least that the bridge's guns are firing smoke charges, not shrapnel or even impact rounds, one of the aircraft is hit. Hit in the tail. It is the middle plane. Immediately it starts to slow down, dropping behind the other planes, grey smoke pouring from its tail, the black puffs of its message continuing for a while, then growing fainter as the plane drops further and further back until it is alongside the train. It does not peel away or take any other evasive action; it keeps the same steady course, but slower now.

Its tail disappears, consumed by the smoke. Still it flies, straight and level. Gradually the fuselage is eaten away. The plane keeps pace with the train and does not deviate from its course, though black anti-aircraft bursts still swarm around it, damage or no. Half the fuselage is gone; it has no tail. The grey smoke starts to eat into the trailing edge of the wing roots and the rear of the cockpit canopy. The plane cannot be flyable; it should have tumbled out of control the instant it lost its tail surfaces, but it flies on, still accurately level with the racing train, and matching its speed. The thick cloud of grey smoke eats fuselage, cockpit, wings, then thins out as they disappear; only the engine cowling and the near-invisible line of the propeller remain to be consumed.

A flying engine; no pilot, no fuel, no control surfaces, no means of lift. The cowling disappears, exhaust by exhaust. Only a few puffs of black smoke bother to follow it. The engine has vanished; the propeller disappears in a sudden thick pulse of grey, then only the boss is left, quickly shrivel-

211

ling to leave a thin grey line; then it is gone. Just blue sky and balloons beyond the whirling verticals and slants of the speed-blurred bridge.

The train jostles and shakes me. I am half awake.

I go back to sleep.

On the journey I had strange recurring dreams of a life lived on land; I kept seeing one man, first as a small boy and then as a youth and finally as a young man, but I did not see him clearly at any stage. It was as though all of it was through some mist, and only in black and white and cluttered with things that were more than just visual images but less than real, as if I watched that life on a distorted screen but at the same time could see into that man's head, see the thoughts inside, the associations and connections, conjectures and imaginings all bursting from him and on to the screen I was watching. It all seemed grey and unreal, and I could sometimes spot similarities between what happened in this odd, recurring dream and what really did happen while I lived on the bridge.

Perhaps that was reality, my damaged memories just restored enough to put on some sort of disordered show and doing their best either to entertain or to inform me. I recall that I did see something that looked like the bridge at one point in my dream, but only from a distance, from a desert coast I think, and besides it was far too small. Later I thought I might have stood underneath it, but again it was too small, and too dark; a minor echo, no more.

The empty train I had stowed away on moved for days over the bridge, sometimes slowing but never stopping. I could have jumped from it a couple of times, but I might have killed myself, and I was still determined to reach the end of the structure. I had the run of only three deserted carriages, two passenger cars – with seats and small tables and sleeping compartments – and one dining-car. But no kitchen-car, no galley, and locked doors at each end of those three carriages.

I hid most of the time, slouched down in one of the re-clining seats so that I could not be seen from outside, or lying in a sleeping compartment top bunk and peeping out through half drawn curtains at the bridge outside. I drank water from the toilet washbasins, and day-dreamed or dreamt about food.

The carriages were unlit at night, haunted by the flickering beams of yellow-orange light from outside. It grew gradually warmer with each passing day, and the sunlight outside became brighter. The overall shape of the bridge outside the windows did not seem to change, but the people I glimpsed occasionally by the trackside did alter; their skins became different colours, darker as the sunlight increased.

After some days, though, everything seemed to get darker again, as I lay, faint with hunger, rattled like something loose in a long, reclined seat. I began to believe that the light had not changed at all, and that it was something inside my eyes that made the people look like shadows. Still, my eyes hurt.

Then one night I awoke, dreaming of the last meal I had had with Abberlaine Arrol, and saw that it was very dark, both inside the carriage and out.

No glow of light came from the bridge outside, no chrome edge of reflecting cabin fitments was visible; neither was my own hand when I held it in front of my face. I closed my eyes and pressed them, only then seeing the false nerve-light that is the eyes' reaction to pressure. I felt my way to the nearest outside door, opened the window and stared out. A strange, thick, heavy smell came into the carriage on the warm air. It alarmed me at first; no smell of salt, of paint or oil or even smoke and fumes.

Then I saw a faint edge of light above me, moving very slowly. The train was still moving at close to full speed – the slipstream poured roaring through the window to tug at my loose clothes – but whatever it was I could see, the light was moving very slowly over it; it must be very far away. A cloudbank, I thought, lit by starlight, then realized I could see that outline of light continuously, without any inter-rupting beams and girders chopping the sight into flickering fragments.

A part of the bridge where the load-bearing structure was beneath the level of the rails? I started to feel faint again.

Then the train slowed for some points, and before it speeded up again I could hear, through the lessened noise of its progress, the distant night noises of a dark, wild forest, and saw that the edging of light I had mistaken for a cloud-bank was a raggedly wooded ridge a couple of miles away. I laughed, delirious and delighted, and sat by the window until the dawn came up and made the green forest steam with fragment mists.

That day the train slowed, and entered the outskirts of a sprawling town. It wound sinuously, slowly, through a great marshalling yard towards a long, low station. I hid in a linen cupboard. The train stopped. I heard voices, the whirring noises of unidentifiable machines inside the carriages, then nothing. I tried to get out of the cupboard but it had been locked from the outside. While I was sitting wondering what to do next, more voices sounded through the cupboard's metal door, and I formed the impression that the train was filling up with people. After a few hours, the train moved again. I slept in the locked cupboard that night and was discovered by a steward on the following morning.

The train was full of passengers; well-dressed ladies and gentlemen who looked as though they came from the bridge. They wore summer suits and dresses; they sipped cocktails chinking with ice at little tables in the observation cars. They looked vaguely disgusted when they saw me led through the train in my crumpled, stale clothes, a railway policeman's hand forcing one of my arms painfully high up my back. Outside, the countryside was mountainous, full of tunnels and tall viaducts spanning boulder-torn torrents.

I was interrogated by one of the train's deputy firemen, a young man in a sparkling white uniform which seemed rather inappropriately spotless given his rank. He asked me how I came to be on board; I told the truth. I was taken back through the train and locked in a bare, barred section of a baggage car. I was fed well, on galley leftovers. My clothes were taken from me, washed and returned. The handkerchief

Abberlaine Arrol had monogrammed, and on which she had left a smudged red image of her lips, came back quite thoroughly clean.

The train moved for days through mountains, and then across a high, grass-covered plain where distant herds of animals scattered and fled on its approach and the wind blew continually. Beyond the plain it started to climb towards another range of mountains. It unwound its way through those, across more spindly viaducts and long tunnels, descending all the time and stopping at small, quiet towns along the way, amongst forests and green lakes and rock spires plinthed in scree. The barred and rattling little cell had only a single small window two feet long and six inches high, but I could observe the scenery well enough, and the fresh, rarefied smells of the mountains and the plateaux leaked through the large baggage door at one end of the car, wrapping me with the scents which I seemed, tantalizingly, to recall from long ago.

I had other dreams, besides the recurring one of the man in the severely beautiful city; I dreamt one night that I woke up and went to my small window and looked out over a boulder-strewn plain, and saw two sets of weak lights as they approached each other over the moonlit wasteland. Just as they stopped, facing each other, the train roared into a tunnel. On another occasion I thought I looked out during the day, while the train ran along the top of a great cliff facing a blue, glittering sea; the cliff-edge was strung about with puffy clouds which we continually plunged into and rushed out of, and a few times in the clear spaces, through a haze of heat, far below on the surface of the sun-burnished sea, I thought I saw two ships of the line sailing alongside one another, the space between them filled with puffs of grey smoke and darting flames. But that was a day-dream.

They left me here eventually, after the mountains and the hills and tundra and another, lower, colder plain. Here is the Republic, a cold, concentric place once known, they say, as The Eye of God. It is reached, from the barren plain, by a long causeway which divides the waters of a huge grey inland sea. The sea is almost perfectly circular, and the large island at its centre is also very close to that same geometric shape. The first I saw of it was the wall; the grey sea wall skirted by low surf and topped by low towers. It seemed to stretch curving away for ever, vanishing in a haze of distant rain squalls. The train clattered through a long tunnel, over a deep moat of water and then another wall. Beyond lay the island and the Republic, a place of wheatfields and wind, low hills and grey buildings; it seemed at once run-down and full of energy, and those grey buildings gave way, every now and again, to immaculate palaces and temples of an obviously earlier age, perfectly restored but seemingly unused. And there was a graveyard, a cemetery miles to each side, packed with millions of identical white pillars spread geometrically across a green sea of grass.

I live in a dormitory with a hundred other men. I sweep leaves from the broad paths of a park. Tall grey buildings rise on all sides, bulking square shapes against the grainy, dusty-blue sky. There are spires and thin towers on top of the buildings; banners I cannot read fly from them.

I sweep the leaves even when there are no leaves to sweep; it is the law. I formed the impression when I first came here that this was a prison, but this is not the case, at least not in the obvious sense. It seemed then that everybody I met was either a prisoner or a guard, and that even when I was weighed and measured and inspected and given my uniform and taken by bus to this large, anonymous town nothing had really changed. I could talk to relatively few people – this came as no surprise, of course – but the ones I did talk to seemed delighted that I could speak to them in my strange, alien tongue, but also rather guarded when talking about their own circumstances. I asked them if they had heard about the bridge; some had, but when I said I came from there they seemed to think I was joking, or even that I was mad.

Then my dreams changed, were taken over, invaded.

I woke up one night in the dormitory; the air was sick with the smell of death, and choked with the sounds of people moaning and crying out. I looked through a broken window and saw the flashes of distant explosions, the steady glow of large fires, and could hear the crump of falling shells and bombs. I was alone in the dormitory, the sounds and smells came from outside.

I felt weak and desperately hungry, more hungry than I had felt on the train which had taken me away from the bridge. I discovered I had lost almost half my weight during the night. I pinched myself and bit the inside of my cheek, but I did not wake up. I looked round the deserted dormitory; the windows had been covered in tape; black and white tape made Xs all over the rectangular panes. Outside, the town was burning.

I found some ill-fitting shoes and an old suit where my standard-issue uniform should have been. I went out into the town. The park which I was supposed to sweep was there, but covered in tents and surrounded by ruined buildings.

Planes droned overhead, or came hurtling down out of the cloudy night sky, screaming. Explosions shook the ground and air; flames leapt into the sky. Everywhere was rubble and the smell of death. I saw a dead, skinny horse, fallen in its traces, the cart behind it half-covered by the ruins of a fallen building. The horse was being carefully butchered by a group of thin, wide-eyed men and women.

The clouds were orange islands against the ink-black sky; fires reflected there on the hung vapour, and sent huge columns of their own darkness into the air to meet them. The planes wheeled, like birds of carrion over the burning town. Sometimes a searchlight would pick one out, and a few black puffs of smoke would darken the sky around the plane still further, but it seemed that otherwise the town was defenceless. Occasionally shells shrieked overhead; twice explosions nearby made me duck for cover as debris – dusty bricks, shards of stone – fell pattering and thumping around me.

I wandered for hours. Towards dawn, as I was returning to the dormitory through this unending nightmare, I found myself behind two old people, a man and a woman. They were walking along the street, each supporting the other, when the man suddenly crumpled and fell, taking the old lady down with him. I tried to help them up, but the man was already dead. There had been no bombs or shells for several minutes, and though I thought I could hear distant crackling small-arms fire, none of it was near us. The woman, almost as thin and grey looking as the old dead man, cried hopelessly, sobbing and moaning into the worn collar of the old man's coat, slowly shaking her head and repeating over and over some words I could not understand.

I did not think the shrivelled old could contain so many tears.

The dormitory was full of dead soldiers in grey uniforms when I returned. One bed was unoccupied. I lay down on it and woke up.

It was the same peaceful, intact town, with the same trees and paths and tall grey buildings. I was still here. The buildings I had seen in flames or in ruins were those that overlooked the park where I worked. When I looked carefully though, in some places I found stones which had not been restored, and which were part of the original buildings. Some of those blocks were chipped and scarred with the distinctive, but weathered, marks of bullets and shrapnel.

I had similar dreams for weeks; always much the same, never exactly similar. Somehow I was not surprised when I discovered that everybody had these dreams. *They* were surprised; surprised that I had never had such dreams before. I cannot understand, I tell them, why they seem frightened of their dreams. That was the past, I say, this is the present; the future will be better, it won't be the past.

They think there is a threat. I tell them there isn't. Some people have started to avoid me. I tell the people who will listen that they are in prison, but the prison is in their own heads.

I sat up drinking far too much spirit with my workmates last night. I told them all about the bridge and that I had seen nothing threatening to them on my long journey here. Most of them just said I was crazy and went to bed. I stayed up too late, drank too much.

I have a hangover now, at the start of the week. I pick up

my brush from the depot and head into the chilly spaces of the park, where the leaves lie, damp or frozen on the ground according to where the sunlight falls. They are waiting for me in the park; four men in a big black car.

In the car two of them hit me while the other two talk about the women they'd screwed that weekend. The beating is painful but not enthusiastic; the two men administering it seem almost bored. One of them cuts a knuckle on my teeth and looks annoyed for a moment; he takes out a knuckle-duster, but one of the other men says something to him; he puts it away again and sits sucking at his finger. The car screams through the wide streets.

The thin, grey-haired man behind the desk is apologetic; I wasn't supposed to be beaten up, but it's standard pro-cedure. He tells me I am a very lucky man. I dab at my bloody nose and puffy eyes with my monogrammed hanky – still, miraculously, not stolen – and try to agree with him. If you were one of ours, he says, then shakes his head. He taps a key on the surface of his grey metal desk.

I am somewhere in a large underground building. They blindfolded me in the car, on the road between the town and whatever city this is. I know it is a city because I heard its noises, and we drove through it for an hour before the car dipped into some echoing underground space, spiralling down and down into the earth. When it stopped I was led out of the car and along innumerable curving corridors to this room, where the thin, grey-haired man was waiting, tapping his grey desk with a key and drinking tea.

I ask him what they are going to do with me. He tells me instead about the combined prison and police headquarters I am now in. It is mostly underground, as I had guessed. He explains, with genuine enthusiasm, the principles upon which it has been designed and built, warming to his subject as he goes on. The prison/HQ is in the form of several tall, buried cylinders; inverted circular skyscrapers interred together beneath the surface of the city. He is deliberately vague about the exact number, but I form the impression there are between three and six of these close-packed cylinders. Each of these huge sunken drums contains many hundreds of rooms: cells, offices, toilets, canteens, dormitories, and so on, and each cylinder can be individually rotated, like some immense battleship magazine, so that the orientation of the corridors and doors leading into and out of each drum can be changed almost continually. A door which one day leads to a lift or an underground car park or a railway station or a certain place in one of the other cylinders might on the following day lead to a completely different cylinder, or to solid rock. From day to day, even – in conditions of high security alert – from hour to hour, this massive gearbox of revolving drums can be moved either at random or according to a complex, coded pattern, thus totally confounding the planning and execution of any attempted escape. The information necessary to decode these erratic transformations is distributed to the police and staff strictly on a need-to-know basis, so that nobody ever knows in exactly what new configuration the composite subterranean complex has been arranged; only the very highest and most trusted officials have access to the machines which set up and oversee these rotations, and the machinery and electronics which are its muscles and nerves are so designed that no engineer or electrician working on any conceivable fault or failure could possibly gain a working overview of the whole system.

The fellow's eyes are bright and wide as he describes all this to me. My head hurts, my vision is blurred and I need to relieve myself, but I agree, quite honestly, that it is a considerable work of engineering. But don't you see? he says, don't you see what it *is*, what it is an image of? No, I don't, I confess, ears ringing.

A lock! he says triumphantly, eyes flashing. It is a poem; a song in metal and rock. A perfect, real image of its purpose; a lock, a safe, a set of tumblers; a safe place to store evil.

I see what the man means. My head throbs and I black out.

When I wake up it is on another train and I've peed my pants.

Miocene

'Versions of the truth disseminated, To the flock like plastic shrapnel, Getting under the skin of most, And on the nerves of some. – Another chip off the old blastoma, Another symptom of the system; The bloom and sump of your diabetical materialism.

'Come give us your excuses, Explain why you did what you had to do; Tell us of your hurting to be kind. You talk of: Bloody Sundays, Black Septembers, And all the time you're wasting.

'We'll smile, dissemble, Case the joint for barricades, Count the weapons, Cost the operation, And mutter back meantime "I believe that's just the way it happened. I'm sure it's exactly as you say." '

'. . . Oh well, very radical. Lot of street cred there.' Stewart nodded. 'I've always said a good poem's worth a dozen Kalashnikovs.' He nodded again and drank from his glass.

'Look, asshole, just tell me if you mind the bit about "Diabetical Materialism".'

Stewart shrugged, reached for another bottle of Pils. 'Doesnae bother me, pal. You just go ahead. That a new poem?'

'No, ancient. But I'm thinking I might try to get some printed. Just thought you might be offended.'

Stewart laughed. 'God, you're a daft bugger sometimes, you know that?'

'I know that.'

They were in Stewart and Shona's house in Dunfermline. Shona had taken the kids to Inverness for the weekend; he'd come over to leave their Christmas presents and talk to Stewart. He needed somebody to talk to. He opened another can of Export and added the ring-pull to the growing pile in the ashtray.

Stewart poured the Pils into his glass and took the drink over to the hi-fi. The last record had ended a few minutes

221

earlier. 'How about a blast from the past?'

'Yeah, let's wallow in nostalgia. Why not.' He settled back in the seat, watching Stewart thumb through the collection of records and wishing he'd been able to think of something more imaginative than record tokens to give the kids. Well, it was what they'd both asked for. Ten and twelve; he remembered he'd bought his first single on his sixteenth birthday. These youngsters already had their own album collections. Oh well.

'Good heavens,' Stewart said, taking out a blue and grey cover and looking slightly shocked. 'Did I really buy *Deep Purple In Rock*?'

'You must have been stoned,' he told him. Stewart turned round and winked at him as he took the record out. 'Oh, eh? Was that a little flash of wit there?'

'Merely a scintilla; put the goddamn record on.'

'Well it hasn't been played for a while, just let me clean it here . . .' Stewart cleaned the record, put it on: *Can't Stand the Rezillos*. My God, he thought, that was from 1978; a blast from the past already, indeed. Stewart nodded in time to the music, then sat down in his armchair. 'I like these gentle melodic songs,' he shouted. The track he'd put the stylus down on was *Somebody's Gonna Get Their Head Kicked In Tonight*.

He raised his can to Stewart. 'God almighty, seven years!' Stewart leaned forward, a hand cupped at one ear. He pointed at the turntable, shouted, 'I said seven years . . .' He nodded towards the hi-fi. 'That: seventy-eight.' Stewart sat back, shaking his head emphatically.

'Aw naw; thirty-three and a third,' he shouted.

I am reduced to telling stories for my living. I raid my dreams for tasty morsels to feed my jealous Field Marshal and his motley band of vapidly murderous ancillaries. We hunker down round a fire of fallen flags and precious books, flames glinting on their bandoliers and bayonets; we eat long pig and drink rough whisky; the Field Marshal boasts of famous battles he has won, all the women he has fucked, and then, when he can think of no more lies, he demands a story from me. I tell him the one about the small boy whose dad had a pigeon loft and who later as a man never felt happier than when his proposal of marriage was turned down, at the top of a pigeon-loft folly of monumental proportions.

The Field Marshal looks unimpressed, so I go back to the beginning.

By the time I recovered from my melodramatic swoon in the office of the grey-haired man with the tapping key and the grey desk, the train I'd been put on had crossed the rest of the Republic, steamed across the causeway to the far shore of the nearly circular sea, and travelled some way across a cold waste of tundra.

I had another new set of clothes; a uniform for the train. I was in a small bunk and I'd wet my pants. I felt terrible; my head was pounding, I ached in various places, and the old circular pain in my chest had returned. The train rattled around me.

I was to be a waiter; one who waited. The train contained various elderly officials from the Republic who were on a peace mission – I never did discover exactly who they were or what sort of peace they envisaged – and I, along with an experienced chief steward, was supposed to wait on them in the dining-car, serving them drinks, taking their orders, bringing their food. Luckily they were drunk for most of the time, these ageing bureaucrats, and my initial gaffes went mostly unnoticed as the steward trained me. Sometimes I had to make beds too, or sweep and dust and polish in the sleeping compartments and public carriages.

If this was a punishment, I thought, then it is very mild. I found out later all that had saved me from a much worse fate was the fact that I was – to these people – illiterate, dumb and deaf. Because I could not understand any conversations I heard, or read any papers left lying about in the cars, I could be trusted and used. Of course I did learn something of the language, but my vocabulary was mostly limited to table matters and the decoding of signs saying Do Not Disturb and the like. I did my job. The train rolled through the wind-

223

swept tundra, passing flat towns and camps and army posts.

The composition of the train gradually changed. As we went further from the Republic the attitude of the officials on the train gradually moved from drunken relaxation to drunken tension; slow columns of smoke climbed blackly on the horizon and occasionally a flight of war planes would swoop, sudden and screaming, across the train. The officials at their tables ducked instinctively when the planes flashed over us, then laughed, loosened collars and nodded appreciatively at the fast-receding dots of the flight. They caught my eye and snapped their fingers commandingly for more drinks.

First we had a couple of flat cars with two four-barrel anti-aircraft guns on them, one just ahead of the engine, one at the back of the guard's van, then later a carriage to accommodate the gun crews and an armoured wagon full of extra ammunition. The military tended to keep to their own carriages, and I was not called on to serve them.

Later, a couple of the public cars were taken off at a small town where sirens and klaxons blared in the distance and a large fire burned near the station. The cars were replaced with armoured carriages containing troops. Their officers took over some of the sleeping cars. Still the people on the train were mostly bureaucrats.

The officers were polite.

The air changed; snow fell. We passed by the side of gravel roads where burned-out trucks lay at angles in ditches, and the trackside and road were pitted with craters. Lines of troops and poor-looking civilians pushing prams loaded with household goods started to appear; the soldiers going in either direction, the civilians only in one; the opposite to ours. Several times the train stopped for no apparent reason, and often, in a siding, I would see a train pass us, carrying sections of track, and cranes, and wagons full of small stones. Often the bridges over the snow-covered tundra were built on the ruins of older bridges, and manned by sappers. The train crossed these bridges at a crawl; I got down and walked alongside to stretch my legs, shivering in my thin waiter's jacket.

Almost before I realized what was happening there were no more civilians on the train; only officers and men and the train crew. All the carriages were armoured; we had three armour-plated diesel locomotives in front and another two behind, there were anti-aircraft flat cars every three or four carriages, covered wagons holding field guns and howitzers, a radio car with its own generator, several flat cars with tanks and staff cars and artillery tractors, many conscript-crammed barrack cars, and a dozen or so wagons full of oil drums.

I now served only officers. They drank more and tended to damage things, but were less likely to throw cutlery if one dropped dirty plates.

The sunlight grew less, the winds colder, the clouds darker and thicker. We passed no more refugees, only the ruins of towns and villages; they looked like charcoal sketches: the black of soot-covered stones and the empty white of clinging snow. There were army camps, sidings full of trains like ours, or trains with hundreds of tanks on flat cars, or gigantic guns on articulated many-axled cars the length of half a dozen ordinary wagons.

We were attacked by planes; the anti-aircraft platforms crackled with noise and sent clouds of acrid smoke drifting down the side of the train; the planes attacked with cannon shell, smashing windows. Bombs missed us by a hundred yards. I lay on the floor of the galley with the chief steward, hugging a box of finest crystal glasses while the windows splintered around us. We both stared in horror as a wave of red liquid spilled from round the galley door, thinking one of the chefs had been hit. It was only wine.

The damage was repaired; the train rolled on, into low hills under dark clouds. The hills were blown clear of snow in places, and though the sun now never rose very far in the sky, the air became warmer. I thought I could catch the breath of the ocean; sometimes there was a smell of sulphur. The army camps grew larger. The hills gradually became mountains, and I saw the first volcano one night while serving dinner; I mistook it for some terrible night attack in the distance. The soldiers gave it only the most cursory glance and told me not to spill the soup.

There were distant explosions all the time now; sometimes volcanic, sometimes man-made. The train rolled and whined over newly repaired track, crawling past long lines of grey-faced men with sledgehammers and long shovels.

We ran from attacking planes; dashing along straights, hurtling round bends – carriages tipping sickeningly – then plunging into tunnels, braking furiously, everything clattering and crashing; the tunnel walls flashing with the light from our howling brakes.

We off-loaded tanks and staff cars, we took on wounded; the debris of war was scattered over these hills and valleys like rotting fruit in an abandoned orchard. Once, at night, I saw the glowing remains of tanks caught in a ruby-red flow. The lava rolled down the valley below us like burning mud, and the wrecked tanks – tracks undone, gun barrels tilted crazily into the air – were borne down on that incandescent tide like strange products of the earth itself; infernal antibodies in that red stream.

I still served the officers their meals, though we had no wine left and our supplies of food were reduced both in quantity and quality. Many of the officers who had joined the train after we entered the battle zone would stare at their plates for minutes at a time, gazing incredulously at what we'd put before them, as confused and disturbed as if we'd just ladled a bowlful of nuts and bolts on to their plates.

Our lights blazed all day; the dark clouds, the vast rolling billows of volcanic smoke, the low sun which we could go days at a time without seeing; all conspired to turn the wreckage-strewn mountains and valleys into a land of night. All was uncertainty. A horizon of deeper darkness might be raincloud or smoke; a layer of white on a hillside or plain might be snow, or ash; fires above us might be burning hill forts or the side vents of great volcanoes. We travelled through darkness, dust and death. After a while it began to seem quite natural.

I believe that if we had gone on, the train – lava-spattered, dust-caked, dented and patched – would have accumulated so much cooled lava on its carriage roofs that from above at least it would have had a form of natural camouflage of rock; an evolved skin, a protective layer grown in this harsh place, as though the metals of the train's own articulated body were spontaneously returning to their original forms.

The attack came in the midst of fire and steam.

The train was descending from a mountain pass. In a shallow valley to one side a loose lava flow ran rapidly, almost keeping pace with the train. As we approached a tunnel through a spur of rock, a vast rising veil of steam reared in front of us, and a sound like a gigantic waterfall slowly drowned out the noise of the train. On the far side of the mist-filled tunnel, we saw that a glacier was blocking the lava flow's way; the ice sheet extended from a side valley, its soiled meltwaters feeding a broad lake. The lava had spilled into the lake, forcing a huge steaming wave of water-cooled debris in front of it.

The train rolled hesitantly forward towards another bank of thick mist. I was making beds in one of the sleeping cars. When the first small rocks started to roll down the mountain-side I left that side of the carriage and watched through an open door as larger and larger boulders came crashing down the mist-shrouded slope into the train, bouncing up to break through windows or battering against the carriage sides. One vast boulder headed straight towards me; I ran down the corridor. The air was full of crashes and thuds and the sound of distant, confused, undirected gunfire. I felt the train shake, then a tremendous bang obliterated every other noise; the lava vaporising the lake, the gunfire, the small rocks whacking on to the sides and roof. The entire carriage flicked to one side, dashing me against the window and then over on my back as the car lights flickered and went out, a breaking, smashing sound seemed to come from all directions at once, and the buckling carriage roof and walls batted me between them like a ball.

Later, I discovered that the carriage had broken free from the rest of the stricken train and rolled down the slope of scree

227

towards the boiling waters of the lake. The Field Marshal's men, looting and murdering their way through the cars, came upon me, mumbling to myself in the wreckage and – so they tell me, though they'd say anything – attempting to put the chief steward's head back on to what was left of his shoulders. I had stuck an apple in his mouth.

Language saved me again. The men speak the same tongue as I do; they took me to the Field Marshal. He was in a small train just up the line.

The Field Marshal is very tall and heavy, with long, disproportionate legs and a huge backside. He has a broad, round face and lank hair, dyed black. He favours garish uniforms with a very high albedo. He was sitting at a desk in his carriage, listening to music on the radio and eating crystallized quinces from a small plate when I was ushered before him, still half unconscious. He asked me where I came from; I vaguely recall telling him the truth, which he found extremely funny. You'll be my valet, he told me. I like a good story at dinner. I was locked in a small cell in one of the carriages while the Field Marshal's men completed their looting and killing. When I was searched, my handkerchief was taken from me. I saw the Field Marshal blowing his nose on it, some days later.

I watched the blood-splashed irregulars of the Field Marshal's force come back from my old train, carrying weapons and valuables; a wind came up and stirred the steam in the valley's cauldron. The lake was almost dry; lava flow and glacier finally met in a series of tremendous explosions which sent chunks of ice and rock hundreds of feet into the air. Our small train escaped, clanking and clattering, away from the wreck on the track behind us, and the elemental cataclysm beyond.

The Field Marshal's train was shorter and less well equipped than the one his men had ambushed. We moved only at night unless there was heavy cloud cover, hiding in tunnels during the day or covering the train with camouflage netting. For the first few days there was an air of tension in the train, but despite a narrow escape from a strafing fighter-bomber, and a hair-raising traverse of a great curved viaduct which was already damaged and under continuing heavy-artillery attack, the atmosphere amongst the motley-uniformed rabble perceptibly lightened as we moved away from the scene of the ambush.

The volcanic activity also decreased; now there were only fumeroles and geysers and small lakes of boiling mud to betray the depths of fire beneath these freezing lands.

It was the Field Marshal's conceit to house the dozen or so pigs he possessed in fine state carriages, while quartering his human captives in a couple of muck-filled cattle trucks at the rear of the train. The pigs were bathed every week in the Field Marshal's own whirlpool bath, which took up a large part of his own carriage. Two soldiers were on permanent pig-husbanding detail, employed to keep clean the nests of sheets and blankets which the animals made of their beds, bring them their meals – they ate the same food as the rest of us – and generally look after their welfare.

Throwing captured soldiers into pools of boiling mud was a comparatively common occurrence, and done just for sport. The Field Marshal could tell I found these practices distressing. 'Ore,' he would say (this was how he pronounced my name), 'Ore, don't you like our little games?' I would smile, dissemble.

The days grew lighter, dormant volcanoes gave way to low hills and savannah. Deprived of his boiling mud, the Field Marshal devised a new sport; he tied a short rope to a man's neck and made him run in front of the train. The Field Marshal took the controls, giggling as he opened the throttle and chased his quarry. They usually lasted a half mile or so before they tripped and fell across the sleepers, or tried to jump to one side, in which case the Field Marshall just opened the throttle and dragged them along the edge of the track.

At the last pool of boiling mud, he had a rope put round the victim, and once he was cooked, dragged him out, covered in a baked layer of mud; he had his men shovel more mud over the twisted figure, then when it had dried left the resulting gnarled statue standing on the ash shore of a salty, foul-smelling inland sea.

We were crossing the floor of a drained sea, towards a city set on a great circular cliff, when the bombers appeared. The train increased speed, heading for a tunnel set underneath the ruined city; the train's few anti-aircraft guns were manned.

Three medium bombers flew straight up the track towards us, not a hundred feet above the rails. They started dropping their bombs, trailing plane first, when they were quarter of a mile away. I was watching from the protruding perspex roof of the Field Marshal's observation car, where I'd been opening a bottle of *eiswein*. The driver braked, throwing us forward. The Field Marshal pushed past me, kicked open an emergency exit and threw himself out. I followed him, thudding into the side of a dusty embankment as the line of bombs stamped down the carriages like a soldier's boots on a train set. The embankment bounded like a trampoline; stones and fragments of train showered from the sky. I lay curled up, fingers in my ears.

We are in the abandoned city now, the Field Marshal, myself and another ten men; all that survived. Some weapons we have, and one pig. The ruined city is full of echoing, flag-hung halls and tall stone spires; we camp in a library because it is the only place we can find anything which will burn. The city is built of stone, or a dark, heavy wood which refuses to do more than glow dull red, even if ignited with powder extracted from rifle cartridges. We get our water from a rusty cistern on the roof of the library, and catch and eat some of the city's pale-skinned, nocturnal inhabitants, who flit like ghosts through the ruins, looking for something they never seem to find. The men complain that these shy but gullible creatures make for poor hunting. We finish our meal. The men pick at their teeth with bayonets; one of them goes to a book-lined wall and knocks down some ancient tomes from this productive face. He brings them back to the fire, twisting their spines and ruffling their pages so that they'll burn better.

I tell the Field Marshal about the barbarian and the enchanted tower, the familiar and the wizard and the witch queen and the mutilated women; he likes that one.

Later, the Field Marshal retires with two of his men and his last pig to his private room. I clean the dishes and listen to the men complain about the monotonous diet and dull sport. They might mutiny soon; the Field Marshal has had no good ideas about what to do next.

I am called in to the Field Marshal's quarters; an old study, I believe. It contains many tables, and one bed. The two men leave, grinning at me. They close the door. Put this on, the Field Marshal says, smiling.

It is a dress; a black dress. He shakes it at me, wiping his nose on the handkerchief he took from me when I was first captured. Put it on, he says.

The pig is lying belly-down on his bed, snorting and squealing, its legs tied with rope to each of the bed's four posts. There is perfume in the air. Put this *on*, the Field Marshall tells me. I watch him put my handkerchief away. I put the dress on. The pig grunts.

The Field Marshal undresses; he throws his uniform into an old chest. He takes a large machine-gun from a book-covered table and shoves it into my hands. He holds up the long chain of cartridges as though it is a thick gold necklace to go with my long black dress. Look at these bullets (I look at the bullets); they are not blanks, see? See how much I trust you, Ore. Do just as I say, the Field Marshal tells me. His broad face is slicked in sweat; his breath is fetid.

I am to poke the machine-gun between the cheeks of his bum while he mounts the pig; this is what he wants. He is already excited, just at the thought. He covers one hand in gun oil and climbs on to the bed over the squealing pig, which he slaps between the legs with his oily hand. I stand at the foot of the bed, gun ready.

I detest this man. But neither of us is stupid. There were faint, regular score-marks round the shoulders of the brass cartridges; they have been held in the jaws of a wrench;

opened and emptied of their powder. Probably the caps have been fired off too.

There is a pillow by the pig's head. The Field Marshal lowers himself over the animal; they grunt together. One of his hands rests near the side of the pillow. There is another gun under there, I think.

'Now,' he says, grunting. I grasp the gun barrel with both hands, lift it overhead and in the same movement bring it down like a sledgehammer on the Field Marshal's head. My hands, my arms and my ears tell me he is dead even before my eyes do. I have never felt or heard a skull smash before, but the signal came quite distinctly through the metal of the gun and the perfumed air of the room.

The Field Marshal's body still moves, but only because the pig is jerking about. I look under the pillow where human blood and pig spittle combine and find a long, very sharp knife there. I take it and open the chest the Field Marshal put his uniform in; I take the pearl-handle revolver and some ammunition, check the door is locked, then change back into my waiter's uniform. I take one of the Field Marshal's great coats as well, then head for the window.

The window's rusty frame squeaks, but not as loudly as the pig. I have both feet on the window-sill when I remember the handkerchief. I take that from the dead man's uniform, too.

The city is dark, and the confused, wandering men who inhabit it bolt for cover as I run softly through the ruins.

Pliocene

She came back. So did Mrs Cramond, looking smaller and older. He had expected Mrs Cramond to sell the house, but she didn't; instead Andrea moved in with her, selling the flat in Comely Bank which had been let out to students in the intervening years. Mother and daughter got on remarkably well. Certainly the house was big enough for them both. They sold off the large basement as a self-contained flat.

It was a good time, after she came back. He'd stopped worrying about his bald patch, work was going well – he was still thinking about joining the other two in a partnership – and his father seemed quite happy on the west coast, spending most of his time at a club for pensioners where he apparently attracted the attentions of several widows (it was only with the greatest reluctance he could be tempted to Edinburgh for even a weekend, and once there would sit looking at his watch and complaining that now he was missing his card game with the lads, and now his bingo, or the old-time dancing. He would look down his nose at the best food Edinburgh's top chefs could provide, and pine volubly for the mince and tatties the others would be having).

And Edinburgh might start to be a capital, albeit in a limited way, once again. Devolution was in the air.

He noticed a little excess weight; just a slight jiggling at waist and upper chest whenever he ran upstairs, but something that had to be dealt with; he started playing squash. He didn't like it though; he preferred to have his own territory in a game, he told people. Besides Andrea kept beating him. He took up badminton, and went swimming at the Commonwealth Pool two or three times a week. He refused to go jogging though; there were limits.

He went to concerts. Andrea had returned from Paris with catholic tastes. She would drag him to the Usher Hall to listen to Bach and Mozart, play Jaque Brel records when he stayed at the house in Moray Place, buy him Bessie Smith albums as presents. He preferred the Motels and the Pretenders, Martha Davis singing *Total Control* and Chrissie Hynde saying 'fffUCKoff!' He thought the classical stuff was having no effect until one day he found himself trying to whistle the overture to *The Marriage of Figaro*. He developed a taste for complicated harpsichord pieces; they made good driving music, providing you played them loud enough. He heard *Warren Zevon* for the first time, and wished he'd heard the man's album when it first came out. And he found himself jumping and pogoing like a teenager to the Rezillos at parties.

'You what?' Andrea said.

'I'm going to get a hang-glider.'

'You'll break your neck.'

'The hell with it; it looks like fun.'

'What, being in an iron lung?'

He didn't buy a hang-glider; he decided they weren't safe enough yet. He went parachuting instead.

Andrea spent a couple of months refurbishing the house at Moray Place, overseeing decorators and carpenters and doing a lot of the painting herself. He enjoyed helping her, working late into the night in old clothes covered in paint, listening to her whistling in another room, or talking to her while they both painted. There was one night of panic when he felt a tiny lump in her breast, but it proved to be harmless. His eyes got tired sometimes at work, looking at plans and drawings, and he was putting off going to the optician' because he suspected he'd be told he needed glasses.

Stewart had a brief affair with a student at the university which Shona found out about. She talked about leaving Stewart, virtually threw him out. Stewart came to stay at his place, worried, regretful. He went to see Shona, driving to Dunfermline to try to smooth things over, describe Stewart's distress and the way he himself had always admired them and even envied the air of calm, steady affection they gave off when together. It felt strange, sitting there trying to persuade Shona not to leave her husband because he'd slept with another woman, almost unreal, almost *comical* at times. It seemed so ridiculous to him; Andrea was in Paris that weekend, doubtless shacked up with Gustave, and he'd be seeing a tall, blonde parachutist in Edinburgh that night. Was it the slip of paper that made the difference, the living together, the children, or just the belief in the vows, the institution, in a religion?

Probably no thanks to him, they patched it up. Shona would only mention it very occasionally, when she was drunk, and with less and less bitterness over the years. Still, it proved to him how fragile even the most secure-seeming relationship could be, if you went against whatever rules you'd agreed.

Oh, what the hell? he thought, and went into partnership with the other two. They found offices in Pilrig, and he had to find an accountant. He joined the Labour Party; he took part in letter-writing campaigns for Amnesty International. He sold the Saab and bought a year-old Golf GTi; he remortgaged the flat.

When he was cleaning out the Saab before taking it to the dealer he found the white silk scarf they had used that day at the tower. He hadn't wanted to leave it lying around for somebody to find, so he'd rinsed it in a burn when they got back down but then lost it; he thought it must have fallen out of the car.

It turned up, crumpled and grubby, beneath the passenger seat. He washed it and managed to get all the footprints off, but the blood stain, dried in a rough circle like some incompetent piece of tie-dying, wouldn't shift. He offered it to her anyway. She told him to keep it, then changed her mind, took it away and returned it a week later, spotless, nearly as good as new, and monogrammed with his initials. He was impressed. She wouldn't tell him how she and her mother had cleaned it. Family secret, she said. He kept the scarf carefully, and never wore it when he knew he'd be getting really drunk, in case he left it lying in some bar.

'Fetishist,' she told him.

The Fabulous Make-Your-Mind-Up Referendum was, effectively, pochled – rigged, in English. A lot of carpentry work in the old High School went to waste.

Andrea was translating Russian texts and writing articles

about Russian literature for magazines. He knew nothing about this until he read something of hers in the *Edinburgh Review*; a long piece on both Sofia Tolstoy and Nadezhda Mandelstam. He was confused, almost dizzy, when he read it; it must be the same Andrea Cramond; she wrote as she talked and he could hear the rhythm of her speech as he read the printed words. 'Why didn't you ever tell me?' he asked her, feeling hurt. She smiled, shrugged, said she didn't like to boast. She'd written a few pieces for magazines in Paris, too. Just a sideline. She was taking piano lessons again, after giving them up in high school, and going to night classes to study drawing and painting.

She was also in a partnership, of sorts; she'd put some money into a feminist bookshop a couple of her old friends had started; other women had come in on the project and now there were seven of them in a collective. Financial madness, her brother called it. She helped out in the shop sometimes; he would go there first when he wanted to buy a particular book, but he always felt vaguely uncomfortable in the place, and rarely browsed. One of the women denounced Andrea at a meeting for kissing him goodbye once, after he'd bought some books; Andrea just laughed at her, then felt very unsisterly. She apologized for the laugh but not the kiss. After she'd told him this, he was careful not to kiss or touch her when he visited the shop.

'Oooohh, shit,' he said, as they sat up in bed in the small hours watching the election results come in. Andrea shook her head, reached for the Black Label on the bedside cabinet.

'Never mind kid; have a whisky and try not to think about it. Think about your top rate of tax.'

'Fuck that; I'd rather have a clear conscience than a healthy bank balance.'

'Tut; you'll have your accountant turning in his filing cabinet.'

Another returning officer announced another Tory win; the Ya-hoos ya-hooed. He shook his head. 'The country really is going to the dogs,' he breathed.

'Certainly gone to the bitch,' Andrea said, swirling her

whisky round in her glass and looking at the television through it, brows creased.

'Well . . . at least she's a woman,' he said glumly.

'She may be a woman,' Andrea said, 'but she ain't no fuckin' sister.'

Scotland voted for Labour, with SNP in second place. What it actually got was the right honourable Margaret Thatcher, MP.

He shook his head again. 'Oooohh, shit.'

The business did well; they had to turn contracts away. Within a year his accountant was telling him to buy a bigger house and another car. But I *like* my little flat, he complained to Andrea. So keep it, but buy another house, she told him. But I can only live in one at a time! Anyway I've always thought it was immoral to have two houses when there's folk going homeless. Andrea was exasperated with him: 'So let somebody live in the flat, or in this house you're going to buy, but remember who'll get all those extra taxes you'll be paying if you don't do what your accountant says.'

'Oh,' he said.

He sold the flat and bought a house in Leith, near the Links and with a view of the Forth from the top storey. It had five bedrooms and a big double garage; he bought a new GTi and a Range Rover, to keep his accountant happy and fill up the garage; the four-wheel drive was useful on business trips when they had to visit sites. They were doing a lot of work with firms in Aberdeen that year, and he dropped in on Stewart's people. On a later trip, he ended up in bed with Stewart's sister, a divorced teacher. He didn't ever tell Stewart, not absolutely certain whether he might mind or not. He did tell Andrea. 'A school teacher,' she grinned. 'An educational experience?' He told her about not wanting to say anything to Stewart. 'Kid,' she said, taking his chin in her hand and looking at him very seriously, 'You're an idiot.'

She helped him decorate the house, bullying him into a complete new scheme.

He was up a ladder, painting an elaborate ceiling rose one evening, when he felt a sudden, dizzying surge of *déjà vu*. He

237

put the brush down. Andrea was in the next room, whistling away to herself. He recognized the tune: *The River*. He stood on the ladder, in the echoing, empty room, and remembered standing in a wide room full of sheet-draped furniture in the house in Moray Place a year earlier, dressed in the same paint-spotted clothes, listening to her whistle in another room, and feeling enormously, simply happy. I am a lucky bastard, he thought. I have so much, so much around me that is good. Not everything; I still want more, I probably want more than I could handle; in fact I probably want things that would only make me unhappy if I had them. But even that's OK; that's still part of the contentment.

If my life was a film, he thought, I'd roll the credits now; fade on this beatific smile in an empty room, the man on a ladder making things better, renovating, improving. Cut. Print. The End.

Well, he told himself, it isn't a film, laddie. He was filled with a surge of pure joy, simple delight at being where and who he was and knowing the people he did. He threw the paint brush into one corner of the room, jumped off the ladder, and ran through to Andrea. She was rolling paint on to a wall. 'God, I thought you'd fallen off the ladder. What's the cheesy grin for?'

'I just remembered,' he said, taking the roller out of her hand and chucking it behind him, 'we haven't christened this room.'

'Well, neither we have. Must remember the smell of paint does this to you.'

They screwed up against the wall, just for a change. Her shirt stuck to the wet paint; she laughed until the tears ran down her face.

He had become a film buff. During the last festival they'd both gone to more films than plays or concerts, and he suddenly realized he'd missed out on hundreds of films he'd heard of and wanted to see. He joined a film society, he bought a video recorder and scoured video shops for films. Whenever business took him down to London he'd try to cram in as many cinema visits as possible. He liked almost everything; he just liked going to the cinema.

A Scottish group called the Tourists had some chart success; their lead singer went on to become half of the Eurythmics. People would ask if he was related to her. No such luck, he sighed.

There were soft voices, nice bums. Andrea had her various flings, and he tried not to feel jealous. It isn't jealousy, he told himself; it's more like envy. And fear. One of them may be nicer, kinder, better man than I am, and more loving.

She was out of circulation for almost two weeks once, having some sort of time-lapse relationship with a young lecturer from Heriot Watt which went from love-at-first-sight to slammed doors, thrown ornaments and smashed windows over the space of twelve days. He missed her, while all this was going on. He took the second week off and headed north-west. The Range Rover and GTi had been supplemented by a Ducatti; he had a one-man tent, a Himalayan-standard sleeping bag and all the best hiking gear; he took the bike roaring up to the western highlands and spent days walking alone in the hills.

When he got back, she'd finished with the lecturer. He talked to her on the phone, but she seemed curiously reluctant to see him; he worried, he didn't sleep well. When he did see her, a week later, there was a fading yellow stain round her left eye. He only noticed it because she forgot to keep her dark glasses on in the pub. 'Ah,' she said. 'Is that why you wouldn't see me?' he asked her. 'Don't do anything,' she said. 'Please. It's all over and I could happily throttle him but you lay a finger on him and I'll never speak to you again.' 'We do not all', he told her coldly, 'resort to violence quite that quickly. You might have trusted me; I've been worried sick the past week.' Then he wished he hadn't said that, because she broke down, and hugged him and cried, and he realized something of what she must have gone through; he felt mean and selfish for adding to her cares. He stroked her hair while she sobbed into his chest. 'Come on home, lass,' he said to her.

He took to the hills a few more times, using the occasions when she went to Paris to get away from Edinburgh and out to islands and the mountains, stopping off to see his father on the way there and back. He was camped one sunset on the slopes of Beinn a' Chaisgein Mor – there was a bothy nearby, but he preferred to pitch the tent if it was good weather – looking out over Fionn Loch and the small causeway he'd be crossing tomorrow to the mountains on the far side, when he suddenly thought: just as he hadn't been to Paris, in all these years neither had Gustave ever visited Edinburgh.

Ahhh. Maybe it was just the effects of the last joint, but in that instant, though they were a thousand miles apart, and all those unshared years away, he felt curiously close to the Frenchman he'd never met. He laughed into the cool highland air; the breeze moved the flanks of the tent like breath.

One of his earliest memories was of mountains, and an island. His mum and dad, his youngest sister and he had gone to Arran for their holidays; he had been three years old. As the steamer paddled down the glittering river towards the distant blue mass of the island, his dad had pointed out the Sleeping Warrior; the way the mountain range at the north end of the island looked like a helmed soldier, lying over the landscape, mighty and fallen. He'd never forgotten that sight, or the medley of accompanying sounds; calling gulls, the slap-slap of the steamer's paddles; an accordion band playing somewhere aboard, people laughing. It also gave him his first nightmare: his mum had to wake him up, in the bed he was sharing with his sister in the guest house; he'd been crying and whimpering. In his dream, the great stone warrior had woken up, and come slowly, terribly, crushingly, to kill his parents.

Mrs and Ms Cramond made the most of their big house; they had social evenings, they entertained; their parties became moderately celebrated. They would put people up; poets giving readings at the university, a visiting painter trying to sell some work to a gallery, a writer the bookshop had invited to a signing session. Some evenings there would be a whole circle of people he didn't recognize at the place; they usually looked less well-off than Andrea's friends, and tended to eat and drink a lot more. Mrs Cramond spent half the day, it seemed, baking cakes and quiches and bread. He worried that even in her widowhood Mrs Cramond was still spending all her time in the kitchen making things for people, but Andrea told him not to be stupid; her mother loved seeing people enjoy something she'd made. He accepted this but watched some of the itinerant denizens of the house stuff cakes and the odd bottle of wine into coat pockets with a nagging sense of vicarious exploitation.

'These people are intellectuals,' he told Andrea once. 'You're starting a *salon*; you're becoming a goddamned blue stocking!'

She just smiled.

Andrea bought a litter of four Siamese cats from a friend. One died; she renamed the two males Franklin and Phineas and the sleek female Fat Freddie; damned nostalgia, he called it. Somebody gave Mrs Cramond a King Charles spaniel; she called it Cromwell.

Just getting ready to go round to the house was enough to make him feel good; driving there would produce an almost childlike thrill in him; the house was another home, a warm and hospitable place. Sometimes, especially when he'd had a few to drink, he had to fight an absurd feeling of sentimentality at the bond between mother and daughter.

He added a Citroen CX to the GTi and the Range Rover, then sold all three and bought an Audi Quattro. He went out to Yemen on business, and stood once in the ruins that had been Mocha, on the shore of the Red Sea; he saw the warm wind from Africa move the sand grains round his feet, and sensed the steady, harsh indifference of the desert, its calm continuance, the spirit of those ancient lands. He stroked his hand over the age-worn, pitted stones, and watched where the waves fell blue, exploding white fists of silk thunder on the open, golden palm of the shore.

He was working in Yemen when the Israelis invaded southern Lebanon because a man was shot in London, and when the Argentinians went ashore at Port Stanley. He didn't learn that his brother, Sammy, was with the Task Force until after it had sailed. When he got back to Edinburgh he argued with his friends; sure the Argentinians ought to have the bloody islands, he said, but how the hell could revolutionary parties support a fascist junta's own little piece of imperialism? Why did there always have to be a right side and a wrong one? Why not just say, A curse on both your houses?

His brother came back, unhurt. He still had arguments about the war; with Sammy, his dad, his radical friends. By the time the next election came round, he was starting to think maybe his pals had been right after all.

'Awww, come *on*!' he said, despairing. Another healthy Labour majority wiped out, votes leeched by the SDP; another surprise Conservative win. The pundits were predicting the Tories would get less of the vote than last time, but increase their majority by a hundred seats, perhaps more. 'Aww *fuck*!'

'This is becoming monotonous,' Andrea said, reaching for the whisky. Margaret Thatcher appeared on the television screen, glowing with victory.

'Off!' he screamed, hiding under the sheets. Andrea stabbed at the remote control unit; the screen went dark. 'Oh . . . God,' he said from beneath the sheets. 'And don't talk to me about my top rate of tax.'

'Never said a word, kid.'

'Tell me it's all just a bad dream.'

'It's all just a bad dream.'

'Really? Is it?'

'Hell no, it's real; I was just telling you what you wanted to hear.'

'Those idiots!' he fumed to Stewart. 'Another four years with that dingbat in charge!' Christ al-fucking-mighty! A senile clown surrounded by a gang of xenophobic reactionaries!'

'Unelected xenophobic reactionaries,' Stewart pointed out. Ronald Reagan had just been elected for another term; half the people who could have voted in the election, hadn't.

'Why don't I get a vote?' he raged. 'My dad lives spitting distance from Coulport, Faslane and the Holy Loch; if that buffoon's liver-spotted finger hits the button my old man's dead; probably all of us are; you, me, Andrea, Shona, and the kids; everybody I love . . . so why the fuck don't *I* get a vote?'

'No annihilation without representation,' Stewart said, thoughtfully. Then, 'Still, on the subject of unelected re-actionaries, what d'you think the Politbureau is?'

'A fucking sight more responsible than that squad of gung-ho-shitheads.'

'. . . .Aye, fair enough. Your round.'

The house at Moray Place, residence of Mrs and Ms Cramond, was now quite well known, especially at Festival time. You couldn't walk into the place without tripping over some up-and-coming artist, or an authoritative new voice in Scottish fiction, or some moody kids with acne who dragged synths and practice amps from room to room, and commandeered the Revox for days at a time. The Last Chance Salon, he called it. Andrea had settled down to a life she found thoroughly fine; still working in the shop, translating Russian books, writing articles, playing the piano, drawing and painting, socialising and partying, visiting pals, holidaying in Paris, going to films and concerts and plays with him, and to the opera and ballet with her mother.

Meeting her one day at the airport, after another jaunt to Paris, he watched her; she walked confidently, head up, out of Customs; she wore a broad, bright red hat, brilliant blue jacket, red skirt, blue tights and shiny red leather boots. Her eyes sparkled, her skin glowed; her face broadened into a wide smile when she saw him. She was thirty-three years old and she had never looked better. He felt, at that instant, an odd amalgam of emotions; love certainly, but also envious admiration. He envied her her happiness, her assurance, her calm way with the troubles and traumas of life, the way she treated everything as one might treat a child making up a story the child really believed in; not patronizingly, but with the same mock-serious frown, the same mixture of ironic detachment and affection, even love. He remembered his

243

talks with the advocate, and could see something of the old man's personality in Andrea.

You're a lucky woman Andrea Cramond, he thought, as she took his arm, there in the airport lounge. Not because of me, and not as lucky *as* me in one way, because I have more of your time than anybody else, but otherwise . . .

Let it go on, he thought. Don't let the idiots blow up the world, and don't let anything else terrible happen. Steady, kid; who are we talking to here? He sold the bike soon afterwards. Things went on; Lennon got shot, Dylan got religion. He could never decide which depressed him most.

His father fell and broke his hip that winter. He looked very small and frail when he visited him in hospital, and much older. In the spring he needed a hernia operation, and fell again, not long after he'd left hospital. He broke a leg and a collar bone. 'Have tae take mair watter with it,' he told his son, and refused to come and live with him in Edinburgh, because his friends were here. Morag and her husband also offered to take him in, and Jimmy wrote from Australia to say why didn't he come out for a few months? But the old man didn't want to move from his own area. He was in hospital for longer this time, and when they let him out he couldn't put back on the weight he'd lost. A home-help came round every morning. She found him, apparently asleep, by the fire one day, a small smile on his face. It had been his heart, too. The doctor said he probably hadn't felt a thing.

He found himself organizing everything, not that there was very much to do. His brothers and sisters all made it to the funeral, even Sammy, on compassionate leave, and Jimmy all the way from Darwin. He had asked Andrea if she minded not coming; she said no, and understood. Once it was all over, it was good to go back to her, back to Edinburgh and work. He never did entirely lose the feeling of numbness which crept over him when he thought about the old man, and though he shed no tears, he knew he'd loved him, and did not feel guilty about that dry grief.

'Ah, my poor orphan,' Andrea said, and was his comfort.

The company expanded; more people joined. They bought grand new offices in the New Town. He argued with

244

the others about their employees' salaries; they should all have a share, he said; they should all be partners.

'What,' the other two said, 'a workers' collective?' They smiled tolerantly. 'Why the hell not?' he said. They were both SDP supporters; worker participation was one of the ideas the Alliance liked. They said no, but started a bonus scheme.

Then one day Andrea got off a Paris flight and she wasn't smiling, and his guts seemed to lurch. Oh no, he thought. What is it? What's wrong?'

She wouldn't talk about it, whatever it was. She said there was nothing wrong, but she looked very solemn and thoughtful most of the time, laughed little, and would often look up, distracted, say sorry and have to have repeated to her the last thing somebody had said. He worried. He thought about phoning Gustave in Paris and asking what the hell was wrong with her, what had happened there?

He didn't call. He fretted, and tried to entertain her, taking her out to dinner or to see a film or over to see Stewart and Shona; he tried to organize a nostalgic evening, eating at the Loon Fung, near his old flat in Canonmills, then taking a taxi to the Canny Man's, but nothing worked. He couldn't decide what it was. Mrs Cramond and he worried together, and individually tried to get the truth out of her. It was the mother who did, though only after three months and another two visits to Paris. Andrea told her mother what was wrong, then went back to France again. Mrs Cramond rang him up. MS, she told him. Gustave had multiple sclerosis.

'Why didn't you tell me?' he asked her.

'I don't know,' she said, listlessly, eyes dull, voice flat. 'I don't know. And I don't know what to do; he's got nobody to look after him, not properly . . .' When he heard those words, a chill settled in him. Poor guy, he thought, and meant it; but once found himself thinking, It's so slow, why couldn't he die quickly? And hated himself for the thought.

Another argument; during the '84 strike he refused to cross a miners' picket line; the company lost a contract.

Andrea spent more and more time in Paris; less people

came to the house at Moray Place now. She looked tired whenever she came back from France, and though she was still slow to anger, and still easy with people, she was slow to laugh now as well, and guarded about taking any enjoyment at face value. When they made love, he thought he could detect an extra tenderness in her, and a sense of how precious and impermanent such moments were. It was less *fun* than it used to be, but somehow the act had gained an extra resonance, become in itself a sort of language.

Sometimes when she was away in Paris he would get lonely sitting in the big house by himself, reading or watching the television or working at the drawing board; if he'd had less than the legal limit to drink he would take the Quattro out and drive to North Queensferry to sit beneath the great dark bridge, listening to the water lap against the stones and trains rumble overhead; he would smoke a joint or just breathe the fresh air. If he felt pity for himself, it was only one timid, tentative part of his mind that felt so; there was another part of him which seemed like a hawk or an eagle; hungry and cruel and fanatically keen-eyed. Self-pity lasted a matter of seconds in the open; then the bird of prey fell on it, tearing it, ripping it.

The bird was the real world, a mercenary dispatched by his embarrassed conscience, the angry voice of all the people in the world, that vast majority who were worse off than he was; just common sense.

He discovered, to his knowing, almost righteous dismay, that the bridge was not painted end-to-end over a neat three-year period. It was done piecemeal, and the cycle lasted anything between four and six years. Another myth bites the dust, he thought; par for the course.

Andrea was away in Paris almost half the time now. She had another life there, another set of friends; he'd met some of them when they'd come over to Edinburgh; a magazine editor, a woman who worked in UNESCO, a lecturer who taught at the Sorbonne; nice people. They were all friends of Gustave, too. I should have gone over, he told himself, I ought to have gone, made friends. Too late. Why am I so stupid? I can design you a structure to withstand hundred-foot waves for thirty years or more and make it as sturdy and safe as any other designer could for the weight and the budget, but I can't see my hand in front of my face when it comes to doing sensible things with my own life. If there is a design to my own existence it escapes me. What was that old Family song? *The Weaver's Answer.* Yeah, well; where's mine, Jimmy?

He bought a Toyota MR2 as well as the latest model Quattro, he started flying lessons, he built up a sound system based on Scottish-made components, he bought the Minolta 7000 camera as soon as it came out, added a CD player to the hi-fi and thought about buying a power boat. He went sailing with some of Andrea's old pals, from the marina at Port Edgar, on the south bank of the Forth, between the two great bridges.

He grew restless with the Quattro and the MR2. There was always some better car; a Ferrari or an Aston or a Lambo or some limited edition Porsche or whatever . . . he decided to stop competing and go for timeless elegance instead. He found a well-looked-after Mk II Jaguar 3.8 through a local dealer; he sold the Audi and the Toyota.

He had the Jag re-upholstered in red Connelly leather. A specialist tuner dismantled the engine, blueprinted it, changed the cams, pistons, valves and carbs and fitted electronic ignition; they completely revised the suspension, fitted beefier brakes, new wheels and asymmetric tyres, plus a new gearbox to handle all the extra torque. He had it fitted with four new seat belts, a laminated windscreen, more powerful lights, electric windows, tinted glass, a sunroof, and anti-theft devices he'd have trusted a Chieftain tank to (but which he kept forgetting about). The car spent three days at another specialist firm having a new sound system installed, complete with CD player. It can make your *ears* bleed, he told people; I haven't even *found* all the speakers yet. Half the boot seems to be amplifier; I don't know which is going to give way under the vibration first; my ear drums or the outside paint job (he'd had it rustproofed and repainted; twelve coats, hand-painted). 'Good heavens,' Stewart said when he told him how much the ICE equipment had cost to install, 'You can buy a new car for that.' 'I know,' he agreed. 'You could buy a new car for the cost of a year's insurance and a new set of tyres for the thing as well. More money than sense.'

Nothing seemed to work quite perfectly. The car had annoying rattles, the house CD player had an intermittent fault, the camera had to be replaced and most of the records he bought seemed to have scratches on them; his dishwasher kept flooding the kitchen. He found himself becoming short-tempered with people, and traffic jams infuriated him; a sort of pervasive impatience seemed to fill him, and a callousness he could not evade. He gave money to Live Aid all right, but his first thought when he heard of the Band Aid record had been about the revolutionary adage which compared giving to charity under capitalism to putting a Band-aid on a cancer.

The 1985 Festival couldn't even revive his spirts. Andrea was there for part of it, but even when she was with him, in the next seat at a hall or cinema, or in the passenger's seat in the car, or beside him in bed, she wasn't really with him, not all of her. Part of the woman's thoughts were not free, not for him. She still didn't want to talk about it. He heard cir-cuitously that there were complications to Gustave's MS; he tried to bring the subject up but she would not co-operate. It dismayed him there were things they could not talk about. It was his own fault; he never had wanted to talk about Gustave. You couldn't change the rules now.

He had dreams about the dying man in the other city, and sometimes thought he could see him, lying in a hospital bed, surrounded by machines.

Andrea went back to Paris half-way through the Festival. He couldn't face the cultural equivalent of a thousand-bomber raid alone, so he borrowed a friend's Bonneville and took off for Skye.

It rained.

The company went from strength to strength, but he was

starting to lose interest. What, in the end, am I really doing? he asked himself. Just another fucking brick in the wall, just another cog in the machine, if a little better oiled than most. I make money for oil companies and their shareholders and for governments that spend it on weapons that can kill us all a thousand times over instead of just five hundred; I don't even operate at the level of an ordinary decent worker, like my dad did; I'm a fucking *boss*, I *employ*, I have real drive and initiative (or I used to); I actually make it all run just that little better than it might if I wasn't here.

He cut the whisky out again, spent some time drinking only mineral water. He gave up dope almost completely once he realized he wasn't enjoying it any more. The only times he did smoke was when he went over to see Stewart. Then it was like old times.

He started to take coke regularly; it got to be a Monday morning ritual and the natural start to an evening out until one night he was watching the television news and cutting up a couple of generous lines before he went out drinking. There was a follow-up report on the African famine being shown. He looked away from a child with dead eyes and skin like a bat's wing; he looked down to the mirror on the table he was hunkered over and saw his own face looking back at him through the shining granules of white powder. He'd stuffed three hundred pounds' worth of this stuff up his nose the previous week. He threw the razor down. Shit, he said to himself.

A bad year, he told himself. Just another bad year. He started smoking cigarettes. He finally accepted he needed glasses. The bald patch on his head was the size of a bath plug-hole. He seemed to feel the restlessness of youth and the last-change urgency of age at the same time. He was thirty-six years old, but he felt like eighteen going on seventy-two.

In November Andrea told him she was thinking of going to stay in Paris, to look after Gustave. They might have to get married, if his family insisted. She hoped he understood. 'I'm sorry kid,' she said, dull voiced.

'Yeah,' he said. 'Me too.'

Ah shit, I suppose I canny really complain; I've had a good innings and all that stuff, but Jeez I don't feel like giving it all up right now; once a swordsman always a swordsman, I gess. Bloody few get to this age, let me tell ye; I'm exceptional; it's a fact. Suppose I might no have made it without the wee bam on the showlder, but I don't let him know that; he's uppity enough without me swelling his head even more so. Still, he didn't come up with a solution for our little problem though; namely, growing old. Wee bugger wasn't that clever.

Anyway, here I am, sitting up in the bed, watching the closed-circuit TV screens and thinking dirty thoughts, trying to get a hard-on. I'm remembering Angharienne and what we used to do. The stuff we used to get up to! Ye'd hardly credit it, but when you're young you'll try anything. Ah well, you're only young once, like they say (the wee familiar disagrees with this, but he's yet to prove otherwise). I suppose three hunner odd years is no a bad score, but bugger it, I still don't feel ready to die, but it looks like I've got no choyce in the matter. The familiar tried a few things (no choyce for him either; he's stuck with me), but nothing's worked so far and I think the wee bastard's run out of ideas; trust him to bugger things up now, when I could really do with his help. He says he's still got some irons in the fire, whitever that's supposed to mean. Either giving up golf or thinking about torchering somebody. Wee bam's sitting on the table by my bed; all shrivelled up and grey looking, so he is. He hasn't sat on my showlder since we got the flying castle (he calls it a ship, but then he likes confusing things; calls the bedroom the ship's bridge, too). What happened was, we got back to the sorcerer who'd helped me get into the Under-world, and the two of them – the sorcerer and the wee familiar – had a battle; hammer and tongs stuff it was and I had to watch from one corner, frozen stiff from some spell the bloody familiar had cast over us. Eventually the familiar won, but then, just when I might have got rid of the wee bugger, he found he couldn't do what he wanted to, which was take over the body of the sorcerer; seems that wasn't possible; against the rules, sort of thing; I could bring him out of the Underworld, but he couldn't take over a living body; had to stay in an inannimate object. That was him; totally scunnered and bombed-out. Trapped in the wee familiar-body, so he was, and no way out of it. He got all upset and started breaking up the sorcerer's magic celler, and I thought he might start on me for a while, but he didn't, he calmed down after a while like and came back to my showlder and released me from the spell. Explained that we really were stuck with each other for good or ill, and we'd both just have to make the best of it, this time.

Maybe it was for the best, you never know. Doubt I'd have lived this long without him; some of his ideas were pretty smart. His first was to go back to see that young witch I'd been doing the business with no long before I rescued the familiar from Hades. Angharienne, that was her name; the familiar thought me and her might be able to come to some sort of arrangement, he said. She was pretty duebious at first, thought the familiar was trying to pull a fast one, going to try and take over her body or something like that, but they had this dead complicated talk, and they both did some magic, and went into one of them trances (dead bloody boring that was); they woke up all smiles and agreement. Familiar told me that we were going to have a trial troylistic arrangement. OK, I said, as long as there's nothing dirty involved. Anyway, I guess that was how I got be an old swordsman.

'What *are* you doing? Trying to raise the dead already?'

'Shut up you; none of your business.'

'Of course it is my business; what if you have a heart attack or something?'

'Well why no magic up one of them whouris for me then?'

'Certainly not; you'd be sure to pet out then. Just stop that; it's so unseemly in a man of your age. Your brain may still be retarded but your years are advanced.'

'It's my willy and it's my life.'

'It's my life too and you can't play with one if it means playing with the other as well. Have a sense of proportion, man.'

'Och, I'm no really wanting a wank, just to see if I can get it up still. Go on; show us a dirty video, eh?'

'No. Keep watching the screens.'

'What for?'

'Just keep watching. You never know what might happen. All is not yet lost.'

'We should have kept looking for that Fountain of Youth, so we should.'

'Ah . . . you'd probably just have pissed in it.'

'Aw, fuck,' I says, and just lie there with the arms folded feeling sorry for myself.

The flying castle is sitting on this hillside; we landed it here weeks ago after visiting this planit where they claim to be able to make people live for ever. Whatever they did, it didn't work on me and the wee familiar (they said they'd no experience with something like us, a swordsman and a familiar). I wanted to go to one of these fancy cities here on Earth and take some of those magic drugs they've got nowdays; a few weeks of fun burning yourself up like a young man, then you pop your clogs, quick and painless and you've had a lot of fun in the innterim, but the familiar wasn't having it; pilated the castle here to the middle of nowhere, on this cold and windy hillside, and dismissed all the guards and servants and that and even shooed off a couple of the great-grandchildren and gave away half the magic gear that we had – crystal balls that fortel the future, enchanted sub-machine-guns, magic missiles and that sort of stuff. Seemed to want to give everybody the impression we were getting ready to die, but didn't give all the good stuff away; kept the flying castle itself and some bits and pieces like a jacket that flies, the Universal Translator and a few tonnes of invisible platinum in the hold, Even found some new batteries for the old dirk; the 'knife missile' as the familiar calls it. Its batteries ran out about a century ago and it was just a no very sharp knife after that what I kept for sentimental reasons. Wee familiar was dead snooty about it at the time 'Just a cheap copy, I told you so,' it said, but it found new batteries for it just recently and put it in charge of security, guarding the flying castle's door. Fuck knows why; the familiar's getting ecsentric in its old age.

Still canny stop thinking about the wife. Popped her clogs nearly half a century ago, but I can still see her bonny face like she'd just croaked yesterday. Turned out she wasn't as young as she looked; never did find out how old she was, but the familiar thinks she was a thousand or so at least. She wouldn't grow old slowly, like even witches are meant to; did the magic on herself so that she stayed looking just out of her teens until right to the end; burned herself out staying young; can't say I blamed her but it catches up on ye in the end. She became a statue; a wee dark wooden carving, all hard and dark and old-looking; left instructions she was to be planted in this forest near where she was born, where she's become a wee tree, no long since. The familiar says the tree will probably go from being wee and shrivelled to big and tall and younger, and then shrink like it's going back in time until it becomes a sede, and after that even it doesn't know what'll happen. It seems sad when it tells me all this, because it knows that when I die – when we both die, because it can't live without me – it'll just disinntigrate into dust and that'll be that; no even an existence in the Underworld for it after that. Tough titty; I'll probably no even be allowed *in* to hell after what happened the last time I was there; the wee familiar still chuckles when we talk about the old days and me rescuing him; seems they had to alter the whole rejeem down there after that bloke Charon turned into stone; couple of characters called Virgil and Danty took over temperarily and they're still there. Fuck knows what sort of receptcion I'll get when I turn up at the perilly gates or whatever it is they've got now. Probably let me in all right but have something really nasty arranged, I'll bet. Ye can see why I'm no so keen on kicking the bucket, anyway.

'Ah-ha.'

'Ah-ha *whit*?'

'I thought you were supposed to be watching the screens.'

'I am, I am, I just – aw *wait* a minute! Who the fuck's that?'

'No one who wishes us well, that's for sure.'

'Aw shite!' Coming down the hillside there's this muscley punter with blond hair and a fucking great sword. Bloody great broad shoulders and sort of metal straps all over his body, big boots and a wee sort of loin cloth thing. Some sort of helmet on his head with a wolve's head on it, snarling like. I sit up in bed, feeling scared already; I'm dead stiff these

253

days (all ecsept the bit I'd like to be), and what with the roomatism and that, and the way my hand shakes nowdays, and needing glasses and so on, I really don't fancy squaring up to some young fit warrior with a dirty great sword. 'Whit happened to the fucking total exclusion zone then, eh? I thought people were meant to fall asleep if they tried to come up to the flying castle!'

'Hmm,' the familiar says, 'must be that helmet he's wearing; probably contains some neuroscreening device. Let's see if the laser can deal with the fellow.'

The big berr with the muscles marches on down the slope, staring up at the castle, big blond brows knitted together, muscles rippling, the big muckle sword swinging. Suddenly he looks surprised, and starts swinging the sword even faster, so it's a blur all around him; next thing I know there's a flash and the screen goes dead. 'Aw naw! Whit now?' I'm trying to get out of bed, but my old muscles seem to have turned to jeely or something, and I'm sweating like a pig. The screen comes alive again, showing the door of the castle from the inside.

'Hmm,' the wee familiar says again, as though it's dead impressed or something. 'Not bad. Some sort of limited prescience involved there, I'll warrant; he *knew* the laser was about to fire on him. Probably only a few seconds into the future, but enough; he's going to be difficult to stop. Nice trick with the laser too; probably some sort of mirrorfield in the sword. Reflecting the light back into the cameras might have been coincidence, but if not then it was *very* cheeky. Quite an adversary, what?'

'I canny move! Do something! Fuck being a wonderful bloody adversary; get us away from that bastard! Get the castle moving!'

'Not enough time, I'm afraid,' the wee familiar says, calm as ye like. 'Let's see if the knife missile can stop him.'

'Fuckin marvellous! Is that all we've got between us and him?'

'I'm afraid so. That and a couple of not very intelligent or strong airlocks.'

'Is that *it*? You stupid *bastard*; why the fuck did you let all the guards go, and the—'

'Error of judgement, I suppose, old son,' the wee familiar says, and yawns. He hops on to my shoulder and we both watch the inside of the castle door. The tip of a sword appears through the metal and cuts a circle out of it; it falls to the floor and the big blond bastard steps through. 'Fields,' the familiar says quietly, nodding by my ear. 'That airlock door had monofilament re-inforcing; cutting it cold like that would need some pretty neat blade-fields. Quite some weapon the lad's equipped himself with . . . though it could be the other round, of course.'

'Where's that wee bastard of a dirk?' I'm shouting now; bloody petrified, ready to shite the bed so I am. The big blond bastard is tramping down the castle hallway, looking dead wary but all determined like, and swinging the sword like he means business. He looks to one side and glowers.

The wee dirk comes at him, but far too slow; almost like it was hesitating. Blondy keeps glowering at it. The dirk stops in mid air, then just falls to the floor and rolls away into a corner. 'Aw naw!' I'm shouting.

'Told you it was a cheap copy; they had to equip it with an IFF circuit. Probably our chum's sword – or that helmet – fed it a fake Friend signal. The real things are free agents, smart enough to make up their own minds . . . which is why they're quite useless for the likes of you or me, of course.'

'Stop talkin like a fuckin arms salesman and *dae something*!' I scream at the wee familiar, but it just shrugs its wee grey shoulders and sighs.

'Too late, old son, I'm afraid.'

'*You're* afraid!' I tell at it, shouting into its face. 'You're no the one they're waiting fur doon in Hades pal; three hunner years they've had to think up somethin really sore and nasty fur me; three hunner fuckin years!'

'Oh calm down man; can't you face death with some dignity?'

'Bugger dignity! Ah want tae *live*!'

'Hmm. Good,' the wee familiar says, as the big blond bastard disappears from the screen. There's a banging noise somewhere outside the door of the bedroom, and the floor shakes. 'Aw naw!' I wet the bed; just like that; canny stop myself. 'Mammy, Daddy!'

The door bursts open. The big blond bastard stands there, filling the doorway. He's even bigger than he looked on the screen. Fucking sord must be nearly as long as I am. I cringe doon in the bed, whole body shaking. The warrior has to duck as he comes through the door, to avoid banging the wolf-head helmet on the roof. 'Wh-wh-what's yer problem, big filla?' I says.

'Now problem moy son,' the bloke says, and comes up to the bed. Bloody man-mountain. He raises the sord up over me.

'Aw geeze a brek pal, *please*; ye can have anythin ye—'

Wallip.

Shock like nothing I've ever felt in my life before, like God slappin ye, or a billion volts going through ye. Stars and light and dizzyness. I can see that sword falling towards me, flashing in the light, see the look in the big bastardin warrior's face, and hear a wee noise at my ear; a wee funny noise, like a chuckle; I'd swear . . . like a chuckle, honest.

The auld punter in the bed wiz deid; skul split open like a rottin coconut. The wee thing on his shoder vanishit in a puf aw smoake. Ah felt ded dizy an ah saw stars and stuff. Ahd sware the giy in the bed lookd difrent from when adh cum intae the room; his herr hadnae bean that sorta blond-grey culur, had it?

'Well . . . heck and hot-dickety, damn transference worked. How're you feeling, bonehead?' It wiz the helmet tolkin. Ah sat doon on the bed an took it of to look at the woolfs heid. 'Ahm feelin a bit funy,' ah toald it. 'Not yourself,' it sed, and the wee woolfs heid noddit at me, an grind. 'Hardly surprising. You'll come to; my vast intellect has survived the transcription perfectly whole and intact, so I can't imagine that such an enormous library of a mind having been faithfully transmitted there is even the remotest possibility that your pamphlet of a consciousness hasn't come through undamaged. Anyway, back to business; the ship's circuits have finally woken up to the fact that there's an interloper aboard; they won't accept that you're the rightful owner, and I still need a little more time to re-arrange the telepathic circuits in this ridiculous helmet, so let's depart before the ship scuttles itself; that involves a thermo-nuclear explosion as I recall, which I doubt even I or that wonderful sword you're holding can protect you from at quite such close range, so, time to go.'

'Fare enuph pal,' ah sez, an gets up, puttin the helmet bak on. Felt grate apart from ma heid; wiz like ahd had a dream but ahd just woke up, ye ken. Sumthin abowt bein an old man; like the wan in the bed. Nevir mynde. Wurk it oot layter. Bettir get oot the cassil if the woolfs heid sez so. Ah liftit up ma sord and ran fur the ootside door. Nae fukin tresshir agen, but ye canny win them aw. No tae wury; plenty mair cassils an majishins an auld barbareyins an whitevir . . .

Whit a life, eh? This is the gemm!

Quaternary

'You know I had that damn record for three years before I realized Fay Fife's name was a pun; you know; "Where are you from?" "Ah'm fay Fife," ' he told Stewart, shaking his head.

'Aye,' Stewart said, 'Ah ken.'

'God I'm so stupid sometimes,' he breathed, gazing sadly at his can of Export.

'Aye,' Stewart nodded. 'Ah ken,' he said, and rose to turn the album over.

He looked out through the window to the view of the town and the distant bare trees of the glen. His watch said 2:16. It was getting dark already. He supposed they were near the solstice now. He drank some more.

He'd had five or six cans, and it looked like he'd have to stay over with Stewart, or get a train back to Edinburgh. A train, he thought. He hadn't been on one for years. It would be good to take a train from Dunfermline and go over the old bridge; he could throw out a coin and wish that Gustave would kill himself, or that Andrea would find herself pregnant and want to bring her child up in Scotland, or—

Cut it out, you idiot, he told himself. Stewart sat down again. They had talked about politics. They'd agreed if they were sincere about what they said they believed in they'd be out in Nicaragua, fighting for the Sandinistas. They'd talked about old times, old music, old friends – but never about her. They'd talked about Star Wars – SDI – which Britain had just signed up for. It wasn't that distant a subject for them; they both knew people at the university who were working on optical computer circuits; the Pentagon was interested.

They'd talked about the new Koestler chair of parapsychology at the university, and about a programme they'd both seen on television a few weeks earlier, on lucid dreaming; and also about the hypotheses of causative formation (he said sure it was interesting, but he could remember when Von Daniken's theories had been 'interesting').

They'd talked about a story mentioned on television and in the press that week, about an *émigré* Russian engineer living in France who'd crashed his car in England; a lot of money had been found in the car and he was under suspicion of having committed a crime in France. He had apparently gone into a coma, but the doctors seemed to think he was faking. Devious bastards us engineers, he told Stewart.

They had talked, in fact, about almost everything except what he really wanted to talk about. Stewart had tried to bring the subject up, but each time he had found himself sliding away from it; the programme on lucid dreaming had come up because it was the last thing he had had an argument with Andrea about; the causative formation hypothesis because it was probably the next thing they'd argue about. Stewart hadn't pressed him on the subject of Andrea and Gustave. Maybe he just needed to talk, about anything.

'How're the kids anyway?' he asked.

Stewart had something to eat and asked him if he wanted anything, but he didn't feel hungry. They had another joint, he had another can; they talked. The afternoon darkened. Stewart felt tired after a while and said he'd have a snooze. He'd set the alarm and be up to make the tea later. They could head out for a pint after they'd eaten something.

He listened to some old Jefferson Airplane on the headphones, but the record was scratched. He looked through his friend's collection of books, drinking from the can and finishing off the last joint. Finally he went and stood by the window, looking out across the slates to the park, the glen, the ruined palace and the abbey.

The light was slowly going from the half-clouded sky. Streetlights were on, and the roads were filled with parked or slowly moving cars; doubtless full of Christmas shoppers. Light-sapped skies hung over the glen. He wondered what this place looked like when the palace was still a place for kings.

And the Kingdom of Fife. A small place now, but big enough then. Rome had been small too, to start with, and it hadn't stopped her; what would the world have been like if some part of Scotland – before such a state existed – had blossomed the way Rome did . . . No, there wasn't the background, the legacy of history here at that time. Athens, Rome, Alexandria; they had libraries when all we had were hill forts; not savages, but not civilized either. By the time we were ready to play our part it was already too late; we were always too soon or too late, and the best things we've done have been for other people.

Well, sentimental Scottishism, he guessed. What about class consciousness rather than nationalism? Well, indeed.

How could she do it? Never mind that this was her home, that this was where her mother lived, her earliest friends, where she had so many of her earliest memories formed, and her character; how could she leave what she had now? Forget about him; he would willingly leave himself out of the equation . . . but she had so much, to do and to be . . . How could she do it?

Self-sacrifice, the woman behind the man, looking after him, putting herself second; it went against all she believed in.

He still hadn't been able to talk to her properly about it. His heart beat faster; he put the can down, thinking. He didn't really know what it was he wanted to say, only that he wanted to talk to her, to hold her, to just be with her and tell her everything he felt for her. He ought to tell her all he'd ever felt, about Gustave, about her, about himself. He should be totally honest with her, so that at least she would know exactly what he felt, be under no illusions about him. It was important, damn it.

He finished the can, put the roach into it, then folded the red tin neatly. A little beer dribbled on to his hand from the folded corner of aluminium. He wiped his hands. I ought to tell her. I ought to talk to her now. What was she doing this evening? They were at home, weren't they? Yes, they both are; something I was invited to, but I wanted to see Stewart. I'll call her. He went to the phone.

Engaged. Probably another hour-long call to Gustave; even when she was here she still seemed to spend half her time with him. He put the phone down and paced the room, his heart thumping, his hands sweating. He needed a pee; he went to the bathroom, washed his hands afterwards, gargled with some mouthwash. He felt all right. He didn't even feel stoned or drunk. He tried the phone again; same signal. He stood at the window. The Jag was visible, if he stood close to the glass and looked right down. A white, curved ghost on the dark street. He looked at his watch again. He felt fine; perfectly straight. Just ready for a drive.

Why not? he thought. Take the albino Jaguar off into the gloaming; head for the motorway and blast over the road bridge with the sounds cranked up high as they'll go; an arrogant grin and a blast of aural pain for whatever poor bastard takes your toll . . . shee-it; very *Fear and Loathing*, very Hunter S. Thompsonish. Belay that, laddy; damn book always did make you drive just that little bit faster afterwards. Your own fault for listening to *White Rabbit* a few minutes ago; that's what's done it. No, forget about driving; you've had too many.

Aw hell; everybody does it at this time of year. Damn it, I drive better drunk than most people do sober. Just take it easy; you can make it. Isn't as though you don't know the road, after all. Drive real careful in the town, just in case some kid runs out in front of you and your reactions are affected, then nice and easy on the motorway; legal limit or even less, none of this blowing away the local boy-racer in his Capri or giving nasty surprises to glassy-eyed BMW drivers; just don't get intimidated, just maintain concentration, don't think about Red Sharks or White Whales, testing the suspension over concrete walls or controlled drifts round an entire clover leaf. Just take it easy, listen to the sounds. Auntie Joanie maybe. Something soothing; not soporific, but steady, not *too* exciting, not the sort of the thing the right foot just hears and floors on; nothing like that . . .

He tried the phone one last time. He went through to see Stewart; he was sleeping quietly, and rolled over when he looked in, away from the hall light's glow. He wrote him a note and left it by the alarm clock. He took up his old biking jacket and the monogrammed scarf and let himself out of the flat.

Getting out of town took a while. There had been a shower; the streets were wet. He was playing *Steeltown* by Big Country as he edged the Jaguar through the traffic; it seemed appropriate, in Carnegie's birthplace. He still felt fine. He knew he ought not to be driving, and he dreaded to think what he'd register on a breathalyser, but one – undrunk – part of him was watching and evaluating his driving; and he'd do, he'd get by, providing his concentration didn't slip and he wasn't unlucky. He wouldn't do it again, he told himself as he at last found a clear stretch of road, heading for the motorway. Just this time, because it is important after all.

And I'll be very careful.

It was dual carriageway here; he let the car leap forward, grinning as his back pressed into the seat. 'Oh I just love to hear that engine snarl,' he murmured to himself. He ejected the Big Country tape from the Nakamichi, frowning at himself for exceeding the speed limit. He let the car's nose drop again, slowed.

Something not too raucous and adrenalin-encouraging for the approach and traverse of the great grey bridge. *Bridge Over Troubled Water?* he thought to himself, grinning. Haven't had that in the car for yonks, Jimmy. He had Lone Judgement, and Los Lobos' *How Will the Wolf Survive?* on either side of the one tape, he picked it up, glanced at it as he approached the motorway itself. No, he wanted the Texican boys right now, and he didn't want to wait for it to spool back. Just have to be the Pogues then. *Rum Sodomy and the Lash;* fuck nice steady driving tunes. Nothing wrong with a bit of raucousness. Keeps you awake better. Just don't try to keep pace with the music all the time. There we go . . .

He joined the M90, heading south. The sky was dark blue above the patchy clouds. A very mild evening; hardly even cool. The road was still wet. He sang along to the Pogues and tried not to go too fast. He felt thirsty; there was usually a can of coke or Irn Bru in the door pocket, but he'd forgotten to replace the last one. He was forgetting too much these days. He put his main lights on after a few people flashed him.

The motorway crested a hill between Inverkeithing and Rosyth, and he could see the road bridge's aircraft lights;

sudden white flashes on the spires of the two great towers. Shame, really; he'd preferred the old red lights. He pulled over into the nearside lane to let a Sierra past, and watched the tail-lights disappear, thinking, You wouldn't get away with that normally, chum. He settled back in the seat, his fingers on the small steering wheel beating in time to the music. The road headed for a stepped cutting through the rocks which formed the small peninsula; the sign for North Queensferry flashed by. He might have gone down there, to stand under the rail bridge again, but there was no point in making this journey any longer than it had to be; that would be tempting fate, or irony at least.

What am I doing this for? he thought. Will this really make any difference? I *hate* people who drunk-drive; why the hell am I doing it? He thought about heading back, taking the road down to North Queensferry after all. There was a station there; he could park, take the train (in either direction) . . . but he'd passed the last turn-off before the bridge. The hell with it. Maybe he'd stop on the far side, at Dalmeny; park there rather than risk this expensive paint job in the pre-Christmas Edinburgh rush. Come back for the damn thing in the morning and remember to set all the alarms.

The road cleared the cutting through the hills. He could see South Queensferry, the marina at Port Edgar, the VAT 69 sign of the distillery there, the lights of Hewlett Packard's factory; and the rail bridge, dark in the evening's last sky-reflected light. Behind it, more lights; the Hound Point oil terminal they'd had a sub-contract on, and, further away, the lights of Leith. The old rail bridge's hollow metal bones looked the colour of dried blood.

You fucking beauty, he thought. What a gorgeous great device you are. So delicate from this distance, so massive and strong close-up. Elegance and grace; perfect form. A quality bridge; granite piers, the best ship-plate steel, and a never-ending paint job . . .

He glanced back at the roadway of the bridge as it rose slowly to its gentle, suspended summit. The surface was a little damp, but nothing to worry about. No problems. He wasn't going all that fast anyway, staying in the nearside lane, looking over at the rail bridge downstream. A light winked at the far end of the island under the rail bridge's middle section.

One day, though, even you'll be gone. Nothing lasts. Maybe that's what I want to tell her. Maybe I want to say, No, of course I don't mind; you must go. I can't grudge the man that; you'd have done the same for me and I would for you. Just a pity, that's all. Go; we'll all survive. Maybe some good—

He was aware of the truck in front pulling out suddenly. He looked round to see a car in front of him. It was stopped, abandoned in the nearside lane. He sucked his breath in, stamped on the brakes, tried to swerve; but it was too late.

There was an instant when his foot was jammed down as hard as it would go on the brake, and when he'd pulled the wheel over as far as it would go in one twist, and he knew there was nothing else he could do. He would never know how long that instant was, only that he saw the car in front was an MG, and that there was nobody in it – a ripple of relief on a tsunami of fear – and that he was going to hit it, hard. He caught a glimpse of the number plate; VS something. Wasn't that a west coast number? The octagonal MG sign on the boot of the broken-down car floated closer to the Jaguar's mascotless snout as it dipped, dug in and started to skid all at once. He tried to go limp, to relax and just go with it, but with his foot jamming the brake to the floor that wasn't possible. He thought, You foo—

The customized white Jaguar, registration number 233 FS, smashed into the rear of the MG. The man driving the Jaguar was thrown forward and up as it somersaulted. The seat belt held but the small steering wheel came pistoning up to meet his chest like a circular sledgehammer.

Low rolling hills under a dark sky; the undersurface of the lowering, ruddy clouds seems to mirror the gentle contours of the land below. The air is thick and heavy; it smells of blood.

265

It is soggy underfoot, but not with water. Whatever great battle was fought here, over these hills that seem to stretch for ever, it drenched the land with blood. There are bodies everywhere, of every animal and every colour and race of human, and many other besides. I find the small dark man eventually, attending the corpses.

He is dressed in rags; we last met in . . . Mocca? (Occam? Something like that), when he was beating the waves with his iron flail. Now it is bodies. Dead bodies; a hundred lashes each, if there's anything left to lash. I watch him for a while.

He is calm, methodical, beating each body exactly one hundred times, before proceeding to the next one. He shows no preference concerning species, sex, size or colour; he beats each with the same determined vigour; on the back if possible, but otherwise just as they lie. Only if they are fully armoured does he touch them, bending stiffly to pull back a visor or disconnect a chest-strap.

'Hello,' he says. I stand some distance away, in case he is under orders to whip everybody on the field, regardless.

'Remember me?' I ask him. He strokes his bloody lash.

'Can't say I do,' he says. I tell him about the city by the sea. He shakes his head. 'No, not me,' he says. He digs into his filthy robes for a moment, then comes out with a small rectangle of card. He wipes it with one strip of his rags, then holds it out. I step forward warily. 'Take it,' he nods. 'I was told to give it to you. Here.' He leans forward. I take the card, step back. It is a playing card; the three of diamonds.

'What's this for?' I ask him. He just shrugs, wipes his flail-hand on one tattered sleeve.

'Don't know.'

'Who gave it to you? How did they know—'

'Is it really necessary to ask all these questions?' he says, shaking his head. I am shamed.

'I suppose not.' I hold up the playing card. 'Thanks.'

'You're welcome,' he says. I had forgotten how soft his voice was. I turn to go, then look back at him.

'Just one more thing.' I nod at the bodies littering the ground like fallen leaves. 'What happened here? What happened to all these people?'

He shrugs. 'They didn't listen to their dreams,' he says, then turns back to his task.

I set off again, for the distant line of light which fills the horizon like a streak of white gold.

I left the city in the dried sea basin and walked the railway track away from it, heading in the same direction as the Field Marshal's train before it was attacked. There was no pursuit, but I heard the sound of distant gunfire coming from the city as I walked.

The landscape changed gradually to become less harsh. I found water and, after a while, fruit on trees. The climate grew less bleak. I saw people sometimes, travelling alone like me, or in groups. I stayed away from them, and they avoided me. Once I found I could walk without danger, and find food and water, the dreams came every night.

It was always the same nameless man and the same city. The dreams came and went, repeating and repeating. I saw so much, but nothing clearly. Twice I think I almost had the man's name. I started to believe that my dreams were the genuine reality, and woke each morning beneath a tree or in the lee of some rocks, fully expecting to wake into another existence, a different life; just a nice clean hospital bed would be a start . . . but no. I was always here, on temperate downlands that eventually became a battlefield, and where I have just met the man with the flail. Still, there is light at the end of the horizon.

I head for that light. It looks like the edge of these dank clouds; a long lidded eye of gold. At the top of a hill I look back on the small, misshapen man. He is still there, whipping at some fallen warrior. Perhaps I ought to have lain down and let him lash me; could death be the only way I might awake from this terrible, enchanted sleep?

That would require faith. I do not believe in faith. I believe it exists but I do not believe it works. I don't know what the rules are here; I can't risk throwing everything away on a long shot.

I come to the place where the clouds end and the dark downs give way to a low cliff. Beyond, there is sand.

An unnatural place, I think, looking up at the edge of dark cloud. It is too distinct, too uniform, the boundary between the shadowy downs with their fallen armies of dead and the golden waste of sand too precisely defined. A hot breath from off the sand blows away the stale, thick smells of the battle-field. I have a bottle of water, and some fruit. My waiter's jacket is thin, the Field Marshal's old coat dirty. I still have the handkerchief, like a favour.

I jump from the last hill over the hot sand, down into the golden slope, ploughing and sliding towards the floor of the desert. The air is hot and dry, devoid of the corrupting odours of the rolling battlefield behind me, but full of another sort of death; its promise in the very dryness of that air moving above a place where there is no water, no food, no shade.

I start walking.

Once I thought I was dying. I had walked and crawled, finding no shade. Finally I fell down the slip face of a dune and knew I could not rise from there without water, without liquid, without something. The sun was a white hole in the sky so blue it had no colour. I waited for clouds to form, but none came. Eventually dark, wide-winged birds appeared. They started to wheel above me, riding an unseen thermal; waiting.

I watched them, through half-glued eyes. The birds flew in a great spiral over the desert, as though there was some immense, invisible bolt suspended over me, and they were just scraps of black silk stuck to its spiralled plane, moving slowly as that vast column turned.

Then I see another man appear at the top of the dune. He is tall and muscular and dressed in some savage's light armour; his golden arms and legs are bare. He carries a huge sword, and a decorated helmet, which he holds in the crook of one arm. He looks transparent and insubstantial, for all his bulk. I can see through his body: perhaps he is a ghost. The sword glitters in the sunlight, but dully. He sways as he stands there, not seeing me. He puts one hand shakily to his brow, then seems to talk to the helmet he holds. He half-walks, half-staggers down the slip face towards me, his booted feet and thickly muscled legs plunging through the baking sand. Still he does not appear to notice me. His hair is bleached by the sun; peeling skin covers his face and arms and legs. The sword drags in the sand behind him. He stops at my feet, staring into the distance, swaying. Has he come to kill me with that great sword? At least it might be quick.

He stands, still swaying, eyes fixed on the hazy distance. I would swear he is standing too close to me, too close to my feet; as though his own feet were somehow inside mine. I lie, waiting. He stands above, struggling to keep on his feet, one arm going out suddenly as he tries to balance himself. The helmet in the crook of his arm falls to the sand. The helmet's decoration, a wolf's head, cries out.

The warrior's eyes turn up into his head, going white. He crumples, falling towards me. I close my eyes, ready to be crushed.

I feel nothing. I hear nothing, either; he does not fall on to the sand beside me, and when I open my eyes there is no trace of him or the helmet he dropped. I stare into the sky again, at the entwined double-spiral of circling birds that are death.

I used the last of my strength to peel open my coat and jacket and bare my chest to the invisible, turning bolt in the sky. I lay, spreadeagled, for some time; two of the birds landed near me. I did not stir.

One of them swiped at my hand with its hooked beak, then jumped back. I lay still, waiting.

When they came for my eyes I took them by their necks. Their blood was thick and salty, but like the taste of life to me.

I see the bridge. At first I am certain it is a hallucination. Then I believe it might be a mirage, something which looks like the bridge reflected in the air and – to my parched, obsessed eyes – taking on its form. I walk closer, through the heat and the slopes of clinging, flowing grains. I have the handkerchief over my head, shading me. The bridge shimmers in the distance, a long rough line of summits.

I come slowly closer to it throughout the day, resting only for a short while when the sun is at its height. Sometimes I climb to the tops of the dunes, to reassure myself it is there. I am within a couple of miles before my confused eyes admit the truth to me; the bridge is in ruins.

The main sections are largely intact, though damaged, but the linking sections, those spans, those little bridges within bridges, they have collapsed or been destroyed, and large parts of the section extremities have disappeared along with them. The bridge looks less like a succession of laterally stretched hexagons and more like a line of isolated octagons. Its feet still stand, its bones still rise, but its linking arms, its connections – they have gone.

I see no movement, no sudden glints of light. The wind sighs sand over the edges of dunes, but no sound comes from the tall ochre skeleton of the bridge. It stands, blanched and gaunt and jagged in the sand, slow golden waves lapping at its granite plinths and lower buildings.

I enter its shadow at last, gratefully. The burning wind moans between the towering girders. I find a staircase, start to climb. It is hot and I am thirsty again.

I recognize this. I know where I am.

Everywhere is deserted. I see no skeletons but I find no survivors. The train deck holds a few old carriages and locomotives, rusted to the rails they stand upon; finally part of the bridge. Sand has blown up even here, shading yellow-gold into the edges of the rails and points.

My old haunt, indeed. I find Dissy Pitton's. It is a fallen place; the ropes which used to attach tables and chairs to ceiling have mostly been cut; the couches and seats and tables lie sprawled over the dusty floor like bodies from long ago. A few hang by one edge or corner; cripples among the dead. I walk to the Sea View Lounge.

I sat here once with Brooke. Right here. We looked out and he complained about the barrage balloons; then the planes flew past. The desert is bright under the high sun.

Dr Joyce's office; not his. I do not recognize any of this furniture, but then he was always moving. The blinds, blowing in and out gently behind the broken windows, look the same.

A long walk takes me to the Arrols' abandoned summer apartment. It is half-submerged in the sand. The door is open. Only the tops of the still sheet-covered pieces of furniture are visible. The fire is buried beneath the waves of sand; so is the bed.

I climb slowly back to the train deck and stand, looking out over the shimmering sands which surround the bridge. An empty bottle lies at my feet. I take it by the neck and throw it from the train deck. It curves, end over end, glinting in the sunlight, towards the sand.

A wind comes up later, screaming through the bridge; scouring me, flailing me. I hug myself in a corner, watching the edge of the wind strip paint from the bridge like some endless rasping tongue. 'I give in,' I tell it.

The sand seems to fill my brain. My skull feels like the bottom of an hourglass.

'I give in. I don't know. Thing or place; you tell me.' I think this is my own voice. The wind blows harder. I cannot hear myself speak, but I know what I am trying to say. I am suddenly certain that death has a sound; a word which anybody may utter which will cause and be their death. I am trying to think of this word when something grates and swivels in the distance, and hands lift me away from this place.

Let's get one thing absolutely straight: it's all a dream. Either way, whatever. We both know that.

I have a choice, however.

I am in a long, hollow, echoing place, lying in bed. There are machines around me, drips into me. People come and look at me, occasionally. The ceiling sometimes looks like white

271

plaster, sometimes like grey metal, sometimes like red brick sometimes like riveted sheets of steel painted the colour of blood. Finally, I realize where I am; inside the bridge, within its hollow metal bones.

Fluid seeps into me through my nose and out again via a catheter. I feel more like a plant than an animal, a mammal, an ape, a human. Part of the machine. All the processes have slowed. I have to find a way back; blow the tanks, pull the cord; floor the throttle?

Some of these people look familiar.

Dr Joyce is here. He wears a white coat and he makes notes on a clipboard. I'm sure I saw Abberlaine Arrol, just fleetingly, a while ago . . . but she was dressed in the uniform of a nurse.

This place is long and echoing. Sometimes I smell iron and rust, and paint and medicines. They took away the card I was given, and the scarf . . . I mean the handkerchief.

Ah, coming round, are we? Dr Joyce smiles at me. I look up at him, try to speak: Who am I? Where am I? What is happening to me?

We have a new treatment, the doctor says to me, as though to a particularly dim child. Would you like us to try it? Would you? It might make you better. Sign this.

Gimme gimme. In blood if you like. Give you my soul if I thought I had one but never mind. How about a tranche on a few billion neurons? Nicely run-in brain here doc; one careful owner (ahem); didn't even take it to church on Sundays . . .

Bastards; it's a machine.

I have to tell everything I can remember to a machine which looks like a metal suitcase on a spindly trolley.

It takes a while.

Just me and the machine now. There was a sallow-faced lad in here for a while, and the nurse, and even the dear good old doctor, but they've gone now. Only me and the machine left. It starts to speak. 'Well,' it says –

272

Look, anybody can make a mistake. Isn't this meant to be the season of – naa, forget it. OK already; I was wrong; mea fuckin' culpa; Joe Contrite here. You want blood?

'Well,' it says, 'your dreams were right in the end. Those last ones, after you left here. That really is you.'

'I don't believe you,' I tell it.

'You will.'

'Why?'

'Because I'm a machine, and you trust machines, you understand them and they don't frighten you; they impress you. You feel differently about people.'

I think about this, then try another question: Where am I? The machine says, 'Your real self, your physical body, is now in the Neurosurgical Unit at the Southern General Hospital, Glasgow. You were moved from the Royal Infirmary in Edinburgh . . . some time ago.' The machine seems uncertain.

'You don't know?' I ask it.

'*You* don't know,' it tells me. 'They moved you; that's all we both know. Might have been three months ago, might have been five or even six. Whenever; in your dream it was about two-thirds of the way through. The treatments and drugs they've been trying out on you have scrambled your sense of time.'

'Do you – do I – have any idea what date it is? How long have I been under?'

'That's a little easier; seven months. The last time Andrea Cramond visited you she mentioned something about it being her birthday in a week and if you were to wake up it would be the best—'

'OK,' I tell the machine. 'That makes it early July; her birthday's on the 10th.'

'Well then.'

'Hmm. And I suppose you don't know my *name*, do you?'

'Correct.'

I say nothing for a while.

'So,' the machines says, 'you going to wake up then?'

'I don't know. I'm not sure what the alternatives are;

what's the choice?'

'Stay under or surface,' the machine says. 'Simple as that.'

'But how do I surface? I was trying to do that on the way here, before I reached the desert. I tried to wake up into—'

'I know. I'm afraid I can't help you with that one. I don't know how you do it, I just know you can if you want to.'

'Hell, I don't know; *do* I want to?'

'Your idea', the machine points out, 'is as good as mine.'

I don't know what they're pumping into me, but everything's hazy at the moment. The machine seems real, when it's here, but the people don't. It's as though there's a fog inside my eyes, as though the fluid in them has darkened, as though they have finally silted up. My other senses are similarly affected; everything I hear sounds mushy, distorted. Nothing smells or tastes of anything very much. I think even my thoughts are slowing down.

I lie, a shallow man breathing shallowly and trying to think deeply.

After a while, nothing. No people, no machine, no sight or sound or taste or smell or touch, no awareness of my own body. Greyness everywhere. Only memories.

I fall asleep.

I wake up in a small room with one door; there is a screen set in one wall. The room is cubical, finished in grey, windowless. I am sitting in a large leather armchair. The chair looks familiar; there is one like it in the house in Leith, in the study. There should be a tiny burn on the right arm where a bit of dope fell out of . . . no; not there. Must be a new chair. I look at my hands. A little scar tissue on the right one. I'm wearing Mephisto shoes, Lee jeans, a checked shirt. I have no beard. I feel thinner than I remember.

I get up and look round the room. Blank screen; no controls. Concealed lighting round the top of the walls. Everything in grey concrete; feels warm. No seams in the concrete; not a bad pouring job at all; I wonder vaguely who the contractors were. The door is ordinary, made of wood. I open it.

There is a similar room on the other side of the door. It has no screen and no armchair; just a bed. It is a hospital bed, empty; crisp white sheets and a single grey blanket pulled back at one corner, as though in invitation.

A noise comes from the room I've just left.

If I go through there, I think, and find an old guy who looks like me, I'm going to get out of there somehow and find that machine and *complain*.

I go through to the room with the armchair. I do not find Keir Dullea in make-up. The room is empty but the screen has come to life. I sit down in the armchair and watch.

It's the man in the bed again. Only this time everything's in colour; I can see him better. He is lying on his front, for a change, in a different bed in a different room. A small ward, in fact, with three other beds, two of them occupied by older men with bandaged heads. There are screens round my man's bed but I am above him, looking down. His bald spot is quite visible. I reach up to my own head; a bald patch. Sure enough, the hairs on my arms are not black but muddy brown. Shit.

It all looks more cosy than I remember. There are yellow flowers in a vase on the small bedside cabinet. There's no chart hanging on the bottom of the bed; maybe they don't do that these days. There's a plastic bracelet on the man's wrist. I can't read what it says.

Noises in the distance; people talking, a little female laughter, bottles or maybe something metallic clinking, and what might be a set of wheels squeaking on a floor. Two nurses appear; they go inside the screens and turn the man over. They plump up his pillows and sit him up a little, chatting to each other most of the time. Infuriatingly, I can't hear what they're saying.

The nurses leave. People start to drift into the picture, approaching the other two occupied beds; ordinary people; a young couple for one elderly man, an old woman talking quietly to the other old chap. Nobody for my man yet.

Doesn't look as though he cares.

Then Andrea Cramond appears. She looks odd from this raised vantage point, but it's her all right. She wears a white trouser suit of raw silk, red high heels, red silk blouse. She puts the jacket – didn't I buy that for her in Jenner's last year? – down at the foot of the bed, then she goes to the man, and bends to kiss him, on the forehead, then lightly on the lips; her hand stays a little while, stroking hair back from his brow. She sits in a chair on one side of the bed, legs crossed at the knee, elbow on thigh, chin in hand. She stares at the man. I stare at her.

A few more lines on that calm but troubled face, just starting; maybe. Those little crinkles under her eyes are still there, but there are slight shadows underneath them now. Her hair is longer than I recall. I cannot see her eyes properly, but those cheekbones, that elegant nose, the wide dark eyebrows, the strong jaw and soft mouth . . . those I can see.

She leans forward and takes his hand, still gazing at him. Why is she here? Why isn't she in Paris?

Scuse me darlin'; you come here oftin?

(Is this now? Is this in the past?)

After a little while, still holding his hand and staring at his white, expressionless face, she slowly lowers her head to the white, turned-over sheet near the man's hand, and buries her face in its starched whiteness. Her shoulders shake; once, twice.

The screen in here goes dark, and then the lights go off. The lights in the room next door with the bed in it stay on.

My subconscious, I suspect, is trying to tell me something. Subtlety never was its strong suit. I sigh, put my hands on the arms of the leather chair, and slowly rise.

I dump my clothes on the floor by the bed. There is a short, rear-fastening cotton night-gown laid out on the pillow. I put it on, climb into bed, fall asleep.

Coda

Fool! Idiot! What the hell do you think you're doing? You were happy there! Think of the control, the fun, the possibilities! And what are you going back to? Probably chucked out of the partnership, certain to be tried for drunk driving (no more flash cars for *you* for a while, lad), getting older and less happy all the time; losing her to another illness, another bedside. You always did what she wanted; she used you, not the other way round; it was role-reversal all right, and you got screwed. She turned you down don't forget; she rejected you; she went on rejecting you and if you show signs of recovery she'll be off again. Don't *do* it, you idiot!'

What else can I do? For one thing they might just turn me off; no doubt my brain shows signs of life, so they know I'm not brain-dead, but if I just lie here showing no other signs of life they might decide to take the drips away, stop the water and liquid foods and let me die.

So, for self-preservation; isn't that meant to be the most important principle?

Anyway, you can't leave her like that. You can't do that to the woman. She doesn't deserve it; nobody does. You don't belong to her and she doesn't belong to you, but you're both part of each other; if she got up and left now and walked away and you never saw each other again for the rest of your lives, and you lived an ordinary waking life for another fifty years, even so on your deathbed you would still know she was part of you.

You have left your marks on each other, you have helped to shape one another; you have each given the other an accent to their life which they will never quite lose; no matter.

You have a greater call on her than the other one only while you are so much closer to death. If you recover, she may well go back to him. Well, tough, You had decided you didn't grudge him that, or was that just the drink talking?

No, it—

Louder.

I said no it wasn't the drink—

Still can't hear you, man. Speak up.

OK! I meant it! I meant it!

Damn it I did, too. And another thing: she still thinks things happen in threes. There was her father, dying in the car; then Gustave, under sentence, slowly deteriorating . . . then me. Another car another car crash; another man she loved. Oh, I don't doubt now that Gustave and I are very similar, and that we both might like each other, and I'm sure he would have got on with the advocate just as I did, and for the same reason . . . but if I can stop the similarities there, by God I will. I will not be the third man! (Pale fingers rise from the screen's black grating, trembling in the night wind like white tubers . . . damn thing's sticked again; the monochrome image peels and bursts, white light behind. Too late again, the sniper first sees then aims then fires and the third—)

No, this little sequence ends at two, if I've got anything to do with it. (And another, slightly sneaky, thought occurs, now that I've realized how alike Gustave and I might be: I know what *I'd* tell Andrea if I was the one slowly deteriorating and she wanted to martyr herself looking after me . . .)

I'll go to the other city; I always wanted to, really. I want to *meet* this man. Damn it I wanna *do* things! I want to travel the Trans-Siberian, go to India, stand on Ayers Rock, get sodden wet in Machupicchu! I want to surf! I *will* get a hang-glider; I want to go back to the Grand Canyon and get further than just the rim rock this time, I want to see the aurora borealis from Svalbard or Greenland, I want to see a total eclipse, I want to watch pyroclastic displays, I want to walk inside a lava tunnel, I want to see the earth from space, I want to drink *chaug* in Ladakh, I want to cruise down the Amazon and up the Yangtze and walk the Great Wall; I want to visit Azania! I want to watch them push helicopters off the aircraft carriers again! *I want to be in bed with three women at once!*

Oh God, back to Thatcher's Britain and Reagan's world, back to all the usual bullshit. At least the bridge was predictable in its oddness, at least it was comparatively *safe*.

Well, maybe not. I don't know.

I know one thing: I don't need the machine to tell me the choice. The choice is not between dream and reality; it is between two different dreams.

One is my own; the bridge and all I made of it. The other is our collective dream, our corporate imagery. We live the dream; call it American, call it Western, call it Northern or call it just that of all we humans, all life. I was part of one dream, for good or ill, and it was half nightmare and I almost let it kill me, but it hasn't. Yet, anyway.

What's changed?

Not the dream, not the result of our dreams which we call the world, not our hi-tech life. Me, then? Maybe. Who knows; could be anything, inside here. Just won't be able to tell until I get back out again, and start living the shared dream, abandoning my own, of a thing become place, a means become end, a route become destination . . . Three of diamonds, indeed, and a quality bridge, an everlasting bridge, a never-quite-the-same bridge, its vast and ruddy frame forever sloughing off and being replaced, like a snake constantly shedding, a metamorphosing insect which is its own cocoon and always changing . . .

All those trains. Going to be on a few more in the future, too. Sure to get banned from driving. Stupid bastard. Writing the car off, drunk-driving just before Christmas; how embarrassing to have to come back to that. At least there wasn't anybody else involved, just me and the two cars. Not sure I'd have wanted to come back if I'd killed somebody, or even injured them badly. Hope whoever owned the MG didn't dote on it too much. Poor Jaguar. After all that time and money, after all the careful, crafted work people put into it. Maybe just as well I didn't have it very long before I wrecked it; might have got sentimental about it, might have come to feel something for it ('Were you very attached to the car, Mr X? '*Attached* to it? I was jammed inside the bastard for three hours.').

And that bridge, that bridge . . . have to make a pilgrimage to it, once I'm better; if I can. Walk over the water (assuming I can walk), cross the river; throw a coin for luck ha ha.

Sections three; first second third Forth Firth . . . loco me loco . . . There were great grey Xs in the road bridge towers too; I remember now. Three big Xs one above the other, like laces or ribbons . . . and also . . . and also . . . what else? Oh yeah and I didn't get to hear all the Pogues tape either. Missed *A Man You Don't Meet Every Day*; fave track that; sing it kid . . . Had the Eurythmics on the other side furra bitta contrast like; young Annie beltin out wiff auntie Aretha; doin' it for themselves and why not? and singin *Better To Have Lost In Love (Than Never To Have Loved At All)*; so it's a cliché? Clichés have feelings too.

I want to come back. Can I come back?

beep beep beep this is a recording; your conscious mind is out at the moment but if you'd care to—

clunk.

Can I? Can I please? I want to come back. Now. Now we try. Sleep; wake. Do it now.

Let's go *there*.

Very soon; waking. Before that, a word from our sponsors. But first, three little asterisks:

*   *   *

I was on the beach at Valtos once, one rainy and not too warm summer. I was with her and we were camping and we took a chemical which altered reality. Rain pattered softly on the tent; she wanted to stay in, looking at a book of Dali's paintings, but didn't mind if I went out.

I walked along the edge of the curving tide, where the waves ate into the golden crescent of sand; I was alone with a warm damp breeze and a mile or two of beach, rain smirring from the greyly wisping clouds. I found razor shells like fragments of a broken rainbow, and watched rain drops fall on some still dry sand as the wind blew over it; the whole beach seemed to heave and flow, like something living. I remember my delight, my childish touching of that sand and its dark spots, the feel of the grains blown across my fingers.

I was on the outer edge of the Outer Isles, rough sea to Newfoundland and Greenland and Iceland and the skull cap of rotating ice above the Pole; there at the end of the Long Isle which is many isles, a curve of broken land lying hard against the sea like a column of spine, like a blossoming of brain above a central system. My mind was that Isle, bared to the sweep of sea and weather by the cutting edge of the drug; a wide escape.

I thought I saw it all then; the way the brain flowers at the end of its articulated stalk; the way, our roots in the soil, we grow and become. It meant everything and nothing, at the time and still.

And to myself I said I've been away a far place . . . because I was my own father and my own child, and I went away for a while but I came back. Child, your father's been away a far place. That was what I said to myself as I headed back: Child, your father's been away a far place.

. . . Yeah, sure, but that was long ago; what about now? I mean, good grief, six months without a drink or a smoke! I've probably been healthier lying here unconscious than I've been in the rest of my adult life; not much exercise maybe, but nothing more dangerous to ingest than whatever it is they shove down this tube in my nose. How the hell has my body *survived* six months without drink and drugs?

Maybe I'll become a reformed character, maybe I'll stop drinking and never smoke or snort or chew anything else ever again and when I do get my driving licence back I'll never exceed the speed limit again, and in future I'll never, never say anything nasty about our legally and democratically elected representatives or those of our allies and I'll have a lot more time and respect for other people's views no matter how fucking stupid they—No; if I was going to do that, why *bother* coming back? Bugger it; I'm going to do *more* of all that stuff just as soon as I can; I'm just going to be a bit more *careful* in future.

Child, your father's—

Yeah I know; so we heard. I think we got that message, thank you. Anybody else . . .?

Our revels now are ended	(thanx bill)
These proceedings are closed	(ta Mac)
Brammer wakes—	(can we get that right, please?)
Brahma wakes	(thank you)
'sokay	(shut up; and get on with it).

Blackness.

No; not blackness. Something. A dark, almost brown red. Everywhere. I try to look away but I can't, so it isn't just the colour of the wall or the ceiling. Is this behind my eyes? Don't know. Dinnae ken.

Sound; I can hear something. It's like, having dived into a pool, floating back up towards the surface again; that sound, a sort of bubbling white noise, slowly altering in pitch from very low to high, and bursting like a bubble itself to—

Conversation, a woman laughing. Clinks and rattles, a wheel or a chair-leg squeaking.

Smell; oh yes. Very medicinal. No doubt where we are now. Something flowery, too; I can smell two scents here. One crude but fresh, one . . . much more . . . I don't know. I can't describe it . . . ah, the first one must be the bedside flowers; the ones in the vase on the cabinet. The second is *her*. Still wearing Joy, it would seem. Must be her; stuff doesn't smell like that on anybody else, even her mother. She's here!

Is this the same day? Will I get to see her? Oh don't leave yet! Stay; don't go!

Move something; go on, *shift*.

Totally disorganized here. Can't see a damn thing and I'm like a dozy puppeteer caught napping, stumbling around behind the scenes trying to find the right lengths of string, getting all in a tangle. Arms? Legs? Tootsies? Which bit works which? Where's the instruction manual . . .? Oh God, we aren't going to have to learn all this stuff *again*, are we?

Eyes; open, dammit!

Twitch, hands!

Feet; come on, do your stuff!

. . . Somebody? Anybody?

Take it easy. Lie back and think of Scotland. Just calm down, laddie. Breathe, feel your blood pump, feel the tucked-in weight of the blanket and sheets, feel the tickle where the tube goes in through your nose . . .

. . . All there. Can't hear anybody talking nearby. Just the hushed rumble of building and city. Slight breeze has taken the smell of Joy away . . . probably not here at all. Still the colour of dried blood behind here . . .

Slight draught again; feels funny on my cheek and the little bit of skin between nose and lip. Haven't felt a breeze there since I was a student; covered by beard all those years . . . grow the thing back if I ever get out of here . . .

I sigh.

I really do sigh; I feel the resistance of the tucked-in bed-clothes as my chest rises higher than normal. The tube which enters me through one nostril slides across the fabric over my shoulder, then slips back as I relax and breathe out. I sighed!

I'm so surprised I open my eyes. The left lid trembles, gummed-up, then clears. Within seconds, though it all looks a bit shaky and bright for a while, everything settles down.

Andrea is sitting less than a metre away, her legs drawn under the small seat. One hand rests on her thigh, the other is holding a small styrofoam cup to her mouth, which is open, those lips parted. I can see her teeth. She is staring at me. I blink. So does she. I waggle my toes and – glancing down to the bottom of the bed – see the white jacket move up and down as I do so.

I flex my hands; damn rough blankets they have here. I am *hungry*.

Andrea puts the cup down, leans forward a little, as though she does not believe what she is seeing; she looks from one of my eyes to the other, apparently checking for signs of sense in both (not an unreasonable precaution, I'll admit). I clear my throat.

Andrea's whole body relaxes. I once watched a chiffon scarf drop from her fingers, and I do not recall that it flowed more gracefully. Her face loses a whole layer of worry, just like that; I – I have remembered my name – am almost embarrassed. She nods slowly.

'Welcome back,' she says, smiling.

'Oh yeah?'

Vonda N. McIntyre
Dreamsnake £2.50

In a world devastated by nuclear holocaust, Snake is a healer. One of an elite band dedicated to caring for sick humanity, she goes wherever her skills are needed.

With her she takes the three deadly reptiles through which her cures are accomplished: a cobra, a rattlesnake, and the dreamsnake, a creature whose hallucinogenic venom brings not healing but an easeful death for the terminally ill.

Rare and valuable is this dreamsnake. When Grass is wantonly slain, Snake must journey across perilous landscapes to find another to take its place . . .

'A very beautiful work indeed . . . richly and beautifully imagined, very satisfying' *THE SPECTATOR*

Robert Silverberg
Sunrise on Mercury £1.95

Here, from Robert Silverberg, the bestselling author of the Majipoor trilogy, is a collection of thirteen stunning science-fiction stories. A 'very, very readable compilation by one of the genre's superior entertainers' THE TIMES

Douglas Adams
The Hitch-Hikers Guide to the Galaxy £2.50

'People of Earth, your attention please . . . Plans for development of the outlying regions of the Galaxy require the building of a Hyperspatial Express Route through your Star System, and regrettably your planet is scheduled for demolition.'

For Arthur Dent, earthling and homeowner, a severe case of planning blight is the overture to a remarkable set of travels, guided en route by an equally remarkable book, *The Hitch-Hikers Guide to the Galaxy*.

All these books are available at your local bookshop or newsagent, or can be ordered direct from the publisher. Indicate the number of copies required and fill in the form below.

Send to: **CS Department, Pan Books Ltd., P.O. Box 40, Basingstoke, Hants.   RG21 2YT.**

or phone: 0256 469551 (Ansaphone), quoting title, author and Credit Card number.

Please enclose a remittance* to the value of the cover price plus: 60p for the first book plus 30p per copy for each additional book ordered to a maximum charge of £2.40 to cover postage and packing.

*Payment may be made in sterling by UK personal cheque, postal order, sterling draft or international money order, made payable to Pan Books Ltd.

Alternatively by Barclaycard/Access:

Card No. | | | | | | | | | | | | | | | | | | |

Signature:

Applicable only in the UK and Republic of Ireland.

While every effort is made to keep prices low, it is sometimes necessary to increase prices at short notice. Pan Books reserve the right to show on covers and charge new retail prices which may differ from those advertised in the text or elsewhere.

NAME AND ADDRESS IN BLOCK LETTERS PLEASE:

....

Name ————————————————————————————

Address ————————————————————————————

————————————————————————————

————————————————————————————

3/87